CONVICTION

By the same author

Suspense

Trinity Calhoun Mysteries:
Can't Go Home
No Safe Haven
Better Left Behind

Lockwood Gate Thrillers:
The Replacement
The Echo
The Choice

Women's Fiction:

Snapshots By Laura
Long Way From Home

Romantic Suspense:

Hostile Ground
Tangled Ground

Deceptions & Desires
Pinups & Possibilities

The Hostage

(Additionally, Melinda's 15 HRS titles can be found on the Harlequin website)

Romantic Comedy

Training the Temp
Lie to Me
Unsolicited Advice

After Hours
Before Dawn

Mile High Weekend

Young Adult

Counting Scars
Racing Hearts
Normals Kids

CONVICTION

A Novel

by

Melinda Di Lorenzo

MELINDA DI LORENZO

con·vic·tion (noun)

1: the process of finding someone guilty of a crime, in a court of law

2: a strong persuasion or belief

3: the act of compelling the admission of a truth

MELINDA DI LORENZO

Welcome to Meridian, British Columbia, Canada

Established, 1953
Population: 5013

MELINDA DI LORENZO

1
Ten Hours After Escape

The Convict

He lit a cigarette, and he watched.

She was so still she could've almost been dead. He knew better.

A sheen of sweat covered her. It started at her delicate, brown hairline. It slithered down her throat and into the curve of her perfect breasts, which didn't heave under the thin Tshirt as one might think they ought to.

It still made him smile. Which, in turn, drew his attention to *her* mouth. So succulent and somehow begging for attention in spite of the fact that it hung open, exposing the very high truth of her vulnerability. It was evidence that she could be broken—*had* been broken. A chipped front tooth. A lip split by the now-jagged edge of that shiny enamel.

Funny, that I didn't notice that while it happened.

For a second, he puzzled at it, wondering how she acquired this particular injury. He was sure he could accurately catalog every bruise, every scratch, every scar-to-be. Until now. He felt almost betrayed by the not-knowing. With his irritation, his smile faded. Became a grimace.

Quickly, he tossed aside all other thoughts in favor of running over the events that had led to this moment. At last, he seized on one.

Her. Tumbling down. Him. Dragging her up.

Ah, yes. Her face hit the pavement.

He inhaled deeply, satisfied by the connection. He went back to examining her, his eyes drawn repeatedly to that small wound.

The newly acquired imperfection should've made her sweet features less appealing, but it didn't. Instead, he liked the little bit of broken, the little bit of suffering. It made him... proud.

She looked up at him, her wrists bound and her eyes wide with terror.

"You scared?" he taunted.

She nodded weakly.

"Not good enough. You should be fucking terrified."

She opened her mouth as though she were about to speak, and he shut it down with a look. Her gaze flicked to the closed door, and for a moment he thought she was just trying not to meet his eyes. He was about to demand her full attention, but her face came back to his, and he realized her slip had nothing to do with him at all. It made him furious.

"Are you thinking about what's in the other room?" he asked, soft but with an edge.

Another limp nod. A mistake.

He balanced his cigarette on the lip of the half-empty whiskey bottle. Carefully. He didn't want to waste either. He didn't know how soon he'd be able to acquire more.

He saw the way she noticed. He saw the way she swallowed nervously, the way she cringed as the motion disturbed the bruising on her neck. His eyes lingered on those bruises. Hand-shaped. If he put his fingers there, they might fit perfectly.

Almost, he felt bad. But feeling bad was close to feeling guilty, and guilt wasn't in his repertoire of emotions. Not at all.

He left the cigarette and the whiskey, and he crossed the room. She shrank in the chair.

Good.

He reached for her. His hands closed on the rope, wound tightly around her wrists, and he dragged her to her feet. She trembled under his hold. She quivered.

Blood rushed from every part of his body and straight to his groin. Zero to sixty—zero to hard-as-fuck—in eight seconds flat.

It took all of his willpower to keep from shoving her back to the chair, to keep from pushing up that short, nearly sheer, floral-print skirt, to keep from taking what he wanted, right then and there.

No.

He satiated himself with a taste of her bruised lips instead. Tinged with the rusty flavor of blood, they did nothing to ease his arousal. He flicked his tongue into her mouth. He ran it over that broken tooth, and she let him do it.

"Aren't you going to fight me?" he growled as he pulled away and pressed his rough cheek to her skin.

She shook her head, and he exhaled then shrugged.

"Too bad," he said. "Might've saved you from being forced to take another look."

She started to shake again. He ignored it and yanked on the rope. Her urge was to resist; he could tell by the way her bare feet, with their chipped polish, dug into the low carpet. She wasn't strong enough to fight him, though. Not for long. He pulled harder, and she followed, eyes cast down. Like a dog being punished.

Christ, is she sexy.

He shoved down the distracting observation and swung open the door to the adjoining room.

There he is.

What was left of him, anyway. A body. Vacant eyes. A bloody mess in the center of his torso.

"Look."

The command was sharp, and she obeyed. Quickly. Then dropped her eyes back down to her feet.

"Not gonna cut it," he murmured, and he dropped the rope so he could grab her chin instead.

She didn't use the freedom to jerk away. She didn't try to bolt across the room or attempt to block out the carnage by closing her eyes. She knew she wouldn't win. Being sure of that made him feel a little smug as her gaze slid to—and stayed on— the dead man.

He stroked her, shoulder to hip, then back again. "I still think it's a shame we won't get to use that bed."

She flinched, just enough that he noticed. He laughed, low and dark, before he slipped his hand to that soft skirt and rolled his fingers over the fabric. Its texture reminded him of her. Filmy. Ethereal. Pleasant against his rough hands.

He bent to speak against her battered throat. "Don't worry. There'll be more opportunities."

Her breath caught. He felt it as much as he heard it. In response, he eased up and pushed out his tongue to touch her ear. He traced the salty curve down to the lobe, then closed his teeth on the skin there. He sucked off the dried sweat, relishing the way she shook.

He reached down, prepared to pick up the rope that held her —it would be easier to drag her to the wide, smooth dresser if he had it in his possession—but an engine in the distance stalled his intention. Seconds later, it was joined by a second. Instinctively, through some innate sixth sense, he knew they were headed his way.

He pulled back and looked the girl's way. Her eyes went wider. Worry. Fear. Hope. Impossible to know which emotion dominated her pale, pale gaze as it flitted around the room from him to the corpse to the door, then back to him again.

Then...she ran.

His attention shifted to her bare feet; he was surprised by their swiftness. He couldn't move or look away as they flew over the carpet past the bed that housed the doughy body. They smacked onto the tiles of the adjoining bathroom as she whisked herself inside. She slammed the door shut, and they disappeared. From behind the wooden barrier, there was a silent pause. Then the sound of a window sliding open.

He stared at the door, a growl forming in his smoke-raw throat.

Still. He didn't go after her. He didn't pound on the door or rack his brain for a way to stop her. He wouldn't stoop to giving in to his emotional needs. Instead, he moved to the bed and—ignoring the violent tableau beneath him—snapped up a corner of a pillowcase and yanked it free.

Without pausing, he trod back into the tiny, separate living space. He picked up the shrinking cigarette from its spot on the whiskey bottle and took a slow drag. He closed his eyes.

He could hear the crackling burn, despite the sirens. He let the smoke swirl inside his lungs. It was dark and dangerous and sweltering. It matched his heart and his mind, and he held it there for a long moment before he released it into the air. Then he lifted his lids. Slowly. Purposefully.

He twisted the cheap piece of bedding into a skinny, dart-like point and forced it into the whiskey. Down, down, until the fabric met the liquid gold and sucked it up.

Outside, the noise was reaching a crescendo. The police cars couldn't be more than a street away. In seconds, they'd arrive at the motel. Their drivers would storm the building, clearing its seedy occupants.

They'd search.

They'd find them.

Or rather...

They'd find *him.*

At the thought, he felt a little thrill. There was nothing to liven things up like a little cat-and-mouse. They'd try to catch him, they wouldn't dare give up. Not even if they had her first.

He lifted his eyes to the mirror and stared at his reflection, unable to help but wonder if they'd prefer her to become a martyr to their cause.

The fact that her life still burns bright... Maybe to them, it's nothing more than a happy accident.

Because *he* was the killer. The kidnapper. The very bad man.

Ellis Black.

His pursuers knew him and his deeds, and there was nothing they wanted more than justice.

That didn't mean he had to make it easy for them.

He took a final pull from his dwindling cigarette, then pushed the burning stub to the twisted pillowcase.

2
Ten Months Before Escape

The Preacher's Daughter

Themal air smelled like bleach. Distinct. Clean and acrid at the same time. Reminiscent of sanitized bathrooms. Spotless hospitals. Here, it seemed out of place.

Roni turned in a circle, closed her eyes, and inhaled.

Deep.

Deep.

Deeper.

Yes, bleach. No doubt about it. But under that sterile scent was something else. Something that couldn't quite be driven away, no matter how thoroughly the janitors wiped every surface. Old sweat and masculinity.

Roni drew in another breath then held it for a second before blowing it out. She was twenty-two years old, and she'd never attended high school, but she imagined the lingering smell was the same one that would permeate a boys' locker room. Which wasn't a particularly pleasant association, to be honest. Jockstraps and dirty jokes weren't exactly high on her list of enjoyable things, and thinking of them only added to the unease she couldn't quite shake.

She opened her eyes and let them skim over her surroundings. Absently, she recalled that she'd heard once—she couldn't remember where now—that Canadian prisons were a cakewalk compared to those found in the United States. But she supposed it was relative. Nothing about this place made her feel easy in any way. Not the fact that it *was* a Canadian prison nor that she had never left her home country for a vacation let alone to visit a correctional facility similar to this. The waiting room into which she'd been buzzed lacked any kind of warmth. A perfect match for the bleach-covered scent of sweat. The walls were painted brick, which Roni suspected was for effect rather than function. They were definitely crafted from stuff hardier than mortar.

The room also had a vibe as strange as the smell, and she couldn't pinpoint the source. Was it the décor? Maybe the lack thereof?

There were no chairs, no tables. Nothing but the blank, off-white walls and two, enormous metal doors on either end of the room.

No, she decided after another second. Not the décor.

Residual sadness? Desperation? A feeling of waiting for something hopeless to happen? The thought that other people's emotions could stay behind and color a room was as romantic as it was disheartening.

Roni swallowed. An urge to leave swept in, demanding to be heeded. But a disembodied voice crackled to life from some unseen speaker.

"Veronica Hollister?" it said.

"Roni," she corrected automatically.

"Well," replied the voice. "All right then. Roni. You can come through."

The heavy door on the other side of the room buzzed, and when Roni stepped forward and put her hand on the door, it opened easily, assisted by some mechanization invisible to the eye. She stepped through and took yet another breath. This time, she regretted it. The smell emanating from the hallway almost overwhelmed her. The bleach was preferable.

Fighting a gag, she focused on the uniformed man in front of her. Standard tan pants and a weapon at his hip. A clipboard in his hands and a small smile on his face. He exuded an underlying sense of power. Maybe not *actual* power. Just the knowledge that he was in control.

Or maybe you're just reading too much into it.

The man's smile stretched wide in a way that made Roni want to smooth her skirt to make sure it covered her knees properly.

"Hey," he said, his voice a match to his expression. "You're the preacher's kid, right?"

For the barest second, Roni bristled. There was always so much pressure—so much *stigma*—attached to being the only child of a man of God. Especially in a town as small as Meridian. No matter that her father had never been the preacher *here*. And no matter, either, that he'd been forced into retirement by his battle with cancer before they'd so much as set foot in their home on the outskirts of town, three years earlier. Word got around, and there were an awful lot of people who bowed their heads a little when he walked by. Who didn't care that he received his income in the form of a disability check now and not from a physical church. Many who still reached out with spiritual questions. And they all called him Father.

But as quickly as the resentment came, it dissipated again. After all, Roni *was* there at the behest of her father. At his order, actually. He'd made the arrangements because this visit was Roni's punishment. Her penance. Like the men locked up in here—and as cliché as it was—she'd done the crime and therefore had to do the time.

The fury on her father's face when he'd caught her perusing a violent headline in the local paper remained fresh in her mind. She could still hear his voice in her head.

You like to read about crimes *in the news, baby girl?* he'd said. *Maybe you ought to get a taste of it for real. See why we stick to reading the Bible in this house. In fact, you can take the good book with you, and you can* keep *taking it with you until you've saved us a soul.*

18

Roni placed her hand over her skirt pocket. She hadn't brought a full Bible, but she *had* brought a small notebook of quotes she thought might be relevant. As any good preacher's daughter might.

She tipped her head to smile at the uniformed man, and she managed to make it sincere. "Yes. That's right. I'm Father Lee's daughter."

"Not the same last name, huh?" he replied.

"No. My mother thought she was being modern and gave me hers instead."

"Hmm. Well. Your dad sure must've pulled some strings to get you in here."

"What do you mean?"

His face was unpleasantly smug. "We don't normally allow women to have one-on-ones with our inmates."

Roni blinked at him, and she realized that he was trying to intimidate her. It sparked an unusual trickle of defiance in her heart. The bristle came back. This time, she couldn't so easily dismiss it.

"What about their mothers?" she asked.

The guard returned her blink. "What?"

She lifted her head. "The inmates. They're allowed visitors, aren't they?"

"Er. Yes."

"And they have mothers. And sisters. Maybe daughters or wives?"

"Um."

"And last time I checked, there were also female lawyers. Counselors. Clergy."

"Well."

"So, unless the prison is in the habit of violating rights, I assume that women come in here regularly."

The guard went silent, so Roni met his eyes without wavering. He shifted in place. Tapped his fingers on his thigh and averted his gaze while clearing his throat. He actually looked *nervous*. Which made her far more gleeful than she ought to be. She felt a little like laughing. She settled for a dignified nod instead.

"Should we go then?" she prodded.

The man's mouth worked for a second, then he scratched his head, sighed, and held out his clipboard. "All right. This is the sign-in. Says you understand the rules and will obey them. We're medium security, so you can get away with a little more. No touching, but—"

She missed the rest of his words.

No touching?

For some reason, the idea struck her hard. She hadn't, until that moment, considered it at all. She'd envisioned a brightly lit room. White walls. A table in the center, and a man in an orange jumpsuit seated across from her. But where were their hands in the imaginary scenario? She wanted to close her eyes and think about it. What if they wanted to clasp fingers in prayer? What if she wanted to issue a reassuring squeeze of his wrist as he broke down and confessed his remorse? Touch was a valid form of therapy. An essential part of humanity. How could the men inside these walls ever be rehabilitated if they were denied that basic right?

"Ms. Hollister?"

She breathed in and blinked that guard. "Yes?"

"Did you understand everything I just said?"

She nodded and vowed silently to make amends for the non-verbal lie later. "I'm ready."

"All right. Follow me and keep to the right."

For a second, the order puzzled her. There seemed to be plenty of room to allow them a side-by-side journey. But as she walked along behind him, her legs taking two steps for every one of his, she quickly figured out why he'd issued it. A second guard, this one accompanied by a man with shackled ankles and handcuffed wrists, approached from the opposite direction. Even the width of the hallway barely allowed them to pass comfortably. And when the prisoner lifted his eyes— oh-so barely, almost like it hurt him to do it—comfort was nowhere to be had. His gaze was cold. Devoid of anything Roni would call connection. A full-body shiver racked her so hard that she stumbled, one of her flat, Mary-Jane-style shoes sliding forward and tapping the guard's heel.

The man whipped around and put out a hand to steady her. "You all right?"

"I just..." She fought her fear and lost. "That guy back there..."

The guard's eyes followed her nervous gaze. "Ah. Julien Jones. Dangerous man. But nothing for you to worry about. The guy you're here to see is pretty harmless. Bobby Lines. Only reason he's in a facility as strict as this one is because it's his fifth strike. Judge was trying to knock some sense into him."

She took a breath. "What did he do?"

"You don't know?"

She didn't tell him that her father had deliberately withheld that information from her. "No, I don't."

"He stole a pizza delivery car. With the driver inside."

The guard offered her a smile, then a chuckle. It made Roni wonder how someone got to the point that he not only found grand theft auto and kidnapping not to be a big deal but also thought it was *funny*. She made herself bite her lip to keep from asking.

You're here for the inmate, not the guard.

Of course, everyone could use a little salvation. That's what her father always said. And she believed it. Heartily.

They reached their destination—a wide metal door with an eight-inch square window. It would've been at eye level for anyone over five and a half feet. Which, of course, Roni wasn't. But she didn't need to see in, anyway. She was going inside no matter what.

"Still good?" the guard asked.

"Still good," she confirmed, squaring her shoulders.

"Got the rules up here?" he tapped his own forehead.

She nodded wordlessly.

"Okay, then. I'm going to hand you off to the guard inside. He'll go over the rules again, then he'll leave. And once you're in, you're in pretty good—the door closes and locks automatically. But I don't want you to think you can't get out at all, okay? I'll be standing right out here, and so will the other guard. You need anything, you can just stand up and knock."

"Thank you."

He looked amused by her gratitude. "S'what I get paid for."

He lifted a set of key cards from their spot on his belt and stretched out the retractable chain. Without looking, he selected one and jammed it into the slot on the door handle.

For a second, an overwhelming sense of foreboding struck Roni so hard that she almost stumbled.

This is it. The point of no return. Once you go in there, you can't undo it.

Licking her suddenly dry lips, she shoved aside the inexplicable dread and forced her feet forward. Thick knots of worry pressed at her so hard that the world grew blurry. As the first guard passed her to the second, she couldn't distinguish between them. She was aware that they exchanged greetings. That one gave the other a friendly clap on the back. But she couldn't have repeated the specifics; she could barely hear the words over her own breaths. When the first of the tan-clad men left, she was sure that at any moment the second one would note the syncopated rhythm of her inhales and exhales and send her away. Maybe she hoped he would.

He didn't.

He seemed to see her as little as she saw him. His bored voice droned like a bee, buzzing into her ears, rolling off the same warnings she'd already heard. One of his feet tapped against the tiles in a quick, get-this-over-with drumbeat.

Vaguely, she saw him gesture upwards, and her eyes followed automatically. She spotted the camera, blinking red in a corner where two of the sullenly yellow walls met. She hadn't really heard what he said, but she nodded her understanding. She'd be further protected from the serial thief by the recording.

"Everything clear?" he said at last.

Everything was just the opposite, but Roni blew out a breath and nodded for what felt like the twentieth time. "Yes."

"All right. Holler if you need us."

"Okay. But where's the—" She cut herself off as the guard moved aside and revealed the answer to her incomplete sentence.

There he sat. She didn't know how she'd missed him in the first place.

3
Ten Hours After Escape

The Policeman

Flip Farriday—the decorated captain of the Meridian PD and current head of the hushed, hours-long manhunt plaguing his town—stepped around to the rear courtyard of the Meridian Motel and stopped short. He blinked slowly, wondering if sleep deprivation had finally gotten to him. A woman was wiggling her way out of a second-floor window. Her floral skirt flapped in the wind, revealing enough skin that Farriday felt like a voyeur.

Lifting his police-issue ball cap, he ran his hand over his sparse hair, then looked around to see if anyone had spotted the same display. None of the men on his small force were in sight. Not the regular duty cops nor the three reserve officers they'd pulled in to help out. It was quiet and still. Far quieter and stiller than anything had been since the call came late last night.

Farriday's eyes lifted to the window again. The woman was gone. The absence didn't last for more than a moment, though, before a pair of legs slipped out in place of the skirt.

The rest of her bottom half followed.

"Well, I'll be damned," Farriday said under his breath.

Not imagining things after all.

He didn't have to think hard to infer what the woman was doing there. There was only one cheap motel this close to town, and it'd seen its fair share of illicit behavior over the years.

He shifted focus and glanced around the rundown courtyard. The rest of his team was still nowhere to be seen. He could hear them on the other side of the building, shouting muffled orders to one another. This little search had been peripheral. More of a rule-stuff-out kinda deal. No one expected a tip called in by some well-known drug addict to pan into anything real. Heck. The same guy had spotted aliens in the woods just last week, and he'd been so hysterical that Farriday had been forced to send a squad car. No little green men anywhere. Surprise, surprise.

There was another, non-urgent shout from the front of the motel. Closer now. Farriday sighed. His team's movement meant *his* movement. Truth be told, he was tired as all getout. Yeah, he wanted to catch their target. With more fervor than most. But he was days away from retirement. His bones ached, giving away his age more than his thinning hair and thickening paunch.

Lord help me just get this over with.

His eyes slid back to the prostitute—or what he could see of her, anyway—and he sighed a second time.

Should I do something about it?

Under normal circumstances, it wouldn't be a question. He would've hollered and stopped her. Slapped her with a warning, probably. In this case, though, Farriday barely had time to breathe, let alone add in something else. As if to hammer home that point, the radio on his shoulder squawked to life with one of his officers announcing that the exterior of the building had been cleared.

But it's not quite clear, is it? he thought, eyeing the woman, who still hung from the window.

Had she put a leg back in again? She was going to fall and crack open her head.

"Not very good at that, are you?" he muttered.

Then he gave himself a mental kick.

The woman wasn't a prostitute. It was her. Veronica Hollister. The very victim they'd been so desperate to find. The one last seen being dragged away at knifepoint from Meridian Penitentiary.

"I'll be damned," Farriday repeated.

The fact that she was climbing out could only mean one thing. She'd managed to free herself from Ellis Black. No way would she be on the move if the man in question had any clue. The fact that Veronica was intact at all... well, that was a minor miracle.

And you should be running.

Logically, he knew it. Probably starting with grabbing the radio and calling for some backup. Let the younger men on the force help the girl down. Give them a bit of a rush. A bit of glory. Have them on hand, too, in case Black reared his head.

But something kept him pinned to the spot. He didn't run. He just lifted his cap again and scratched the stubs of his hair, considering what to do about this unexpected development. He had a few seconds. He was out of view, hidden by the cover of a thick-trunked tree.

The capture of an escaped convict—or at least the rescue of his hostage—would be a damned fine way to go out. A nice little cap to end his reign. And there was some poetic symmetry to it, too, considering that Ellis Black's arrest had been the thing that revitalized a career that nearly didn't happen. So instead of announcing the sighting, he reached up and dialed back the volume of his radio so it wouldn't interrupt him again. Or spook the girl.

With that in mind, he sidled over to the slab of not-so white-washed stucco below Ms. Hollister, his focus no longer on what her rear end was up to, but rather on taking credit for saving it.

Heard something around the side of the building, he'd say. *Saw her climbing out and knew right away it was her. Didn't stop to think. Just acted on gut instinct.*

Farriday smiled a little to himself. He wasn't egotistical, but who didn't love seeing their name in the papers? And the news loved stories where cops used their instincts to solve crimes. It would be a win, all around.

He moved to position himself under the girl, and he didn't have to wait long. As soon as her shoulders came out the window, the rest of her dropped like a stone. She slammed into him, letting out a screech. He stumbled backward but didn't fall. With his teeth gritted against the sound of her shriek, he held her shoulders and spoke into her ear.

"Hey," he said, trying to keep his voice as soothing as possible. "It's okay. I've got you."

She was frantic, though. Too frightened to recognize that she was being held by someone safe. She kicked and writhed so hard that the captain couldn't quite help but lift her from the ground.

"Hey!" he said again, this time a little rougher.

Her hollering didn't stop. If anything, the wailing got louder.

Holy Hannah, Farriday thought. *She's like a banshee.*

He brought up his hand and pressed it gently against her mouth, just hoping to grab her attention and quiet her. She bit into his palm. Hard.

"Shit!"

The curse escaped before Farriday could think to let his professional decorum stop it. Worse than that, though, was the way he let her go. He loosened his grip. She toppled to the ground, her screams finally cutting off. Then her head whipped up and she caught sight of him. She pushed herself backward, seemingly unaware—or maybe just uncaring—of the pavement that scraped over her bare thighs.

"You!" she gasped.

Farriday blinked, taken aback. "Me?"

"You. You have to help me."

He let out a breath. "That's what I'm here to do, kiddo."

He took a small step toward her and put out a hand. She stared at it for a second, her expression a mask of distrust.

"C'mon," Farriday urged. "You recognize the uniform. I know you do. Good old Captain Flip. That's me."

Her eyes skidded across the navy-blue getup. Rested on the holster that held his gun in a way that made him itch to cover it. Then came back to his face.

Lord, she was skittish. A few hours with Ellis and the girl was a mess.

"You've got this, Ms. Hollister," he said. "I know you do."

Slowly—like his hand might actually be covering a venomous snake—she reached up and grasped his fingers. He noted that her touch was hot and sweaty. As wild as her face. He held onto her firmly anyway, and he pulled her to her feet. She collapsed into his arms just as the pound of boots on pavement greeted his ears.

Farriday looked up. Three officers—a quarter of the whole force—had come around the corner, weapons raised, face shields down, and bodies stiff.

"It's all right, boys," Farriday called. "This is Ms. Hollister. She's alive and well."

One of the other cops—a kid named Brody—lifted his mask. "What about Black?"

In Farriday's arms, Veronica shivered.

"Inside," she whispered.

"In the hotel?"

She nodded into his chest.

Farriday narrowed his eyes at the crew. "Thought you boys said it was clear."

"It is," one of them—another fresh hire—said.

"We did the perimeter like you told us to do," Brody added.

"Did you go door to door?" the captain asked.

The new hire shifted from foot to foot. "Well, not yet, Captain, because—"

"Because *what*, son?" Flip replied, waving an arm at the rest of them. "One of you spit it out."

No one answered. Every one of them had turned his attention up to the open window. A puff of dark smoke drifted out.

What the—

"He's burning it," Veronica said.

"What?" Farriday looked down at the girl, whose green gaze had lifted as well.

"He's burning it," she repeated. "Maybe because he thinks I'm still trapped inside, too."

4

Ten Years Earlier
Forty-Eight Hours Before Arrest

The Policeman

T he squawk of the in-dash radio dragged Flip from dead asleep to full-on awake—and full-on panicked —in about one second flat. His heart smashed to his ribcage, and it took him yet another four seconds to acclimatize to his surroundings. He was in his squad car. Parked on the side of the road. His head throbbed in a way that didn't match up with his uniform or his job, and his brain refused to answer for the messy state.

The radio crackled again, making him wince at its sharpness, and Danielle from dispatch spoke. "Flip, you copy?"

Rubbing his eyes, he grabbed the handset. "Yeah, I'm here. I mean... copy."

"Are you in car four?" said the dispatcher. "I need your help."

His gaze drifted to the identifying number on the dashboard, but the clock got his attention first.

7:12 am.

Whoops.

His shift started twelve minutes ago. Mentally, he flailed for an excuse, but as he opened his mouth to spit one out, a hazy memory resurfaced, and his jaw clamped shut again.

Quit or be fired, the captain had said. *Beginning of the day tomorrow, you give me your answer, or I'll give you mine.*

Twenty-three years of dedicated service. Following in his father's footsteps. A good cop with a run of bad luck. A few mistakes and an argument with his superior, leading to a metaphorical slap in the face. And as a result, Flip wasn't *supposed* to be in car four. He wasn't supposed to be in *any* police car. But an impulsive moment, fueled by his imminent termination, had driven him to snag the vehicle on the way out of the station. He was probably lucky they hadn't radioed in before now.

Probably? I think you mean for damn sure.

"Flip, seriously," said Danielle, her voice taking on an urgent edge. "Do you copy? Are you in car four?"

He cleared his throat and answered casually—like he didn't suspect that her so-called favor was tracking down the vehicle where he sat now. "Yeah. Copy. I'm in car four. What's up?"

"We need someone to follow up on a dropped called situation. Your car is showing as the closest. Can you attend?"

Flip's puzzlement about the call to action overrode the call itself. This was more than just a check-in on the whereabouts of the car. Which meant Danielle hadn't been informed of the ultimatum delivered by Captain Dax. His fingers tapped his thigh.

Should he tell her the truth? Or maybe just deny the request and make an excuse, letting her figure it out on her own later? Or should he simply take the request? Pretend like his boss had actually given him a choice in whether or not he walked away from his decades-long career. It was a little underhanded, but it would become Dax's problem, not his own.

"Flip?" Danielle pressed. "Are you there?"

He suppressed a sigh. "Still here. But are you sure you want *me* on this one?"

"What kind of question is that? Didn't you hear me? You're the closest."

"Did you run this by the captain?"

A long silence followed the question. He was about to speak into the radio again, but as his thumb found the button,

Danielle's voice crackled through.

"Oh, God," she said. "You don't know."

"What?"

"The captain is dead."

Flip sat up a little straighter and repeated himself. "What?"

"Last night. He had an anaphylactic reaction to something. They think maybe cross-contamination with nuts?" Her shuddering breath made the radio whine. "It's chaos here. Charlie is at the hospital with the captain's wife. Cliff is attending a hit-and-run, and Sammy already pulled a double. He literally just went home."

"Damn."

"I know. So can you check it out?"

Flip knew he should say no. There was a chance Dax had filed the paperwork prior to his unexpected death. Maybe the pink slip and the final pay stub were already in the mail.

Or not, said a considering voice in his head.

His boss was—or had been—a bit of a slacker on the paperwork front. Add in the fact that the other man had wanted to make it look like Flip's decision, and there was a chance this could turn out to be a karmic break.

Could I actually be that lucky? He winced, thinking of just how *un*lucky it'd been for Dax.

"Flip?"

"Give me the details," he replied, his tone full of new authority. "You said it was a dropped call?"

Her relief was palpable. "A double hang-up from the same number. And the callback wasn't answered."

"Right. Okay. What's the address?"

"It's the Black place. Do you know it?"

Distaste surged through Flip. He knew the house in question, and the thought of dealing with the family made his teeth grit together. Dad was big and mean. Good with his fists and not much else. Mom was beautiful. In another life, she could've been a model. Son was a delinquent with an attitude. And the daughter was a sad story all by herself.

"Hey. Are you okay, Flip?" Danielle asked. "You seem… off."

"Crappy sleep," he replied. "Just gotta grab a coffee. Which I promise can wait until after I've taken the statement from the Blacks. And yeah, I do know the place. I was out for a domestic a few months back."

"Bad situation, right?"

"Not the best."

"I guess we can hope that the call was a misdial?" Danielle said.

"Can't hurt to want the best," Flip agreed. "I'll head out now."

"Thanks. I'm glad you're able to go." The dispatcher's gratitude sounded genuine, and he smiled to himself despite the task ahead.

"Just doing my job, Danielle," he said.

"Aren't we all?" Her sigh was another crackle. "You wanna hear something funny before you head out?"

"Sure do."

"When we got here this morning, and you and car four were missing, Sammy said it was the first time you'd ever beaten him out of the station. He thought maybe you'd quit the force, stolen the vehicle, and gone for a joy ride."

Flip's smile dropped, but he forced a laugh and hoped the woodenness wouldn't carry through. "What kind of cop would I be if I stole a police car?"

The dispatcher laughed. "Not a very smart one!"

"Exactly. I had an early morning obligation today, so I took the car home last night."

"Good thinking."

"Worked out well. I'll report back ASAP," he said. "Over."

"Over," she replied.

The radio went silent. The key hung in the ignition, ready to go. After a few seconds of collecting his thoughts and shaking off his disquiet, Flip decided to take the whole thing as a dark, cosmic sign that he was doing exactly what he was meant to do.

5

Ten Hours After Escape

The Preacher's Daughter

round Veronica, the world moved in slow motion. The captain blinked. Once. Twice. His grandfatherly features filled with surprise.

His men shifted uneasily from foot to foot as if unsure what to do.

The tendril of smoke grew thicker, an inch at a time.

And no one spoke.

Had it really not occurred to them that Ellis might try to kill her? Hadn't they predicted that as his endgame?

As damaged as she was, Veronica had no problems seeing it. Her body might be broken, her spirit bent, but her mind was sharp enough to see that death was the only out. For her. And for the man who'd tied her to the chair. Taunted her. Tasted her.

She shivered, and the captain's reassuring grip on her body tightened. He spoke, too, and his voice vibrated against her. Whatever he said was gentle, but it had a wobbly, underwater quality that made it seem utterly unreal and impossible to understand.

Just like the rest of it.

Veronica's teeth squeezed together in the way teeth liked to do when they wanted to keep something out. Or in. A compulsion to free herself of the thick man's hold swept through her.

But would that make me appear ungrateful?

She almost laughed. Kidnapped. Assaulted. The target of death by arson. Yet here she was, worrying about what these men might think of her.

Wrong. So wrong.

Still, things moved oh-so slowly.

The police were speaking, arguing. She couldn't hear them. Not really. Tone but not words was the only thing she caught. Though she tried hard to focus, language was elusive. Something about firefighters? Or no. Until at last someone said something clear.

"Captain, maybe if you let her go…"

The captain did. His arms dropped, and Veronica could breathe.

"Where is he?" asked Captain Farriday.

She got the impression he'd directed the question her way several times already. Just a hint of impatience had entered his voice.

Please don't be mad.

"Kiddo," he said, "we just want to help."

She shook her head, and it made the scenery vibrate. "I can't. I won't."

"We can keep you safe," he added. "But not if we don't know where he is." *Safe.*

The concept was laughable. But she couldn't explain that. Couldn't reveal the fear in her heart.

If I'm caught… If I'm trapped… No.

The words dried up in Veronica's throat. As weak as it was, she wouldn't reveal him, wouldn't give him away. And the law wouldn't punish her for that. Would it?

The cops were talking again, their sentences fragments around her.

"In shock…"

"Back at the station…"

"Maybe…"

"Hospital…"

"Ellis…"

His name made all her wounds ache.

Then, abruptly—belatedly—an alarm sounded from within the motel, and the world's pace picked up. Not just to regular speed, but to turbo. A hair dryer on the hottest, windiest setting. Or maybe she'd only imagined its slowness.

The captain yelled something.

The cops took off at a run.

From somewhere at the front of the building, a woman shrieked.

Then. *Then.* Thumping and pounding, around the corner he came. *No.* Not he came. But rather, *he* came.

A monster of a man. Over six feet tall, and wide, wide, wide. Muscles that bulged, muscles that dominated and frightened. Hair cut short. Two days of beard growth as obvious on his face as his scowl. Soot. Everywhere. His hands. His clothes. His twisted lips. His eyes, though… They were clear. Focused on Veronica.

I'm coming for you, they said.

She stared back, the world whipping all around her. More sirens—the fire engine this time—echoed over the terrible beat of her heart.

The captain was already moving, already dashing toward Ellis as fast as his frame would allow. For a second, Veronica thought the cop would simply shoot the other man. But she had a funny feeling that a bullet would pass straight through him.

Farriday doesn't know that.

He'd already drawn his useless weapon.

Veronica dived forward, frantic to issue a warning. She made it only two steps before another policeman came barrelling around the corner. Yet another jumped in. It took all three of them to take Ellis down.

A pair of arms around his legs.

A knee into his back.

A set of hands, securing his wrists with cuffs.

But they couldn't control his stare. They couldn't stop it from burning into Veronica, and they couldn't silence his dangerous promise.

There'll be more opportunities.

She was so sure that hadn't changed. Even as they dragged Ellis Black away. Even as they loaded her into the ambulance. Even as they promised to keep her safe. He would find a means. It was just a matter of how long.

6
Twelve Hours After Escape

The Preacher's Daughter

Too clean.

The phrase kept coming, and every time Veronica tried to dismiss it, the stark whiteness of the room would hit her like a smack, and it would echo again.

Too clean.

"Ms. Hollister. Are you still with us?"

She snapped up her head at the question. It came from the woman who'd stationed herself in the corner of the room, a watchful eye trained on Captain Farriday more than on Veronica. A lioness in a white coat, ready to pounce at the slightest misstep. That wasn't what Veronica wanted. Protection from the man in uniform wasn't a concern. But she said nothing to make the woman leave, too afraid that anything that came out of her mouth would be wrong.

The lioness in the corner spoke up again, her voice reassuring. "For now, sweetheart, the police don't need a detailed account. Just your best summary. I'll be here if you need me to stop things or if anything is too triggering. Stick to the truth in your own words, and you'll be fine."

The truth.

Veronica inhaled. One person's truth was another person's lie. Easy enough to twist. Even through the pain, Ellis had taught her that. Beaten it in. But it wasn't something she could say aloud. It wasn't something she wanted in her own head. And if the lioness was in there, probing around... God only knew what she'd find. What she'd drag out. Terrible things. Things that didn't need to be pulled from her head into the light. Things that made this Veronica's fault.

"If you don't feel like you're ready, Ms. Hollister, you don't have to do this," added the woman, taking a step closer and addressing the captain now. "I told you. She's not ready. You can't force her."

"Lives could be on the line," Farriday replied.

"I understand, officer, but—"

"Captain."

"I understand. *Captain*. But—"

"I want to go home," Veronica said.

Two sets of eyes found her. Judging. Questioning. Making her want to shrink in on herself. But she shook her head and cleared her throat.

"I don't want to stay here in the hospital," she said.

"Ms. Hollister," said the other woman, "this is the safest place for you. You're getting the best medical care available. If you're not ready to answer questions, that part can wait."

Veronica shook her head again. It was true she didn't want to answer a hundred questions, but stalling wouldn't do any good. It wouldn't change what had been done. She just didn't want to do it here. Not with the bleachy smell and the beeping machines and the prying eyes.

"Just him," she said abruptly. "And then I want to go home. Please."

The lioness appeared not to understand. "Just who?"

Veronica made herself nod toward the policeman, the bob of her head turning the clean, white room into a snowy blur. "Him. I'll talk to him."

"The captain?"

"Yes. Please."

"You're sure?"

You don't owe him anything, even if he saved you, said the woman's face.

But I do, thought Veronica nodding. "Yes."

"I… Okay. Yes. Give us a moment."

Veronica closed her eyes as the captain shuffled backward to join the lioness in her corner. And she did her best to tune out their conversation, struggling to ignore words like *victim* and *transference* and warnings for Captain Farriday to be cautious in the right way. But blocking out the world around her gave her mind time to wander. Time to find the fresh memories. The motel room. The chair. The rope, tightening on her wrists.

"Ms. Hollister?" said Farriday.

Not here. No rope. No Ellis.

A cool hand landed on her arm, making her jump, then sink back into the bed as her eyes opened. She genuinely couldn't tell which one had touched her. The captain's gaze was on her, the lioness's on the monitor beside Veronica's bed. The heart-rate line danced up and down erratically, and the machine emitted a piercing warning. It made sense, really, with the way her chest thudded.

"Sorry," Veronica said.

"I can stay," the lioness replied.

Veronica breathed in, trying to slow her pulse. "No. That's not what I want."

"You're sure?"

Hadn't the woman already asked that? Veronica's head was fuzzy. But she needed to focus or they might find a way to make her stay here in this bed.

"It's…" *God, give me strength.* "Captain Farriday reminds me of my father. I *want* to talk to him. I want to help him."

The two exchanged a glance. Concerned. But a bit relieved, too. Now they understood why she—the victim— would want to speak to a man, even after her traumatic experience. Acceptable transference. The captain in lieu of her murdered parent.

"Please," said Veronica. "And after I'm done…"

"You want to go home," replied the lioness in an easy,people-pleaser voice. "I caught that. But do you think you could give us twenty-four hours, Ms. Hollister? Just to make sure you're all right."

Twenty-four hours.

It was too long. Veronica shook her head, and a lock of hair dropped into her face. Immediately, she wished for a ponytail holder or an elastic band. Her loose curls were too wild. Too wanton. They made her self-conscious.

"Can I have a hair elastic?" she asked abruptly.

The other woman blinked. "Pardon me?"

Shouldn't have asked.

Ashamed, Veronica looked down at her hands. They'd been washed and dressed, but she could see the bloody and bruised edges.

"Ms. Hollister?"

"Never mind."

But Captain Farriday jumped in. "Just get her a damned hair elastic, Dr. Yves. And unhook these machines as soon as you can."

The fact that the lioness was a doctor surprised Veronica, though it probably shouldn't have. And knowing it somehow cut away a bit of the other woman's fierceness.

Veronica watched the woman purse her lips. But she didn't argue. The captain was the cop. And even if the hospital belonged to the lioness—Dr. Yves—ultimately her patient would leave, taking with her the memory of the crime rather than leaving it here in the bed. Veronica would carry it inside, always. In that way, she was more a part of the captain's future than of the doctor's. If anything, she was already a part of the other woman's past.

Veronica's gaze drifted back to her hands, waiting for the doctor to leave. She didn't look up again until the door to the hospital room clicked shut.

"You ready, kiddo?" Captain Farriday asked.

"Will you let me go home?" she inquired in return. "I'll do

what I can. I promise."

Veronica met his gaze with as much steadiness as she could muster. "Where do you want me to start?"

"How about at the beginning," he suggested.

She hesitated. "The beginning?"

"If you're up to it."

Her palms were suddenly sweaty. Itchy under the bandages. She wanted desperately to scratch. To rip off the gauze and tear into the tingling skin with her chipped nails. But she didn't dare. Doing it might bring back the doctor, when all she needed was the sergeant.

Trying to ground herself, her eyes moved around the room in search of a focal point. She finally realized what it was that bothered her about the hospital. It reminded her—rather solidly—of the prison. How could it not? Bleach and sweat and sickness. Had no one ever noticed how closely the hospital's atmosphere matched that of the home for the incarcerated?

And that was as good a starting point as any, she decided.

"The first thing I remember," she said. "Is the smell. And then him. Ellis. When I still thought he was Bobby."

7

Ten Months Before Escape

The Preacher's Daughter

He wore a slate gray jumpsuit rather than an orange one, but that gave her no excuse. The man was enormous. Based on the height and length of the table, she'd guess him to be six foot five, at least. His legs jutted out under it, and his torso loomed over it. And he had to weigh two hundred and fifty pounds. More, maybe. Hadn't she heard that muscle was heavier than fat? Roni couldn't imagine the terror of the pizza guy who'd been caught behind the wheel while this man took his car. Every bit of exposed skin, however minimal it was, showcased scarily defined muscle. Covered in tattoos.

The inked patterns were intricate. Eye-popping. *Unnerving.*

It was impossible to know where to look. Roni settled for his hands.

Her eyes hung there while her tongue glued itself to the roof of her mouth.

His fingers were as long and thick and dangerous as the rest of him. His nails had been cut bluntly short, and though they were split in some places—evidence of physical labor, Roni thought—no hint of dirt touched them. Thick knuckles flexed just a little. A vein on the back of one hand twitched. He rolled his wrists to face his palms up, and she saw what a struggle it was for him to move, even that much. The shackles held him tight. They'd been fastened to his cuffs and the table, and they kept him from adjusting more than a few inches. *No. That's not quite it.*

The chains weren't *attached* to the table. They'd been run *through* it, then hooked to an anchor in the floor.

In spite of the fear that permeated her body and mind, Roni winced sympathetically. Wasn't it overkill, even for a man who was on his fifth strike?

She didn't realize she'd spoken the words aloud until the prisoner's rumbling voice echoed the question back to her. "Do *you* think it's overkill?"

"Yes," she admitted, inching closer to the table.

"So why didn't you say something to the guard?"

She flushed. She couldn't very well tell him she hadn't noticed him there until the guard had already walked out. It was absurd.

"What would I say?" she countered instead. "I can't tell the guards how to do their jobs."

"Not even if the way they're doing them is immoral?"

It was a valid query. Where did the line get drawn? Prisoners were prisoners. They were paying a debt to society. But what rights did that take away? Some? All? Did *not* being chained to a table fall under the heading of human rights? Roni wasn't sure. She just knew when something felt wrong. And seeing Bobby Lines held this way definitely seemed off.

But saying all of that seemed like a dangerous way to start off a conversation with an incarcerated man. So, she refrained and drew out the chair opposite the man instead.

"Do you know who I am?" she asked.

For the first time, he lifted his gaze. Sharp blue eyes pinned her to the spot, one hand on the back of the chair, one foot poised to swing around it.

He was young. Far younger than she would've thought — not all that far off from her own age, she suspected. It made her want to rail against the injustice. To stand up and demand to know what had led him down this path when there were so many more years in front of him. Or maybe just drop to her knees and pray for a way out on his behalf.

But then he spoke—"*Sit.*"—and she had to acknowledge that the quietly authoritative expectation of obedience bred more than a sliver of gratitude for the chains. She dragged the chair out anyway, then perched on the edge.

"I know who you are," Bobby said. "The church guy's daughter."

"I prefer being called by my name." "Do you, Veronica?" He sounded amused.

She refused to be baited. "It's Roni. And don't *you*?" He lifted one of his eyebrows. "Doesn't suit you too well. And I suppose."

She wasn't going to let it go that easily, though she couldn't have said what it was that made her want to persist. "I think it suits me just fine. And you *suppose*? Would you like it if I called you by whatever number they've given you in here? Or by your crime?"

For a moment, his features became shadowed. Then his lips pursed like he was trying to hold something in. And it turned out he was—a laugh. Deep and as slick as the blond hair he had pulled back into a short ponytail at the nape of his neck. It filled the room in an utterly out-of-place way.

Roni stared at him, startled by his mirth. It took several seconds for his laugh to taper into a chuckle, and when it finally did, he leaned back as if he wasn't locked down, and fixed her with a grin. She'd been wrong to think his calm face was frightening. This look was far worse. It sent a lick of something deeply unpleasant through her. Almost, she bolted. Only her sweat-inducing willpower kept her feet from moving.

Bobby gave her a nod. "You've got more guts than a girl named Roni."

"That sounds like a compliment," she replied. "But it feels like an insult."

"Just not what I expected."

"What *did* you expect?"

"Dunno. Long skirt. Ugly blouse."

Roni glanced down without meaning to. Her skirt brushed her ankles; her blouse was bland. She yanked her head back up to meet Bobby's gaze again. He looked even more amused than he had before.

"Still," he said. "As gutsy as you are, you didn't complain about my chains."

"I told you—"

"I know. It's not *your* job to tell them how to do *their* job." He studied her for a second, his eyes assessing. "But whose job *is* it?"

Roni sank into the chair. "Their supervisors."

"And if the supervisors are complicit?"

"Are they complicit?"

"For argument's sake, let's say they are."

"Well. Then I think there's a board of directors."

"And if they do nothing as well? Does it just keep going all the way up the chain until it reaches God himself?"

"I guess..." She trailed off, unsure what to say.

"When do people come into play, Nic?"

She blinked. *Nic?* Had he somehow managed to come up with his own name for her in just five minutes? There was something too intimate about the idea. But maybe that was his game. Maybe it was an intimidation tactic. Or simply a way to throw her off.

Or maybe it doesn't mean a lick. Because what makes you sure he has *a game?*

Nothing. Except that her heart told her it was true. The smiles and the questions and the sly look on his face now... Yes. He had a game. And she was pretty sure he was waiting for her to make the next move. So she kept silent. Patience and quiet were two things she was very good at. But the same couldn't be said for him, apparently. Mild annoyance crossed his features as he waited.

He finally sighed. "No answer to that?"

Feeling triumphant, Roni nodded. "Everyone answers to God. But that doesn't mean we don't have a responsibility here on Earth."

"So why not in this case? Why not question the shackles?" He rattled them for emphasis. "Have ten minutes behind these walls already corrupted you?"

"Of course not."

"You sure about that?"

The devious look in his eyes didn't give her quite enough warning. His chair skidded forward, driving his chest to the table, and his hand shot out. The chain scraped up, up, through the hole. And like lightning, his fingers closed on hers, clutching oh-so tightly.

Warm. Rough.

Surprisingly pleasant.

Frightened by the last one, Roni tried to jerk her hands away. She failed. His grip was demandingly solid. Not one she wanted to engage in a tug-of-war.

So she lifted her eyes and offered him a cool stare instead. "You're not allowed to touch me."

"But I am," he pointed out.

"You need to let me go."

He didn't. Instead, he pulled a thumb over the back of her hand in a way that made her shiver in fear. Her eyes sought the video camera. And she saw something she hadn't before. It was closed. A lid covered the lens. So in spite of the red, flashing light, she knew without a doubt that she was truly alone with this behemoth of a man. Who was smiling a slow, danger-laden smile now.

"Doesn't it seem like cruel and unusual punishment?" he asked.

"What?"

"The lack of human contact."

"I—" She cut herself off abruptly.

"You what?"

She licked her lips nervously. Lying felt wrong. But so did admitting that the very same thought had crossed her mind just a few minutes before.

Minutes that feel like hours.

"If I don't let you go..." There was a teasing undertone in his voice. "Are you going to tattle on me?"

"Yes."

"And you think that'll get me in more trouble than I'm already in?"

"Won't it?"

He shrugged, but he didn't let her go. "Solitary. Maybe."

She breathed in, trying to focus on anything but the feel of her hand clasped in his. "That can't be something you want."

"Gives me time to think."

"About what?"

His eyes ran over her face slowly. Then dropped. Then seared across her chest and slid over her breasts slowly.

She fought an embarrassed gasp. The heat in her face, though, couldn't be beaten down. She kept her head up anyway, refusing to let his lewdness get to her.

"What were you expecting to hear about?" he asked in a low voice. "My musings on Descartes?"

"I have no idea what goes on in the mind of a criminal," she informed him stiffly.

He dropped her hands, dismissive. "Well, Nic. The things that go on in the mind of a criminal are simple. He thinks about all the things he *can't* do behind bars. Crack a beer. Watch a first-run movie. Fuck a pretty girl."

Now she did gasp. And push to her feet.

He shot her a darkly amused look as she scuttled backward. "It'd be naïve of you not to accept the truth of it. But I guess that's a thing for you, hmm?"

The assumption—however true—piqued her anger. "You don't know anything about me."

"I know enough."

"You don't." Petulance rang through the denial, and Roni's cheeks warmed all the more. "I'm leaving."

"When are you coming back?"

"It should be pretty obvious that I'm not."

"Why? Did you reform the troubled Bobby Lines?" The convict's question was a sneer that managed to be underlined with amusement at her expense. "Did you get through to him? Accomplish what you came here to do?"

"I don't—" Roni stopped herself just in time.

I don't know what I came here to do.

That's what she'd been about to tell him. But it was untrue. She knew exactly why she was there. Her father had told her she *had* to go, so she'd come. She could only imagine what the man sitting across from her would say if she admitted that to him.

Why do you care what he thinks?

"Second thoughts, Nic? Want to stay a little longer and find out what *I* can offer *you*?"

She said nothing. Instead, she banged on the door, careful to make sure the knocks didn't sound as panicked as the thuds of her heart. And when the door opened, Roni pushed through the hall, ignoring—or maybe not really hearing, if she was being honest—the parting words of the guards. Each step made her queasier, and the fluorescent lights and crushingly white walls didn't help.

She needed air. Non-bleach-y, non-recirculated, non-Bobby-Lines air. Was desperate for it.

Please, please.

She didn't know what she was pleading for. But whatever it was, she didn't get it as her hand closed on the cold door handle, nor as she flung herself into the cloying July sunshine. The first gulp of oxygen she got wasn't enough to stave off the nausea or to hold in the heave of her stomach. She couldn't even dredge up enough dignity to glance back to see if anyone was watching as she leaned over the nearest bush and threw up. Once, twice. A third time. And a fourth, which was nothing but acid that burned her throat.

At the end, she collapsed to her knees. The rough concrete stairs dug into her skin, and she was almost grateful for the way it hurt. At least she knew the pain to be specific. At least she knew its source. Unlike whatever it was that tore at her heart. That, she didn't recognize.

Roni pressed her hands to her thighs, trying to sort out the rush of emotions that made her head spin. It seemed like an impossible task. Too many feelings vied for supremacy. She was confused. Surprised. And angry. That one was a given. At herself, for letting him get under her skin and for not doing what she came there to do. At him, for calling her out. For laughing at her expense. For stating opinions that mirrored her own and for making himself seem *moral.*

But what did you think would happen? asked a small voice in her head. *Did you think he'd fit some pre-established mold?*

She sucked in some more warm air. She knew very well how multi-faceted people were, so trying to tuck the inmate into some tidy package made no sense. But she hadn't been anticipating having anything in common with the man. Even before she learned what his crimes were, she'd made certain assumptions. Categorized him. Thought of herself as better. Which wasn't the case at all. They were both human. And that made them equal under God. She was no less righteous, no less sinful. And she had no right to put herself on a pedestal.

The realization made her press her palms to her thighs and arch her neck enough that she could see the outline of the prison.

The building was a single story. It sprawled across the naked ground, its octagonal shape deceptively still. It reminded her of something, though she couldn't put her finger on what it was exactly.

Roni blew out the breath she'd drawn in. In spite of the sickness that still tugged at her guts, she had an odd urge to go back in and apologize. To ask Bobby Lines to forgive her for doing him such a terrible disservice.

For a moment, the need to do it pulled at her so strongly that she actually pushed to her feet unconsciously and moved forward. She had to force herself to hold still. To turn. To leave behind the compulsion and remind herself that if her penance didn't come from this, it *would* come from elsewhere.

As she stepped away from the jaws of the prison, she managed to get almost all the way to the bus stop before hazarding a final glance back. And she figured out what the prison's shape brought to mind.

A coiled snake.

Watching.

Waiting.

Deadly.

8
Nine Months, Six Days Before Escape

The Convict

E llis flicked the key across his fingers, watching absently as the silver-tinged metal moved from knuckle to knuckle like some oddly themed magic trick. The noise and feel of it—tick, tick, tick and flash, flash, flash—provided a small sliver of comfort in the void of his empty cell. It was two in the morning, but there was no one to complain about the distraction. He was one of the few cellmate-less guests at Meridian Correctional Facility. The separateness was one of those conundrums. "Blessing," he said to the key.

Tick-flash-tick.

"Curse," he added.

Flash-tick-flash.

Alone.

Flash-flash. Tick-flash. Flash-tick.

Lonely.

At the beginning, he'd been like everyone else. He'd had a cellmate. Charles. Chuck. C-man. The block Perv, incarcerated for multiple counts of possession of child pornography but deemed to not be a threat to other inmates. Unless the inmate was a just-turned-seventeen-year-old boy, of course.

Tried as an adult—but still very much legally a child— Ellis had walked the line of risk himself. His violent history was a proven fact. His confession was as gruesome as his crime. His age, though, made things uncertain. Youth were malleable. Not fully formed. There might've been hope for reformation.

Flash-flash-tick.

Tick-tick-flash.

Still. Sticking the Perv in with the Kid seemed like an odd thing to do. Bad planning on the prison's part, Ellis supposed. Or maybe overcrowding. Fuck. It was quite possibly intelligent design. Hard to say.

Flash-flash.

Tick-tick.

Self-defense, they called it after. It was true. Waking to find a man's hand between his thighs, night after night had grown to be too much to bear. What else could he do to protect himself?

Though Ellis had a lot of rage to start with, even before that. More than his share of teen angst; he could admit it. All of the *'me-me-me'* mentality and a refusal to regret things that seemed a necessary evil. Was he a narcissist? A sociopath? Something else? Who could say? It was such a long time ago now. The system hadn't given him a label, and the doc deemed him capable of understanding the difference between right and wrong.

Self-defence against Chuck, yes. Not culpable on that count? Harder to be sure.

He'd used the soap pump to do it. Mostly because the opportunity had presented itself.

Pump-pump went the pink, commercial-grade foam after he'd taken a piss.

Snap-snap went the dispenser, breaking straight into his palm.

At first, Ellis had thought someone might notice. They didn't. A day went by. Then two. A week. The Perv wasn't much into hygiene. The guards were overworked and underpaid, and their cell inspections were half-assed. So Ellis held it. Three days more. Under his pillow. In the strange little dip in the wall, right beside his bunk. Then in his hand. The metal was warm. Secure. Deadly when coming up against a man who'd put his hand between Ellis's legs.

Fucker.

Well. Not after that.

Ellis had woken in the infirmary, covered in blood that wasn't his own. The doctor told him he was fine. Badly bruised, but he would be okay. The small, lab-coat-wearing man had seemed apologetic. Maybe he realized that Charles and Ellis were a bad match. Maybe he wished he could say so. He didn't.

Ellis heard the whispers only later. Rumors about the small, jagged-edged soap pump. Lodged in Chuck's eye. The screams that carried through the prison.

Tick-flash. Flash-tick.

For a time after that, Ellis was alone. Not lonely. He didn't know how long. He wasn't one for counting off days on the wall. He didn't request a calendar. It might've been a year. It might've been two. He did the work he was assigned. Collected his prison pay—how laughable he found that, being able to earn an income in here better than he ever could out there—and minded his own goddamn business. Then came the new cellmate, and he seemed innocuous enough. To start. Simon was his name.

He had a sense of humor, which was a rarity behind the walls. He made jokes. *Simon says, get in line for an ass-whooping. Simon says, pay off the guards. Simon says, keeps smiling.* Ellis laughed, even when it wasn't funny.

Thinking back, maybe there were signs the man wasn't all right.

"So many maybes," Ellis murmured, pausing in his flip-flip-flipping to study the edge of the key.

Simon sold drugs. In the prison and out of it. Heroin, mostly. A bad batch had killed sixteen people, elevating Simon to mass murder status. His official charge, though, was involuntary manslaughter.

Simon says, he didn't want those people to die.

One of them was a thirteen-year-old girl.

The story came out slowly. It might've taken another year. Ellis still didn't count.

There were secret celebrations. Booze made from potatoes stolen from the mess hall. Dope. Consumed using smokeless pipes crafted from scrap metal and scrap glass and scrap plastic. Bit by bit, the confession leaked out. Like puss from a festering wound.

The thirteen-year-old was a whore. Thrown out by her mother. Starving on the streets for months. Simon took her in. He didn't need to pay her because she'd perform for ramen noodles and cable TV and tiny tastes of poison.

Simon says, it was consensual.

The thirteen-year-old got a little too comfortable. Hot meals. Warm bed. The thirteen-year-old got a little too pregnant. Hot water. Burning soul.

Simon says, he had a wife who wasn't too impressed.

Bad heroin wasn't all that hard to come by. Not when you were Simon, the man with the ready smile and the readier connections.

Sixteen people died. One of them was a thirteen-year-old girl. She was found in a dumpster, her body bloated and old beyond its years. No autopsy was performed; the cause of death was obvious.

Simon says, it's too bad she had his driver's license in her pocket or else he might've gotten off completely.

The guards found him one morning. Simon couldn't say much at all after that.

Ellis, though, was out in the yard, lifting weights. A newfound passion. A means of blowing off steam and blocking out the way a man's face looked when the oxygen stopped coming.

Suicide.

Death by self-asphyxiation.

The books said so.

After that, Ellis didn't get another cellmate. Fine with him.

Most often, it was nothing more than boredom that reigned. Though he could admit that he was a bit lonely, now and then. If he had to guess, he'd say that's why the pretty little thing got to him. Why he couldn't get her out of his mind. Even the way the key danced over his knuckles made him think of her. Rhythmic. Pulsing. Sensual without meaning to be that way.

Veronica.

The name had sharp edges that pricked at the tongue.

"Nic," he murmured, pleased with himself for the personal claim that shortening laid on her.

Not cute like *Roni,* as she claimed to like to be called. Not soft, like *Sarah* or *Melissa.* In the dark, thinking of her made him the opposite of soft, actually.

Tick-tick—

"Hey, Black!" The voice cut through the otherwise endless, sleepless night.

He said nothing back.

"Black! I know you're awake. I can hear you slapping your cock. What's on your mind, Black? Thinking 'bout that sweet little sister of yours?"

The question brought no shame. A guilty conscience was a luxury only the *un*incarcerated could afford.

"Shut up, fuckwit!" called someone else. "Let the man masturbate in peace."

That comment filled the block with laughter, and the laughter brought the guard, who made a beeline for Ellis' cell. In the dark, the uniformed man swept a flashlight over the six-by-eight room.

"Watcha got there, Black?"

Ellis flipped the key a little faster and blinked into the yellow beam. The guard on the other side of the bars was new, and he was full of cocky, authoritative self-assurance that made Ellis wonder what would happen if he was stripped of his power. Rather suddenly.

There was always a pecking order. At school. At work. In a home. The prison was no different, though the system seemed overly complex. There were offenses to consider. Durations of sentencings. Repeat offenders. Physical size. Gang affiliations. Economic status and race. Willingness to commit crimes of varying nature while inside. Which dick was being sucked, and who was doing the sucking. Who liked whom at any given moment.

Take the current senior guard, for example. *He* liked Ellis. Called him a lone wolf. A prince among thieves. Ellis didn't know why. If he wore a crown, it would be tarnished and broken. Stolen off the head of a king he'd killed himself.

Truthfully, though, he didn't care if he was liked or not. Except when it brought him the occasional privilege. Protection from the other guards. A spontaneous visit with a pretty girl because someone was willing to let him use a dead man's name.

Bobby Lines.

Poor fucker had expired in the lunch line three days earlier. Too bad the paperwork got "lost in the mail," and Bobby's scheduled appointments hadn't been canceled. Too bad this morning's guard had been willing to let that detail slide when a God-fearing man's fine young daughter showed up for a visit.

Ellis smiled.

Flick-flick-flick. Tick-tick-tick.

There was no real reason for Ellis to have gone out of his way to see the girl. Nothing specific he'd had in mind. Just the satisfaction of thwarting the system was enough—and there were guards aplenty who like to exercise their control of that system by manipulating it, too. The whole thing was as hardon-inducing as Veronica herself.

"Asked you a question, Black." The guard's voice cut off his happy-ending reverie. "What the hell have you got there? A fucking *key*? Hand it over."

The other man stepped closer, and Ellis was up, his arm a bolt of lightning. Hand through the bars at hip height. Fingers on the man's belt, pulling him fast and hard against the slots. Before the guard could react, Ellis had used his other hand to unsnap his baton from the man's side, jerked it into the extended position, and had it pressed to his chin.

"Move," he growled, "and I'll use this to break your fucking windpipe."

The guard twitched.

Up and down the cell block, silence hung thick.

"You're new," Ellis said. "But I promise you, *I am not.* I've been living in this block, in this exact cell for a decade. You were probably in grade school the day I checked in. You'll probably get tired of this place – sick of it, let it make you crazy – before I'm done. Maybe you'll make it to retirement. But I doubt it."

"You son-of-a-bitch, I'm gonna—"

"Gonna what? Tell the chief guard? Go ahead. See what he's got to say about *you* letting *me* relieve *you* of your one and only weapon. Explain to him that the reason you're alive is that I let you go."

In his grip, the man quivered.

"That's right," said Ellis. "No need to think it through. You can't come out on top, friend."

"You'll get sent to solitary."

"Maybe."

"No. Not may—"

"You think that matters to me anyway? You think I haven't been sent there before, or that I *mind*?" He pressed the button up hard enough that the other man gagged, and he called out, "Hey, Dan!"

A reluctant response carried from the cell beside his own. "Yeah, Black?"

"Tell the new guard how I feel about solitary."

A sigh echoed through the block. "He doesn't care, man. Some of us go crazy. Most of us, I guess. But Black... I think he might like it."

Ellis might've laughed. If only it weren't true.

9

Twelve Hours After Escape

The Policeman

arriday leaned forward, eager to hear what the girl was about to say.

She met his eyes, fear, exhaustion, and the effects of whatever the hospital was feeding her through the IV marking her gaze. She bit her lower lip, and the split there brightened with a fresh drop of blood.

Farriday's eyes hung on it for a moment. He felt sorry for her. He really did. She was a sweet kid, even broken and battered as she was at the moment. Where it wasn't bruised and scraped, her skin was creamy and unlined. Young. So young. He regretted that Black had marred that and harmed her. But he wanted—no, *needed*—to know what else the son-of-a-bitch had gotten up to during those hours between leaving the prison and getting captured. Who had he spoken with? Who else had he hurt? More importantly, who was he *going* to harm, and had he told Veronica Hollister any of his plans? Farriday's gut was screaming that simply getting away wasn't Ellis's endgame.

So, he needed her to talk more. To give her statement about the parts that mattered, while it was all still fresh in her mind. No matter how much it pained her. It was for the greater good. And currently, her eyes appeared to be doing their damnedest to close. What she'd told him so far was nothing but background noise.

"Kiddo." He said it patiently and kindly despite his eagerness for answers. The girl deserved nothing if not that. "You're safe here with me."

She didn't respond. The bead of blood on her lips had lengthened, and now it threatened to drip down to her chin. She showed no sign of wiping it away. Maybe she didn't know it was there because she was trapped in some dark memory from her recent trauma.

Farriday wanted to push her, but he was sure Dr. Yves was lurking somewhere out in the hall, waiting for an excuse to come back. The woman was a physician who fancied herself a psychiatrist. And as much as he valued the medical professionals, they always believed that patient care outweighed crime solving. It made little sense to him. What good did it do to handle a person so carefully that it risked endangering the lives of others?

He suppressed an urge to glance over his shoulder. He kept his eyes on Veronica. Would it help if she understood what it meant to him—personally—to know how that son-of-a-bitch had orchestrated an escape? Would the human connection prod her to disclose more?

Her eyelids fluttered just then, and she lifted them to meet his gaze. "Do you know him?"

The question was so close to his train of thought that it caught him a little off-guard, and it made him hesitate in his reply. He could tell her. All he had to do was give her enough that the disclosure evoked some trust.

"I made the arrest, ten years ago," he said.

"When he raped and killed his sister?" As blunt and dark as the question was, Veronica's tone was hollow.

Farriday remained impassive as he nodded. "Emily. I like to use her name."

"Yes. That's good. Emily."

"Did Ellis tell you that himself? About me knowing him and his sister?"

"He talked about you a lot," she said. "He blames you for what happened to him."

He nodded again. "I'm sure he does. But he confessed to the crime, Ms. Hollister. He pled guilty in a court of law."

"He said you caught him—" She drew a shuddering breath and tried again. "Caught him in the act. He told me how you found him. What it looked like. What his sister—what Emily looked like in that moment."

Anger made his fist tighten and this time, it was harder for Farriday to maintain the even tone. "I'm sorry you had to hear it."

"It's my own fault."

"You know that's not true, kiddo. Ellis Black is a very bad man."

"But I let him in." Her voice cracked.

Farriday reached out, but Veronica flinched away, and he dropped his hand without touching her. *For the best, anyway.*

"You did nothing wrong," he said. "From what the prison guards tell me, you were trying to help Ellis."

Her eyes closed again, but her breathing stayed hitched. Her hands flexed a few times, and he was sure she was fighting tears.

"My dad..." She trailed off and swallowed.

"I'm so sorry," Farriday replied.

"We didn't always see things the same way," she said without opening her eyes. "But he wanted to bring his version of God to even the most undeserving of men. That's why he sent me to the prison."

"His death isn't on your hands. Ellis killed him." He paused. "Veronica... Roni... I really need to ask you some questions about those hours between the time Ellis escaped and the time when we found you." She inhaled. Exhaled. Met his gaze once more.

"When you saved me, you mean," she said. "We were just doing our job."

"Thank you."

"You're welcome."

Sensing a window, he opened his mouth to ask a more direct question, but a light rap on the door stopped him and made him turn instead. A uniformed officer stood on the other side of the glass with a nervous look on his face. When the officer saw that he'd caught Farriday's attention, he gestured for the captain to join him.

What now?

"Is everything okay?" Veronica asked.

Farriday had no idea, but he sure as heck wasn't going to tell that to her, so he nodded anyway. "Give me one second, all right?"

"Sure."

Trying to hide his irritation, Farriday waited until he was in the hall with the door closed behind them before addressing the young officer.

"Better be good, Constable," he said. "I'm working my butt off trying to get a statement from a traumatized witness."

"Sorry, sir. You weren't answering the radio." The officer's eyes flicked over Farriday's shoulder, curiosity marking his features.

The captain repositioned himself to block the view.

"Like I said. Getting a statement. Now spit it out."

"Ellis Black is gone."

If Farriday had been expecting to hear anything in particular, it wasn't that. The floor dropped out from under him, and he grabbed hold of the railing on the wall in order to keep from swaying. For a good second, he truly believed he might be having a stroke. But as he righted himself and straightened his shoulders, and the world stopped swimming, he realized the reality of the situation was no less heinous.

Ellis Black is on the loose. Again.

"Hell," he muttered. "*Hell.*"

"Sir?" said the uniformed man.

Farriday stepped closer and dropped his voice. "How did this happen?"

MELINDA DI LORENZO

"I..."

The young officer's Adam's apple bobbed. His boss's tone clearly surprised him; Farriday wasn't in the habit of giving his men flack. But this situation called for action. Softness wouldn't do.

"Where was he?" he asked, no less brusquely.

"The interrogation room, like you said to do."

"At the table? Locked down? Door guarded?"

"Yes, sir," said the constable. "All of that."

"Tell me you didn't step into the bathroom?"

The other man was quick to shake his head. "No, of course not. But I wasn't at the door anyway, sir. It was Constable Lauren. And for the record, it wasn't negligence. Ellis uncuffed himself, opened the door, then knocked Constable Lauren unconscious before managing to sneak out."

"How?"

The constable cleared his throat. "Apparently he used his fist."

The impatience that had been building up inside Farriday burst to the surface. "Not how did he knock him out, man. How in God's name did Ellis Black get a set of keys to a pair of police handcuffs?"

But as soon as the words were out, he recalled a moment in the parking lot. Veronica had been clinging tightly to Farriday, propelled into his arms as Ellis went past, just a couple of inches away. Ellis had brushed up against him.

"Hell," he said again under his breath.

They weren't equipped for this kind of chaos. Infractions in town were minor and also few and far between. The occasional bar fight. Disagreements between neighbors. As a result, Farriday's men were soft and inexperienced and unused to having to be on their toes. In all his years as a cop here in town, the worst thing he'd had to deal with was a drunk, pissed-off teenager who'd stolen a car and purposely driven it into his parents' living room.

Worst thing to happen since Ellis's sister was killed, you mean?

"Should we put out the APB, sir?" asked the constable.

Farriday lifted his cap and ran his hand over his head. Black needed to be caught. Stopped immediately before this could blow up worse than it already had. But did Farriday want this little debacle all over the news? Not if he could help it. Not so close to the final moments of his career.

Just a bit longer.

"How long ago did he get out?" he asked.

"They found Constable Lauren about five minutes in," replied the uniformed man.

"And you came here right away?"

"I tried to call you three times on the radio and twice on the phone. Then I came. I'd say that took no less than ten minutes, no more than fifteen?" *Twenty minutes, max.*

How far could Black have gotten in that time? It depended. Did the man have new transportation? A fresh disguise? Was his intention to go somewhere at all? The captain's gut was kicking up another fuss. "Sir?" the constable said. "An APB?"

Farriday cleared his throat. "Who all has gone home? The reserves?"

"Only the guys on duty stayed behind. We sent the others home when we caught Black the first time."

The first time. Lord how he hated that phrase at the moment.

"Let's play this cool," he said. "Set up a roadblock on Route One with all hands on deck again. Reserve, too. Call it a DUI check for any civilians who pass through. And Hilltop PD still owes us that favor?"

The constable nodded. "Yeah. We sent Brody over to help man their parade a few weeks back."

"Perfect," said Farriday. "I'll call Merkle, give him Ellis's description, but tell him to keep it on the down low. If one of his guys spots *our* guy, I want them to call me directly."

"What about a warning for the public?" The constable's expression said he regretted the question as soon as it was asked, but he didn't retract it.

"We don't want to needlessly alarm the whole town. That'll wreak more havoc and probably interfere with our investigation," Farriday replied. "We caught him quickly once, didn't we?"

"Yes, sir."

"If there's a threat, we'll deal with it. And realistically, Constable... I don't think Ellis Black is going to put himself on display. Why risk his freedom? But if I'm wrong about that, I'll take responsibility for any fallout. You wait here and station yourself outside Ms. Hollister's room for the duration of her stay, all right?"

"Yeah, I can do that."

"Good man." Farriday clapped him on the back. "We'll put a car outside, too."

Trying to come up with the best thing to say to Veronica Hollister—because he couldn't leave without a word—he stopped with his hand midway to the door. He could see her through the window. One arm was tucked up beside her body, the other flung wide across the bed. Her eyes were closed, her mouth a little open as her chest rose and fell in steady breaths. *Asleep.* This time, he was thankful for her exhaustion.

He addressed the constable. "If Ms. Hollister wakes and has questions, call me. Don't let it slip about Black's escape."

The kid nodded. "Got it."

Farriday cast one more glance at Veronica. Did she know anything that could help him search out the convict? Had Ellis said something that might give him a clue as to the other man's whereabouts? Possibly. Even if she didn't know it. But he didn't have time to coax it out of her slowly now. He had a man to catch. No way in hell was he going to let Ellis Black ruin the career that he's spent the last ten years so carefully rebuilding.

10

Nine Months,
Fifteen Days Before Escape

The Preacher's Daughter

"Roni!"

Her name was like a gunshot, piercing the mindless task of washing the dishes. She turned and flashed a guilty look in her father's direction. He sat at the table, smoke curling from the pipe he held clenched between his teeth. Despite the cool breeze blowing in through the screen door, he had a sheen of sweat covering his exposed chest and wrinkled face. That sticky shine was always there, especially when he smoked. A vice he acknowledged. One he said God acknowledged too, in the form of high blood pressure and a bad heart.

He lifted an eyebrow. "Said your name three times, baby girl. You lost in la-la land, or what?"

She opened her mouth to answer, but a voice in her head spoke up before she could. *Do you think maybe that's because he called you Roni?*

It was an absurd thought.

Would you have heard him if he'd called you Nic instead? asked the same voice, now sounding far too familiar.

Bobby Lines.

His name wasn't a bullet like her own had been. It was an

ice cube, dropped down the back of her shirt. Roni's fingers weakened, her breath stuck in her throat, and she fumbled with the plate in her hand, catching it just before it could slip out and clatter to the ground. Carefully, she set it in the drying rack. The extra moment of silence gave her father another chance to speak.

"Wanted to know how that thing went the other week," he said. "Been meaning to ask about it for a while now. Don't know how it got away from me."

She'd been waiting for the query. Dreading it. And she was sure it hadn't slipped his mind at all. Rather, he'd held onto it until he felt like bringing it up.

Nic, Bobby's voice repeated in her head.

She almost lost the next dish, too, but managed to keep her response steady. "Not so well."

"No?"

"It wasn't what I expected, I guess."

"Good."

She disagreed, but she clamped her lips together and kept that to herself. Her father disliked being argued with. And Roni was a peacekeeper.

"Least you'll know what to expect when you go back," her father added.

This time, the dish fell for real. It was only a fork, but when it slipped from Roni's hands, it hit the counter, bounced off, and skittered across the tiles, coming to rest at her father's feet.

She scurried over to grab it. "Sorry."

She sensed the hand coming down before she felt it, and it gave her enough time to brace for the touch. His fingers ran over her hair, just this side of roughly. The strands caught on his skin, pulling hard enough to sting.

"You've got a duty to God, baby girl," her father said.

"I know," she managed to say through her wince.

"And to me."

"I know."

"You thought you wanted to see what that world had to offer, didn't you?"

It was a trick question. Roni knew it. If she agreed, it would be an admission that the macabre story in the paper interested her. If she argued, it would open the door to accusations of being a liar.

"The fork, Daddy," she said instead, slipping into the childish moniker unconsciously.

His hand tightened. Almost a yank.

"Don't be giving me any bull about expectations," her father ordered. "Not when it comes to that prisoner and your obligation to do good. The only expectations you need to be concerned about are the ones the Lord and I set for you. And we're the only ones who will decide when you're done. Understand?"

Veronica tried to nod, but it hurt. "I do."

"You don't want to let me down, do you?"

"No."

"Your mother let me down."

"I know, Daddy."

"You know what happens to good girls who let people down," he said.

"Yes, I do," she replied.

For another few seconds, he held on. "Good, good."

Roni wasn't sure how much longer she could keep herself from crying. Her father didn't like it when she cried any more than he liked it when she disagreed with him. Tears weren't a sin. But they were a weakness. And ironically, if they did make their way to the surface, he would only do things to keep them coming.

I'll give you something to cry about, baby girl.

But in the current moment, his grip at last released. "You get those dishes done, then get yourself to bed. I've got work to do outside."

Breathing out, Roni obeyed. She stepped to the sink and submerged her hands in the water, scrubbing in a way that couldn't quite be called vicious.

Her father's footfalls—heavy boots on linoleum—announced he was leaving, as did the squeak of the backdoor as it opened. But the burn of her scalp didn't fade along with his presence. And it was a good reminder to stay vigilant. She didn't let her shoulders drop or urge her pulse to slow its nervous thrum. Not yet. She was glad of it, too, a heartbeat later, when her father's voice carried through the screen.

"Roni?" he said.

She worked to keep the tension from her reply. "Yes?"

"Pray on what day you'll visit the prison again."

"I will."

"You make it soon."

"I will," she repeated.

"I'll be watching."

"Okay, Dad."

The kitchen went quiet, and it stayed quiet except for the clink of dishes and slosh of suds. Still, Roni kept her guard up until she was done. Only once she'd climbed the stairs to the second floor of their home, stepped into her bedroom, and closed the door behind herself did she feel some loosening of the tension in her chest.

In all honesty, she didn't want to do what her father had asked. She had no desire to pray or to ask for spiritual guidance in the matter of visiting Bobby Lines again. Mainly because she didn't want to go back at all. She hadn't planned on it. The idea of doing it terrified her.

His eyes. His voice. The look on his face as his gaze rakes over me.

She shivered. She wasn't afraid to admit that it made her pulse quicken and her lips go dry. Or, to be more truthful, she wasn't afraid to admit it in her own head. But her father wouldn't understand. For all his rough parenting, he was a man who truly believed that the Bible was absolute and that God wanted things from His people on earth. More importantly, her father would *know* if Roni didn't follow through. He always did.

So as much as she told herself she wouldn't do it, the more minutes that ticked by, the less firm her resolve became. By the time she'd peeled out of her clothes and slipped into her nightgown, she was already mentally preparing how to tackle it. Looking for a prayer loophole. But after she'd brushed her teeth and run the wide-toothed comb over her hair for exactly two dozen strokes, she knew she wouldn't find one. Because there *wasn't* one.

Feeling more powerless than she had when she'd been left alone with Bobby, she stood in the center of her bedroom. She swept her gaze over her belongings, trying to get a hold of some mental strength through the familiar objects.

The vanity with its mirror, which had a crack down the middle.

The white-framed daybed that had been Veronica's for seventeen of her twenty-two years.

A bright white teddy bear that sat on a wall-mounted shelf alongside a few other childhood mementos. A stack of schoolbooks from the many years of home learning.

The Bible sitting atop the overturned box she used as a nightstand.

None of it helped.

The room felt small. And small*er* by the second.

Around her the walls pressed in. The paper that covered them—cream in color, yellowed with age and water—seemed to bend and warp. Veronica's lungs tightened. She clutched at her own chest as she fought for air.

God, help me, she thought, her eyes sinking shut to block out the encroaching nausea.

She didn't mean it as a prayer, but the silent plea no sooner came than an answer followed. Except once again, it was the inmate's derisive voice that spoke in her head.

You think this is small? he sneered. *Try an eight-by-six cell.*

It was so real that Veronica's eyes flew open and she flung a look around, half expecting to find his hulking frame crouched in a corner of her room. The fact that he wasn't there didn't make her breathe any easier. And in that, she found her answer. Like it or not, she did have to go back. Not because her father said so. But because Bobby Lines was in her head.

11

Ten Years Earlier
Forty-Seven Hours Before Arrest

The Policeman

As Flip reached the edge of the property that belonged to the Blacks, he had no choice but to slow the cruiser.

Until that point, he'd had his foot down hard. Lights flashing, sirens off. His renewed dedication to his job was already in full effect. He'd disposed of the empty whisky bottle that had led him to the low point. Since getting rid of it, every moment seemed brighter. He would do this. He would push past his dead boss's ultimatum and prove the man wrong. The dropped call from the Blacks' place was just the beginning. He knew from experience that their driveway was long and narrow, made of packed dirt, and embedded between two lines of trees. Not a good place to be flooring it. So as much as his urgency propelled him forward, his need to get to the house in one piece was stronger.

Can't be a good cop if I'm a dead cop, he told himself as he tapped the brakes. *Sorry, Captain.*

He let a small smile creep onto his face in response to his own joke, but it dropped away immediately as the trees parted and the house came into view.

"Holy crap."

He braked even harder, almost stopping.

Flip could swear his last visit had been only six months earlier. Since then, the place had taken a serious turn for the worse. The front of the house featured a shattered window. A chunk of shingles was missing from the roof. The surrounding grass, which had already been overgrown, had become a calfhigh mess, dotted with dandelions and buttercups and other unidentifiable weeds. A truck with only three wheels and no passenger side door lay on its side a few feet from a broken toilet. What the hell had happened?

As he got nearer, he swept his gaze over the scene a second time, and he spotted something he hadn't noticed before—a teenage boy, sitting on the front porch.

Smart-mouth punk, he thought, remembering the way the kid had laughed in Flip's face when he'd dared to ask if he felt safe in his home.

Flip continued studying the kid as the car crawled along. The boy was seated, but it was easy to see he appeared tall and skinny. His legs were bent up in front of him, his knees almost reaching his forehead. He held his arms wrapped around his chest, squeezing himself and emphasizing his thinness.

They're twins, Flip remembered suddenly. *The boy and the girl.*

On that domestic disturbance call, the two kids had been out in the yard, away from the violent episode that occurred in their parents' bedroom. The girl had been the taller one, those few months ago. Obviously, the boy had gone through a growth spurt since then. Likely, he towered over his twin sister these days.

Flip frowned, trying to recall the kid's name. The girl was Emily. She'd announced it loudly, and her brother had elbowed her and told her to be quiet. But what was the boy's name? Ethan? Evan? Something that lined up with Emily, that much he knew. After another second of trying to remember, he gave up. He'd find out soon enough, anyway.

He cruised to a halt beside the battered truck, then cut the engine. The youth on the porch didn't move. Not so much as to look up.

A prickle crept between Flip's shoulder blades. He didn't know if it was worry on behalf of the unmoving boy or if it was concern for his own wellbeing, but either way, he wasn't taking any chances. He put his right hand on his weapon—something he also shouldn't have been in possession of, given his conversation with Captain Dax yesterday—and swung open the door with the other. When he stepped to the ground, he noted two more oddities. One, a shovel sat at the kid's feet. And two, the boy was covered in fresh dirt.

"Hey, buddy!" Flip kept his tone friendly as he called out from behind the relative cover of the car. "Your mom or dad around?"

The boy jerked his head up, seeming to be genuinely surprised by Flip's presence. For a second, he stared. Then he unfolded from his odd position and pushed to his feet. He really *was* tall. Over six feet, for sure. It made Flip nervous for a moment, and he thought of the bulky father. But there was no sign of the man, and he could see that the son's hands were empty. No weapon, no sign of a threat in his body language, despite the slightly sullen look on his face and the purple bruise under his left eye.

"What do you want?" the boy said.

"Got a couple of dropped calls from your address," Flip replied. "Standard procedure is to check it out."

"I don't need help."

Flip ignored the snarky tone. "I'm sure you don't, but I'm obligated to be here, nonetheless."

"Are you gonna call child services?" asked the kid.

Flip couldn't cover a frown. "Why would I do that?"

The boy shrugged and dropped his eyes to the ground, not in deference but rather as though he might have a secret to hide. Flip glanced toward the house. The prickle was back. Something else was going on. His fingers itched to find his gun again, but he ordered himself not to do it. No need to escalate anything.

He moved closer, lowering his voice for the kid's ears only. "Did your dad do something? You can tell me if he did."

"Like fuck," the kid muttered.

"You recognize me from the last time I was here, don't you?"

"Maybe."

"Remind me what your name is."

The teenager lifted his eyes, and he fixed Flip with a sharp look. "Don't you guys keep track of this shit?"

Flip's teeth tried to clench. *Not the time to lose your patience.*

He breathed out. "We do. But I got this call while I was on the road, and I wanted to come as quickly as I could, so I didn't stop to review the file. Cut a guy some slack, okay?"

The kid's expression didn't change. "Fine. My dad sure as shit *did* do something."

"All right. I'm listening."

"He died."

Flip thought he'd either misheard, or the kid was messing with him. His eyes slid to the dilapidated property, then back to the boy, who lifted a hand and ran it over his shaggy hair. The motion exposed a crudely done —undoubtedly homemade—tattoo on his forearm. It was a serpent of some kind, and Flip's attention hung on it, unease making him want to twitch.

He forced himself to acknowledge the boy's statement as though he believed it. "I'm sorry to hear that."

The kid clearly didn't buy the condolences, and he offered a sneer that went far beyond his age. "I don't care if you think I'm lying or not, *officer*."

"All right. Look. I'm sorry, and—"

"Don't be. My dad was a piece of garbage who liked to beat on my mom for fun. Broke my arm last summer because I didn't get out of the bathroom fast enough. And if I didn't need your help with all that, then why the fuck would I need it now?"

Flip's hands flexed with irritation, but he drew a breath and

channeled some extra patience. "This will probably go a little faster if we go inside and talk to your mom."

"Can't."

"Pardon me?"

"My mom's gone. She took off a month after our dad died. Haven't seen her since then." The kid jammed his hands into his pockets. "It's Ellis, by the way."

"What is?"

"My name."

Flip was starting to feel like the kid was getting the better of him somehow, and he didn't like it. Maybe he *would* call child services. Get this family the help it needed. If the parents were gone, and the two kids were on their own, it was an obligation, wasn't it?

He cleared his throat. "How old are you, Ellis?"

The kid narrowed his eyes. "Almost seventeen."

"And your mom has been gone for how long?"

"Dunno. Longer this time than the last time, but not as long as the time before."

"Okay. Listen. Why don't you invite me in, let me take a look around, and see if we can't figure out why the station got a dropped call from your residence."

"You got a warrant?" Ellis replied.

Flip stifled a sigh. "Do I *need* a warrant, son?"

"Pretty sure it's your job to know that."

"Unless you've got something to hide, there's nothing to worry about."

Ellis met his eyes. There was a sharpness in them. True intelligence. And resignation.

"I'm a sixteen-year-old kid with a record for theft, vandalism, and mischief," he said. "My dad is dead, my mom is M.I.A., and you're a cop. I think all of that makes a pretty compelling argument for not wanting to 'invite' you in, regardless as to whether or not I have something to hide, doesn't it?"

Flip had to concede that the boy had a point. Several,

actually. But there was still the matter of the dropped call.

"You got a cellphone, Ellis?" he asked.

"Who *doesn't* have a cellphone?" the kid replied.

"Mind if I take a look at yours?"

"Yeah, I mind."

"Well, it's going to be a choice then. I can either come in—no warrant needed because the dropped call gives me probable cause—or you can let me see your phone so I can determine if it was you who made the call." Flip held out his hand.

After a narrow-eyed glare, Ellis reached into his jeans and yanked out the device. He smacked it with a few vicious stabs, then handed over the phone.

Flip didn't comment. He tapped to the recent call log, saw what he needed to see, and gave the kid his cell back.

"So?" said Ellis, crossing his skinny arms over his chest.

"So," Flip replied. "You want to tell me *why* you called us and hung up?"

"It was an accident."

"Twice in a row?"

The kid's hands dropped into fists at his sides. "My dog died, and I wasn't sure what to do."

Whatever Flip had thought he might hear, that particular statement came nowhere close to it, and it caught him off guard enough that he blinked. The moment of silence made the kid sigh.

"I really didn't know what to do, okay?" he said again. "I wasn't sure if I was allowed to bury him on the property, or if that was illegal, or... I dunno. I freaked out a little."

Flip's eyes roved over the kid's dirty clothes then slid to the shovel on the porch before he answered. "I guess you figured it out, then?"

"Yeah."

"Son..."

"What?"

"I need to take you in," said Flip.

The kid lifted an eyebrow, suddenly looking twenty years

older. "What will you do? Wrestle me to the ground?"

Flip's skull throbbed at the mere thought of it. "Only one of us would be in the wrong in that situation."

"Oh, yeah? Would it be me? The kid without any parents around, who was suddenly attacked and profiled by a cop who smells a little like booze?"

The kid had a point. Flip didn't *like* it, but he had a point.

He plowed forward with his next statement. "Here's what I should do. I should bust my way in and make sure neither you nor anyone else is in danger. I should call social services and wait for them to get here. But I'm trusting you when you say no one's life is on the line, and the truth is, the police department has a fair amount of stuff going on at the moment, so it's your lucky day. You're going to get a reprieve. But I *will* be checking on you. And soon. You guys can't live here unsupervised indefinitely. You understand that, right?"

"Yeah, okay. I get it." Ellis sounded relieved and resentful at the same time.

"I hope you do."

It wasn't until Flip was already back on the road, heading into town, that he realized something. The kid had talked about himself. He'd talked about his parents. And the dog. One thing he hadn't done, though, was mention his twin sister.

12

Eight Months, Nineteen Days Before Escape

The Convict

Ellis lifted the barbell from his chest in a steady rhythm, his grunts and breaths setting a pace that was internally hypnotic.

Breathe out, press up.

Breathe in, drop down.

Inhale, up. Exhale, down.

In.

Out.

In-out, in-out, in-out.

There was no denying the sexual undertone of the action, so Ellis didn't bother to try. If anything, he reveled in it.

He was half-hard, and it felt fucking good. Pun intended.

In-out, in-out.

Ver-on.

I-ca.

In-out, in-out.

Ver-on, i-ca.

The pretty little thing hadn't left his mind. If anything, she'd become a fixation, strange and dark. Three times in the past week alone, Ellis had woken from the same dream of her. His hand on her throat. Her dress ripped open to reveal her braless state. Nipples erect. Mouth open in a cry, tears sliding past her pale lashes.

Christ.

The dream did something to Ellis. Awakened something in him that he hadn't felt since... since when?

Since me, said his sister in his head.

Her face flashed to the front of his thoughts, and he closed his eyes in an attempt to get rid of her.

Fuck off, Emily.

It wasn't quite enough to do the trick. Her honey hair and blue eyes and childlike smile danced across the inside of his eyelids. Smiling. Always fucking smiling. The way a three-year-old might smile to herself as she sat and played alone. But Emily hadn't been three. She'd been sixteen. With a woman's dangerous body. Curves and dips and tempting things that she had no right to have. Who could resist?

In-out. A grunt. "No." *Up-down.*

"Re..."

A thick breath.

"Morse."

He pumped the weight harder, grabbed hold of thoughts of Veronica, and held on. Blonde. Innocent. So very much in need of a man like Ellis to control her.

His dick hardened even more.

Lust wasn't foreign. Not at all. Neither was the need to dominate. To punish. Plenty of men found outlets in prison. There were more than enough inmates to punish and to *be* punished. But Veronica was shiny and new. The first concrete target Ellis had found for the drive of his thoughts in an insurmountable length of time. There was a reason she'd been put in front of him. He just hadn't yet figured out what the fuck it was.

In, out. Up, down.

As he expelled a groan, he felt a subtle change in the air. One he was sure a free man wouldn't have sensed at all. But a man like him—caged among other, equally feral men—had no choice but to develop a radar for it. A form of self-preservation.

Someone was watching him. Waiting. Ellis didn't care enough to open his eyes. Intimidation meant nothing to him. His fellow inmates rarely got closer than a dozen feet away, and that was how he liked it. Today, though, he silently dared the newcomer to approach. Let him try something. Ellis needed an excuse to lash out. He'd fucking *enjoy* giving some new guy a piece of his fist.

He kept up his rhythm. Increased it, even.

In-out, in-out. Veronica.

His erection grew to full mast. It had to be visible under his coveralls. The watcher didn't budge. Not all that surprising.

Little was sacred behind these walls.

In-out, in-out.

Her creamy throat.

Up-down, up-down.

Ellis wondered if he could climax on a thought alone. He felt close to it already.

In-out. Up-down.

A thrust inside her. Violent. Pleasure and pain.

The intruder chose that moment to interrupt, clearing his throat and compelling Ellis to address the fucker.

He set the barbell down on the rack, rasping a statement as the metal on metal clanged through the covered courtyard. "If you want to suck it, you need to make an appointment. And not during gym class, either"

"Thanks for the offer, but you're not my type," replied a voice he didn't recognize. "I like my dates with a little less... rape and murder. Assuming you're Ellis Black, that is?"

It was enough to make Ellis's temper surge. It was a quick transition. Natural. Lust to fury. Red emotions. Blinding. And in a slick move that he knew belied his size, he came to his feet and lunged, hand out, ready to grasp the nearest piece of exposed flesh. His fingers found only air. The man had sidestepped—just the tiniest bit, and in a calculated way rather than out of fear. It caught Ellis in the unusual position of being off-guard. He hit the ground, chin first. A familiar, rusty flavor filled his mouth. The motherfucker had split his lip.

Panting, he rolled over and prepared to defend himself. No attack came. It wasn't even another fucking prisoner who stood a few feet away, staring down at him. It was a guard. Another newb. His shirt was crisp, the baton on his belt unmarked. *More fresh meat.* Ellis eyed him up and down, not bothering to hide his contempt for the man's slick hair and shiny shoes, then spat out a mouthful of blood.

"I'm going to cut you some slack and assume that nobody gave you the memo," he said. "This hour is mine, I don't like to be bothered, and the warden and I have an understanding."

"Oh, I'm aware of your reputation," replied the other man. "But *I'm* going to cut *you* some slack and assume you've never tried to fight someone with three black belts and a boxing title. Nothing you come at me with is something I haven't seen before. You want to try it, or you want me to give you the message that the other guys thought it would be funny to see me deliver?"

Under normal circumstances, Ellis probably would've taken him up on the offer to fight. But something stopped him.

"What's the message?" he asked, his skin prickling in a way that was utterly foreign to him.

"You have a visitor. A woman. Preacher's daughter, from what I hear."

Veron. Ica.

"Take me to her," Ellis growled.

The guard shifted. "You want a second to clean up?"

Ellis swiped a hand over his bloody mouth. "This will be fine."

The guard looked dubious, but Ellis didn't care. Because it had just struck him. Veronica's purpose in his life. She was going to be his ticket out.

13

Eight Months, Nineteen Days Before Escape

The Preacher's Daughter

Roni was mad. Foot stomping, fist clenching angry. And embarrassed, too, if she were being honest.

She wanted to blame the prison itself. But she knew the real source wasn't the institution. It was the man who she was there to see.

The liar.

She resisted a need to pace the tiny room where she waited. She pushed back an even stronger urge to fling open the door and simply leave.

"I'm doing this," she said. "Even if it's just to tell him that I know."

She hadn't stopped dreading the trip. Not for a moment. She'd had to drag herself there. In fact, she'd made herself tell her father the exact day and time of the visit so that she'd have to answer for it if she didn't follow through. Accountability.

Obligation.

"Honesty."

Except then she'd arrived at Meridian Penitentiary, and the truth had been revealed. There'd been a mix-up, they told her. The man she'd thought was Bobby Lines was actually someone else entirely. Ellis Black. And yes, Roni could have turned away.

She could've gone home and found a way to tell her father what had happened. Maybe he'd have understood.

Who knew what *this* man's crimes were? Roni stayed anyway. She felt she was owed an explanation for the deception. But now she'd been waiting for almost an hour inside the tiny room. The vent was blowing hot air instead of cold. Sweat made her hair stick to her face, and the cotton fabric of her dress clung to her body.

Patience is a virtue, she reminded herself firmly. *This is nothing more than a test of that.*

She still heaved a sigh of relief when the tap of approaching feet announced that she was, at last, going to see some progress. She straightened her shoulders as the door opened to reveal the same guard who'd led her through the halls on her last visit.

"Is everything sorted out?" Roni asked.

He nodded. "As sorted as it *can* be, under the circumstances. Ready?"

Roni nodded back, then followed him out, paying far less attention to her surroundings than she had the previous time she'd been sandwiched between the walls. She was too busy grabbing hold of her anger. She knew she was going to need to use it as a shield, and also as a means of propelling forward with an atypical boldness.

When they reached the room where Ellis Black undoubtedly sat chained to the table, the guard faced her before opening the door.

"I have to ask…" he said. "Are you sure you want to do this, Ms. Hollister?"

"You did ask. Six times."

"Make it seven, then. Ellis Black is a different kind of man than Bobby Lines."

She narrowed her eyes. It was on the tip of her tongue to ask if he really expected her to believe that he hadn't known it was Ellis Black in there the last time. He *had* to have known.

The only other option was complete and utter

84

incompetence.

Still believe this is a mix-up, Nic?

No, she most certainly did not. The difference between then and now wasn't what the guard knew about Ellis's real identity. It was that he knew that *she* knew.

"Ms. Hollister?" prodded the guard.

She cleared her throat. "I understand, and I'm not going to change my mind."

The uniformed man looked as though he might add to his argument, but he just shook his head and twisted the knob to let her in. Roni took a breath. Fear gripped her. She stepped forward anyway. She had her question—her accusation—ready. But the words died on her lips. The big man—*Ellis Black,* she reminded herself—*was* seated at the table. His hands *were* secured much as they had been on the previous visit. A few things, though, were different. Markedly so. His face was covered in dirt, and fresh blood marked his mouth. A small rip decorated the collar of his gray jumpsuit, too. He looked as though he'd come out on the wrong end of a fight.

Alarmed, Roni tried to face the guard again, but he'd already closed the door. She took a small, automatic step toward it. Maybe she was trying to escape, or maybe she wanted an explanation. Either way, the prisoner's laugh—that same, darkly amused one he'd offered her last time—made her pause and spin back again instead. She found Ellis watching her with a macabre crimson smile.

"What?" he said. "Have you changed your mind about trying to do something about my living conditions? Or have you already forgotten what I told you last time about how things work?"

Defensiveness crept up, and Roni ordered it back, keeping her reply cool. "No, I haven't forgotten. But there's a difference between keeping you chained to a table and causing bodily harm. If the guards did that to you, they *should* have to answer for it. And if it was another inmate, then they should make *him* answer for it."

"It's so sweet of you to care, Nic." He leaned back as much as his chains would allow, and he gave her one of his slow once-overs, his attention hanging on the spots where the sweat-damp dress hugged her body the tightest. "You want to come closer and show me just how much?"

Roni's face warmed. Her gaze slipped to the door again. She truly believed she was right about someone answering for the injuries. And the marks on Ellis's face were evidence. Quantifiable damage. But the guards and their sins weren't the reason she'd come. They *really* weren't the reason she'd stayed. That focus belonged to the gray-clad man. He owed her. And he was clearly both deflecting her attention *and* trying to make her uncomfortable. She refused to let him do either.

"Why did you lie to me?" she asked, lifting her chin with a hint of defiance.

"I would never lie to you, baby." His teeth flashed, bright white behind the red, completely at odds with his teasing words. "I respect you far too much for that."

Roni fought a shiver. "You lied to me about who you are."

"It wasn't a lie. I didn't say that I was Bobby Lines. You used that pretty little head of yours to make an assumption."

"You let me *think* you were Bobby. On purpose. Semantics don't make that not a lie."

"All right," he said. "I'll concede that to be true."

She let herself feel the tiniest sliver of triumph. "So why did you do it?"

"Being Bobby Lines meant meeting *you.* Isn't that enough?"

"That's not what I mean. I understand why you'd pretend to be him in the first place. It can't be pleasant sitting in an eight-by-six cell all day, every day. But why did you let me keep believing, even *after* we met? You had to know you'd get caught."

Ellis shifted and lifted an eyebrow. "Would you have stayed, if I'd told you the truth?"

Roni exhaled, then dared to pull out the chair across the table from the cuffed man so she could sit down. She saw the way Ellis's gaze grew hungrier as she got closer. Despite the fact that she was overheated, it made her wish she could wrap herself up to help keep his lust at bay.

It's not what you're wearing that makes him an animal, she reminded himself. *But what you say might help tame the beast.*

And thankfully, he managed to keep his thick hands to himself this time.

"Was that a trick question, a second ago?" she asked. "You weren't interested in keeping me here, regardless of whether I thought you were Bobby or not."

"You seem different today," he stated, his sharp blue gaze holding her. "Maybe it's better that I'm not Bobby."

His words brought an idea into her head, and she spoke without thinking. "Is it because you're more ashamed of being *you* than you would be of being *him*?"

It was a mistake. Roni saw it right away. Ellis's jaw ticked. His hands clenched, unclenched, and clenched again.

"Bobby was a juvenile fuckwit," he growled. "He was so dumb that he couldn't think of a more creative enterprise than robbing cab drivers, and he failed at that, too. Dying was the smartest thing he did in his entire life."

Roni sensed her guess had held some truth. She should've backpedaled right away. But for no good reason—no sane reason—she pushed on instead.

"What did *you* do, that was so much smarter than that?" she asked. "Do you want to tell me about it?"

Ellis flattened his palms on the table, and somehow, it seemed like they took up half the metal slab. The position made him appear bigger, too.

The room crowded in on Roni, and she inhaled, trying to steal back some of the space the convict had taken in his small move. Immediately, she wished she hadn't breathed in at all. Her nose filled with the scent of blood and sweat and something she could only describe as danger. The energy changed to match it.

Then Ellis spoke, his voice low and edged with violence. "Do

I strike you as the kind of man who likes to *talk*, Nic?"

She inched back, realizing she'd become too complacent over the last few minutes. "I didn't mean—"

"You did," he said. "You mean exactly what I think you mean. What you're here for is my soul."

The words caught Roni off-guard in an unsettling way. It was as though he were accusing her, personally, of trying to steal his quintessential life force. And Ellis seemed to read the train of her thoughts, too.

"I'm not saying you're the Grim Reaper, sweetheart." He'd dialed his tone back from overtly threatening. "But I've been around the prison long enough to know when someone is getting ready to throw a fucking Bible at my face. That being said, if you want a look inside my head, then I think it's my turn to ask a question."

Roni swallowed. "What do you want to know?"

He relaxed his hands. "No."

"Sorry?"

"I want some assurance that you're going to answer me honestly first, Nic."

"I can't make you a promise that I'm not sure I can keep."

He tilted his head, studying her with thoughtful eyes. "All right. Don't let anyone tell you that I'm incapable of compromise. I'll ask my question. If you can't be honest about an answer, then don't give me one. Yet."

Roni nodded, her palms sweating. "Fair enough."

He didn't answer. Instead, he adjusted in the chair, somehow producing a cigarette and a match from inside his sleeve. As Roni blinked in surprise, he bent over and lit the former with the latter. He took a deep inhale, then exhaled a puff of perfect rings that might've seemed ridiculous if not for the man blowing them out. The smoke reached the ceiling in seconds. An alarm blared to life, sending Roni's heart rate soaring.

"Sweetheart?" Ellis spoke loudly enough to be heard over the cacophony, smiling as he did. "What I want to know is how far you'd go to *get* this soul of mine."

The statement provoked answers Roni didn't want to think about, let alone do. Her skin prickled unpleasantly, and her stomach churned. Her mouth was dry, too. But before she could moisten her lips to gasp out a response, the door swung open, and the guard swept in.

"C'mon, man," he said. "You *know* you can't smoke in here."

Despite his words, the guard didn't take away the cigarette. He just addressed Roni as Ellis continued to bend over and take another inhale.

"Come on, Ms. Hollister, I'll take you out front. Someone else will come and get Mr. Black."

Feeling slightly dizzy—maybe from the smoke, maybe as an after-effect of the convict's words—she pushed to her feet. And as she followed the guard out to the hallway and through the pneumatic doors, it struck her that Ellis had lit up on purpose. A way to end the conversation on his own terms.

So she *couldn't* answer.

"What did he do?" she blurted.

The guard, who was walking a couple of feet in front of her, almost tripped. "Sorry?"

"What was his crime? Why is he in prison?"

"We don't talk about it."

"I don't understand."

The guard sighed. "At Mr. Black's request, we don't discuss his crimes."

"How is that possible?" Roni replied. "He's in here for a reason. It can't be a secret."

They reached the main lobby, and the uniformed man stayed quiet as they passed by a few other visitors and guards, but he spoke up again when they reached the exit.

"Ellis Black is in good with the warden," he explained in a low voice. "Got there by saving his life. One of the regular lowlifes damn near shanked the boss, and Black put himself in between them. Took a shiv to the gut. So, Mr. Black wants a few privileges, he gets 'em." He pushed the door open and raised his voice. "You have a safe day, Ms. Hollister. Maybe we'll see you again?"

She nodded faintly, then stepped outside, trying to process what she'd learned. It seemed too daunting. What was the man in prison for? Why would he go out of his way to save the warden? He hardly seemed like the type to risk his life for his own jailer. Was he dangling the prospect of saving his soul over her head, just because he could? Or was there an actual possibility of redemption there? Roni suspected that the only way to find out would be to come back. And maybe that was part of Ellis Black's plan, too.

14
Fifteen Hours After Escape

The Preacher's Daughter

Veronica jerked awake, her heart thudding and her brain disoriented. Her thoughts came in a jumble of questions and answers.

Where am I?

This is Meridian Hope Hospital.

Why do I feel so funny?

They gave you a sedative to help you stay calm and something for the pain, too.

What happened?

There was a longer pause before the next reply came, but when it did, any residual effect of the medication zapped aside.

Ellis happened. Ellis Black.

Veronica sat upright, yanking her IV with her. Pain shot up her hand, but she ignored it in favor of assessing her safety. For a heart-thumping minute, she swore that the hulking man was stationed in one corner of the room. Dressed in the familiar gray. Ready to pounce.

She tensed, waiting for it now. It didn't come.

His name slipped from her mouth in a trembling whisper. "Ellis?"

But when she was met with silence, she blinked, and the shape came into focus. It was a privacy curtain, suspended from the ceiling and partially draped over a visitor's chair.

The concern didn't quite taper off though, and her gaze darted furtively around the room, seeking out some other hiding place. But every space was as empty as it ought to be. The door was closed. The lights were dim. The steady beep of machinery filtered through the air. It was almost soothing.

Veronica lay back and let her eyes sink shut.

She hadn't meant to fall asleep. She'd wanted a moment of rest. A moment not to dwell on everything that had happened. Now that she'd been afforded that very thing, it felt strange to be alone. For the preceding hours, Ellis Black had stayed within ten feet of her. Even when she'd gone to use the bathroom, she'd been hyperaware of his presence. Those intense eyes holding her to the spot so thoroughly that he didn't need his hands. But his hands were sometimes there anyway. Pinning her down. Grappling with her hair. Securing her with rope.

Nic.

Veronica shuddered and redirected her thoughts. Her mind went to the policeman. Where had he gone? She needed him. He'd been so intent on questioning her that it seemed incongruous that he'd left without a word. Another little stab of concern sidled up beside the existing anxiety.

"It's okay," she said, her voice sounding too echoey in the empty room. "I can do this on my own."

Trying to stave off the ensuing panic, she tossed aside her blanket, scooted to the end of the bed, and swung her legs off. Her bare feet met with freezing cold linoleum. Right away, she shivered. The air, too, was more chilled than Veronica would've liked, covering her whole body in goosebumps. The hospital robe covered far too little to keep her warm. She pushed off an urge to climb back into the bed and pull the covers up. But she didn't rush to stand. She needed to think. To plan. And to figure out how badly she was hurt. She needed to know how equipped she was to handle what was coming next.

Because there *was* a next. That much she was sure of.

All right. Thoroughness is key.

She closed her eyes again, this time with stronger intent.

Carefully, she searched out what she could feel, both from the inside and the outside. Her hands followed her mind.

Head. It did ache. But not so much that she suspected a concussion. And there were no bandages there either, so whatever hits she'd sustained hadn't damaged her skull.

Face. The skin there was sore, too. Throbbing a tiny bit near her left eye and the corner of her mouth on the same side. She almost wished for a mirror, but then thought better of it.

Upper body. Scratches, scrapes, and so many bruises. Veronica knew about those already. She'd thought at one point that maybe she'd cracked a rib, but the fact that the hospital hadn't wrapped her torso made her believe there was no fracture. In fact, the part that hurt the most was the IV.

Lower body. She wiggled a little in place, testing for pain. Like the rest of her body, it was sore. One spot—right above her left hip—seemed particularly tender. Her legs themselves felt pretty okay. Like she'd fallen from a bike but managed to get back up to ride again.

What about what's between *your legs?* The question cropped up before Veronica could stop it, and she drew in a sharp breath and shook her head. *Don't. Not now. Not yet.*

Compartmentalization was going to be key. She could see that.

Slowly—with extra care to compensate for her injuries, including any she might not yet be aware of—she pressed to her feet. She swayed for a second. Then steadied.

"Okay. I'm okay."

She grabbed hold of the IV pole and took an experimental step. Then another. Her legs protested a little, but no more than they would have if she'd spent a few hours sleeping somewhere uncomfortable under better circumstances. Gripping the metal, she rolled the medical device the rest of the way across the room. At the door, she paused, nerves alight.

Doing her best to find an inner calm, she leaned forward and peered through the glass.

Just outside her room, she could see a police officer. He was positioned to the left of the door, sitting in a chair against the wall. His feet were stretched out straight, and his head had slumped a bit in the other direction. He looked like he was sleeping, which made Veronica's heart trip. What good was a guard who couldn't keep himself awake?

It's fine, she assured herself. *He wouldn't be sleeping if he was worried.*

She tugged at her robe, pulling it tighter then smoothing it down as she tried to convince the nervous thump of her pulse that it was a correct inference.

She lifted her eyes higher, past the sleeping cop, searching the area for some sign of medical staff. There *was* a nurse's station in view. But the desk appeared to be empty.

Probably doing rounds, she rationalized. *And it's evening now, so the hospital's less busy in general. Fewer visitors, if any. Doctors only coming and going as needed.*

It was true. But that didn't mean it was the *only* thing that was true.

Veronica took a small step. The tiniest step. Her feet were heavy, and the sensation outweighed the cold. Still, there were goosebumps over every inch of her body, and she couldn't shake the neck-prickling feel that something was off.

Her attention went back to the nurse's station again. Had the staff been gone long? Shouldn't someone be there pretty much all the time?

She waited for a nurse to make an appearance. Counted up to thirty in her head then counted back down to zero, dragging out the final seconds as long as she could. Still, no one came.

Where are they?

She slid her eyes back to the police officer. His position hadn't changed. He was the very picture of exhausted repose. Veronica wished she could say something remotely the same about herself. But nerves flicked through her like fireflies in the night. After another second, she clenched her fingers into a fist and raised it to knock on the glass so she could grab the cop's attention. She only got her hand halfway up before some movement up the hall caught her eye. Alarms went off in every part of her. She turned her head anyway, hoping to find one of the nurses. But she found Ellis Black instead.

This time, he wasn't an illusion; she was sure of it. His clothes gave it away. Her imagination wouldn't have conjured up a wardrobe change. His prison-gray jumpsuit was gone. So were the white T-shirt and sports shorts he'd donned after his escape and had still been wearing when the police took him in. In their place was a pair of faded jeans and a thick, black hoodie he'd pulled up to cover his head. The piercing stare Veronica had been thinking about minutes earlier captured and held her.

He'd escaped again. Just as he'd promised.

Veronica's breaths shortened. She should've been calling for help. Any reasonable person would have screamed already. But reason eluded her. She simply stood and watched as he pointed toward the feet of the cop guarding her room. Automatically, she shifted her eyes to see what he wanted her to look at. And she spied it right away. A note. Scrawled directly onto the linoleum. The only reason she hadn't noticed it before was that she hadn't looked directly at the ground. Now, though, it held her attention for a dozen humming-bird-fast heartbeats.

I'LL BE WAITING, it read in all caps.

With all she knew of Ellis, Veronica was sure there was more to the message than another promise. He wasn't a man who waited. He was a man who took. Who demanded. Who slammed through obstacles with his fists out and his teeth bared.

I'll be waiting.

No, not a promise. Not a threat. An exercise of control.

He only waited because he *could.*

It wasn't until she heard feet hitting the ground that Veronica yanked her head back up. Ellis was already gone. She didn't get a chance to decide belatedly what to do about his message or his presence, because right then, a nurse finally stepped out of the room next door and turned right. The same direction the convict had gone.

At last, Veronica felt properly compelled to move. With complete disregard for the IV attached to her hand, she jolted forward. The pole clattered to the ground. The machine beeped a protest. And the tube ripped from her hand as she burst the rest of the way through the door. She ignored it all. The noise. The blood dripping from her hand. Everything.

The nurse was already hurrying toward her, concern etched into her fifty-something features. "Ms. Hollister, what are you —"

"He's here!"

"Who?"

"Black. Ellis Black."

The nurse's eyes widened, but she shook her head and placed a hand on Veronica's elbow. "That's impossible Ms. Hollister. The police arrested Mr. Black. It was on the news. And you're bleeding. We've got to get some pressure on that."

Veronica pulled free. "Where did Captain Farriday go?"

"I'm not sure." From somewhere, the nurse pulled out a fabric compress, pressed it to Veronica's bloody hand, and continued to speak, all calmness. "Maybe home for the evening, but I can try to have someone call him for you. Or you can speak to the constable."

The constable.

Veronica spun back. The man was slumped over. His eyes were closed, his mouth agape, and for a second, she thought he was dead. But when she took a step in his direction, she noted the telltale rise and fall of his chest. She saw something else, too. A syringe sticking out of his thigh. It had to be one of the ones he'd taken from the prison infirmary.

Planning. Always planning. A step ahead.

I have to get out of here.

The need was physical. "I have to go."

The nurse looked from her to the drugged constable then back again. "I can't let you do that."

"Are you going to physically hold me here?"

"No, but—"

"I'm going!"

She pushed past the other woman, who called out something Veronica couldn't hear. She made it all the way to the end of the hall before she clued in to just how illogical she must seem. How irrational. Running through a hospital in a robe, hand bleeding from the IV, no shoes on her feet. With no sane reason to be heading into the unknown while Ellis Black was on the loose. But she couldn't stop herself. Luckily, when she rounded the corner, she crashed into exactly the right person—Captain Farriday.

The policeman put both hands on Veronica's arms, steadying her and halting her progress at the same time. "Whoa. What's going on here? Why aren't you in your bed?"

"I want to go home," she replied.

She met his eyes and absently noted that she managed to hold an evenness in her own voice. But her heart was a mess, bouncing with seemingly no rhythm against her ribcage.

"Did something happen?" His posture tightened, and his gaze lifted over her shoulder.

He knows, Veronica realized.

She took a step back. "How?"

"Ms. Hollister…"

"No. Don't lie to me. Because I swear to God, if you're not honest with me, I'll walk out of here like this."

"Ms. Hollister," he said again. "We should go back to your room. Let the nurse put your IV back in."

She shook her head. "Not a chance. He was here, Captain. He left me a note. He drugged your guy."

"He… damn." The captain's response seemed less an underreaction than more like a true loss for words.

"I want to know what happened. I think I have a right to be told."

Farriday ran a hand over his head, and he shifted from foot to foot. "He managed to get a hold of the handcuff keys."

"Handcuff keys…" Veronica trailed off. "You mean he got

away before he was even processed?"

He nodded. "I swear to you that we're going to find him. And in the meantime, we can protect you."

"Protect me? Stop him from killing me, you mean?"

"Yes, if necessary."

"I don't think he wants me dead, Captain."

His eyebrows came together. "What do you mean?"

She clamped her lips together to keep from saying aloud what was in her head. But one of her hands did its best to creep up to her abdomen. She forced it down.

"Take me home," she said. "Please. I'll still give you your statement, and I don't care if you want to post a guard—" She paused and almost laughed. "You might want to post a *few*, actually. One clearly didn't work. But I want to be in my own house."

The policeman's mouth opened, then closed, then opened again. "Let me deal with the situation here and make some arrangements."

"I'm not going to wait long," she warned. "I don't think I *can*."

Farriday nodded. And ten minutes later, Veronica was wrapped in a blanket, sitting in the passenger seat of a squad car, headed for home.

15

Ten Years Earlier
Forty-Four Hours Before Arrest

The Policeman

Flip tapped his thumbs on the steering wheel and cast a look—not quite a glare—toward the Blacks' driveway.

He couldn't actually see the split in the road through the thickness of shrubs where he'd stowed the squad car. All the same, he knew its exact position. He hadn't taken his gaze off it for more than a second or two since sliding the vehicle into its current hiding place.

He strummed a little faster. He was aware he was riding the line of sitting in the spot for too long. It'd been two hours since his nagging subconscious had forced him back. In fact, he hadn't made it all the way into town.

It wasn't just that he felt wrong about leaving the boy there, though his training and common sense said it wasn't the best decision. But he *was* confident that Ellis wasn't in danger. Flip had encountered his share of scared folks, trying to hide something. This feeling wasn't about that. This was... something else.

Minutes after leaving the kid, he'd pulled a wide U-turn, coasted into his current hiding place, then made his followup call to Danielle in Dispatch to let her know he'd be a while longer. After that, he'd hunkered down to wait. For what, he wasn't entirely sure, but he'd figured he'd know when he saw it.

Except whatever "it" was, it hadn't shown itself. Now his body ached from being stuck in the driver's seat. He still hadn't had a coffee, and if he didn't get some soon, the dull throb of caffeine withdrawal would become a roar.

Probably time to call it quits.

He no sooner reached for the keys, though, than the rumble of an engine carried out from the trees surrounding the Blacks' property. A few seconds later, a motorcycle tore up from the driveway and disappeared down the road in a cloud of dust. There was no mistaking the rider. Long and lanky and helmetless, Ellis Black was easy to identify.

An the moment the boy was out of sight, Flip realized *this* was what he'd been waiting for— an opportunity to explore the property at a leisurely pace with no eyes on him. It took only another moment to decide the best thing to do was to maintain some secrecy in his approach.

He counted to sixty to be sure the kid was really gone, then guided his car from its hiding spot out to the road. From there, he drove straight to the property next door to the Blacks' place. It was a rundown, formerly agricultural acreage, like the one where Ellis and his family lived. But this one's owners had abandoned it years earlier, turning it into an excellent location to stash the vehicle while he proceeded on foot.

Eager to make use of whatever window he might have, Flip moved quickly. He made his way across an abandoned pasture, then skirted past a ramshackle barn and a roofless shed. He bypassed a mound of gravel, slipped through what might've been an orchard at one point, and in minutes, he reached his destination—the perimeter of the Blacks' property. There, he slowed. He continued his approach more cautiously, on full alert. With his hand on his weapon, he let his eyes roam in search of any potential threat. He found none. The air was still and quiet, and the nearer he got to the house, the more certain he became that Ellis had been the only one there. His conclusion was further cemented by the fact that when he reached the front, he found the door hanging open, moving slightly in the breeze.

Just to be sure, he stopped at the bottom of the porch and called out, "Hello? Is anyone here?"

As anticipated, there was no response.

Flip moved up the stairs, paused at the top, and projected his voice toward the open door. "This is Officer Farriday from the Meridian PD. Back again, hoping for another chat."

He got nothing but silence in return.

Can't call it breaking and entering when there's no breaking, right? he thought, twisting his lips and casting a quick look over his shoulder before nudging his way into the small foyer. *And an open door is pretty close to probable cause. Add the dropped calls to that, and I'm golden. Or close enough, anyway.*

The interior of the home was in far better shape than the exterior. The floor, though well-worn, was spotless. Two jackets hung from hooks on the wall and several pairs of shoes sat tidily under on a shelf below. The smell of fresh paint vaguely permeated the air. Another step, and Flip spotted a throw-covered couch, a mismatched loveseat in olive green, and a well-used coffee table. There was no dust, no garbage, no dishes. No sign that anything was amiss. Flip frowned. Based on the immaculate state of the home, whatever he was searching for, it wasn't going to jump out at him.

"That's fine," he said under his breath. "Police work is what I'm being paid for."

Careful to leave no trace of his presence, he began a search. He started by checking the usual places for clues. Shelves and tables. Behind or under every item he could see. He made quick work of the living room, kitchen, and master bedroom. The former two were set up in a minimalist way—necessities only, and little in the way of personal touches. The latter appeared to have been stripped down to guestroom status. A double bed sat on a plain black frame, a white dresser with broken handles rested against the wall, and a framed watercolor flower was its only adornment. The closet did house a single plastic bin, and a peek inside told Flip that it was full of women's clothing, likely belonging to the M.I.A. mother. Nothing of value, nothing of note. It was almost as though someone had gone out of their way to scrub the place clean of the family's life.

But when Flip stepped into the next room, the illusion broke.

He blinked as he was transported into a sea of bubble gum. Everything was pink. Much of it was sparkly, too. One wall was covered in boy-band posters, and another showcased glittery silver letters that spelled out E-M-I-L-Y. The décor looked more like it belonged to a ten-year-old than a girl in her mid-teens, and it made Flip shake his head as he turned in a circle, seeking an anomaly.

Right away, a slip of something sticking out from under the mattress caught his eye. He bent down and pulled it free. Then nearly dropped it. A chuckle escaped his lips, sounding out of place in the pink-frilled bedroom. But not as out of place as the magazine in his hands. The cover featured a topless man in an overtly sexual pose, and the caption promised to unravel the secrets of the male mind. A quick rifle through the pages told him more than he wanted to know about Emily's interest in boys. Things were circled with hearts and marked with stars, and several photos had been dotted with lipstick smudges.

"I wonder... does your brother know about this?" he murmured, tucking the magazine back into its spot.

He visually sought any other incongruous items. Nothing stuck out, so he did a quick look through the rest of the bedroom and then moved on, this time to what he realized was his ultimate goal.

Ellis's room.

With anticipation looming, Flip paused outside the door. A giant drawing of a middle finger was tacked to the wood. Under that was a fist-shaped hole. Both were a sharp contrast to Emily's sparkly nametag.

"Angry son-of-a-gun, aren't you?" Flip said, lifting a shirt-covered hand to the knob.

He almost *enjoyed* opening the door. It made him feel in control. Purposeful. But when he stepped into the room, the first wave of true disappointment hit him. The space was tiny. Not much bigger than a closet. In fact, there *was* no closet. No dresser, either. Only the smallest of windows. Posters covered the walls—rock bands rather than boy bands—and a stereo was tucked in beside the single mattress. A stack of folded Tshirts and jeans rested against one wall.

"Where do you hide your secrets, Ellis?" Thinking of the magazine in Emily's room, Flip bent down and heaved up the mattress, then balanced it against the wall. "Jackpot."

A flat envelope was lying on the floor, stark white against the brown wood. Flip didn't hesitate. He picked it up, lifted the flap, and peered inside.

Photographs.

Cautiously, he slid out the first one. It was a shot of Emily, head back, mouth open in laughter. She really was pretty enough to be a double-take kinda girl. Thick blond hair. Full lips and a dimple in one cheek. Full of joy and life.

"Why are you hiding these in here, Mr. Black?"

Flip slid the picture back into the envelope and moved to grab another, but a distant noise made him freeze. He cocked an ear. There it was again. An engine. Getting louder. Closer.

"Dammit," he said under his breath.

What to do now?

Part of him wanted to simply steal the envelope and its contents. He was sure it was key in some way, to the thoughts brewing in his head. He knew, though, that an illegal search and seizure wouldn't get him the results he wanted.

The engine noise reached a crescendo then cut out.

"Dammit," Flip repeated.

Regretfully, he set the envelope back down, dropped the mattress on top of it, and hurried out of the room.

16
Nineteen Hours After Escape

The Convict

Ellis stood outside the cop's house, anger writhing through him. He let it come. He let the red cloud his vision and the oily black fury slide inside him. Ten years, he'd been filling this cup. Ten years, needing a place to throw the rage with the violence it deserved. Captain Flip fucking Farriday. The cop who knew it all. Who'd pursued Ellis with a dogged commitment that put all others to shame and caught him in the act.

"Fucker."

He pulled a cigarette from the package in his pocket. Lit it. Smoked the whole thing without taking a step.

Revenge was a powerful thing. An all-consuming one. A remarkable number of hours could be dedicated to violent plotting. To dark, creative matters. Drawn-out. Pain-inducing. So many blood-thirsty promises made in the never-silent confines of his cell.

How many times had he listened to the other men explain what crimes had put them behind bars? How many times in the months since meeting sweet Veronica had he wondered if any one of those things would fit with his plan to flay the cop alive?

Now he was here. At this moment. The man who'd put *him* away lived in this very house, and Ellis could think of many,

many ways to destroy it. Except he didn't move. Not yet. Some measure of self-control was required. A window smashed... a fire that left the place a husk... neither was enough. Short-term gratification wasn't what he was after. He wanted it slow. Done bit by bit by bit. A gnawing retribution that would leave the policeman second-guessing every moment. That was why he'd planned so carefully. Why he'd used his resources inside the prison to ensure that things could be done *just right* when the time came.

Ellis closed his eyes, an erotic charge running through him.

He thought of the girl, lying in her hospital bed. Of her delicate arms and legs, bruised and sliced. Of her vulnerability. Of the look on her face when she spied him in the hallway. He was sure it was his presence alone that had woken her.

He could've gone in. Taken her again. Tasted her lips as he had so many times over the last day. Sweetness and fear and pain in the form of a little blood. It would've wreaked havoc then and there.

Where would the fun in that be?

"Too quick," he said, his voice thick with a lust he couldn't suppress.

He wanted to savor the time this would take.

Leaving the girl where she was had served another purpose anyway—it'd made certain that Farriday would be distracted. There was no doubt he would take personal responsibility for her.

If he hurts her...

The thought came from nowhere, and the anger surged again, more aggressively than before.

"Mine," Ellis growled to himself. "I'll kill him three times instead of just once."

He opened his eyes. A starting point came to him then, and he smiled and unzipped his pants. He pulled out his half-hard dick and turned sideways. Moving slowly toward the front door, he let out a steady stream of piss along the walkway. It would likely dry before Farriday returned, but the amount of fucks Ellis gave about that came to a total of fewer than zero. *He* would know he'd done it, and that was enough for him.

Still smiling, he zipped his pants and reached into his pocket to pull out the tools he'd grabbed from a local gas station. Even though it'd been years since he'd needed to pick a lock, it still took under a minute to get the door open.

The house was dark when he stepped in, but he didn't turn on a light. Just being inside the cop's space was already triggering enough. Seeing where Farriday lived—really being forced to look at the details of his non-confined life—was the last thing Ellis needed. He had a mission. A designated task. Until he completed it, he couldn't move on. He couldn't snatch the girl away. He couldn't leave town. This right here... this was the reason he'd risked the escape in the first place.

He pushed aside his need to destroy and moved through the house in the dark in search of the perfect spot to lay down his threat. It didn't take long to decide there was only one choice. The master bedroom. The master's *bed*.

Ellis took the stairs, two at a time. Instinct guided him past three doors and straight to a fourth, and without hesitation, he shoved it open. He took a step and narrowed his eyes, contempt rising up as the moonlight shined onto the unmade bed. A pile of dirty clothes sat at the foot of it, and a crumb-crusted plate and some sticky-looking cutlery rested on the nightstand, too. The prison had higher standards, for fuck's sake.

"How many girls have you brought here, you lazy bastard?" he said, wishing he'd saved a little piss for this moment, too. "How many times did you fuck someone in this bed while I stared up at the ceiling in my cell?"

Hate clouded both his vision and his mind. He wanted to grab the filthy knife from the nightstand and drive it into the mattress, slashing it open. He wanted to tear the sheets into tiny pieces, pile them up, then drop a match and watch them go up in flames.

Destruction is easy, he reminded himself. *So is violence.*

He'd known that even before setting foot into Meridian Penitentiary. He'd lived it. His incarceration had only enhanced it. What prison had also given him, though, was a special kind of patience. Ellis drew on it now. He reached into his back pocket and pulled out the little gift he'd brought along for Farriday. It was more of a *re*gift, really. Something the cop had used against Ellis. A knock-out punch, demonstrating the power of the justice system.

"Fuck you, Farriday. You aren't going to know what hit you."

He dropped the item onto one of the pillows, pulled the sheet overtop of it, and spun away. He almost made it out. *Almost.* At the last second, though, he couldn't take the thought of not leaving some more violent mark on the place.

He drew back a fist, then smashed it straight into the full-length mirror in the entryway. The glass shattered. Ellis could feel blood seeping from his hand. He let it drip on the floor for a second. Another warning. Then he grinned and walked away, leaving the door swinging wide open.

17
Seven Months,
Seven Days Before Escape

The Preacher's Daughter

A s she followed along behind the now-familiar guard up the now-familiar hallway to the room where Ellis waited, Roni was nervous. Which should've been expected. And normal. The man she was here to see wasn't a friend. And had it been a social visit, the prison was still an unnerving place to be. Even for the third time. Even when someone, like her, had been steeling for the sights and sounds and smells and feelings for a month. But the way her pulse skittered around was different this time than it had been before. It was thicker. Harder. In fact, the rush of blood through her whole body was so loud she almost couldn't hear the guard speak as he reiterated the rules and opened the door. The moment he was gone—the moment Roni locked eyes with the gray-clad man at the table—her heart silenced.

This was a bad idea, she thought immediately. *I should've found a way to stay away.*

But it wasn't an option. Not according to her father. She swallowed thickly, her mind sliding to the way he'd looked at her when she'd explained why *this* visit had to be delayed. The flash of anger. The blame. As though it was Roni's fault that she hadn't been able to come as planned.

Don't think about that right now.

But her tongue appeared to be stuck, and Ellis stayed quiet, too. Watching her with a predatory look in his eyes. He was smoking again. And Roni noted that although his cigarette was half gone, and the guard must've seen it, there was no reprimand this time around.

"Hello, sweetheart." The greeting dripped with false tenderness. "You came back."

She forced in a breath and gave a quick nod and managed to find her voice. "Yes."

"And have you missed me the way I've missed you?"

"I suspect not."

One of his dark chuckles filled the room. With someone else, it could almost have been a parody. A caricature. With Ellis, it just fit.

"No," he said. "I guess you don't have nearly as many hours to fill with fantasies as I do."

"I try to keep busy," she replied.

"Still." He leaned forward. "You're here. So that must mean that you spent at least a little time thinking about me and the question I asked last time."

Trying not to flinch back from the undisguised look of expectation on his face—as though she'd already acquiesced to some dark need of his in exchange for saving his soul—Roni squared her shoulders. "Yes, as a matter of fact, I *have* spent some time thinking about it."

His eyes glittered. "And?"

"I won't commit a sin, in order to absolve you of yours."

"Is that what you think I want? Which sin do you think I'm after, Nic? Pride? Greed or gluttony? How about some wrath or envy, topped with some sloth?"

She knew he'd deliberately left out the only one that mattered. *Lust.* And she also knew he was daring her to call him out for it. But she'd promised herself she wasn't going to be steamrolled today.

She met his challenging stare. "I had a fair bit more time to think this over than I'd initially assumed, actually."

"I'm honored to have found my way into your head."

"It was the extra *time* that was unexpected. Not the extra *you*. And I would've been here again a while ago, but you were indisposed, from what I hear. Fifteen days in solitary? That doesn't sound like fun."

For the first time since meeting him, she saw a flicker of genuine surprise on Ellis's face. She'd caught him off guard.

And that was good.

"Do you want to tell me what happened?" she asked.

"Seems like I don't have to. Did you and the warden become texting buddies? Maybe something a little *more* than that?"

"I don't have a cellphone. And I haven't had the pleasure of meeting the warden. But the prison called the week before last to tell me not to come."

"How courteous of them."

"Do you really think that coming here is as simple as walking up to the door and ringing the bell?"

"I didn't know there *was* a bell."

She shook her head and ignored the way he was trying repeatedly to undermine her. "My visits here are all preplanned. Pre-vetted. The only reason we're not talking through Plexiglass is because I'm willing to jump through those hoops."

"I *am* curious about why you're so determined," Ellis replied.

"Everyone deserves a chance," she said, deliberately avoiding mention of her father and his heavy-handed ruling on the matter. "And even if I can't pretend to understand a man like you, that doesn't mean I don't want to help."

"I'm surprised you waded through my sins and still found something there that's worth absolution." He paused and studied her face, his cold gaze growing surprised for a second time as he read the flicker she couldn't quite cover. "You didn't do it. You didn't look up my record. Why not?"

"I don't have a computer," she admitted.

"No internet. No cellphone. Do you live in a convent, Nic? Have I been fantasizing nightly about a nun?"

"No. Of course not. My father is very traditional, and he thinks technology is dangerous. If I *did* have a phone or a computer, he'd be watching it closely. I don't rock the boat, that's all."

"What stopped you from finding a computer somewhere other than at home?"

Roni's lips pressed together for a moment. Truthfully, she *had* thought about going to the library to research Ellis Black's crimes. A dozen times or more. Once, she'd gone so far as to drive to the parking lot. She'd stayed there until Angus Clyde —a local wood carver who was well-known in Meridian— had pulled up alongside her and waved. She'd waved back and gotten out of there as fast as she could. Curiosity was eating at her. But fear of what she'd find held her back. And she'd convinced herself that he ought to be the one to tell her.

"It doesn't matter," she said. "I just didn't. But I have an offer for you."

"What could you possibly have to 'offer' me?" He sneered as he said it, but the words held less ferocity than they might have.

Feeling emboldened by that, Roni cleared her throat and uttered the words that had been in her, making her nerves jump since she'd first had the epiphany. "I'll keep coming back, so long as you're willing to keep talking."

She held her breath as he stared at her, his gaze unwavering. There was a tension in the air, and she felt sure it was because Ellis was on the precipice of admitting that having her there was feeding some need of his. But when he spoke, he said something else. His voice was soft and dangerous in a way that made Roni want to slide her chair back.

"I want more than that, Nic," he said.

This time, she didn't think his intention was to scare her. And ironically, that scared her even more. Fear sliced through her, cold and true. And it only grew worse.

"Did you forget to put on a bra today, sweetheart?" Ellis asked.

In the space of a heartbeat, she felt her face heat then drain as the blood dropped away. Without meaning to, she looked down at her chest. She was already in the prison parking lot when the front clasp had suddenly snapped. She'd pulled over and tried to no avail to find some way of securing it. Her only choice had been to take it off. But she'd checked —triple-checked—that nothing was showing. She jerked her attention up to Ellis's face. He definitely knew.

"You remind me of my sister in so many ways," he said. "Not in the intellect department. God knows she was lacking there through no fault of her own. But your sweetness. Your innocence. She was naïve like that, too. Not knowing how she could affect a man."

The words sent yet another cold wave of fear through her.

"I'll take your deal, sweetheart," he added. "I'll talk if you do. I'll tell you my story if you tell me yours. But I promise you this. I *will* twist everything. I'll manipulate you. I'll use you. I'll fuck with your head. All in the name of getting the thing I want, and when it's done... you won't be able to say I didn't warn you."

Roni didn't want to answer him, but she couldn't stop herself. "What is it you really want?"

"Freedom from this hellhole."

"That's impossible."

"Nothing's impossible, Nic," he said. "Isn't that what your God teaches? And you *will* help me. Even if I have to drag you, kicking and screaming."

She stared at him, quite sure he meant the threat literally.

18
Twenty-Two Hours After Escape

The Policeman

Captain Farriday was simultaneously exhausted and keyed up. After securing Veronica Hollister in her home—literally tucking her into her bed—and then performing a perimeter check and stationing a man and a car outside, he'd gone on to personally check in with each of the units at the roadblocks. No one had spotted Ellis Black. No one had seen anyone who remotely resembled the man. The only small relief was that no one had leaked the second escape to the press.

Not yet, anyway, he thought as he navigated toward his street.

The station's media liaison had given a statement to a local news outlet before Ellis had gotten away. So as far as the Meridian townsfolk were concerned, the PD was so efficient that the prison escape was barely a blip. They hadn't even known about it until it was over. How much better could their cops do?

Now all Farriday wanted to do was go home, pour a stiff drink, and work at figuring out how the hell to get the other man back into custody before anyone found out. His fellow officers would only be content to keep it quiet for so long.

"Not that I blame them for that," he said.

No one wanted a murderer running amok in their town.

With an agitated grunt, he flicked on his turn signal and pulled over in front of his house. For a moment after he cut the engine, he sat there.

His head ached, but his thumbs tapped restlessly on the steering wheel. Part of him—a big part —wondered if he should go back to Veronica's place and relieve the uniformed officer he'd left behind. Between the knocked-out man at the station and the drugged-up one at the hospital, Farriday thought it was safe to conclude that none of the constables would be capable of outwitting Ellis Black. Maybe they just had too little experience in dealing with situations of this magnitude. Giving out speeding tickets and issuing fines for public drunkenness hardly compared to trying to chase down an escaped murderer. In any case, Farriday couldn't rely on them. But the bottom line was that if Black had wanted to take Veronica again, he could've done so at the hospital. Speaking of which, why the hell *had* the man gone there in the first place, if not to grab the girl?

Farriday shook his head. He didn't know, but the lack of a repeat kidnapping was enough to make him conclude that Ellis wanted something other than the woman he'd held hostage.

Would it be better—easier—if he's already left the Meridian area completely?

He shook his head again, this time in answer to his own silent question. It might seem better or easier in the current moment, but once it hit the news, it would be a whole other story. Farriday's retirement would be on the line. His unmarred reputation and his ten years of even-keeled captainhood would evaporate. Letting the convict get away and become someone else's problem wasn't an option.

Sighing, Farriday climbed out of his car. He needed a reset. To get himself cleaned up a bit. Maybe take a ten-minute power nap. Then a very strong cup of coffee. After that, he'd be in a better place to go after his target. But he only made it three steps toward the house before he stopped. The front door was wide open.

Ellis.

"Crap."

Farriday swept his gaze over the house, then up and down the street, then back over the house again. Everything was dark and still. That didn't mean that the escaped convict wasn't waiting for the right moment to pounce. There was something in the night air that made Farriday's nose twitch and his skin crawl.

His right hand went to his weapon, and his left hand went to the radio on his shoulder. Then he paused. He knew he should be favoring the latter of the two items. Calling for backup, however limited his current resources might be. But a split second of debate made him rule in favor of relying on the former instead. He wanted to end this himself. The crimes for which Ellis had been convicted were heinous. Even if he met his demise on the wrong end of Farriday's weapon, he wouldn't become a martyr.

Farriday drew the gun, inching toward the door and calling out as he did. "I'm armed, and I'm coming in, ready to shoot."

There was no response from within.

Farriday moved closer and spoke up again. "Ellis Black, if you're in there… I'm warning you… I won't hesitate to take you down at the slightest threat."

There was still no answer.

Come out, come out, wherever you are, Farriday thought, tightening his grip on his weapon. "Final warning, Mr. Black. I'm coming in hot."

He crept forward, ready to defend with force. Slowly and carefully, he made it to the front door. No attack came, and he stopped outside to listen for sounds of an intruder. He heard nothing. Less than nothing. Not a breeze nor a creak. He slid forward a bit more then stopped again. Shattered glass spread out across the tiled entryway, and a multitude of crimson droplets spotted the ground between the shards. He recognized it for what it was.

Blood.

Farriday drew in a breath that shook. More than that,

it sliced cold in his chest. Ellis Black had no concern over leaving his DNA everywhere, that much was obvious. And a man who felt he had nothing to lose wouldn't hold back. Except, of course, Ellis *was* holding back. The murderer had the advantage of surprise, and he hadn't taken it.

Why not? He answered the question as quickly as it came. *He wants to make you suffer the way you made him suffer by putting him behind bars for all those years.*

The thought was a chilling one. And not exactly unlikely. Hadn't Veronica Hollister stated that the convict laid the blame squarely at the captain's feet?

"Maybe it's true," he said quietly to the empty air.

Ellis was to blame for his sister's death. And the deal he made in exchange for his confession hadn't changed. He had more to lose than just his freedom. Medium security prison close to home wasn't exactly a day at the spa, but it could've been worse. So why would he screw himself over with this stunt? What had changed?

Pushing the questions aside, Farriday stepped into the house a little more, picking his way around the broken mirror to examine the surrounding area.

"If you're in here, Black... you should come out and face me like a man!" he yelled.

The holler elicited no response.

Farriday rolled his shoulders and began a full, cautious sweep of the house. It quickly became evident no one else was there. Aside from the destruction in the entryway, things were undisturbed. Nothing broken, nothing stolen. No one hiding in a nook or cranny.

Farriday made his way back to the front entryway and examined the mess. He knew he ought to be calling in the B&E and the destruction of property. Heck. He should probably be asking someone else to come and sweep the house, too.

Not going to do it, though, are you?

"No, I'm not."

He didn't want anyone else to know about this. He didn't

want people—especially his fellow cops—delving into this as something more personal. Fewer than two days. That's how long he had until he hung up his badge for good. Why make things more complicated now? It was bad enough as it was.

He stowed his weapon and finished locking the doors—making sure each slide lock was engaged from the inside and all of the windows were secure, too—then got to work on the mess Ellis had left behind.

As Farriday worked, he rolled it all over in his head a little more. The man had kidnapped the girl and escaped but then stayed close to home. He'd been caught, then escaped again. Only instead of making a break for it when he could, he used the second escape to come to both the hospital and Farriday's home, where he'd done little more than play bogeyman. What else did he have planned?

Farriday put away his broom, tossed the blood-stained cloth into the garbage, then made his way up to his ensuite bathroom, where he scrubbed his face and continued with his evaluation of the situation.

"Maybe Ellis *wanted* to get caught again," he said to his own reflection.

He frowned. The idea felt like it fit. But why? He ran a hand over his chin, then slipped out of his button-down uniform top. Despite what his gut was saying, at least one thing didn't line up. If Ellis's goal was to get caught a second time, then why had he gone to the trouble of freeing himself?

Trying to come up with a plausible explanation, the captain exited the bathroom and moved to his closet to grab a T-shirt. Nothing came to mind as he slid the cotton over his head.

All it did was to again beg the question of what Ellis Black was trying to accomplish with this little game. Psychological warfare? If so, Farriday wasn't going to fall prey to it. He was the cop. The good guy. Ellis was scum, born and raised. The only proof needed was in their living arrangement. Ellis had a six-by-eight room and had to use the toilet in view of his equally scummy peers. Farriday owned this nice little house in a nice little suburb where there was no one to bother him but the neighborhood kids.

What do you want, Ellis Black, after all these years?

He flopped back onto the bed, then turned on his side. Something scraped against his upper arm, halting his musings.

With an inexplicable trickle of apprehension running through his body, he sat up and pulled back the sheets. And went very still.

Apparently, while Black hadn't taken anything, he *had* left something. A photograph.

Slowly—aware that he was damaging evidence—Farriday picked it up. He didn't have to study it for more than a heartbeat to know that he recognized it. Though the picture was a decade old now, it was in pristine condition. Emily Black's sweet smile shone up at him, frozen in time. Forever sixteen.

For a few seconds more, he continued to sit there, staring down at the girl's pretty face. Farriday rarely allowed himself to think of her. Her death had reinvigorated his career—given him the opportunity that had otherwise eluded him— and it wasn't always easy to reconcile that with his conscience.

Now he wondered if he should've considered it more often. Run over the details more thoroughly. Crossed more Ts, dotted more Is. Of course, a guilty plea negated the need. So did arresting the girl's brother while he leaned over a brutally beaten body. Now self-doubt crept up, and Farriday ran a finger over the image. Had he missed something? Had he—

"Shit," he said, dropping a rare curse as his brain finally caught up to the situation.

Most things related to policework—maybe *all* things, he wasn't sure—were digitized now. Paperwork, crime scene photos. All logged on a computer and stored on a server somewhere, quadruple-backed-up by some group of tech gurus. Even hard evidence was photographed and uploaded. It was practical. But the originals had to be kept. The majority were sent to a central storage place, but for some cases, Farriday preferred to use his own station's meager facility. Ellis Black most definitely fell into that category. *This photo* fell into that category. It hadn't been in Ellis's possession in ten years. Not since Farriday had removed it from the Blacks' house, logged it into evidence, and put it in the PD basement for safekeeping.

19
Six Months,
Twenty-Seven Days Before Escape

The Preacher's Daughter

Heart beating wildly, Roni positioned herself in front of the mirror and aimed the camera at her reflection.

Are you really doing this? she asked herself.

Her arms dropped as doubt wormed its way in. She studied her appearance. She'd fixed her hair into a side braid, and her face was makeup free. Her clothes were carefully modest, as always. She wore a pale blue blouse, buttoned to her throat. Her legs were covered in a navy skirt that hit her ankles. There was nothing—less than nothing—about her appearance that was inappropriate.

She swallowed. "It's just a picture."

But her hands didn't bring the camera up again. Because the problem wasn't the photo itself. It was the purpose behind it.

She'd met with Ellis two more times since he'd agreed to her deal. But both visits had been nothing more than a frustrating dance of words. He asked a lot of questions. Things about her life in Meridian and things about being brought up by a single father. Details of where she saw herself in five years, or ten. His curiosity about her upbringing made her squirm. She knew it was unusual. Not the homeschooling itself. Not the overt religious zealotry. Not even the combination. But her acceptance of it. Her lack of rebellion. Two things that made Ellis raise his eyebrow and twist his mouth while also creating just a niggling of doubt in her own heart.

It was just the way things had always been.

Roni had been answering patiently. Vaguely, when possible. Specifically, when it couldn't be avoided. She got the feeling that Ellis was testing her out. Building a foundation of possible trust. And although her fear of him hadn't eased in the slightest, she at least felt like she was doing what she'd come to do. She'd been priming to ask him a few direct questions of her own. But the previous week, he'd startled her with a different query—the one that had led to this moment. As she thought about it now, it came back in perfect clarity.

"Give me a gift, Nic," he said, *"and I'll tell you a story about my life before this."*

Right away, Roni's palms started to sweat. "What kind of a gift?"

"A photograph."

"Of what?"

"Of you."

"I don't think I—"

"I'll make sure that you're allowed to bring it," he told her.

She swallowed. "No, I'm not worried about that. But I don't have a picture of myself."

"So get one taken. Take one yourself. Bring me what I want, and you won't be sorry," he promised.

Then their meeting had ended, and Roni had gone home with zero intentions of following through on the request. Just the thought of Ellis Black having an image of her in his cell— or anywhere near him, really—was enough to keep her up at night. It *had* kept her up at night. Mostly because she'd walked into her room that same evening and spied her mom's old camera up there on the shelf.

For two days, Roni had ignored it. On the third day, she'd caved a little and pulled the camera down and given it a falsely disinterested once-over before putting it back. On the fourth day, she'd checked it over more thoroughly, noting that it contained film and seemed to be in good working order. She'd wondered if there were even places that *developed* film in the time of digital photography. The next evening—yesterday — when Roni had gone to pick up a last-minute grocery item at the local convenience store, she'd spied a sign that promised one-hour prints. And the clerk had confirmed that yes, they really did still do film. Today she'd given in and acknowledged that the universe wanted her to do this. It was what she needed to do in order to move forward with Ellis.

She took a shaky breath and lifted the camera again. She held it in what she hoped was a good position, closed her eyes and clicked. Then she realized what she'd done, and she groaned. Opening her eyes, she tried again. She clicked. The flash came on brightly as she took the shot, and Roni winced. There was no way the picture wouldn't be obscured by the light. She turned the camera over, adjusted the settings, and aimed once more. But as soon as she clicked again, she wondered if she'd closed her eyes this time, too.

She tapped the button once more, lost her grip on the camera, and had to bend to catch it mid-fall—just as it took another picture.

And this... this *is why digital photography was invented,* she thought ruefully as she righted herself.

"Okay," she said. "One more try, and Ellis Black gets what he gets."

She'd already decided that she'd use the remainder of the film to take pictures of the scenery around her house. She'd give those to him, too. Maybe he'd appreciate a little glimpse of the natural world more than he would a picture of Roni.

Or maybe it'll remind him that he's stuck and infuriate him, and he'll burn them in his cell. She shook off the thought. *Whatever he decides will be on him.*

For the umpteenth time, she brought the camera up and angled it just so. She curved her lips up in the smallest smile—

no need to look miserable *or* excessively pleased—and pushed down with her index finger. The moment she did, she heard her bedroom door open. A heartbeat more, and she would've had time to hide the camera. But it was too late.

"What in the love of heaven are you doing?" Her father's eyes met hers in the mirror, then went from her to the camera and back again before hardening. "Is this... are you making *pornography*?"

Roni sucked in a startled breath at the absurd question, and she faced him. "What? No! I—"

The back of his hand on her cheek cut off her words with a crack she could hear as well as feel. The hit was unexpected, and she fell over sideways, her temple thumping the vanity so hard that her vision sparkled. The camera flew from her hands. From where she landed, Roni watched it skitter across the floor until it came to a stop under her bed. For a second, a dreadful silence hung over the room. Then her father delivered a second blow, this one with his foot to her abdomen.

"Who have you been seeing?" he demanded.

The tears were unstoppable, but Roni did her best not to cringe away from him. "No one."

"God doesn't like liars."

"I'm not lying. I swear."

"Your mother was a liar."

She swallowed. "I know. But I'm not like her. You know I'm not."

"She thought she was smart. She thought she could hide it from me. But I could smell it on her, every time." He took a deep inhale. "I swear to the almighty God above that if you're out there, letting some man under your skirt..."

She shook her head, feeling the throb caused by the blows he'd delivered. "I would never."

He narrowed his eyes, and she waited for him to ask why she was taking the pictures, if not for some indecent purpose. She truly didn't know what he'd do or say in response. Reason was a blurred line for her father. He might accept it. Or it might draw more ire.

But after another few moments, his furious breaths leveled, and he asked one of his favorite questions instead.

"You're a good girl, aren't you, Roni?"

She let out a small breath. "Yes."

"My good girl."

"Yes."

"And you'll always be my good girl, won't you?"

"I will."

He nodded once, then headed for the door. But he paused again before fully exiting.

"I don't have to ask if you remember what happened to your mother," he said. "But just in case... I'm reminding you now. The Lord sees all, and He is not shy with punishing those who refuse to repent."

Roni didn't answer. She knew he wasn't expecting her to. She also didn't move until she was one hundred percent sure her father was out of earshot. When she did finally get up, she did something that surprised herself. She didn't simply grab the camera and put it away, though she probably should have. Especially considering the fresh stings from the hits her father had dealt. She'd obeyed him her whole life. But this once, she thought maybe he was wrong about what God had in mind. So what Roni did instead was to carefully close the door, and *then* retrieve the camera. Slowly, she stood up and turned back to the mirror. Without looking, she took seven quick shots in succession. For the final photo, she stepped to the window, aimed at the horizon, and clicked once more.

20
Six Months,
Twenty Days Before Escape

The Convict

Ellis was fucking antsy. It was an unusual sensation for him. The cuffs on his wrists felt too tight, even though the guard—by unspoken understanding—left them just loose enough to not be quite uncomfortable. The chains were too short today, the small room too warm. He'd left his cigarettes in his cell. Under the table, his knee bounced for a second before he ordered it to stop.

Where the hell was the girl? She was coming. He knew she was. Or else they wouldn't have bothered to bring him here. Rarely had he had to wait more than a minute or two. The prison was nothing if not efficient. Now, though, he'd been sitting there for ten minutes. The analog clock overhead was about to click over to an eleventh one, too.

He was riding a line. He needed the girl to trust him a little. Not in an unreasonable way. Her fear was a continuing necessity, too. That little bit of faith, though, was what would carry him to the other side. Veronica Hollister would be lulled just enough. Then he'd slam in. Rip out the metaphorical fucking rug to get what he desired.

If she ever shows up.

At last—on the thirteenth minute—the door creaked open. Veronica stepped through, pausing to say something over her shoulder to the guard before closing it behind her. Head down, hair hanging over her face, she stepped forward.

Ellis had a contempt-filled accusation on the ready. It died, though, as she lifted her head and met his eyes. A mottled blue and purple bruise marred the perfection of her cheek. That creamy skin that *he* dreamed of marking on a nightly basis had been damaged by someone else.

An unexpected emotion surged through him, whitehot. *Jealousy.* He was enraged. The girl was his. He'd spent hours mapping out the things he was going to do to her once he got free. Now this. Someone—another man, undoubtedly— had damaged his property.

"What the *fuck* happened?" he growled.

"Sorry?" she replied.

"Your fucking face, Nic."

"Oh." Her hand came up to touch the bruise. "I fell." It was a lie. An obvious one.

"Bullshit," Ellis said.

She blinked, then dropped her gaze. "I don't want to argue."

"I don't argue, and I'm not a patient man."

"Mr. Black…"

He slammed his hands hard against the table. "Tell me what the fuck happened, or I'll stop talking altogether."

Veronica drew in a sharp breath, and she quivered. Ellis expected her to acquiesce. Instead, her eyes came back up to his, and they were flashing.

"You haven't even *started* talking yet," she snapped. "You haven't told me about your crimes. You haven't told me why you were in solitary the other week. I don't know anything about you except for the fact that you're pretty good at manipulating the system in which you've been living for the last decade. How about you actually give me something before you threaten to take it away?"

"You shouldn't ask questions that you don't really want to know the answer to, Nic."

"Why do you *care* what happened to my face, Ellis?"

She said something more, but he missed all of it, because she'd used his given name for the first time. Hearing her sweet voice wrapped around it provoked a violent need in him. He wanted her to whimper it. To beg him for mercy, using it.

Oh, the things I'll do to her once I'm free.

His imagination slid somewhere primal, and it took some effort to focus on the here and now. Veronica was looking at him expectantly, her cheeks still flushed from her minute-earlier outburst. Had she asked another question? Ellis had no fucking clue. He didn't care, either. She was a tool. Weak and soft. Malleable. Needed for only a short while.

He stared at her bruise for a second longer, then took control once more. "Why did you keep him a secret from me, Nic?"

"What?"

"Your boyfriend. Were you ashamed that he hurts you? Or did you feel disloyal to one of us?"

The pink in her cheeks deepened. "I don't have a boyfriend."

"Then who hit you?"

She didn't answer. Pressure built up inside Ellis's chest, and he forcibly molded it into cold calmness.

"Come here," he ordered.

"I—"

"Now."

She tossed a backward glance at the door, and Ellis thought she might make a run for it. She didn't. She took a visible breath and stepped nearer.

"Sit down," he said.

She bit her lip—he could see she had a small abrasion there, too—and obeyed him. He could smell her light soapy scent. It made his mouth water. Briefly, he toyed with the idea of giving her another order. Something more sinister.

"I'm not here to offer my services as some kind of dark knight," he told her. "I just want to know which one of us is the other man."

Her eyes widened, and a small laugh burst from her pretty

little mouth. It was a pleasant sound. Totally unsuited to either the prison or Ellis's mind.

"Well, if there *were* another man in this scenario, you'd be able to rest assured that it's not you. This..." She touched her bruise again, her smile dropping away. "Is courtesy of my father."

Her father.

"Is hitting you a big part of his traditionalism?" He sneered. "No internet, no cellphone, and a beating on the side?"

"He has high expectations. If I let him down, he makes sure I know it." Her voice was too flat for him to believe she simply accepted the situation as normal, even if she accepted it as fact.

"How old are you, Nic? Remind me."

"Twenty-two."

Twenty-two. And still under her dad's thumb like a small child. Not a bad thing. Not for me.

"What rules could your father possibly hold you—a twenty-two-year-old woman—to?" Ellis asked.

"Actually, in this case, it was about you and the picture you wanted," she replied, her expression as unmoving as her tone. "So, feel free to take credit for my bruises if that makes you feel better."

He narrowed his eyes, momentarily distracted by thoughts of his own hands on her creamy flesh. How long until the mark left by her father faded back into perfection?

"I don't do things secondhand, sweetheart," he said.

She blinked in that surprised way of hers. "What do you want me to say to that? Should I be *glad* that you have a preference for hurting women, one-on-one?"

His mouth twisted. "Better than getting someone else to do your dirty work, isn't it? I take back what I said about being a dark knight. If I were a free man, I'd beat your father to a bloody fucking pulp."

Veronica sucked in an audible breath. "I *did* bring you the picture that cost me this bruise. I brought all of them, actually. And it took some convincing, but the guard agreed to let me give them to you. He's going to leave them in your cell. But I promise you that I won't be coming back unless you tell me that story like you said you would."

"It doesn't matter what I tell you," he said. "What I did ten years ago... it can't be undone."

He studied her face. It was open. So full of innocence. If he'd had any conscience left at all, he might've felt bad for what he was going to do to her.

"Well?" she said.

"I had a sister," he replied, the words coming with true reluctance.

Veronica nodded. "You mentioned her before. You told me I reminded you of her."

"Emily was my twin. Three minutes older. She was born with my umbilical cord wrapped around her neck, and the oxygen deprivation gave her brain damage. Not something you'd notice from looking at her. But she was... lacking in intellectual sophistication."

Sympathy filled Veronica's eyes, and Ellis opened his mouth to tell her where she could shove it. And why. Before he could speak, though, he felt the light touch of her fingers on the back of one of his clenched hands.

Fuck.

He wanted to spin her wrist and yank her closer and make her cry out. He forced himself to keep still.

"Emily was sweet. Totally oblivious to her own so-called disadvantage. It made people like her. Except our dad. He could barely look at her, most of the time. The only upside was that the bastard didn't beat on her like he did me and my mom. He blamed me for Emily's condition." A dark chuckle escaped. "Bad before I was even born."

"You know it wasn't actually your fault, right?" said Veronica.

He met her eyes, and he could read her expression perfectly. She saw his little anecdote about his birth and the reveal of his family dynamic as a crack in his damaged psyche. If she could fix that, she could fix him. But she was barking up the wrong fucking tree. It was time to tell her.

"Emily is the reason I'm in here," he replied.

Puzzlement crinkled her brow. "What?"

"Rape and murder, sweetheart. Those are my crimes."

Her eyes went impossibly wide, and her face paled. "I..."

"You *what*?"

"I..."

Another heartbeat went by before she yanked her hand from his and scraped back her chair. Ellis looked away. He heard her feet scuttle across the floor, followed by the creak of the door opening. Air rushed in. There was an echoing click.

Then the room went still and silent.

She'll come back, he told himself.

She had to.

21
Five Months, Twenty-Four Days Before Escape

The Preacher's Daughter

R oni held out for as long as she could. She immersed herself in tasks that kept her body and mind occupied.

She completed some overdue housework and repainted the kitchen chairs. She did some baking and weeded the flowerbeds. She finished a book she'd been putting off reading. She distracted her father with games of cribbage and questions about his old parish. Every time her mind tried to slide to Ellis and his dark confession, she recited the alphabet backward. One thing she didn't do—and which maybe she should have done, considering the circumstances—was seek solace in her Bible. But she didn't want to dwell on that, either.

Ultimately, Roni lost the battle. It was sleep deprivation that did it. Weeks of restlessness. Several nights that didn't amount to more than a few minutes of eyes shut tightly while begging her body to nod off. All that alongside the extra bursts of physical labor. And she was done. She *had* to think about it. If she didn't, she would go crazy. She was halfway there already, wondering how she'd thought she would be able to help a man like Ellis in the first place. Knowing nothing about him except that he was a convicted criminal should've been enough to tell her otherwise. But she had no choice; she had to face what he'd done, or it was going to haunt her mind forever.

So, with exhaustion dragging at her, she made a fake grocery list, said goodbye to her father, then headed for the library. She drove in a haze and climbed out of her car like a zombie. She made it up the cement stairs and through the doors without issue. But as those same doors closed behind her, the unnatural hush of the library settled over Roni, and a half dozen thoughts rushed in, each one as unsettling as the next.

Am I doing the right thing? Can't I wash my hands of Ellis Black and be done with it? Is he really worth this risk? I don't rebel. Not for anything. And yet, here I am. For this. For him. Why?

She stood in the lobby, heart tapping unevenly. The rows of books—seven feet high and intimidating in the current moment—loomed in front of her. She very nearly left again. In fact, she *did* turn. But she didn't leave. She couldn't. Because another patron was entering the library. A man she knew. A man who knew her father. The head of Meridian Alliance Church. Pastor Benson.

Roni froze. The pastor stood in the doorframe, his attention on someone out in the lot. Any second, he'd find her there. And while it was unlikely that he'd make an effort to reach out to her father just to inform him of her presence in the library —it was hardly a deviant venue—there was a good possibility he'd bring it up inadvertently in the future. And Roni knew how that would go. She could imagine the look on her father's face as he realized she'd deceived him for some reason. What excuse could she possibly have for lying about this trip? The conclusion her father would come to was singular.

Were you meeting a man, Roni? Who is he? What did you let him do to you?

She shook a little at the thought of what would come next. But there was no time to dwell on fears of the future. She needed to focus on the current problem and get out of Pastor Benson's line of sight.

Spinning away from him, Roni sought easy refuge. Right

away, she spied the women's bathroom. On silent feet, she headed for the swinging door. She almost made it. But a new problem arose in the form of yet another contact from Meridian Alliance. It was one of her old Sunday school teachers. A throwback to the days before Roni's father decided he was the best one to impart the Bible's words to her. The woman—who had to be in her nineties and who was partially blind, thank God—was stepping out of the children's section.

What is this? Roni thought. *Church reunion day at the library?*

Groaning to herself, she made a sharp turn at the nearest aisle. There, she pressed her back to one of the shelves and held her breath as the Sunday school teacher toddled by. As soon as the older woman was out of view, Roni exhaled sharply. Her shoulders sagged even as her pulse continued to thud. She eased away from the shelf and started to exit the aisle, then jumped back once more as she saw that Pastor Benson was headed her way.

Seriously?

Knowing the pastor wasn't impeded by poor sight like the Sunday school teacher, Roni decided not to take a chance and wait for him to pass. She scurried off in the other direction, turned up another aisle, then made a quick dash for the space set aside for the library's computers. Thankfully, each one of those was tucked into a private cubby. Sinking into a chair put Roni out of public view. It only took a second for her to catch her breath, and then she brought her attention to the task she'd come there to complete.

"No point in wasting time," she said to the keyboard, typing in Ellis's name.

The computer, on the other hand, had a different idea. A spinning circle appeared in the middle of the screen, and Roni rolled her eyes as she waited for it to load.

Her mind wandered to the absurdity of the current situation. Sneaking through a library. Running from church folk like they'd burn her alive for being there. A laugh tried to escape, and she covered her mouth with her hand, but that only made her want to laugh harder. A snort got out instead.

Then a giggle. But her amusement died as the search engine on the computer finally chose to do its thing and loaded up the results.

The row of headlines was disturbing. Breath-cutting. And Roni couldn't stop her eyes from moving over them.

Meridian Resident Found Raped and Murdered: Suspect in Custody.

Victim in Homicide Identified as 16-Year-Old Emily Black.

Suspect Revealed: Meridian Teen's Brother Under Arrest.

Ellis Black, Twin Brother of Emily Black, Pleads Guilty.

And the list went on, all the way down the digital page. Their meaning was unequivocal; Ellis had committed the heinous crimes.

He'd been sixteen, going on seventeen. Roni would've been twelve at the time. And she would've been living nearby. How could this have slipped past her? As closely as her father guarded her, she surely should have heard something. Seen something. A whisper. Any tiny thing. And yet she hadn't.

She stared blankly, thinking about it. *Where was I when it happened? What was I doing when she was raped and murdered by her own brother?*

But she knew the answer. She'd been in her room. Or out in the yard. Not allowed to interact with her peers, not allowed to peruse the news. And that year—the transition from preteen to teen—had been particularly rough for her father. Or he'd been particularly rough on her. Kept her home more than usual. Punished her more often.

He was protecting you, Nic, said Ellis's voice in her head. And maybe you can see why?

"I can," she whispered.

She could understand not wanting a child to hear about this. Really, truly. And once that year had ended, once Ellis had confessed and been put away, she could also understand why no one would want to relive it.

Woodenly, Roni clicked on one of the articles at random. A

photo popped up. It displayed a sullen teenage boy sitting in a courtroom. Though he was younger and lean to the point of gaunt, there was no denying it was Ellis. His eyes gave him away. Cold. Angry. Him to the core. He'd pushed his chair back from the table in front of him and had his long legs spread out in a careless way that was at odds with the proceedings going on around him. Even his lawyer stood away from him as though trying not to get too close.

The article that accompanied the picture started out by painting a sad story. An abusive father. A neglectful mother. Two children who had to fend for themselves. There wasn't a soul left to mourn the girl.

Sympathy hovered in Roni's heart. Empathy, even. She knew what it was like to be parented in this way. But the feeling didn't last long. Because the story changed. It branched into darkness that became an abyss. Ellis's petty crimes. His trouble at school. His sister's missing status and the dogged work of a particular police officer who worked to unravel it. When the article began to describe the gruesome details of the find, Roni clicked it closed. Nausea rolled up, stronger than it had been even after her first prison visit. Swallowing, Roni stared at the blank screen.

I sat across from him, she thought. *I touched his hand. I looked him in the eye, and I believed there was something there that could be saved.*

"But not from this," she whispered.

How could anyone be forgiven for such atrocity, even by God himself?

22

Ten Years Earlier
Forty Hours Before Arrest

The Policeman

Flip paused outside the steel and glass doors at the station. He'd successfully escaped the Blacks' home without drawing notice, issued two speeding tickets on his way back into town, and managed to snag a coffee, too. He'd just been settling into his car and putting the cup to his lips when Danielle had radioed in with a friendly heads-up. Cliff Sunder had taken on the role of interim captain and was asking for him. The latter thing by itself wasn't a surprise. The man was a brown noser, through and through. The thing that was making Flip hesitate now was the fact that Cliff had specifically asked for him.

Between interviewing Ellis and following up on the surety that there was something more to be had of the situation, he'd somehow managed to forget that he'd been— nearly—fired the day before. Now he couldn't help but wonder if the recently deceased captain's paperwork had been filed after all. Was he about to be caught? He supposed there was little he could do about it now. Denial would probably be his new best friend.

Flip took a breath, put his hand on the door handle and a smile on his face, and stepped into the familiar space. There was an unusual quiet inside. The hum of the station was muted. Understandable, given the circumstances. But

Flip couldn't let it unnerve him. Not now. He straightened his shoulders and kept going. He shook his head in silent forgiveness when Danielle mouthed the word *sorry* at him as he slid past her office. Then he stopped in front of his new—still unofficial—boss's door, adjusted his stance again, and gave a firm rap. One that said he was supposed to be there. That he belonged. Because he did.

"Come in!" called Cliff.

Flip pushed his way into the office. "You wanted to see me?"

"Close the door."

The words irked him, but he maintained an outward calm and did as requested.

"Have a seat," said the other man.

Flip did that, too. "Thanks."

Cliff waited until he was settled, then cleared his throat. "Are you doing okay, Farriday?"

"Tip-top, all things considered," Flip replied. "Why do you ask?"

"I had an odd report a short bit ago from a citizen. He said he saw someone who fits your description hanging around outside the Black property."

Flip quickly calculated the benefit of lying versus the cost of it and decided to hope that Cliff would see reason. He recapped the dropped call and his interaction with the boy but left out the part where he went into the house. Confessing that wouldn't help him in the slightest.

"Something's wrong out there, Cliff. I can feel it," he said at the end.

"We don't use feelings. We use evidence."

"That's crap, and you know it. We rely on our guts all the time."

The other man sighed. "It's not crap, Constable."

Flip ordered his teeth not to grit together. "This has something to do with the girl. Emily. I was going to put in a report about the dropped call and—"

"Tell me you have something more than 'a feeling,' and we'll talk."

"I don't understand the problem of looking into it a little more."

"The fact that you don't understand *is* the problem, Constable."

Flip refrained from reminding the other man that they'd had the same rank right up until this very moment. "Pardon me?"

Cliff sighed yet again and leaned back in his chair. "Do you know how many calls we've had out there in the last ten years?"

"Not precisely, no."

"Exactly."

"I'm not following."

"Good police work requires more than showing up."

Wasn't that precisely what Flip had just said? He opened his mouth, but the interim captain spoke more quickly.

"You took the boy's statement," said Cliff, "and that was the extent of what you were asked to do. Now you've brought your concerns to me, and I've told you it's nothing to worry about. You went ahead and took matters into your own hands once already, and I need that to stop. Here. Now. Today."

"I was trying to do more than show up," Flip argued, desperately trying to keep his tone free of emotion.

"What you should've done is to put in the ten minutes to do some research."

Cliff slid a folder across the desk, and Flip had little choice but to open it up. There were dozens of pages, but six stood out because they were marked with brightly colored sticky notes.

Flip went to the first one and skimmed over the report. It was a call taken a month earlier. It'd been placed by Ellis Black, who'd claimed someone had followed him home. Meridian PD had found nothing suspicious. The second sticky note showed another call placed by Ellis, two months before that. This one was a report that someone had been in their house while he and Emily were at school. Again, Flip's fellow officers had determined the claim to be bunk.

"You see?" said Cliff. "The kid has a habit of reporting things that never happened. If you go back two years, you'll find out the brother called in a missing report on his sister another time. Turned out to be as false as the rest of the stuff."

"This is..." Flip rubbed his neck, trying to tamp down his percolating frustration. "It's different, Cliff. I *know* it."

The other man sighed again. "You don't know it, Flip, because it's not true."

"I just want a bit of leeway."

"No."

"Cliff."

The acting captain pulled the file folder away and slapped it shut. "Things are going to be in an upheaval for a while around here. I think we can all agree on that."

"Sure, but—"

"Did you know that my wife and Captain Dax went to high school together?"

Flip tensed at the unexpected question and what it might mean. "I don't think so, no."

Cliff nodded. "They did. That's why I took this low-man posting in Meridian rather than a captain's position elsewhere. Sherry—my wife—didn't much care for city life. Had enough of it, and she wanted to come home. So we did. Happy wife, happy life, and all that. Anyway... she reconnected with her old friend, which led to family dinners, and a closer relationship between me and Dax."

Flip's muscles were so bunched that his body ached, and it was all he could do to force out a neutral response. "Makes sense."

"I want you to know that the captain always left work at work. A true professional. But he said something to me a short while ago, purely out of worry. Because he was also a good guy. Which is why I feel like he wouldn't mind if I told you this now.

Maybe he'd even want me to. So here it goes. He was concerned about you, Flip. And I can see why."

Flip waited for more—for the revelation that Captain Dax had told Cliff about his plan to let Flip go. That he'd told the other man over beers that if Flip had had a future in police work, it would've taken off by now. It didn't come.

"I want you to do something for me," Cliff said instead. "I want you to take the rest of the week off. Get yourself into the right headspace."

"You just told me everything was in upheaval," Flip pointed out.

"I know. And that's why I want you to take this little break. I need to smooth out as many wrinkles as I can, and now I'm concerned about how you're pushing this thing with the Blacks."

"I—no. You know what? Fine."

"Yes?"

"Sure."

"Good," said Cliff. "Report back to me next Monday, okay?"

"You got it," Flip replied.

He turned to go, but the other man called out to him as his hand closed around the door handle. "Constable?"

He held in his irritation. "Yeah?"

"It'd probably be best if you started calling me Captain from here on out."

"Will do. *Captain.*"

Flip barely managed to keep from storming off.

Probably what Cliff wants *me to do,* he thought as he stepped through the station at a clipped pace and kept going straight through the front door. *Probably what he was* hoping *I'd do. Give him the excuse that he—*

Flip stopped short. Both mentally and physically. Ellis Black was on the other side of the street, his skinny rear end planted on a bench, a cigarette dangling from his lips. His eyes fixed directly on Flip. There was dark anger in his gaze, palpable even from the distance between them. But it was smug, too. And it occurred to Flip that Cliff hadn't said *who* had placed the call to complain about his trip out to the Black property. Who was to say it wasn't the boy himself?

For a good few seconds, the kid stayed there. Like he wanted to make sure Flip had seen him. Then he tossed his butt to the ground, stood up, and strode away.

Flip only hesitated for a second—the length of time it took him to glance over his shoulder to check if anyone from the station was paying attention—before booking it after Ellis Black. There was no doubt the kid was up to something. Baiting him, possibly. No way was Flip letting him get away with it. The promise he'd just made to Cliff notwithstanding.

His boots hit the ground in a quick, thumping rhythm. He darted across the street, and a group of teens waiting at a bus stop scattered in his wake.

Ellis veered left at the end of the block. Flip picked up his pace and did the same. For a moment after he made the turn, he lost sight of the kid. But a heartbeat later, he noticed a cluster of shrubs on the side of the road was shuddering though the air was still.

Flip took off again. In seconds, he was at the foliage and pushing through them. On the other side, he paused and glanced to each side. It was a private residence. A large yard with a birdbath in the middle of it. And no sign of Ellis.

Where did the kid go?

Flip's eyes landed on a gate on the far side of the yard.

"Jackpot," he said.

Ignoring a woman who hollered out a window that she was calling the cops, he ran toward the fence, clicked open the latch, and pushed. As he swung it open, a motorcycle engine revved, and Flip knew he'd lost this particular battle. But that didn't mean he was giving up. No matter what his so-called captain said.

23

Twenty-Three Hours After Escape

The Policeman

Farriday unlocked the station door and eased through it, stifling a sigh as he eyed the dispatch office. Danielle sat inside, her platinum blond head visible above the lip of the window that looked out into the lobby. She wore her headset, but there was an open book in front of her on the table, so he knew it was a quiet evening in Meridian. As was the norm on a Thursday.

Yes. Totally quiet and normal. Except for that pesky matter of the convicted murderer who's on the loose.

He shoved aside the sarcastic—and far too true— thought and stepped reluctantly toward the office, wondering how quickly he'd be able to get away. He'd thought it was Danielle's night off, and he obviously wasn't in the mood for small talk. Didn't even have time for it. But while anyone else would've been satisfied with a wave, the longest-standing employee at Meridian PD—aside from Flip himself, of course —always expected a proper greeting. If he didn't stop and say hello, she'd call him out for it later. Loudly. Probably publicly. Drawing more attention to a situation that already garnered far too much.

He gave her open door a light tap and smiled. "Working the night shift tonight?"

Danielle lifted her head and laughed, not startled or put off by his presence at all. "Well, I'm not here for my health, honey."

"Funny as always," Farriday said. "What happened to the new girl? Isn't this her shift?"

"You mean Clara? I don't know if she's going to last much longer, Flip. This is the third night this week that her kid is allegedly sick. Georgie and I have been covering her all week."

"Did it occur to you that her kid might actually *be* sick?" he asked, raising an eyebrow.

She wagged a purple-painted nail at him. "You're far too nice to be able to tell when someone is lying."

"Ouch. Doesn't say much about my policework, does it?"

"I don't mean nice like *that*. I mean that when you see a pretty face, you assume the best."

"How is that any better than the other thing you said?" He winked. "Besides, which… yours is the only pretty face I notice, Danielle."

"Flattery will get you everywhere," she replied. "What brings you in tonight, honey?"

"Just wanted to look through some old case files," he told her honestly.

"That sounds… boring."

"It will be, I promise." He grinned. "You want to come?"

"That's a hard no," she said.

"You sure? I'm going to cozy up in the bad lighting with that wonderfully damp basement scent all around me."

"As appealing as *that* is… still no."

He shrugged. "Suit yourself."

"I always do," Danielle replied. "Is this about that horrible man who attacked Constable Kinsley earlier in the interrogation room?" *Dammit.*

He hadn't wanted to talk about Ellis at all, but of course, the dispatcher would know already what was going on. He couldn't deflect the question. Or simply lie about it.

"Crossing and dotting my you-know-whats," he said, his voice far easier than his mind.

"I heard from Georgie that there was blood up and down the whole hallway after it happened. I told her head wounds do that. But still… I hope you catch him soon. We don't want that kind of violence out the streets, do we?" Danielle paused. "He's the one from all those years ago, isn't he? He killed his sister. And there was the whole thing with Cliff out in the barn."

"That's the one," Flip said.

"Damn shame."

"Damn shame," he echoed.

A pall hung over the already quiet station.

"Honey?" said Danielle. "You okay?"

He opened his mouth to offer a reassurance that he was fine. But the switchboard buzzed with an incoming call, saving him from answering. Relieved, he made a zipped lips motion as Danielle picked it up with the standard intro—*9-1-1, what's your emergency?*—and he used the moment to slip away.

He hurried down the hall to the stairs that led to the basement and descended quickly. There was one room below ground level, and access was limited. Only Farriday had keys, and only he could let someone else in.

Until now, he thought, bending down to examine the lock.

It didn't appear to have been tampered with, but that didn't mean anything. Ellis had been a sneaky bastard all those years ago, and prison had probably only made him all the more cunning.

Ordering his mind to stay on track, Farriday unlocked the door, then stepped inside the room and flicked on the light. A yellowish glow—he hadn't been kidding about the quality of the illumination nor about the smell—bathed only the smallest of areas. It didn't matter. He didn't have to think about which shelf housed the correct box. Or which box was the right one, for that matter. He moved toward it by feel, pulled it down, then carried it over to the makeshift examination table on the edge of the room. Without hesitation, he lifted the lid. A moment of relief hit as he spied the contents. Familiar evidence bags, almost all of which contained a single photo each.

But where's the dress?

It was the only other item that had been kept in the box. Emily's clothing.

Farriday put a hand into the cardboard, swishing around in search of it. As the bags moved, his heart lurched. His stomach churned. They were photographs, all right. But they weren't the correct ones. They weren't from the stack found in Ellis's room, proving his debauchery. These were fresh pictures, taken on an instant camera. Feeling sicker by the second, he flipped through them. They were all of *himself*. All taken at varying intervals over the last two days. Ellis Black had been following him. Documenting his movements as he undertook the search for the man himself.

Is this why he stayed in town?

The thought made Farriday tense. It was further evidence that the convicted murderer was after more than freedom.

Slowly, he set the lid back in place. He needed to think about what to do next. Whether he needed to set aside his pride and his reservations so that he could get himself more protection. If Black was in the process of dragging out some kind of revenge plot, then Farriday had to consider his own well-being. He had zero interest in dying.

"So what do I do about it?"

As if in answer to the question, his phone buzzed in his pocket, making him jump. He pulled it out, his heart rate increasing when he saw that the call was coming from the man he'd stationed at Veronica's house.

He tapped the screen and lifted the phone to his ear. "This is Captain Farriday."

"Hey, Captain. It's Bose," said the man on the other end. "We've got a situation here at the Hollister place."

Dread crept up. "What is it?"

"Ms. Hollister found something. It's a dress, Captain. And it looks like it's covered in dried blood."

24
Five Months,
Three Days Before Escape

The Convict

Ellis ran his thumb over Veronica's image. It was the eleventh picture in the small stack, which meant that about six weeks had passed since he'd confessed his sin. Six long weeks since the girl had stumbled out in horror. He'd been savoring the photos. Removing two each Monday—one in the morning and one in the evening—since the guard had left the envelope on his cot. Examining them. Studying every detail.

Some of the pictures had been a mess. One—the eighth one, he thought—was a blur of nothing. Yet he hadn't set it aside and rushed to the next. He far preferred to take his pleasure slowly. Achingly.

This one he held now was his favorite so far. In it, Veronica looked angry. Her brow furrowed, her eyes flashing. Her hair —which had been in a tidy braid for the first few pictures and partly unraveled in the latter ones—was wild. A mane that begged to be fisted up and pulled hard as Ellis did darkly unimaginable things to her. In the shot, there was a smudge of red on her cheek in the exact spot where the bruise had been on her last visit. It made him sure she'd taken the picture within minutes of the abuse. Knowing that simultaneously aroused and disgusted him.

What did the fucker who'd hit her look like? He half-hoped that the last photo in the bunch would be of her father.

He'd love to destroy an image of the man who'd marred the creamy flesh Ellis wanted to claim as his own. He closed his eyes and let himself sink into the fantasy of driving his fist into the unknown man's face. Perversely, it was nearly as satisfying as the ever-growing list he had for Veronica the moment he was free to get his hands on her delicate skin.

But she hasn't come back again, has she? The thought sneaked up, unwelcome, and Ellis answered it aloud in a low snarl. "I'm aware of that fucking fact, thank you very much."

The statement didn't change anything. The doubt still lingered. It was infuriating. Nagging away at him. He hadn't been all that surprised when Veronica hadn't turned up the first week, or the second. She'd need time to process his depravity. Day twenty had been the first time he'd really questioned the lack of her presence. It'd only built up from there. Had he revealed too much to the girl, too soon? Or maybe it was too much, in general?

"No," he growled at full volume, slamming his fist into the mattress at the same time.

A responding holler came from one of the other cells. "Is that what all the girls used to say when you pulled out that tiny dick of yours, Black?"

For once, Ellis ignored the jibe. He had more important things to think about, and he refused to accept the idea that the girl wasn't going to turn up. She *wanted* to help him. She looked at him, and she saw a project for her God. A God who was all fucking powerful and all fucking forgiving. It was just taking longer than expected for her to remember that. Longer than *he* wanted it to take.

Ten years is plenty enough time.

A buzz sounded then, signaling that the cells were about to open so the inmates could head for breakfast. Ellis jerked his head up, set down the photo, and put his hands on his knees. Typically, he ate alone. He liked to make his choices from the canteen and have his food delivered rather than joining the others in gen pop. Today, though, he was expecting a guest alongside his meal. His plan B.

For a few minutes, the air was filled with the sounds of men making their way out of their respective cells. Jeers and shoves and laughs, punctuated by the guards' orders. The noise faded quickly. Ellis stayed where he was, not looking up until he heard the shuffle of feet directly in front of him.

"Fifteen minutes," said an authoritative voice. "Don't say I never did anything for you."

Ellis nodded at the guard, who walked away. Then he met the eyes of the prisoner standing just inside his cell. Evidently, the man was surprised to find himself deposited in Ellis's space. He frowned, then glanced over his shoulder as though expecting the guard to inform him of a mistake. Not that Ellis could fault him for it. Rarely did he willingly address the men who might be called his peers. If he *did* happen to initiate a conversation, it wasn't about something pleasant. Except for today.

"Morning, Steeler," he greeted with as much sincere-sounding pleasantry as he could muster. "You doing okay?"

"As fine as a man can be behind these walls, Black," replied the other inmate, his voice somehow wary and cocky at the same time.

"Glad to hear it."

"I doubt that very much. And I assume you didn't drag me here to chat about our living conditions?"

"Come a little closer, Steeler, so we can talk," Ellis replied.

Brow crinkling, the other man glanced over his shoulder again and didn't budge. "Sounds like a good way to get my head shoved straight up my ass."

"You want me to say this quietly." Ellis flashed a dark smile. "Trust me."

Steeler stepped a few feet nearer, smirking. "Doubt there's anything you could say to make me trust you, Black. But here I am."

"You're a cop."

"What the actual fuck?"

"Don't bother trying to lie. I *know* it's true. You were sent here as a plant to try to get some info from Jimmy Chin."

False bravado gone, Steeler dropped his voice low. "I don't know what the hell you're playing at, but—"

In one fluid motion, Ellis stood, grabbed the other man by the collar, and pushed him—not gently—to the wall then leaned in to speak into his ear. "You're not Daniel Steeler. You're not in here for shanking someone in a prison somewhere else. You're Evan Lochiel, and you work for a federal organization that's partnered with Meridian Penitentiary to find an in with Chin's boss. Is that enough detail for you?"

The other man sputtered out a cough. "Fuck."

Ellis dropped his hand and stepped back. "All I need from you is a small favor."

"What is it?"

"A credible message, sent directly to Captain Flip Farriday at Meridian PD. I want him to hear it from you that a woman named Veronica Hollister is in imminent danger. Strongly suggest that he ought to check on her well-being." Steeler—aka Lochiel—swiped his sleeve over his mouth. "How am I going to make that credible?"

Ellis shrugged. "You won't need to do much more than mention my name, and Farriday will be all over it. The fact that it comes from you will give it that extra punch. And if anyone questions your source, tell them you got the info from Henry Bains."

"And if they go back to Henry?"

"Henry will be dead by noon today."

"Are you telling me that you're going to kill a man, Black?" Steeler asked.

Ellis shook his head. "Not me. But I know for a fact that he'll be dead before lunch. There's nothing you can do to help him, so don't try."

"How—"

"A side of poison with his peanut butter and toast."

The other man narrowed his eyes. "You know an awful lot for someone who keeps to himself."

"I listen, Steeler," said Ellis. "Works better than talking, most of the time."

"And let me guess… in exchange for this 'favor,' you're going to keep your opinion about who I am to yourself?"

"I'm a far nicer man than you're giving me credit for. If you get the message out for me by tomorrow, I'll tell you how to get Jimmy Chin to talk."

Steeler reached out his hand, clearly expecting to shake on it. Ellis laughed. Maybe there was honor among thieves, but the same thing sure as fuck didn't apply to murderers, rapists, and undercover cops. He slid back on his cot and picked up his picture of Veronica. He took no note of how many seconds went by before the other man walked out. He was already reimmersed in his dark fantasies.

25

Five Months, Three Days Before Escape

The Preacher's Daughter

Roni was about halfway up the driveway when she spied the flash of red and blue. Normally, noting the presence of police at her house would've been cause for immediate alarm. She would've worried that something was wrong with her father. Maybe a small part of her brain would've asked if he had *done* something wrong. She would've pressed a little harder on the gas pedal and gotten up the driveway as fast as she could. But not today. Today, the hair on the back of her neck tingled, and she put her foot on the brake in order to come to a stop. Her mind was racing with some other unidentifiable concern. One that had nothing to do with her father.

What is it?

Uneasily, she cut the engine altogether and got out. She drew a few deep breaths, hoping the fresh air would calm both her mind and her pulse. It did nothing for either. If anything, her heart only beat harder as she stood in the middle of the winding, tree-heavy driveway. Her eyes pointed toward the house, but she couldn't see much more than the roof. The only reason she'd spotted the police car was because of the lights—without those, she wouldn't have noticed it until she was right in front of it. That was a good thing. It made her invisible to whoever was up there.

And why don't I want them to see me?

The question hung in her mind. Roni didn't know the answer. But after a few more seconds, her body decided on a course of action on its own. Her feet began to move. They guided her deeper into the cover of the trees, then took her on a zigzag route up the hill. The two-minute hike led her to the rear of the house, where she paused behind the rundown shed her father used to store wood for their fireplace. Faintly, she could hear voices. If she wanted to know what they were saying, she'd have to get closer.

Darting a look around first, she ducked low and jogged from the shed to the side of the house. She pressed her back to the exterior wall. She gave herself a second to catch her breath, then crouched down and made her way to the living room window. It was usually open at least a crack, and this was no different. The moment she poised her body beside it, her father's gruff timbre rumbled from the other side of the screen.

"For the umpteenth time, officer," he said. "No, my daughter does *not* have a cellphone."

"Captain," corrected a male voice Roni didn't recognize.

"Captain." Her father's eye roll was practically audible.

The policeman cleared his throat. "It's just unusual, sir."

"You accusing me of lying?"

"Of course not. I only want the same thing you do—to make sure Roni is safe."

"So run it past me again, *Captain*," her father said. "Because I feel like either I'm missing something, or you're leaving something out. Why would my Roni be the target of some killer? And how on God's green earth would this killer *get* to her, officer?"

"I don't know," replied the captain. "But it's my job to follow up on threats like this one, which came from an undercover officer inside the facility."

The man continued talking, but Roni missed whatever he added. *Ellis.* Was he trying to have her killed? Did he have some outside connection who was coming after her? The thought chilled her. She very nearly popped up and exposed herself before she remembered something Ellis had said to her. *I don't do things second-hand, sweetheart.* Those were his exact words. And she was one hundred percent certain he'd meant them. There was no way he'd send someone else to harm her.

You don't think I want to hurt you, Nic? said Ellis's voice in her head.

"I do," she replied in the barest whisper. "I really think you do. But you want to do it yourself."

Imaginary Ellis spoke up again. *Why would I send the police captain on a wild goose chase, then?*

Roni eased away from the wall as an explanation came to mind. Ellis was angry that she hadn't come back, and he wanted to punish her. It would work. Her father would be humiliated by the fact that the police had come to his house. There was a good chance he'd think that she'd been lying to him about her time at the prison, too. And maybe she had been. After all, Ellis Black wasn't the person her father had sent her to see at the beginning, and she'd never corrected it.

Fear seeped in. Her father's wrath would be swift and violent.

And how is that not *second-hand?* she asked the mental edition of the convict.

Her subconscious offered no response, and quite suddenly, it made her angry. Furious enough that she needed to leave before she did something stupid and gave away her presence.

Moving as quickly as she dared, she retraced her steps to the car. She climbed in, started the engine, and backed out of the driveway. She took off down the road, her foot pressing harder and harder while the speedometer swung higher and higher. In moments, she was above the posted limit.

Let the police catch me, she thought. *After all, they're already trying to find me, aren't they?*

Her fury spiked even more.

It wasn't *fair.* Her father was not a kind man. He wasn't a just man. His methods were Old Testament, his heart a vicious whip. But she forgave him. For peace. For God. For reasons that were guarded closely to her heart. But he was her father. The man who raised her. Fed her. Clothed her. Cared for her after her mother was gone. Ellis was none of those things, and she wasn't going to let a murdering rapist dole out some penalty because she'd hurt his *feelings.*

The gas pedal was nearing the floor now, and her speed was probably approaching dangerous. Roni didn't care. The faster she got to the prison, the better.

26

Twenty-Four Hours After Escape

The Preacher's Daughter

Veronica blew out a small breath, drew her blanket a little more tightly over her body, and studied the patrolman from her spot on the couch. Her personal guard had his back to her, and his posture was combative. Braced for a confrontation. For the last ten minutes, he'd been prowling the interior perimeter of her house. Every window, every door. He checked them at measured intervals, pausing so predictably that Veronica could practically count the seconds at each one without fail. She knew he was making sure things were secure. More than that, she knew he was waiting for Captain Farriday, who should be there at any moment. He wanted to be told what to do. The proof was in the fact that he hadn't once looked toward the dress.

Emily's dress.

Veronica knew it was the dead girl's. *Knew it.* She flicked a look toward it now. It hung from the doorframe between her kitchen and the living room, fluttering a little in some unfelt breeze. It was a pretty dress. Not unlike something she might've chosen for herself. It was a subtly eye-catching fabric. Small yellow and pink flowers on a background of cream. The hem was just past knee-length, the sleeves capped and summery. Buttons lined the front from the round neck to a spot about mid-thigh. It would part when the wearer took long strides, and it would expose a little bit of skin. A little *too* much, probably. But it wasn't a sexy style. It was simply functional. Easy movement. Yes, Veronica would likely have bought it if she'd spied it on a rack. Except, of course, for the blood stain that marred one side of it.

The rusty splotch caught her attention again, and her heart quickened. She squeezed her fingers around the slip of paper she held in her left palm. It was a note. Penned in red ink. Lettered in all capitals, just like the one that had been left on the linoleum at the hospital.

PUT ME ON, it read.

It'd been attached to the dress with a safety pin, and the policeman had no idea it existed, let alone that Veronica had it. She'd torn it off right before her scream had brought the cop running in from his post outside.

She bit her lip and exhaled a heavy breath. For as long as she'd been clutching the note, she'd also been deliberating on what to do with it. She was completely sure what the right thing was— telling the cop that she'd unthinkingly ripped it off the dress. But she knew what the consequences of not obeying a command from Ellis Black were.

If he wanted her to put on the dress—blood and all— then he had a reason for it. She might not be aware of what that reason *was*, but there was no doubt that Ellis had his motivation. And Ellis was a man who got what he wanted. At all costs.

Veronica glanced toward the policeman again. She couldn't remember his name. For some reason, that seemed important. Maybe because he seemed even younger than she was. In another life, he might've been the sweet little brother of a friend. Instead, she was responsible for a situation that could wind up with him dead. And she'd have bet that right up until now, he probably hadn't done much more than issue a speeding ticket. Shoving aside the guilt over what she was about to do, Veronica cleared her throat.

"You okay?" the constable asked, sounding like he really hoped her answer would be in the affirmative.

She nodded. "I'm fine. But could you do me a favor?"

"Sure, Ms. Hollister. What do you need?" His hand seemed to be twitching toward his weapon.

"My throat is feeling a little dry." She forced a small cough. "Would you mind getting me a bottle of water from the garage? There's a door off the mudroom at the back of the kitchen."

"No problem. So long as you're sure you'll be comfortable here for a minute?"

"Yes. But I can grab it myself if you'd rather keep watch."

He shook his head. "No. Safer if you stay put. I'll be right back."

"Thank you."

Veronica waited until he was out of sight, then jumped to her feet. With her eyes on the spot where the constable had just disappeared, she slipped off her nightgown and traded it for the dress, not bothering with the buttons as she slid it over her head. Breathing a little heavily, she put her nightgown on the hanger. She pushed to her tiptoes and hooked it over the lip of the doorframe, then sank back down on her heels right as a sharp inhale announced that the cop had re-entered the room. Guiltily, she faced him. His eyes roved over her and the dress, and he took a small step back as understanding passed over his features.

"I can explain," she said in a small voice.

The constable's Adam's apple bobbed up and down in his throat. She knew, even when she showed him the note, he'd wonder why—*how*—she could've put on the dress at Ellis's behest. She'd wonder too, if she were him. And maybe it was a bad excuse, but she was going to say it anyway.

I'm used to obeying unreasonable orders. I know what happens when I don't listen.

"Ms. Hollister," said the uniformed man, "I don't think you should—"

A sharp rap on the door cut him off and made both of them

jump.

"It's the captain," Veronica stated.

The officer regained enough of his composure that he managed to move in front of her, shoving the water bottle at her as he went by. With his hand poised near his weapon, he strode to the door.

"Identify yourself," he called out.

"It's Captain Farriday," came the muffled reply. "Let me in, Doyle."

Doyle, Veronica thought, trying to commit the name to memory this time.

But a moment later it went out of her head again, because as the door swung open and Captain Farriday's gaze found her, his expression was the only thing her brain had room for. His face wasn't just pale; it was colorless. Almost transparent. His eyes were wide and haunted, his jaw slack. One of his hands sought the doorframe in an obvious attempt to keep upright.

He was afraid. Far more scared than his younger counterpart. More fearful than Veronica herself. She'd never seen a man—never seen a *person*—look so frightened.

"He wanted me to wear it." She tried to speak softly, but her voice cracked, and it sounded loud in the otherwise silent house.

"Lord, help us," Farriday said under his breath as he made a visible effort to move his eyes to her face and keep them there. "Was he here? Did he talk to you?"

"No. He left a note." Veronica held it out, and the captain took it and read it.

"We can fix this, Ms. Hollister," he said. "You take off the dress and—"

"I'm selling the house," she blurted.

"What?"

She took a deep breath. Let it out slowly. She hadn't meant to tell him. But now that it was out, there was no reason to hold back.

"There was a guy here last week," she said. "A developer.

He offered my dad some money—a lot, I think—to take the property off his hands. I'm going to do it as soon as I can."

The captain's attention flicked to the other officer. "Constable, do you think you could give us a minute? Maybe wait in the patrol car? I'll get your account of things after."

The younger cop nodded, then slipped out. Farriday closed the door behind him.

"Ms. Hollister..." he said, still seeming to have to work not to look at the dress. "You have to know that it's not safe for you to leave Meridian while Black is on the loose."

She met his eyes. "Do you think it's safe for me to *stay* in Meridian while he's on the loose?"

His answer had an evasive feel. "Here, we can keep an eye on him."

"You can't keep an eye on *him.* You can keep an eye on *me.* And even Ellis is doing a better job than you are. He was in my house. He's gotten by your guys twice now. That's not counting the fact that he broke out of prison *and* your station." She paused and bit her lip. "Sorry, Captain. No offense."

"None taken," Farriday replied. "Trust me when I say that I want to catch this guy as badly as you want him to be caught. We can do more. Put you in a safe house. Station some more—"

"No. I'm doing this. And not because I'm scared. My father is dead, I have no reason to stay in Meridian. I want to move on."

"Selling a house doesn't take a day, Ms. Hollister. And it's not something to do impulsively."

"I know that. I know both of those things. But honestly... it's not as reckless as it sounds. I only stayed as long as I did because I thought my father needed me. Now that he doesn't..."

The captain's fingers tapped a momentary beat on his thigh. "How about you sleep on it? I'll switch out with Doyle and stay here for the rest of the night. I can park myself in your driveway, or I can park myself on your couch. Either way, Ellis Black won't get past *me.*"

Even though she knew she wouldn't change her mind

about the house, Veronica nodded. She could feel exhaustion encroaching. She needed sleep more than she needed an argument.

"Good," said Farriday. "I'll go let my constable know." He closed a hand on the doorknob then paused without exiting. "And while you have a second, you should take the dress off. It's evidence. Again."

"I can't take it off," Veronica replied. "I still don't know why Ellis wanted me to put it on."

A brief battle of uncertainty waged on his face before he sighed and answered her. "I'm pretty sure I know why. And I'm pretty sure you've already satisfied his need."

"What do you mean?"

"I think all Ellis Black wanted was for me to see you wearing it."

27

Ten Years Earlier
Thirty-Two Hours Before Arrest

The Policeman

F lip could only distract himself from thoughts of the delinquent kid for so long. No matter what Cliff might want. There were only so many games of solitaire to be played, only so many pages of the newspapers to look through, and only so many online videos to watch before he was bored to tears. Plus, he kept hearing that damn motorcycle engine. And he could no longer tell when it was real or imagined. If it was real or imagined.

No fewer than six times, he got up and peered out the window, expecting to see the bike and its rider sitting at the end of his block. He also couldn't shake the sensation that he was being watched. Ellis Black was in his head. No doubt about it.

And there has to be a reason for that, Flip said to himself as he eyed his keys and narrowed his glare, his palm itching.

Part of him also kept expecting Cliff to call. Not to retract the order to take time off, but rather to tell Flip he'd reconsidered his thoughts on the Black situation in general. Surely, that had to happen. The idea of *not* following up on it was absurd. Any second now, the interim captain had to realize it, too. Teenagers weren't equipped to be on their own. Especially not the ones like Ellis Black. The kid might be a delinquent, but he wasn't a fool. There was a sharpness in his eyes. A cleverness. He was the type to play this to its fullest. But no call came.

Another hour passed.

Flip did a jigsaw puzzle. He stared at the clock, and he had to concede that maybe Cliff had no real interest in what was going on after all. He supposed the other man could be tied up with his sudden new role, but either way, that meant Flip was the only one focused on Ellis. The only one thinking about what the boy was up to.

I should've done something about it then and there. He stood up and paced the room. *It was stupid to delay. Stupider to look in the house and not find some excuse to make it valid.*

Going out to the property now was a risky move. Cliff might be keeping an eye on him somehow. But what choice did he have? The longer this went on, the more the window closed. Things could get worse. A delay might result in someone else spearheading things. And that wouldn't be good. Not if Flip still wanted to use this to catapult his career to where it ought to be already.

More minutes ticked by. Outside, an engine revved.

Flip checked through the blinds, found nothing, and paced some more. Eyed his keys again. Stared at his phone. Thought about Ellis. The kid's knowing gaze. The dead dog. The dead father. The missing mother and the unmentioned sister. The more time went by, the surer Flip became. Ellis was the one who'd called in the complaint about him being on the property.

And there has to be a reason for that, too.

But what was it? Simply to torment an officer, or something more? Drawing attention to himself hardly seemed smart, given his circumstances.

Flip paused his pacing, eyes narrowing yet again. It occurred to him—belatedly—that he could just do what he ought to have done in the first place and call social services. Sure, it would still be going against what his so-called boss had said to do. Insinuating himself into the situation. But it'd also be doing the right thing. Cliff would be hard-pressed to argue it wasn't.

Flip let his imagination run through it for a second. Making the report. Having a couple of child welfare workers pay a visit to the home. Them realizing the boy was alone. They'd take him away. Immediately. That'd stop him from making false claims and plaguing Flip's existence. They'd look for the sister properly, too.

What will that mean for me? he wondered.

Cliff wouldn't be pleased. Maybe it would backfire and the captain would send the blame Flip's way.

He paced some more. The bottom line was that the simplest thing to do was to follow his gut. After that, he could do what the new boss wanted and find some solid evidence. Multiple things if he timed it right. He couldn't leave things to chance. It wasn't possible.

Unable to fight the need for action for one second more, he snagged the keys and headed out. He was almost at his car — and almost convinced he was making the correct choice, too —when he caught his foot on something and lost his balance. It was dark out. Flip's hand flailed to catch himself before he fell. He didn't succeed. Face first, he smacked into his vehicle. Pain shot through his nose and into his skull. He couldn't quite manage to break his tumble after that, either. His chest hit the concrete, leaving him breathless.

Still think you're doing the right thing?

The snide question was one part Cliff and one part Ellis, and it earned a snarl from Flip. But the feral sound cut itself off, midway to leaving his mouth.

"What the hell?" he said instead.

A coldness slid over his skin. The item he'd tripped over sat a few feet away, completely out of place. It was a woman's shoe. A flat slip-on. Bathed in the low glow of the moon, showing off its color. Pink. *Bubble gum pink.* Like Emily Black's childhood bedroom. Except for the toe, which was marked with flecks of brown that could be only one thing. Dried blood.

28
Thirty-Three Hours After Escape

The Policeman

The moment the sun crept up over the horizon, Farriday threw aside his blanket and swung his feet to the ground. A groan escaped his lips as he sat up. If he'd slept at all, he didn't know it. The whole night, he'd felt the weight of Ellis's unknown plan hanging over him. The image of Veronica in the dress wouldn't leave him, either. Every time he closed his eyes, he saw it. The little flowers. The blood.

Goddamn, Ellis Black.

The man wanted to get to Farriday, and it was working. At the current moment, he couldn't even decide if he was thankful Veronica had invited him to use the couch. His body ached from lying on the springs. His *mind* ached from going over the same facts, again and again. And he wasn't any further along in his conclusions, either.

Stretching and trying to shake off the weariness, he came to his feet. Then immediately staggered back. A figure stood on the other side of the living room, silhouetted in the window. It took Farriday a good five seconds to realize it was Veronica. She stood, unmoving, with one hand pressed to the pane. Her hair hung down her back, resting against the fabric of her white nightgown. Her pose was somehow unnatural.

Ghostly, almost.

At least she's not wearing Emily's dress.

As true as the thought was—he was most definitely thankful she'd taken it off—it still was somehow a gut punch. It also reminded him that he still had to send the dress back to evidence. He'd bagged it up properly but had put off the loathsome task under the excuse that Veronica needed him here. He didn't even want to think about it, really. It brought back too many violent memories. Maybe he could pass the task off to one of the constables. He probably should've done it already.

He stood there for a few seconds, waiting for Veronica to say something. She didn't. Her focus was on her yard, and she seemed unaware of his presence at all.

"Ms. Hollister?" he finally said, his voice low so as not to startle her.

Slowly, still seeming ethereal, she turned his way. Her face was pale, the cuts and bruises standing out starkly against her fair skin. She looked like she hadn't slept any more than he had. What really struck him, though, was how young she looked. She could've passed for a teenager. Her naïveté was practically visible, too. She radiated an alluring kind of innocence.

No wonder Ellis glommed onto her, Farriday thought as he cleared his throat and addressed her again. "Are you all right, Ms. Hollister?"

"You're going to catch him, aren't you?" she replied.

"And make things right?"

"That's my plan."

"Will you kill him?"

"Not unless I have to."

"But you *want* to?" she asked.

Farriday answered carefully. "It's not my job to pass judgment in that way, and I believe in our justice system."

"Even though it fails, sometimes, and the bad guy gets free?"

"We don't always get it right the first time. But we have to keep trying."

"What about evil? Do you believe in that? Because Ellis does." Veronica's eyes went back to the window. "He thinks evil can't be cured. That it can't be caged inside a prison. You have to kill it to get rid of it. It's death or nothing."

"He talked to you a lot, didn't he?"

"Yes. When he wasn't doing other things to me."

"I'm sorry he put you through that."

"Don't be," she said. "*You* didn't do it. And my father always said that the Lord doesn't give us more than we can handle. Although I'm not sure what that says about Ellis's sister."

Farriday flinched. "Ms. Hollister, are you sure you don't want to discuss this with someone at the hospital?"

Her gaze swept his way. "Why?"

"Pardon me?"

"Is it too much for you?"

He blinked. "For me? No. Not for me."

"But you think it's too much for me?"

Farriday didn't immediately answer. The girl needed help. Much more help than he could give.

Why did I let her talk me out of keeping her in the hospital?

"Look at me," she said. "Please."

He didn't even realize he'd looked away, and he forced his eyes back to here. "Ms. Hollister…"

"Is it so bad that you *can't* look at what our justice system brought me?" There were tears on her cheeks. "My father would say that I'm ruined and going straight to hell."

She moved forward, grabbed his hand, and placed his palm on her stomach.

"Just flesh," she said. "Is it that hard to resist?"

He tried to pull away, but her grip tightened. Farriday met her eyes. There was a darkness there he wasn't expecting. A wildness.

Ellis had done this to her. *Ruined* her, as she put it. Lord, how Farriday needed to get the man behind bars again before he did any more damage.

"Ms. Hollister, I'm honestly not equipped to—"

"Men always take, don't they?" she whispered. "Why is that? Are they animals?"

"Ms. Hollister—"

"Do they assume we *want* to be taken? Or is it just that they don't care? Do you hear us if we say no? Because I think they see what they want to see. Hear what they want to hear. Even when they know something's wrong, they give themselves permission to do it anyway. Then they say we were asking for it." She tipped her face up, then backed away. "Well, I'm not staying that way. I'm going to do something about it."

Farriday didn't like the sound of that, but he didn't get a chance to express his concern. The crunch of tires on gravel pulled his attention away.

"Who's that?" he said, reaching for the weapon he still had at his hip.

"The realtor," Veronica said right away. "I asked him to come as soon as he could."

Farriday froze with his hand on his gun. "I thought we agreed to sleep on it."

"We did. And I think we can also agree, Captain, that neither of us will be sleeping too well until we know Ellis's whereabouts." She started for the door but paused, mid-step. "I'm not going to wind up dead in a barn, like Emily."

Farriday's brain did a record scratch. *The barn.* The scene of the crime. Of the arrest. It was the perfect place for Ellis to hole up.

29
Five Months, Three Days Before Escape

The Convict

Ellis let the key pause on the knuckle at the base of his index finger, then flicked it into a spin. It'd been hours since he'd sent the undercover cop on his little mission. Breakfast had come and gone. So had lunch. Flip Farriday hadn't shown up with an interrogation. Nor had he sent some lackey to do it on his behalf. Ellis hadn't expected him to. Setting foot in the prison would've been an admission that they had someone on the inside. It also would've violated a decade-old promise the cop had made to never get within ten feet of Ellis and the filth he represented. By now, though, something should've happened. He was starting to think he'd misjudged Steeler's ability to get shit done.

Or maybe you didn't scare him enough. Maybe the threat of exposure needed some added punch. Literally.

He narrowed his eyes, contemplating the idea of calling in another favor so he could pay Steeler a visit. The thought of sinking his fist into something was tempting. He flipped the key over the rest of his knuckles and imagined them driving hard against the other man's stomach. In his mind, he let himself hear the pain-filled grunt that followed a blow like that. But he didn't smile like he normally might have. Just this once, he didn't want an excuse to kick someone's ass.

He flicked the key into the air and let it land on his pillow as the rattle of a different set of keys drew his attention to the corridor outside his cell. Finally, a guard—one of the regulars, who had a serious hard-on for getting under his skin — appeared outside the bars.

"You're one lucky son-of-a-bitch, aren't you, Black?" said the uniformed man.

"You wanna trade places and find out exactly how lucky I am, Liam?"

"I've got zero interest in your living space. Your pretty visitor, on the other hand. Her, I'd be willing to trade for."

Not reacting violently required effort. The relief that his plan had worked helped a little. The fact that Veronica Hollister was there in the prison, at that very second, helped more. Ellis wasn't going to risk losing his only chance at keeping her right where he needed her. He shrugged, his reply coming out with little more than mild annoyance.

"If you think a girl like that is going to be interested in a fat old fuck like you, then I welcome you to make a move," he said.

"Don't get snarky," Liam replied. "You want to see her, don't you?"

"See her?" yelled someone down the block. "Pretty fucking sure he wants to do more than that."

The guard laughed, jammed the key into the lock, and slid the gate open. "Nah. He'll be a good boy and keep it in his pants. Won't you, Black?"

"Only because I'm saving it all for you," Ellis replied.

"We both know I'm neither young enough nor... familial enough to get your dick worked up." Liam leaned a little closer. "And if it weren't for your special privileges, I'd be happy to discuss that with you in further detail."

Thinking about how it would feel to press a thumb straight into the other man's eye, Ellis smiled. "I'll make sure to schedule an appointment the moment the warden retires."

Liam made a sour face, clearly unimpressed at not being able to set the right bait. "C'mon. Let's go."

He said nothing else as he led the way from the block into the visitor's wing, and Ellis counted it a win. He liked the silence from the douchebag almost as much as he would've liked coldcocking him. His gloating was cut short, though, once he was in the room with Veronica Hollister. She stood in a corner, and she was in a ragged state. One foot was bare. Her dress had a jagged tear down one sleeve, and her face was filthy—covered in dirt, except for a few clear streaks down the center of her cheeks. There was also a fucking *leaf* in her hair, and for once he was too confused to be furious. He let Liam chain him to the table without protest, and even after the other man had exited, Ellis stared in silence before he finally found his voice.

"What the fuck happened to you?" he demanded.

"*You* happened to me," she retorted.

"I didn't do this."

"No, Ellis? Are you sure about that?"

His mouth twisted, because he couldn't even take the time to enjoy hearing her lips wrap around his name. He rattled his chains at her.

"Relatively fucking sure, sweetheart," he said. "Last time I checked, I'm not in a position to go around stealing women's shoes and tearing their clothes."

"Maybe not." She crossed her arms. "But apparently you *are* in a position to make threats on my life."

For a good second, he wondered if Steeler had misunderstood his instructions and actually sent someone after her rather than just making sure Flip Farriday thought that was what was happening. Then sense kicked in. Unless the girl had become a ninja over the last two weeks, she wouldn't have won in any kind of fight.

He leaned back. "Whatever the fuck happened... it wasn't me."

"Oh, really? So you didn't tell someone that you were going to make something bad happen to me?"

"Oh, *that* I did." He let a smirk creep up. "What I didn't do is chew you up and spit you out looking like *that*. If something happened to you for real, you can go ahead and blame your God."

She threw up her hands. "You know what? Maybe you're right. Maybe He made my car break down two miles from here, and maybe He made me fall into a ditch because He was giving me a sign that I shouldn't give in to my anger and come here to confront you."

"Have you decided to stop listening to Him, then?"

"No."

"So why did you come?"

She swallowed, her vulnerability reappearing despite the hint of sarcasm in her response. "I guess that explanation that God might be trying to stop me occurred to me too late."

"You mean I pointed out that it's not *my* fault too late," he replied.

"It doesn't matter."

"It does matter. To me."

"Why would it possibly matter?" she asked.

He tipped his head and studied her grime-laden face. "I don't think that's the complete question."

"I don't know what you mean."

"I think you do. What you *meant* was... why would it matter to a man like me? Why would a man like me give any fucks at all if he got blamed for the mess you're in at the current moment? Or any moment, for that matter."

She neither moved nor broke eye contact nor answered. Ellis knew he had to move forward with the gentlest touch, despite gentleness not being in his usual repertoire of tricks. He wanted her to stay. *No. That wasn't quite right.* He needed her to leave. Then come back again. He'd torn down the possibility of his redemption by letting her into his darkness. Let her see the evil. Now he had to convince her—just enough—that the opposite was true. That he was somehow deserving of help.

"You looked me up," he said.

She started a headshake that ended in a nod. "Yes, I did."

"You didn't like what you found."

"Would anyone like those things?"

"Can I ask you something, Nic?" He didn't bother to wait for her to respond. "Did I ever say that I wasn't the monster in this story?"

Her reply was a whisper. "No."

"Maybe I even warned you that I was."

"Maybe you did."

"Good. I think we already agreed that honesty is something we both appreciate," he said. "So I'll admit something. The reason it matters to me is because I like to be right. I like to be in control. Power is... *everything*... for a man like me."

The girl blinked. "You're behind bars. Any power you have is an illusion."

"Is it?"

"Yes."

"Then come over here," he suggested. "If I have no power, then get close enough to me to prove it."

She sucked in a breath. "I'm not allowed to do that."

"I can't reach my own pocket, sweetheart, so you're going to have to do it for me."

Even with the dirt marking her cheeks, the sudden pink was visible. "I'm not doing that."

"What I want you to get is on the left side."

"I am *not* putting my hand in your pocket."

"Then I guess I'm right again."

"That's—"

"Not fair? Is that what you're about to tell me?" he said. "Do you think I give a fuck about *fair*? Either I have power, and you have no choice but to stay over there, or it's an illusion, and you have no choice but to come over here and prove that you're right."

"Or I could leave," she replied.

"Still means I'm right."

"The last time I came close to you, it didn't end well for me."

"I'll behave."

Her eyes closed for a long second, and she spoke softly. "Do you have *any* idea what's going to happen to me when I get home and have to answer for this? The kind of hell I'm going to have to pay for what you told the police?"

He couldn't help but like the way the word "hell" sounded coming out of her mouth, and he smiled. "My dad was a giant fucking prick, sweetheart. I know a little bit about misguided anger."

Her eyes opened and focused on him. "I think…"

"What?"

"Nothing."

He was going to argue that she was lying—her nothing was definitely something—but she moved, and suddenly she was beside him, bending down and slipping her hand into the pocket of his coveralls.

Jesus wept.

Her touch was quick and light, but it still sent violent need coursing through him. She smelled like dirt and flowers and a sultry hint of sweat. His promise to behave fell away with the tidal wave of lust. He was already adjusting in his seat, his fingers desperate to close on some part—any part—of her body. She was too efficient. By the time Ellis had yanked his chains sideways, Veronica was already a few feet away, holding a square of white fabric in her hands.

"What is this?" she asked, stepping around to her side of the table.

Fuck. Fuck, fuck, fuck. *Breathe, you idiot. And answer her.*

"What does it look like?" his reply was just this side of a snarl.

She didn't seem to notice. "It looks like a handkerchief."

Why didn't I grab her when I had the chance? Silently, he answered himself. *Because it would've been a stupid fucking move, that's why.*

"Ellis?" she prodded.

Fuck again.

"It looks like a handkerchief because that's what it is," he said.

"But... why?"

"You've got a little something on your face."

Her eyes came up, startlement filling them. "Oh. You want me to wipe my face?"

"I thought *you* might want to," he replied, still speaking through his teeth.

"Thank you." She sat down, then lifted the cloth and rubbed it over her cheeks, chin, and forehead.

"How the hell did you convince them to let you in here, looking like that?" he asked.

"I cried." She held out the handkerchief.

He shook his head. "Keep it."

She tightened a fist on the fabric and sighed. "Why did you work so hard to get me to come back here, Ellis?"

Dark and delicious answers swirled through his head, and he dropped his voice low. "I happen to like you, Nic."

"You like me?" she replied. "Or you want to hurt me?"

"What makes you think they aren't one and the same for me?" He offered her a toothy grin.

"Maybe they are." Her lower lip slipped between her teeth in the most distracting way possible, and she tilted her head, her green gaze considering as she stared at him. "Do you remember what you told me you really wanted?"

"Freedom." The word came out rawer than he meant it to sound.

She simply nodded. "And I understand that. It's... oppressive in here. I actually threw up the first time I walked out. But I don't think that it's physical freedom that you need. I think it's spiritual. Or mental, I guess, if you're not comfortable with anything that sounds too close to God. And I'm not the one who's going to have to be dragged along, kicking and screaming."

"What led you to all those unpleasant conclusions, sweetheart?"

"Because you're not sorry for what you did."

Anger surged up at the statement, and Ellis beat it back with a stick. "What about your dad? Is *he* repentant for all his sins against you?"

"His sins have nothing to do with yours," she replied.

He didn't wait for her to add that her father's injustices were a far cry from the deviance on Ellis's rap sheet. His goal here was to breed connection. To tear open cracks in Veronica's mind and fill them with him*self*.

"He hurts you. He takes out his own inadequacies on you. I hardly know a thing about you, but I've seen the marks he leaves on your face. There's no part of me that believes he's anything but cruel to you at the best of times. Your actions —your thoughts—are all reined in because you're terrified of what will happen if you make a misstep."

"That's not all true."

"Which part isn't?" he asked. "I'd really like to know."

Her mouth opened, and her lips quivered, but she said nothing.

Ellis leaned forward. "Tell me you can leave home any time you like."

"He's my father," she replied in a small voice.

"Yes. The man who's supposed to protect you and love you and not make you scared to go home. Why does he do it? Why does he keep a beautiful, twenty-two-year-old woman all locked up at home and punish her for any transgression against his wants?" He paused. "I might be a fucking degenerate, but I have no illusions about who I am. So maybe I'm not the only one who needs an awakening, Nic."

He pulled back again and let his eyes roam over her body, not disguising in the slightest that he intended his words to be laden with innuendo.

"I have to go," Veronica said, the words sounding raw.

"Go ahead. Go home to Daddy."

She stood. "Bye, Ellis."

"What, no kiss?"

CONVICTION

Two spots of color appeared in her cheeks, and her eyes dropped to his mouth for a second so quick that it was nearly indiscernible. But Ellis saw it, and he smiled. She could rush out all she wanted; he knew a crack was opening. The moment he could, he'd slide right in.

30
Thirty-Six Hours After Escape

The Policeman

Captain Farriday came to a coasting stop at the end of the driveway on the property where the Blacks had once made their home. Tensely, he cut the engine and surveyed the space in front of his car. It'd been ten years since he'd set foot in this particular place, and a lot had changed. The dilapidated home had been leveled. The remnants of it— beams and insulation and some furniture— simply sat rotting. A display of unfinished destruction. The random debris that littered the yard had now been reclaimed by nature. Budding flowers poked out from between the slats of a pallet, a thorny bush of some kind had wrapped its way around a three-wheeled wagon, and a frog sat on the edge of an upended fridge.

Years ago, the property had been seized for taxes owing, but it'd never sold.

Farriday shook his head. It was a waste. Some nice family— people completely unlike the Blacks—could've made this place their home. Or a developer could've turned it into a row of tidy townhouses, bringing more prosperity to Meridian in general. But the taint of rape and murder stopped everything. The crime was a blight on the town.

Should've done something about it when I still could, he thought. *Too late now.*

He stared for another second before narrowing his eyes and ordering himself to stay focused on the current task.

Slowly, he brought his hand to the door handle of his squad car. He eased it open a crack, then waited, listening for the sound of any unwanted company. The only noise was the wind, whistling through the overgrown grass. He wasn't naïve enough to be convinced that it meant he was alone. His target could be waiting. Trying to reverse the roles of hunter and hunted. It was why, as he pushed the vehicle door wider, he readied his weapon and didn't immediately exit. This wasn't a suicide mission.

Admittedly, it'd crossed his mind a dozen times that lone wolfing it might not have been the best idea. Right about now, it'd have been nice to know that one or two of Meridian's spry young constables had his back. But the more hours that slipped by—the more not-so-subtle hints that were left behind —the surer he became that for Ellis, this was all about the two of them. Man to man. One on one. Bringing backup would only have driven the convicted murderer back into hiding. And Farriday wanted to take him down. Again. Maybe—despite what he'd said to Veronica—more permanently this time.

Shoving aside the dark thought, he cleared his throat and grabbed hold of his most authoritative tone. "Ellis Black, if you're out here, make yourself known!"

His voice echoed back at him, but there was no other sound. Slowly—on high alert—he finally climbed out and positioned himself behind the car door. He scanned the area again. There was no sign of anyone, so he shuffled out the tiniest bit and waited for a reaction of some kind. Of any kind, really. A physical attack. A flying bullet. A simple holler. None came. Even when he lost his grip on the door as he closed it and it slammed noisily shut, he didn't get a response other than his own startled jump.

All right, Farriday, he said to himself after a few seconds. *Time to pull up your big boy pants and take care of this.*

With his weapon in his hand and his eyes continuously

seeking danger, he started toward the barn. He picked his way past the destroyed house and kept going. In some places, his boots squelched in mud. In others, they crunched on dried bits of God knew what. One step in a divot almost cost him his balance. But there was no outside impediment to his progress. There was also nothing to make him think that this space had been recently disturbed by anyone other than him. A niggle of doubt crept in. If Ellis had come through here, he'd done it with more stealth than Farriday was using now.

What if I'm wrong about this?

"Doesn't matter if I am," he muttered. "I'll find another way to catch him."

A few more steps, and the worry slipped to the back of his mind. Just ahead, the barn was at last visible. Its worn roof peeked out from behind the cover of several sparsely leaved trees, and a rusted weathervane jutted above that, drifting a little in the wind. As he paused to stare, a strange feeling—one part déjà vu and one part immediate foreboding—settled in the pit of Farriday's stomach. He had to force it aside in order to keep going.

He stepped through the trees and came to another stop a dozen feet away from his destination. Yet again, he glanced around in search of watchful eyes. There was no one within his sightline.

Rolling his shoulders and adjusting his weapon, Farriday turned his attention to the barn. Unlike the Black family home, the structure remained intact, albeit a little worse for wear. A very large, visibly rusty padlock was attached to a latch on the doors, but from where he stood, he could see that it hung open anyway. Under other circumstances, he might've deemed that fact fortuitous. Right now, it felt like a setup.

But knowing it's a setup kind of takes the wind out of the sails, doesn't it?

Dipping a nod in affirmation, he moved forward again, careful to flick a look around in case of an ambush. Somehow, the air seemed even quieter now. The only sounds were the ones he produced. The thump of his feet was far too loud, and his inhales and exhales were coming out heavily. When he stopped in front of the doors, he could hear the blood rushing through his head in a way that made him dizzy. It worsened when a vaguely familiar, rusty smell carried to his nose. What was it? He drew in a deep breath, trying to place it. Then wished he hadn't. Because he knew why he recognized the scent. It was blood.

"Crap."

Farriday went still, wondering if this was enough of a sign that he ought to turn around. Or maybe radio in for some help. But he rejected the idea as quickly as it came. He was tired. He wasn't in the mood to have to justify his actions, and he didn't want to lose momentum or the chance to confront Ellis. He had no choice but to push past the red flag.

More apprehensive than ever, he set an elbow to the door and applied some pressure. For a second, the hinges protested. But when he leaned in a bit harder, they gave way. A resounding creak broke through the air. In response to the discordant noise, a dozen or more birds screamed to life from somewhere in the trees behind him, then flew off. Farriday's pulse soared right alongside them. His unease only deepened as he stepped a little farther into the barn. It was dark inside. Far darker than it ought to have been. The off-ness was so pervasive that he was tempted to step back out again. Before he could do it, though, the whole place lit up as though a spotlight had been shined down on it.

"Holy Hannah," Farriday said, stumbling a little at the sudden brightness.

But as his eyes adjusted, he realized that the exclamation wasn't close to adequate. In front of him was a spread of fresh hay. And on top of that was a body.

31

Five Months, Three Days Before Escape

The Preacher's Daughter

R oni stood beside her car, waiting with as much patience as she could muster. The man from roadside assistance was working at changing her tire, but—according to him, anyway—rust and age and warping were slowing the process.

The seconds were crawling by, and Roni ached, head to toe. Her body wasn't accustomed to making a four-mile roundtrip trek in a day, let alone within a few hours.

Particularly when that trek involved only one shoe.

And speaking of the one shoe…

She shifted in place, trying to find a way to ease the bite of small rocks under her bare foot. It would've been easier in the short term to have asked for help getting from the prison to this spot here, where her car had blown its tire. But she hadn't dared do it.

She bit her lip. She'd told Ellis a bit of a lie. And while she shouldn't be feeling bad about it… she did. Yes, she'd really cried at the counter when the guard there had tried to deny her entry into the prison. And yes, that had made him concede. But the very moment she'd gained access, she'd realized that someone there would likely tell the police about her presence. They *were* looking for her, after all. And then they would tell her father.

Panic had set it in. It made her irrational. Impulsive. And she'd done the first thing that popped to mind. She'd offered the guard eighty dollars—all the cash she had—to keep her visit to himself. She had *bribed* him. An officer at a correctional facility. Bought his silence. So she could go in and yell at a man who was guilty of rape and murder. The same rapist and murderer who was trying to get under her skin. Who was maybe even succeeding a little, if Roni was willing to acknowledge that her mind had been in upheaval since she first laid eyes on him.

"Miss?" said the mechanic, yanking her from her thoughts. "Are you all right?"

She jerked her focus to him. He was watching her with a concerned look. She flushed. Obviously, he'd been trying to get her attention and she hadn't noticed.

She forced a smile and a hollow laugh. "Sorry. Off in my own world."

"No worries," he said. "Been rough for you this afternoon. Although when you think about it, it's straight-up lucky that your tire blew this close to a gas station. If you'd been a few miles in the other direction, the next nearest thing would've been the prison. Not sure they'd be so amenable about letting you use their phone."

Roni did her best to ignore the lightheaded feeling that tried to encroach. "Right. That might not have gone over well."

"Might be time to give in and get a cell phone, huh?" His smile made the words sound like less of a criticism, but she still regretted admitting to him that she didn't have one.

"I guess I'll have to think about it," she lied.

He nodded like he believed her. "Anyway, the busted tire's off now. Looks like you managed to get a piece of metal jammed up in there pretty good. I put it in your trunk, but it's not salvageable. Spare is in good shape, though, so you should make it home without any issues."

"Thank you."

"Anything else I can do for you?"

"No, I don't think so."

"You sure?" he said hopefully. "I'd be happy to drive along behind you to make sure you get home safe."

Roni shook her head and fought a blush as she realized the guy was picking the most inopportune moment to flirt with her. For a crazy second, she wondered what would happen if she reciprocated. What if she asked him to follow her into town for a drink? He was her age, she thought. There was no ring on his finger and no tell-tale tan line where one might've been.

An awakening, Nic? Ellis's voice said in her head. *This isn't quite what I meant.*

Face burning hot now, Roni shook her head again. "I'll be fine. Really. My dad is probably worried about where I am."

"All right. Here are your keys." He held them out, and she took them quickly so as not to prolong any unwanted contact.

It was a relief to get onto the road. Even the slightly off-feeling roll of the smaller spare tire was soothing. Or at least it started out that way. But the closer she got to home, the more trepidation slithered through her. What was her father going to do when she told him the lie she'd prepared? Would he believe her? Would he give her a chance to finish before he lashed out? By the time Roni reached the driveway, her stomach was roiling with fear. And it didn't help that she kept hearing Ellis in her head, mocking her inability to leave.

He doesn't understand, she told herself. *How could he?*

If it was that easy, Roni would've walked away a long time ago.

Tightening her hands on the steering wheel, she brought the car to a coasting stop in front of her house. Then she went still. Her father was sitting on the porch in his rocker. In his hands, he held a mug of steaming liquid. And when he spied her, he stood up and took several steps forward.

Roni climbed out and watched her father's face as he took in her appearance. She moved toward him, bracing for an attack as she reached the stairs. Instead, she was met with concern.

"You look a right mess, girl," her father said. "I expected you home from the shop an hour ago, and I've been worried sick. What happened?"

For a second, his words startled her into silence. A tirade or an accusation would've been expected. This... not so much.

Don't look a gift horse in the mouth, she thought, then drew a breath and launched into her altered version of events.

Blowing a tire. Having the ridiculous notion that she might be able to fix it herself. Realizing she needed help, but somehow taking a terrible wrong turn when seeking a phone. Stumbling through the woods and having to find her way out. At last, arriving at the gas station and calling for help.

"I'm sorry," she said at the end of her story. "I really should've called you, too, to let you know what happened. I wasn't thinking, and I just wanted to get home."

"Glad you're safe," he replied, sipping from his mug. "Why don't you go ahead and go inside and get cleaned up? I'll take a look in the garage for a proper replacement for that tire of yours."

"Thanks, Dad."

Roni pressed to her tiptoes and gave his dry cheek a quick kiss. It wasn't until she was already in the bathroom with the tub filling that she wondered why he hadn't mentioned the visit from the police captain. She nearly went back and asked before remembering that she wasn't supposed to know about the cop at all. With a sliver of apprehension slipping through, she stripped out of her dirty dress and stepped into the tub.

Maybe he didn't want to worry me, she reasoned.

It was a sound explanation. But as the bubbles crested over her stomach, her father came calling, bursting the hope that things were going to stay smooth.

"Roni!" Her name was an angry bleat that carried through from the other side of the door. "Get your Godforsaken self out of there and explain this."

Expelling a breath, she eased to a sitting position and

feigned complete ignorance of his angry tone. "Dad?"

"Show your face right now."

"Okay. Give me a second. I just got into the bath."

"A second is going to get this door kicked down."

Nerves lighting as she realized he probably meant it, Roni clambered out. She grabbed her towel, wound it tightly around her body, and put a hand on the knob. She sent up a silent prayer, then opened the door. Her father stood on the other side, his face red with anger, his hand clutched around a small piece of paper that was marked with blue ink.

"I found this in the console of your car," he said, shoving the note hard against Roni's chest. "Care to revise your story about getting lost in the woods?"

Her eyes dropped to the paper, and horror and fear built up as she read the words there.

In case you ever really do get that cell phone, here's my number. Stan (aka, your friendly neighborhood tow truck driver).

Roni lifted her gaze. She knew what was coming, but she still didn't react quickly enough, and the sting of the incoming slap was amplified by the wetness of her skin. Her heels slid on the tiles, and she barely managed to stay on her feet. It might actually have been better if she'd fallen, because being upright put her in grabbing distance. Her father took advantage. He snagged her wrist so hard she expected to hear a crack. She bit down to keep from yelping. But she couldn't hold in her cry as he yanked her to the stairs and started down, towing her along with entirely more force than necessary. Pain shot up her arm. And halfway down, she lost her footing. She toppled sideways, smashing her forehead into the handrail.

Her father didn't even pause. Another sharp tug on her arm sent her thumping to the bottom landing, where she cowered against the floor, clutching her towel around her sopping-wet body.

"It's not what you think," she gasped. "Please let me explain."

Her father's face was red with anger. "No explanation is

going to make this note disappear."

"I didn't know about the note," she said quickly. "I swear. But you're right. The guy who changed my tire *was* interested in me. I told him no."

His expression changed—still angry, but a little less targeted at her. "Did he put his hands on you, Roni? Did he do something to you?"

"No," she replied, being careful to meet his eyes. "I would've told you. But I just got in my car and drove home right away."

He heaved a sigh. "I wasn't going to let you know about this, Roni, but a policeman came by today. He said that fellow you've been helping down at the prison was out to get you. Worried the daylights out of me until he called a while later and said it was a false alarm. Been thinking about that all afternoon. Why some pervert would have his eye on you."

Ellis's penetrating stare passed through her mind, and she shook it off. "I don't know."

"You're my good girl, aren't you, Roni?"

"Always."

"I know you are. I *know* it. But the problem is that men out there... *they* don't know it. They see a pretty girl like you, and they get ideas." He gave her a scrutinous look. "The bigger problem might be that *you* don't know. The effect you might have on those men."

Yet again, Ellis made his presence known in her psyche. This time, to remind her that he'd said something just like that about his sister. How she did things to a man without even knowing it.

"I think..." said her father. "It might be time for you to learn a little lesson."

Roni cringed back, sickness welling up inside her. For all the times he'd hit her—for all the abuse she'd suffered at his hands —he'd never touched her like that.

And I won't let him. Not now. Not ever.

Grasping at some strength she didn't know she had, she pushed to her feet with the intention of making a run for it. But she was too conditioned to listening to her father. So when he spoke again—just as she took her first step away—she couldn't stop herself from pausing.

"Get the scissors, baby girl," he said.

Automatically, she turned back. "What?"

"Perception is the devil's plaything," her father replied. "And as much as it pains me to say it, the first thing a man perceives when he sees that hair of yours is something wild."

Her brain caught up to his meaning. "You... want to cut my hair?"

"The Lord demands it," he corrected.

A hysterical laugh built up in Roni's chest. She ordered it down. How could she have thought her father would commit such an atrocity against her?

Easy... said her subconscious. *Ellis made it seem possible.*

Internally, she started to nod. But before she could complete the affirmation, the convicted man filled her head with his own response.

Did I, Nic? Was it really me *who made you question his moral integrity? Or did I nudge you in that direction and help you see what was already there?*

For a second, she met her father's eyes. There was nothing in his gaze but the expectation of absolute obedience.

Roni swallowed. Then she wrapped her towel a little tighter and went to do as she was told.

32
Thirty-Eight Hours After Escape

The Preacher's Daughter

Clutching the necessary papers tightly, Veronica stepped out of the squad car and offered the constable behind the wheel her best approximation of a smile. She knew he didn't like this. None of them did. They felt she should stay locked up until they'd caught Ellis. They wanted her to check back into the hospital. To speak to a counselor.

They're probably right, don't you think, Nic? asked Ellis's voice in her head.

But the reality was they couldn't *make* her go anywhere. She was accused of no crime. Nothing more than a witness. A victim. And they couldn't hold her prisoner, no matter how they tried to phrase it as being for her own good.

Oh, so now *you're standing up for yourself?* Ellis's voice added.

She ignored imaginary him and focused on the constable instead. She *could* do this. And she would.

"I'll only be a half hour or so," she said. "I don't know if you want to get a coffee and come back?"

The young policeman smiled back. "I've got orders, Miss. I'll be waiting right here. And you know I'd be coming in, too, if not for that whole attorney-client privilege bit. See you shortly, all right?"

Veronica nodded, closed the car door, and faced the law office. For a moment that was probably too long, she stood there, studying the embossed letters on the door.

It was hard to believe—truly—that things could move this quickly. Two days ago, the house where she'd grown up had belonged to her father. Yesterday, it had become hers. She'd been stunned and pleased to hear from her father's lawyer. For all that he'd put her through, she couldn't quite believe that he'd put her name on the title of the house. She'd been wordless. It made her heart ache, too. So hard that she'd had to call the lawyer back after she'd collected herself somewhat. But through the grief and guilt, she also felt relief. A weight lifting for how much easier this made things.

A week from now, the home would belong in trust to a man she'd never met. Cyrus Little, owner of Little & Co., a well-reputed development company. He'd been transparent about his plan, which was to turn the small acreage into ten desirable home to then sell at a profit. The real estate agent had wanted to make sure Veronica understood it would be torn down. And she did. She understood it perfectly. Not only that... she *welcomed* it. In fact, being told that the place would be leveled had pulled away a fog from her head.

Her father was dead, and that was sad, regardless of how he'd treated her in life. But if she didn't move past it now, she might never do it at all. Being back in the house after her brief stint in the hospital had shown her that. The house was her past, and its weight was crushing. If she had to stay there, she'd lose her mind. Herself. Any hope of becoming who she wanted to become.

Inhaling, she took one step forward, then another. When her fingers closed on the cool metal door handle, her confidence swelled more. The strange feeling of detachment that had been hanging over her all morning at last sloughed off, and her smile became genuine as she greeted the woman —gray-haired and dressed in a power suit—who sat at the mahogany desk.

"Hi there," she said. "I'm here to see Leigh Childress?"

The woman stood up, smoothed her skirt, and held out her palm for a handshake. "I'm Leigh. You must be Veronica Hollister." She paused as she released her warm grip from Veronica's. "Well... for now, anyway. I understand a name change is on your list of things to do today?"

The lawyer's tone—easy and not at all curious or judgemental—made Veronica relax. "In with the old, out with the new. Completely, in this case."

Leigh gestured to the chair across from her desk. "Have a seat."

Veronica did as asked, then set the paperwork out in front of her. "I think everything is here."

"Veronica... is it okay if I call you that, for now?"

"Of course. It's who I am for now, right?"

Leigh nodded. "Good. Okay. I just want to make you aware that I *do* know who you are. Your story's been all over the news for the last couple of days."

"It's been impossible to get away from," Veronica replied. "That's why I need this."

The lawyer's hand came out to cover Veronica's, offering a tight squeeze of reassurance. "You don't have to explain yourself to me. I've helped my fair share of women get out of bad situations."

"People kidnapped by escaped convicts?"

"Well, to be fair... you're my first one of those."

A real laugh—the first one in what felt like forever—escaped Veronica's lips. "I guess I should be thankful there aren't more of us around."

"The world definitely doesn't need more of that," Leigh agreed. "And just so you know... anything you *do* choose to tell me is protected by professional privilege."

"Thank you."

"So. Let's get to work then, shall we? One house sale, one expedited name change, and one fresh start, coming up."

Once again, Veronica was surprised at how quickly things

moved. In a matter of minutes, the details for the sale of her home were complete. A short bit more, and her I.D. was on its way to being updated. Leigh helped her arrange for a P.O. box, secured under the new name.

Veronica almost felt guilty about how simple it was. But it also showed her how little of her own identity she really had. Her driver's license and her birth certificate were the only two things that proved who she was—who she'd been. Even her bank account was joint with her father.

"It'll be a smoother transition to open a new one under the new name," Leigh told her as she handed over the last of the witnessed documents. "In the meantime, is there anything else I can do for you?"

"I feel like I could use a hug." Veronica blurted the words without thinking and her face warmed.

But the lawyer either didn't notice or didn't care about her embarrassment. Immediately, she pushed away from the desk, came around to Veronica's side, and held out her arms. Veronica stood and accepted the embrace. The other woman smelled faintly of lilac and fabric softener, and for some reason, it made tears want to come. It was strange to be so close to her. Almost unnatural.

When was the last time I hugged another woman?

Veronica truly didn't know. Her mother had been dead a long time. And she had no female friends. She had no friends at all. Because she'd never been *allowed* to have any. Her father had been picky about who she'd talked to as a child. Pickier still when she'd become a teen. Even the other church kids—back in the days when they still went—were off-limits the moment Sunday ended. Veronica's existence had been solitary, always.

Until Ellis.

For all that had happened, she definitely owed him some credit for letting her see that her life had been incomplete. Maybe incomplete wasn't the right word. Maybe she hadn't even started living yet.

"Thank you," Veronica said, pulling away at last.

"I hope you find what you're looking for," Leigh replied.

"I think I will."

With light steps, Veronica made her way out of the office and back to the police car.

"Constable?" she said as she opened the door, climbed in, and settled into the seat. "Do you think we could make another quick stop?"

"I've got nothing but time, and this is far more pleasant than walking a beat," he replied easily. "Where would you like to go?"

"I'm not sure, exactly. Somewhere I can buy a cellphone."

"Like... the disposable kind?"

"You tell me," Veronica said. "I've never had one before."

His glance was disbelieving. "Really?"

"Really."

"All right. Well, we can swing by just about any corner store to grab a pay-as-you-go deal."

"Perfect. You pick."

And seven minutes later, Veronica had paid for both a phone and a much-needed coffee—one for herself and one for her bodyguard policeman, too. Feeling pleased, she pushed her way back out through the door of the convenience store. She barely made it a foot before an arm snaked around her. A hand —rough and familiar—closed on her mouth, sending her paper cups flying as she was dragged around to the other side of the building.

33
Thirty-Eight Hours After Escape

The Policeman

I t took at least a full minute—maybe closer to two—for Farriday to realize that what he was staring at wasn't actually a body. He was frozen. Professionalism and experience nowhere to be found. At last, he clued in. It wasn't a repeat of the ten-year-old crime. It was a picture of the original. Or to be more accurate, it was multiple pictures of various body parts, all taped together to create a whole. Not just *any* body. It was the prosecution's favorite shot of Emily Black. Laid out just as she had been ten years ago, in just the same place, in just the same way. Nude. An arm thrown up. Legs spread wide. That dress of hers covering her face.

Fighting an instinctive desire to back away, the captain moved a little closer to the macabre display. Right away, he spied the source of the blood-tinged scent that permeated the air. Ellis had taken an extra step in an already elaborate endeavor. He'd dripped fresh crimson liquid over the photograph. He'd done it with precision, too. The splashes and droplets lined up perfectly with the ones in the image.

Bile rose up. Farriday leaned over, and he retched. The stale bagel he'd eaten between leaving Veronica Hollister's house and arriving at the Black property spattered onto the hay near Emily's foot. It only made him gag more. When there was finally nothing left to come up, he staggered back and whipped a look around, half-expecting to see the girl's brother watching him with a smile. But the barn was as empty as it had been when he'd stepped through the doors.

"Was the recreation really necessary, Black?" he muttered, swiping the back of his hand over his mouth.

It wasn't as though Farriday needed a reminder. The memory of that day was burned into his mind. The look on Ellis's face. The blood on his hands. The broken, naked girl on the ground. A man didn't forget something like that. Nor did he want to relive it.

The only good thing about the forced revisit was that it alerted him to a pattern. Everything Ellis had done so far was a reminder, each one designed to bring Farriday back to the crime. The photo left in his bed. The dress left at Veronica's house. Now this. Ellis wanted him to have all the details fresh in his mind.

And I'm not letting you into my head now, you bugger, he thought.

He stepped away from the regurgitated horror. He knew he had to call this in. What other choice did he have? It wasn't just a professional courtesy. It was inevitable that the rest of the team would realize their search needed to move inward rather than outward. They would revisit everything, and that would lead them here, where his own vomit would make it impossible to deny he'd been there first.

Or... said a devilish voice in his head.

"Or what?" he replied aloud.

You could destroy the evidence.

"And how would I do that? Burn it down?"

It was a crazy idea. Among the worst that had crossed his mind. Not to mention the whole illegality of it. And that it was the complete opposite of what it meant to be captain of the Meridian PD. To be *any* member of any PD. But that didn't mean it held no appeal.

For what felt like the hundredth time, Farriday thought about Ellis's intentions and how they related back to him. He scraped a hand over his jaw. The setup in front of him was all about the two of them. A direct reference to the last time they'd been alone, face-to-face. It would mean nothing to the other investigators except as the former scene of Ellis's crime.

His eyes hung on the pieced-together photograph. Would allowing someone else to examine it put them any closer to finding the convict?

"Possibly," he admitted after a second.

But would it help them find Ellis faster than the escaped man would meet his endgame?

"Not likely," he said.

Farriday strummed his thigh. He considered it again.

Really considered it, imagining the tinderbox of a barn going up in flames. The struggle it would take to get the fire engines in. If they could manage at all.

Finally, he shook his head. As much as he wanted to keep this to himself, arson wasn't the way to go.

But maybe it won't hurt to bag up the evidence myself.

It was a far more workable solution. He could clean up his own puke and dispose of it. Photograph the scene. Take a sample of the blood. And finally, collect the recreated body. Yes, his decision would meet with criticism later. But it was proactive, really. It was just him, doing his job, and doing it before Ellis got another chance to *undo* it. Farriday decided to go for it. Playing it safe never got anyone anywhere fast, anyway.

He retrieved the appropriate tools from his car, gloved up, and got to work. The vomit was scooped into a garbage bag. The pictures were taken, and the blood was swabbed, the cotton-ended stick all bagged up and properly labeled. With that done, he moved on to tackling the pieced-together image. He wasn't sure what the best approach was. The display was large—the size of a human body, obviously. Folding it seemed wrong. But the only other option was to pull it apart and bag the individual photos, and that was equally distasteful.

Trying to come up with some easier solution, he idly

reached out a gloved hand and lifted the nearest corner of the picture. The image rippled with his touch. When he let it go, it settled unevenly, which bothered him. He started to smooth it out again, being careful to avoid the blood, but stopped as something under the paper caught his eye.

Lettering.

His instincts tingled. Frowning, he lifted the picture again, then peered at the underside of it. For a moment, what he saw puzzled him. It *was* letters. Numbers, too. *What for?* Then it clicked. Their arrangement wasn't random. They were coordinates.

"Are you kidding me, Black?" he said, dropping the photo. "You really think I'm going to show up where you want me to?"

But as he made the denial of compliance, he knew that following the trail was exactly what he was going to do.

34
Forty Hours After Escape

The Preacher's Daughter

"You know better than to scream, don't you?" said Ellis, his voice filling Veronica's ear.

She inclined her head in a tiny nod—all that the big man's tight grip would allow.

"And you know what will happen if you do," he added.

She nodded again, and slowly, he released her. His hands came to her shoulders, and he turned her so that she was facing him.

His eyes glittered down at her. "Hello, Nic."

"Ellis," she whispered. "What are you doing here?"

"What can I say? I missed you, sweetheart. I got a little too used to having that soft mouth of yours accessible to me."

"There's a cop waiting for me in front of the store."

"I know."

"He probably has shoot-to-kill orders."

"I know that, too," he said.

She breathed out heavily. "You aren't worried about it?"

"*Should* I be worried about it?" he replied.

"I—"

"Should I be *jealous*, Nic?"

"No!" The word burst out too loudly, and she flicked a look to the side, fearful she might draw attention.

Ellis seemed unconcerned about the volume of her voice,

and Veronica wondered if he had a weapon hidden somewhere. Undoubtedly, he had a backup plan ready, in case he got caught. He wasn't the kind of man who left anything to chance. Not at all.

"He didn't do a very good job of supervising you now, did he?" Ellis asked, pulling a pack of cigarettes from his pocket and tapping one free.

"He swept the inside *and* the outside," she said.

"Shitty effort." He struck a match, lit up, and inhaled. "Should've stayed beside you the whole time. Not turned his back for a second." He blew out a ring of smoke. "Then again... that's par for the Meridian PD course, isn't it? Their own personal M.O."

She didn't argue. She didn't say anything. And Ellis smiled.

"Do you think the nice policeman hasn't noticed how pretty you are?" he added. "How sweet and tempting? Because *I* think that would be impossible." He inhaled and exhaled again. "What's the handsome officer's name?"

"I'm not sure," Veronica said truthfully. "There seems to have been so many of them over the last couple of days."

"Meridian certainly is crawling with useless cops at the moment. It's making things slightly more difficult for me." He took a long drag, then blew out half a dozen smoke rings. "Which is why I need you to do something for me, sweetheart."

"I put on the dress already."

"I know you did."

She blinked. "You do?"

"Of course," he said. "Do you think I'm just sitting by, hoping things will go the way I planned?"

"No."

"Good. I'm always so glad when we understand each other."

She cast another look up the side of the building. Any second, her current bodyguard was going to wonder what was taking her so long. Maybe he'd *already* wondered. Maybe he was looking inside the convenience store, right now.

"Nic." Ellis's growl drew her attention back to him.

Her heart jumped to her throat and stayed there. "Yes?"

"Thank you for putting on the dress. I enjoyed watching Farriday's face when he saw you wearing it."

"You saw his face?"

"There hasn't been more than an hour here or there that I haven't been within easy reaching distance, Nic." He lifted his free hand and slid a finger down her cheek. "I went over the details, didn't I? Minute by minute. So you should know that."

A shiver racked her whole body. "I do know. You keep your promises."

"I do." He dropped his cigarette and crushed it under his foot. "We're still being honest with each other, aren't we? That still holds?"

"Yes."

"Then answer me this, sweetheart. Does Farriday want to fuck you yet?"

Veronica's face flamed. "I... I don't know."

Ellis wasn't the slightest bit put off by her embarrassment. "When he had his hand on you this morning, did it make him hard?"

"I didn't..." She trailed off, swallowed, and tried again. "He wasn't close enough for me to tell."

He studied her as though trying to discern the truthfulness behind her words, and after a second, he nodded. "It doesn't matter. He *will* want to. Even if it's just to punish me a little more."

"Not every man—"

"Yes, sweetheart. Every. Fucking. Man. If he's not gay or impotent or indifferent to sex in general, he wants to do all the terrible things to you. All the things that *I* want. All the things I started to do before Farriday and his men took you away from me."

Veronica's breath caught in her throat, and the air around her grew thinner. "Are you going to take me away again now?"

"I'm going to see my plan through. Every minute still matters, and I need to keep to my timeline. But I have a gift for you."

Ellis stuck his hand into his pocket, and when he pulled it out again, he was clasping a silver chain. He wiggled his fingers, and it shimmered to its full length, showing off the blue pendant that hung from the lowest point.

"Turn around," he said. "You're going to wear this."

Obediently, Veronica spun. She utterly held still as Ellis swiped her hair away from her neck then fastened the necklace with far more gentleness than seemed possible.

"This was Emily's," he told her, pulling her back against his chest and running his hands down the length of her arms. "You remember the story?"

"It wasn't on the body," she replied. "The prosecution accused you of stealing it."

"And the truth, my dearest Nic?"

"You gave it as a gift to your sister on her sixteenth birthday."

"On *our* sixteenth birthday," he corrected.

She inclined her head. "On your shared sixteenth birthday. And you can't steal what's already yours."

"Exactly." His hands found her shoulders again, and once more, he turned her to face him. "Are you missing your father?"

Her eyes dropped. "Yes."

"Then I've got something else I need you to do."

"What?"

He grabbed her chin and tilted her face up. "There's a small box under his bed. It's locked, but the key is in an envelope in his nightstand. Look inside, and you'll remember why he had to die."

She met his sharp gaze. "Okay."

"Promise me."

"I promise."

"Good girl." He pinched her chin a little harder, then swiped a thumb over her lips before leaning close to whisper in her ear. "Maybe tonight...I'll watch you sleep. See you soon, Nic."

The words managed, in typical Ellis fashion, to be both a promise and a threat. And as Veronica's heart slammed a staccato beat against her ribcage in reply, he dropped a slow wink and slipped silently away.

35
Ten Years Earlier
Twenty-Four Hours Before Arrest

The Policeman

Flip had been sitting in the interview room at the station —his station—for a good two hours. And that was following the time he'd spent sitting on his car's rear bumper while waiting for dispatch to send someone out to take his statement and collect the shoe. Both things were ridiculous. Especially in a town as small as Meridian. Especially considering he was a member of the force.

What's their excuse this time? He glanced down at the watch on his wrist. *No more captains to drop dead and slow things down.*

"Maybe Cliff fell and broke his leg," he muttered.

He didn't hope it was true. Not quite. But if he did hope it a little, the hope was dashed as the other man's wide shoulders appeared on the other side of the frosted glass. Flip knew it was him, even though he didn't come into the room right away. That too-confident way he held himself gave it away.

Was his personal presence a good thing, or a bad one? It was impossible to say. And Cliff didn't appear to be in a rush to make the answer known.

"Don't hurry," Flip said. "Nothing to see here but evidence of a crime."

He crossed his arms and waited. Getting up and losing his patience might be what Cliff was hoping for, and Flip wasn't going to give him the satisfaction. Finally, the door opened. But the acting captain didn't rush to come in. He finished whatever he was saying to whoever he was saying it to, paused for a long moment, then at last entered.

"Cl—" Flip feigned a cough to cover the misspeak—no need to start out antagonistic, after all. "Captain. Didn't expect to find you on the receiving end of my call."

"I wasn't," replied Cliff without so much as a hint of a smile.

Flip didn't give up on his cheerful overtures. "Seems like it from here. Glad to see you, either way."

The other man's response was flat. "I asked Danielle to let me know if you turned up on the radar, Flip."

Of course you did, thought Flip, while aloud he said, "Well, I appreciate you wanting to keep tabs on my little vacation, boss. But I wasn't calling in my capacity as an officer of the law. I was calling in a civilian find in my driveway. Speaking of which… What do you make of that shoe?"

"What do I make of it in a way that's a 'civilian find,' or in a way that's in an official capacity?"

Flip worked at not gritting his teeth. "Either or."

"Well, Constable Farriday, what I think of it is that you're fishing."

"What do you mean, Cl—" *Dammit.* "Captain."

"I told you to take the week off."

"I am."

The other man fixed him with a disbelieving look. "You expect me to believe that you just happened to find this woman's shoe in your driveway?"

It doesn't matter! It's Emily Black's! Flip wanted to holler.

He smiled instead. "I agree that it's mighty odd timing. But that doesn't mean we can ignore it. Like you said before. We go on evidence, right?"

"We do."

"So?"

"You touched the shoe," said Cliff.

"I acknowledged that I did," Flip replied. "One of the first things in my statement. Scared the bejeezus out of me when I saw it there, and procedure went out of my head. Grabbed it without thinking."

"We did a preliminary run on the prints, Constable Farriday. And yours are the only ones we found."

Flip made himself keep the smile in place. "Happy to admit that I made the mistake. Can't see how it got left there without the culprit's prints on it, though. Maybe the nonpreliminary check will bring up something else?"

"Maybe."

"On another note, what about the blood?"

Cliff appeared to be trying to stifle the world's biggest sigh. "It's not blood."

"You checked?"

"We will."

Now the smile fell away, and the teeth-gritting overpowered it. "You don't know it's not blood."

"Let me ask you something," said Cliff. "Do you remember a few months back when you decided Jenny Blankenship was in danger, and you burst through her door and found her and her boyfriend mid... ahem... coitus?"

"This isn't the same."

"What *is* the same is the fact that you see things that aren't there, Flip. You put your fingerprints all over something that you thought was evidence. It's a thin line. One where the Meridian PD is at risk. And Captain Dax was patient with you, but I suspect I'm going to struggle to be the same."

"Are you at least going to send someone out to the Black place to check it out?" Flip asked.

Cliff's expression got impossibly flatter. "Why would this shoe have anything to do with the Blacks?" *Crap again.*

He didn't have an explanation. Not one that didn't involve confessing to the minor B&E and suspecting the kid of following him around and making reports about him. So he went with a lie.

"I saw these very same shoes on the sister," he stated.

"When?" replied the acting captain.

"A while back."

"A week? A day? When?"

Flip crossed his arms. "Can't say the exact moment, but I know what I saw."

Cliff shook his head. "Listen to me. I want to say this only once, all right? Meridian is a small town. We have so little crime that we barely earned the officers we had before Captain Dax died. We'll be lucky if we get a replacement for me once I've officially received the promotion."

"I don't—"

"I'm not done, Flip. Let me be thorough. The only monsters living in this town are the ones in the prison. There's no one hiding under the bed. No one out to get you. You have to let this go. Yes, I'll get someone out to check on those kids. *I will.* But it's not crazy for their mom to be gone on a weekend bender. And my guess is that Ellis only wishes his father were dead." Cliff drew a breath. "Let. It. Go. Understood?"

Flip's mouth opened, but his so-called boss didn't wait. He simply stalked out. For a second—for several seconds—Flip stared after him. He didn't know what word best described how he was feeling. Stunned? Offended? Downright pissed off?

After another few moments, though, he decided it didn't matter. He'd just learned something important, and that was that he, Flip Farriday, was the one person he could truly count on.

If you want something done right…

Never had an adage held so much truth. Flip would make that his official policy. He would take matters into his own hands from here on out, consequences be damned.

36
Four Months,
Twenty-Seven Days Before Escape

The Preacher's Daughter

R oni had a speech ready. She swore she did.

She was going to tell Ellis that she would help him. Or at least give him the chance to *be* helped, so long as he agreed to take religious offerings seriously, among other things. It had woken her in the night, thinking of it. A dream where a person with a soul as dark as Ellis Black's was still able to be guided to the light. She'd clung to that dream with fervor. She'd flicked on her lamp and written out a manifesto. Then she'd committed it to memory, torn the paper into a hundred pieces, and flushed it all to keep it from her father's eyes.

Now... it was all gone.

It disappeared the second she walked into the room and saw Ellis. Or, to be more accurate, it evaporated when *he* saw *her*. Because his eyes hung on her sheered hair—the once-long curls now barely touched her chin—and his expression was identical to the one he'd had when he'd spied the bruise on her face before.

He knows what happened, she thought.

It took more than a modicum of self-restraint to keep from bringing up a self-conscious hand. She opened her mouth to say something—Lord knew what—but Ellis beat her to the punch.

"That fucker," he said.

A lie—a vehement denial—sprung into Roni's mind as she sank into the chair across from him, but a hint of the truth slipped through her lips anyway. "He didn't hurt me."

"No. He demeaned you. Stripped you of a little piece of yourself."

"I'm fine."

"I'm an expert on fucked up. Try again."

He stared her down. As much as she wanted to meet his challenge, she couldn't stop herself from dropping her gaze to her lap. When she spoke up, it was in the general direction of her own hands.

"It was just hair," she said.

"What was his reason this time?" Ellis asked.

"He doesn't need a reason at all." Her reply contained far more bitterness than she intended, and she blushed.

"How about this, sweetheart? I'll make you a new offer. Help me get what I want, and I'll make sure that your father understands not to touch a single part of you. Ever."

Pieces of the speech she'd forgotten surfaced, and she looked up again. "It doesn't matter what you offer, Ellis. Getting you out of prison isn't something I can help with."

"Is this still about me and God? Or is it that you think I don't deserve to be free, because I'm incapable of self-control?"

She forced herself to keep meeting his eyes. "Do you *want* to change your violent nature?"

He lifted one of his thick brows. "Tell me something...How long have you been sitting there?"

"What?"

"How long?"

She felt her forehead crease. "More than five minutes, less than ten."

"Right," he replied.

"So?"

He didn't say anything to her little prompt. Instead, he shifted in his chair. He pulled back his hands, sending the cuffs clattering down to the table. Then he stood up, did a languorous stretch, and took a few wide steps toward the back of the room. There, he crossed his arms and leaned against the wall. He grinned one of his dark grins. And finally, he lit a cigarette. Throughout the whole thing, Roni was paralyzed. The only parts of her that seemed capable of moving were her eyes. Those, she could feel getting bigger and bigger by the second.

What.

Spots dotted her vision.

Is.

Dizziness thickened.

Happening?

"You might want to take a breath, sweetheart," Ellis said after another second.

His words made her aware that her lungs were as still as the rest of her body. They burned from a lack of oxygen.

"Nic." Her name was a growl, but it held a hint of worry, and he pushed away from the wall, too.

He's going to come over here, she realized.

Drawing on everything she had, Roni sucked in a mouthful of air. It blasted in and sent her gasping so hard that she had to press her hands to the table to keep from falling off the chair. But thankfully, the world stopped spinning.

"Stay there," she managed to get out.

Ellis fixed her with the stoniest glare she'd ever seen. "Why? Don't you want to put my cuffs back on for me?"

Her attention shifted to the shackles. Without being attached to him, they looked small and useless. So much so that it called into question their effectiveness at all. She looked back toward the hulking man. A brief image flashed through her mind—her tiny hands fumbling with the metal restraints in an effort to reattach them to his thick wrists. It was absurd.

What about the guards?

She didn't mean to say it aloud. She didn't realize she had until Ellis answered. Even then, she wasn't sure if he was just reading her mind the way he so often seemed to be able to.

"You'd be surprised at what those upstanding citizens will do for a hundred bucks." He tilted his head to study her. "Though you might not be surprised to learn what they'll do to keep that corruption to themselves. Threaten their wives and kids and *bam!* Some poor thing like you becomes collateral damage to them."

That means you're completely vulnerable, said her subconscious. *You need to tread lightly. So, so lightly.*

Roni took another breath, this one a bit smoother. "How did you get them off?"

"My dad had a fun trick when I was a kid," Ellis said. "He used to like to chain me to a post in the barn on our property. It was cold as fuck in the middle of January. I had to learn to save myself somehow."

"So you could've done that every time that I've been here?" she asked.

"Not every time. Part of it is holding my hands in the right way to give myself enough slack. I have to have a tool." He held out his palm to reveal a silver, needle-like object that caught the overhead light and glinted wickedly. "And sometimes, the guard who chains me up does it too tightly for me to get out no matter what I do." He closed his hand, then opened it again, and the lockpick was gone. "Thankfully, my dear old dad was usually too drunk to be as effective as the guards." He paused and met her eyes. "What about you?"

She shook her head. "I don't think I could undo a set of handcuffs if you paid me."

"Oh, the things I'd love to say about you in a pair of handcuffs. Nic..." His low chuckle vibrated through the air. "But I meant your father. Does he have any specialties in his punishments? Aside from the haircuts and the smacks? Is he a drinker?"

Heat slid up Roni's neck, and she ordered herself to focus on the latter half of Ellis's comments. "He doesn't drink at all. My mother was killed by a drunk driver."

Something that looked an awful lot like compassion flashed over his features, and his reply had a genuine sound to it, too. "I'm sorry."

"I was five," she added.

"Ah," Ellis said. "So that's why you stay with him."

"I don't know what you mean."

"Sure you do. Something about the way your mother died makes you think that something terrible would happen if you left."

"I didn't say that."

"You didn't have to. In fact, I like it better that way, because I'd prefer to pluck it right out of your head myself. So give me a second to think about it…" He gave his chin a thoughtfully mocking stroke. "It's not that you're afraid of leaving the old bastard alone. And it's not that you feel responsible for your mother's death, either."

Unease tickled at Roni's mind, and she adjusted herself in her seat. "You don't know what you're talking about."

"What was she like, your mother? Was she hit by a drunk driver, or in the car with one?"

"It doesn't matter."

"I think it does. I also think if she were completely innocent, you wouldn't be hedging."

"She was a passenger," Roni blurted.

"And she was… unfaithful." Ellis sounded far too satisfied.

Roni couldn't muster up a denial. "But that doesn't make it her fault that she died."

"No, it doesn't. It's done a few other things, though, hasn't it? It's given you an insidious fear that karma came for her. It's made you worry that if you do anything *close* to what she did— leaving your son-of-a-bitch father, for example —that you'll be punished, too." He paused, and this time the thoughtful look on his face didn't seem phony. "Your dad might've been a piece of shit before, too, I don't know, but your mom's infidelity is probably the reason he keeps you locked up."

"I'm not locked up."

"No? Then tell me the truth, Nic. What made your father decide to shear you like a sheep?"

She bit her lip. She willed herself not to answer. The man had enough power at this moment as it was. For a few seconds, Roni held her silence. But it didn't do any good. Ellis filled in the blanks without her help.

"The haircut was about a man, too," he said.

Her teeth clamped down harder. She tasted blood. But she still didn't reply.

Ellis's voice dropped low. "Was it me?"

Without her permission, her eyes lowered. And she knew the unconscious motion gave it away.

"Not me, then," Ellis stated, his tone abruptly hardedged. "Did you meet someone else, Nic?"

Someone else. The phrase gave her a little start. It made it sound as though *he* had some claim on her. And that was not only disturbing, but it also sparked some anger.

She looked up. "Contrary to popular belief, I'm my own person."

"That doesn't answer my question," he replied.

"Because I don't *have* to answer your question."

"Oh, but you do."

He moved then, and Roni realized she'd made a mistake. She'd let her guard down. She had—somehow—quite literally forgotten that the man across the room from her was a hardened criminal. That he was supposed to be locked to the table in front of her. But she was reminded of it now. Thoroughly. Because he yanked her from the chair, put a hand around her throat, and forced her to the wall.

37
Forty-Three Hours After Escape

The Policeman

Captain Farriday put his hands on his hips and glared at the treeline. It looked just like it had for the last eight minutes. A wall of green and brown. Of unbroken nothing. Which, admittedly, was exactly what he'd been expecting. Because it was exactly what had turned up with his computer search of the coordinates supplied by Ellis Black. Not that being guided to the middle of nowhere was particularly surprising. In fact, if Ellis had tried to guide him somewhere obvious, then that would've been a red flag.

Doesn't mean I like this *any better, though,* Farriday thought, swinging his gaze back and forth again.

Somehow, seeing the blank uniformness in person was different than looking at it on a computer screen.

Grimacing, he pinched the bridge of his nose and closed his eyes. He'd put off the distasteful taste of catering to the convicted man's will and whim for as long as he could, all the while hoping some turn of events would mean he didn't have to do it at all.

First, he'd done what *had* to be done. He'd packed up all the evidence he'd collected and taken it back to the station, where he did—but didn't file, just in case it bit him in the ass —the appropriate paperwork. Next, he'd checked in with his guys. No one had any updates. Even Constable Boon, the young guy guarding Veronica, had nothing to report other than that the girl had spilled a coffee and taken an extra-long bathroom break at a gas station. And finally, Farriday had needed to give in. No one was going to magically spot the escaped man. Not unless that was what the convict wanted.

"Which clearly, he does not," he said as he stepped back and again searched for some sign of whatever he was supposed to find there.

It was more of the same. A five-minute walk up and down the gravel road revealed nothing. Two more minutes of staring didn't change a thing. There wasn't even a break in the trees that might indicate a way to access some point farther into the woods. Then, just when Farriday was about to give up, a small flash of color caught his eye.

Frowning, he studied it from afar. From what he could tell, it appeared to be a bright pink ribbon. Not the kind of tape used for flagging trees to be cut, either. This was more iridescent. It made Farriday's gut churn. Its presence couldn't be a coincidence. He took a couple of cautious strides toward it. The material flapped a little in the breeze, and for a wild second, it felt eerily like its movement was a reaction to his approach. He shook off the odd sensation, took a few more steps, then stopped in front of the flashing pink. Now he recognized it for what it was.

A hair ribbon.

A memory flashed through his mind. A straighttoothed smile. Guileless blue eyes. Blond hair tied into a ponytail, and a cotton candy bow atop those golden locks. *Emily Black.* She'd had a preference for satin ribbons. All her school pictures showed her wearing them.

Farriday lifted his hand toward the one fastened to the tree but dropped his arm again without touching it. Not because of a fear of contaminating evidence, but because he realized right then that the ribbon wasn't alone. A few feet into the trees, another hung from a different branch. Then a number of feet more past that, yet another.

213

Ellis Black's version of a trail of breadcrumbs, Farriday thought, hip lips twisting with disgust.

Wondering what kind of darkness waited for him at the end of it, he moved in the ribbons' direction. What would a man like Ellis use in place of a witch and her giant oven?

As he crunched over the forest floor, he noted evidence of a crudely hacked path that extended past the second and third ribbons. Not only had the convict provided the breadcrumbs; he'd made it easy to access them.

"So thoughtful," Farriday grunted.

He continued on. There was a fourth ribbon. Then a fifth. By that point, he was sweating and sucking wind despite the cutback greenery. He pushed through it for another minute, but when he reached the sixth ribbon, he paused to take a needed breather. Leaning against a tree, he cast a look back in the direction from which he'd come.

The road was practically invisible already, and now that he was standing still, Farriday could see that the trail had taken an excessively meandering path. A few more ribbons in, and any sense of direction would be lost. He'd be rendered helpless to do anything but follow what Ellis had laid out for him. Assuming, of course, that the other man didn't take his Hansel and Gretel theme further and remove the trail markers once their use had been exhausted.

"Dammit," Farriday said.

Should he really keep going? He lifted his ballcap and swiped a hand over his sweaty head, considering. The answer was obvious. No, he shouldn't keep going. But he knew he was going to anyway. Just as he'd entered the barn. Just as he'd follow along with whatever else Ellis threw his way until the cat-and-mouse game was done.

Shoving his hat back onto his head, he started off again. He counted six more ribbons before he started to worry that maybe he'd doubled back on the route and was walking in circles. Though for all he knew, that was what the scumbag wanted. Confusion. Disorientation. Control over Farriday.

He plodded on in spite of his reservations, and at last, a subtle change in the slope of his trek and a thinning of the trees indicated that he'd made progress. Two minutes and two ribbons more, and he was pushing his way out of the woods and into a clearing on top of a hill. And what he saw stopped him so abruptly that he nearly tripped.

In the dead center of the open space was a three-foot-tall, wooden cross, driven into the dirt and strung with more ribbons than he could count. It wasn't as overtly violent as the last gift Ellis had left for him. Yet somehow, this one was creepier. Almost chilling.

He took a small step toward it. Then he stopped again. The chill rose to an icy crescendo as he spotted the name that had been roughly chiseled into the wood.

Francis "Flip" Farriday.

"Lord Help me," he said under his breath.

Rolling his shoulders, he tried to shake off the disturbed feeling that slithered along his spine. The motion did nothing to ease the unpleasantness, and he yanked his eyes away from the cross for some reprieve.

He blinked as he took in the rest of his surroundings. The display had been so distracting that he hadn't noticed anything about where he was. From his current position, he could see much of the outskirts of Meridian Far off to his left, in the deepest dip of the valley beside the town, was the intimidating sprawl of the prison. To his right—and much closer—were the older, bigger properties that had once been farmland. Included in those were two Farriday knew well. The first was the Black property. The other was Veronica Hollister's home.

Until right then, he'd somehow managed to overlook the fact that the houses were that close to each other. Not quite neighbors. But enough that it struck a chord. Ellis had to have chosen this spot for that very reason.

"Why?"

Doesn't matter, he told himself. *It doesn't mean anything.*

He took a step back. But as he did, a curl of black smoke stalled him. There was no doubt about its source.

Veronica's house.

Without stopping to think abut whether it was logical or not, Farriday took off down the hill at a stumbling run.

38
Forty-Four Hours After Escape

The Preacher's Daughter

T he small fire in front of Veronica glowed hot orange. The embers crackled. The smoke thickened. And yet it still didn't seem like enough destruction.
It should be more, she thought. *It should be bigger.*

But she was moving slowly. Burning them, one by one, because she wanted to make sure they all got destroyed. There was no room for error.

She watched the flames, waiting as the paper they consumed curled, then crumbled before she bent down and grabbed the next glossy sheet from the pile inside the shoebox. A girl's face—lips painted a wicked shade of red that contrasted sharply with her wide-eyed expression of innocence—flickered briefly across Veronica's vision. She didn't let herself look. She balled it up and tossed it into the fire.

Her eyes closed for a second, but without the dancing fire in sight, it was impossible not to let her head fill with a picture of her father. And not *just* her father. Her father and the pictures. Her father, the pictures, and the stained mattress that Veronica herself had covered in sheets, week after week, month after month, year after year.

She tried to power past it. But the mental images refused to retreat, and she had no choice but to open her eyes so she could block them out. When she did, she was almost *pleased* to see that her latest addition to the fire had turned acrider than the others. The smoke was blacker. A sour smell permeated the air. And both things were about perfect, as far as Veronica was concerned. She even smiled a little as she dug for another of the abhorrent pictures from the box. But as her hand closed on the next piece of shiny paper, a voice startled her into dropping it.

"Ms. Hollister?"

Quickly, she stood up and spun, heart pounding. Through the smoke, she spotted a bedraggled figure. It staggered toward her. And for a wild moment, she thought it was her father's ghost, come to claim her for her transgression against the man himself. But when she took a step back and wiped her eyes, she realized it was a real person after all. The police captain. A second later, a call from near the back porch— the spot where her bodyguard waited—confirmed it.

"Captain!" said the constable. "I wasn't expecting you."

Farriday waved him off. "No need to come down here. Just saw the smoke and wanted to check in." He brought his attention to Veronica. "Is everything okay here, sweetheart?"

The question was tinged with both kindness and concern, but at that moment, her ears focused on only one part of it.

"He called me that all the time," she said. "Ellis, I mean."

"Sorry. It's probably a bad habit, anyway. Not very modern of me."

"It's fine. I don't mind old-fashioned. In fact, I think it would be kind of nice if *everyone* was a little more that way, you know?"

Farriday frowned, his eyes sliding from her to the fire and back again. "Anything I can do to help you? Did something happen?"

She shook her head, but her shoulders turned in. "It's kind of true, isn't it? What I said this morning."

"Refresh my memory."

"Men. They're mostly animals."

"I prefer to think not."

She met his eyes, and he averted his gaze for a tenth of a second—just long enough that she knew he wasn't being honest.

"You're a cop," she stated. "You must see the worst of humanity. You can't tell me that it doesn't make you question whether all of us have some of that inside of us."

"Well, like you said... I'm a cop," he replied. "So yeah, I see the bad. A lot. Often. Small stuff and big stuff. Stuff I'd rather not have seen. There's more to my job than that, though. The whole point of policework is that there has to be something worth saving, or there's no point in doing what I do."

"That's why I went to Ellis. And why I *kept* going to him," she confessed. "Because I believed I could find that spark. A way out for his soul. But that's not what I found."

"I don't think Ellis Black is the right litmus test for the rest of us."

"No. Maybe not."

She looked away from Farriday, watching the fire again. The flames were still there, though they were flickering now more than dancing. The current piece of evidence was almost gone. But not quite.

"What about my father, Captain?" she said softly.

"Your father?" he echoed. "What do you mean?"

"Is *he* a good litmus test for the rest of you? A former preacher. A single father and a homeowner with no police record whatsoever."

"Better than most, I would say."

She gestured toward the shoebox. "Look inside." He didn't answer. But he did take the suggestion. Veronica waited, listening as the policeman flipped through what was left of her father's unsavory collection.

Only a few seconds went by before Farriday cleared his throat. "This sounds funny to say... but it's just pornography, sweet—er. Ms. Hollister."

"They're *girls*." Veronica's voice quavered. "Just *girls*."

"Underage, you mean?" His eyes dropped to the box.

"Yes."

"Is that why you're burning them?"

"Yes," she said again.

He spoke gently. "Look. There's no way to know that these girls aren't eighteen."

"But even if they're *just* eighteen. That's... it's... it's wrong. My father, looking at these girls who are younger than I am. Girls who are dressed up to look younger than that." She shook her head and met his eyes. "Do you think it's all right?"

"It might feel morally wrong, but we have to assume the best here. And if we do, then we also have to acknowledge that there's nothing illegal about it, whether we like it or not."

"So my father had a monster inside him, too. But I should pretend that he didn't because it was legal?"

"That's not what I said."

"What if I had found these a week ago when he was still alive? What if I had brought them to you?"

"Did you tell Constable Boon about them?" Farriday asked.

"No," Veronica admitted.

"So maybe there's a part of *you* that thinks these are legal."

"Or maybe there's a part of me that's a monster."

"Ms. Hollister. You know that's not—"

"I want to be alone now, Captain. Please."

He nodded, then tipped his face toward the porch and raised his voice. "I'll be turning Ms. Hollister back over to you now, Constable."

"Thanks, Captain!" called the other man.

Farriday nodded once more, then started to spin on his heel. But he stopped short, shot out a hand, and grabbed Veronica's arm, his grip far more aggressive than she would've expected. And his voice was equally rough.

"Where did you get that?" he demanded.

"Where did I—oh." Her fingers came up to the necklace as she realized what he meant. "It was a gift."

"From who?"

The force behind the question made her flinch. It also made

her hesitate because she couldn't recall if Ellis had told her whether or not she ought to admit that it had come from him.

"My friend got it second-hand, but I think a local artisan used to make them," she said evasively. "Do you like it?"

His eyes narrowed, and she braced for him to push again. But the captain seemed to get a hold of himself instead. He dropped her arm and stepped back.

"It just reminds me of someone I knew once." His eyes rested on the necklace for another second. "I'll let you get back to your thing, Ms. Hollister. I'm sure I'll be talking to you soon."

39
Four Months, Twenty-Seven Days Before Escape

The Preacher's Daughter

Ellis's hand on her throat should've made Roni more fearful than it did. Every logical part of her brain screamed it. In fact, the logical parts were demanding to know why the illogical parts weren't doing their instinctive thing and initiating fight or flight mode. She had enough room to lift her knee and drive it between his legs. Her arms were free, too. She could hit. Flail. Aim for his eyes. Not to mention that she had a voice. She could raise it in a blood-curdling scream that would draw the attention of the prison guards. No matter how complacent they might be toward Ellis in general, they would surely burst through the door if they believed she was in peril. But she didn't do any of it. She didn't even squeeze her eyes shut and pray for mercy. Instead, she looked directly into Ellis's face. She took note of the heat there. The violent want. It was the same hunger he'd been tossing her way since the moment they'd met. But now it didn't scare her. It made her feel something else entirely. Something unnatural and dark and tingly at the same time.

God. Oh, God.

She wanted this.

"What's wrong with me?" Roni whispered, her voice catching a little.

"You can't figure it out?" he replied.

"No. I just—" She cut herself off before a hysterical noise — half sob, half laugh—could escape.

"It's simple, sweetheart," Ellis said.

"*How?*"

"You've been conditioned to think you're not worth more than this."

"That's—"

"True." The word was a slap. "You live under your father's thumb. He uses any excuse to hurt you. Shame you. Beat you. He's kept you away from the world so you wouldn't know any better."

"I go out." But the claim sounded hollow, even to her own ears.

"On his whim. On his schedule. On his fucking terms, Nic. Running errands. Coming here. That was all him. You're so used to it that even your heart..." He slid the edge of his hand between her breasts, then flattened his palm there. "Even your heart believes it doesn't deserve anything better than a man who's behind bars for rape and murder."

As though to emphasize the last word, his hand moved to her throat and squeezed for a moment before falling away. But instead of bringing her relief, the loss of contact brought emptiness. Roni tried to suck in a breath. It should've been easier without his large palm clasped around her windpipe. But it wasn't. She failed to pull in the smallest amount of oxygen.

"You shouldn't feel too bad about it." Ellis's voice dropped low, making the words all the more intimate. "After all, I understand you. I understand your life. I know you at least as well as you know yourself. In a lot of ways, I'm the perfect man for you."

"That can't be right." Roni wasn't sure whether she said it for his benefit or for her own.

His fingers came up, and with a flick, he freed the top button on her dress. His rough skin met the tender flesh along the edge of her bra. She shivered. And it would've been a lie to say it was entirely unpleasant.

"It *is* right," Ellis said. "If you think otherwise, you're lying to yourself."

"No."

"Close your eyes, Nic."

She didn't want to obey him. She knew she ought not give him a single moment more of this. Whatever it was. She felt sick at the very idea of it. But she had no control. Her lids fluttered, then sank shut.

Please, God. Help me.

For a moment, there was nothing. No sound except the light buzz of the fluorescent lights overhead. No movement but the quiver of her own body. It was almost as though Ellis had disappeared. Roni nearly opened her eyes again to check. But before she got that far, she felt him again.

His breath came hot against her throat, and his hands landed on her hips, the stretch of them so wide that they seemed to cover her, back to front. It was an all-encompassing sensation, and it grew stronger as he slid his palms up to her abdomen, resting them there for an endless amount of time. His palms were warm. And the heat seeped into her. Insidious. Snakelike. And it was palpably *good.*

The sickness in Roni's stomach grew, which would've been a relief if not for one thing—it wasn't alone. There was another feeling alongside it. A deep ache. A wrong ache.

Ellis's hands moved again. They traveled up her sides, then settled under her breasts, cupping them in a possessive way they had no right to.

Roni was drowning.

I'm going to hell, she thought. *And I deserve it.*

She leaned into the big man. The convict. The murderer. The *rapist.* She reminded herself of the things he was guilty of. Tears sprung up and spilled over. And still... she didn't open her eyes or make the slightest attempt to get away.

"Do it," she gasped.

"Do what?" Ellis growled.

"Whatever you're going to do to me. Just... do it."

"Tell me what you think that is, Nic."

"I don't know."

"Bullshit," he snarled. "Open your fucking eyes."

Her compliance was immediate. Her eyes snapped open, and she found Ellis's face an inch from hers, all hardness and anger. His hands fell away. But his jaw looked tight enough to snap.

"What do you think I'm going to do?" he asked.

Roni had to swallow three times before she could speak again. "Hurt me."

Ellis cocked his head, a dark smile tipping up his mouth. "Is that what you think I'm going to do, sweetheart? Or is that a request?"

"I don't want to be hurt."

"You want something." Fire slid up her cheeks.

"No."

"Yes," he replied.

His fingers found the hem of her skirt and tugged up.

His thumbs coasted along her thighs.

"Is it this?" he asked. "Or something more?"

Roni didn't trust herself to answer.

Ellis tipped his mouth to her ear. "Are you expecting me to fuck you, Nic? Against your will, maybe?"

Finally, reality—if not sense—hit her, and she managed to squirm back a little while also finding her voice. "Isn't that your thing, Ellis?"

He jerked like she'd struck him, took a step back, then pointed to the door. "Get. The. Fuck. *Out.*"

"I—"

"Now, Nic. *Now.*"

She stumbled back. All of the fear that should've been present before came rushing in, like it was breaking through a wall. It slammed into her with an equal force that was almost physical. She felt winded. Dizzy. Ellis's body was a blur, and Roni could barely focus on finding the exit. She fumbled several times before her hand finally found the knob, and, she still couldn't grip it properly on the first try. Her fingers slipped right off.

Gasping now, she squeezed the cold metal and ordered herself to perform this simple task. And it almost worked. She held on. She twisted. But her mouth decided that it needed to make a final comment.

"I've never even been kissed!"

Roni had no idea why she said it. Nor did she have a clue as to why she looked over her shoulder to see Ellis's reaction. As soon as the words were out and the motion made, she regretted them both. Not just because she sounded childish, or because the statement was utterly unnecessary, but because saying it refocused the evil man's attention. His eyes homed in on her lips. He took a step closer. And closer again. The brief moment of control that Roni had over the door handle evaporated. She cowered, her back pressed to the door as though she could melt into it. But of course, she didn't. She stayed exactly where she was as Ellis reached her. And except for an all-over shake, she didn't move as his hands landed on the door on either side of her shoulders.

"Tell me not to do this," he said.

Roni couldn't do it. She couldn't even shake her head in silent denial of what was about to happen. And she didn't blame Ellis for taking her lack of response as acquiescence. Especially since he bent his neck and eased his face toward her so very slowly, and she had plenty of time to try to get away. When his lips met hers, it was soft enough that she could have resisted. But she didn't. Instead, she tipped her head up and returned the undemanding kiss.

Ellis's mouth was warm and firm, and he met her reciprocation with a palm on her cheek and a deepening of the contact between them. His tongue parted her lips, teased her own for a moment, then pulled away. For a heartbeat, he pressed his forehead to hers. It was a gesture that was about as far removed from who he was as it could possibly get. And then he pulled away, too.

"Please go, Nic," he said. "Please."

The words were edged with a desperation so real and sorrowful that Roni's entire body ached for him. She wanted to stay. To offer him some kind of comfort. But nothing in her existence had ever prepared her for a moment like this one. Her head was reeling.

Wordlessly, she grabbed the door handle—with no problems this time—gave it a perfect twist and a yank, and she slipped into the hall without a backward glance.

40
Three Months, Nine Days Before Escape

The Convict

Ellis slammed his tray down on the table so hard that the man at the other end jumped, then steadied his food.

"You got a problem?" Ellis snapped.

He didn't bother to listen for a response. His head was fucked up beyond all reason. He'd never felt so fucking *fucked.* Even in the throes of his sister's murder, even under the ferocious pressure of the trial and the judgemental bastards looking down on him, he hadn't wanted to tear his hair out.

Not like this. Not with this visceral fucking fuckery of need.

A kiss.

Never had his cell been so small. Never had he railed so shit-tastically hard against the six feet of width and the eight feet of depth and the ceiling he could reach if he stretched his arms up *just so.* He deserved it. He deserved the tiny room and the cement walls and the goddamned cold toilet and lack of privacy. Yet here he was, gnawing on a fucking bread roll in the middle of gen pop just to get the hell away from it.

A fucking kiss.

For a decade, exactly two things had dominated his life. The first was an absolute necessity, given his living situation. It was survival in the form of domination—something he was more than good at. The second thing... Well. That was the reason to keep up with the survival piece. The fantasy of destroying Flip Fucking Farriday. Of tearing the man apart, limb by limb. A thing he dreamed of. Literally. Figuratively. Awake. Asleep. In that lull in between the two.

Except now. *Now.* Now, there was a glitch. And it came in the form of Veronica Hollister.

Fuck.

Silent as it was, the word was still a guttural utterance.

He jammed his spoon into his mouth so hard that he tasted blood alongside the fucking mashed potatoes and their shitty-ass gravy.

It's a distraction, he told himself. *It changes nothing.*

That didn't mean he could stop himself from replaying it in his head. It'd been going on for weeks now.

Weeks? he scoffed. *It's been more than a month without her coming back. Hell. Soon it'll be two fucking months, won't it?*

Yet it wouldn't leave him. She wouldn't leave him. Her soft mouth, reddened from the impact of the kiss. The curls her father had lopped off in an attempt to subdue her beauty, but which still managed to frame her pink-stained face. And those eyes. Jesus Christ, those eyes. Just for a second, looking at him like he wasn't a fucking monster.

What kind of woman could see beyond a past like his?

You know exactly what kind.

He chewed hard on a piece of meat, barely noticing its rubbery texture as it slid down his throat.

He did know. And the last person who'd thought he was human had been punished in the most *in*humane way possible. Like Veronica would be punished, once she'd helped him get what he wanted. And he did *not* care. Yes, he wanted to do the exact thing she'd said he did. He wanted to tear aside her dress. Slice through her underwear. Gnash his teeth into her flesh and drive himself deep into her. Caring wasn't a part of the fucking equation. But the kiss... the sweet taste of her... he couldn't shake it off.

And that was the reason Ellis didn't see it coming. It was why he didn't notice that the nervous man at the end of his table had disappeared. It was why the unusual hush that hung over the so-called cafeteria didn't give him pause. It was why, when someone bumped him from behind and sent a green pea rolling off his tray, he didn't clue in that it was a targeted attack, and why his defensive reaction came too late.

A set of fingers pressed to his windpipe, expertly cutting off his air supply and his ability to speak. At the same time, a pair of hands took hold of his arms and secured them behind his back. A tenth of a second later brought an excruciating pain under his left-side ribcage. It was only then that Ellis caught up. They'd fucking *shanked* him.

Belatedly, he tried to fend off the attackers by throwing an elbow, but the agony in his side rendered the attempt futile.

"Steeler wants to tell you you're welcome," said a voice near his ear as the hands released him.

Steeler, his mind echoed through the blinding stab that shot across his abdomen.

If he hadn't been in the process of toppling from the bench, Ellis might've laughed. A retaliation move sent on behalf of an undercover cop. He could hardly believe it. These dumbass lackeys were so clueless it was almost embarrassing. Funny as all hell. A laugh, though, didn't come. The only sound that made its way out was a gurgle, and that was quickly cut short by the smack of his body hitting the concrete floor, face first.

"Fuck," he groaned.

Fuzz coated the edges of his vision. The roar in his skull was immediate, and it was compounded by the blare of the overhead speakers, coming to life as they played a recorded command for the prisoners to go back to their cells. The words ended in a crackle, and then came a countdown from thirty that seemed to get louder with each number.

A conditioned part of Ellis's brain told him he should be following the instructions, too. He even made a weakened attempt to do so. He shifted on the ground, but the movement rewarded him with the feel of something sticky and wet underneath him. Through the haze, he realized that it was his own blood.

And you thought you were fucked before.

"Shut up," he replied, his eyes closing.

This was a different kind of fuckery—the type that could derail everything he'd been working toward since meeting Veronica Hollister.

The countdown on the speakers reached one, and the blast of an airhorn-like alarm followed, lasting far too long. Then came a moment of silence before an unknown male voice broke it.

"Mr. Black? Ellis? Can you hear me?"

Another wave of dizziness hit Ellis. He tried to answer, but as firm as the words were in his mind—*Of course I can fucking hear you. If you were any closer, I'd expect your hand to be down my pants*—he couldn't force them out of his mouth. He ordered his eyes to open. That didn't work either.

"Mr. Black?" the man repeated. "I need you to—Jesus. Nope. Nope! That's not happening on my watch. Guys! Bring that stretcher over here. We need to get Mr. Black to the infirmary right this second."

The infirmary.

A new idea—a modification to his plan—slid into place. With it, came calmness. In his head, Ellis smiled. The idiots on the other end of the shiv had given him a way to un-fuck himself.

41
Three Months, Eight Days Before Escape

The Preacher's Daughter

Roni was in a dream. She knew it because it was the same dream she'd had every night since the day, more than a month ago now, she'd let Ellis kiss her. In the dream, she clawed at her own neck, trying desperately to catch a breath that wouldn't come. Invisible hands held her throat closed. Ellis's. Her father's. She couldn't be sure. Both, maybe. And she tried desperately to wake from it. She was lucid enough that it ought to have been possible. Instead, she was stuck. But dreaming or awake, there was darkness on either side. Sliding back into sleep would let the suffocation win. She would be choked out, over and over in a never-ending cycle. And giving in to full consciousness was almost worse. Because it would mean being in the world where she'd kissed a man guilty of murdering and raping his sister. There was no reprieve from that, either. But in the end, it was the latter that won out.

Roni's eyes opened. The invisible hands lost their hold, and nausea set in. She rolled to her side, propped herself up onto her elbow, and threw up into the bucket at the side of her bed. The last four nights had taught her that she wouldn't make it to the bathroom in time. With her stomach emptied, she sank back. She wondered when this feeling would subside. If it ever would. She couldn't undo what had been done. What *she* had done. But she wasn't prepared to face it, either. What terrible things would she find out about herself if she did?

Don't you want *to know, Nic?* said Ellis in her head.

"No," she replied aloud. "I don't think I do."

She wasn't expecting a response of any sort. But she got one anyway.

"You need something, baby girl?" said a sleep-roughened voice.

She sat up so fast that the room wobbled, as did the figure in her doorframe. For a terrible, wild second, she thought Ellis had escaped and come to claim her. Then sense kicked in. It was her father.

"Dad?" she said.

"Expecting someone else?" he replied.

He was clad in his boxer shorts. His skinny shoulders were hunched over in their usual way, giving the illusion that he was weak. Making his words sound less threatening than they were. But his eyes gave away the truth. They were sharp. Mean. They held Roni for a second before sliding to the bucket.

"Sins manifest themselves in physical ways," he said. "Have you been sinning?"

She was thankful that the dark covered the heat in her face. It wasn't close to the first time her father had asked this particular question. But it was the first time she'd felt like maybe she ought to answer in the affirmative.

"It's still just this flu," she stated hollowly.

"Then I guess you don't want to hear about your boyfriend."

"About my—"

He moved so quickly that Roni didn't have a second to process what was happening. His hand slammed to her shoulder, and his bare foot hit her knee with so much force that she screamed. The sound pierced the air and filled her mind with images of shattering glass. It was an awful sound, and she wanted to cringe away from the self-created noise. But it didn't deter her father from coming at her again.

"I knew it." One of his heels landed on her stomach, and she flew backward against her nightstand. "I knew, the second I heard that boy's name. *Ellis Black*. Dirty scumbag." A palm met the side of her head, drawing a cry. "He's had his hands on you. A whore. Just like your lying mother." Spital flew from his mouth. "I've been waiting all these years to see if the lust would take you. If the devil was in you, like it was with her." His long, grizzled fingers closed on her forearm, squeezing. "And now I have my proof."

She tried to plead with him to stop. To ask him what he meant and beg for forgiveness. But she was shaking too hard to form the words. And the destruction had extended to her surroundings. The bucket had been upended, the mess spreading over the floor. Her lamp was broken. Her mattress had fallen from its frame. For some reason, the ruination of her personal space hurt almost as much as the bruising blows.

So fight back, Nic, said imaginary Ellis. *Fight the fuck* back.

And for a moment, she thought she might muster up some counterattack. But the idea was fleeting. Her father already had the upper hand, and his fury was fueling his strength all the more. He yanked her hard across the floor, then into the hallway, punctuating the violence with further insults.

Slut.

Jezebel.

Ingrate.

Roni could barely hear them over the sound of her own pounding heart. This was bad. The worst it'd been. And she didn't know what to do. So she did nothing.

Down the stairs, he dragged her, unheeding of the way her body bounced and banged along.

Through the living room, he pulled her, ignoring it when her head smacked the couch and she whimpered.

Out the front door, he hauled her, seemingly indifferent to the freezing cold rain.

He kept going. And going. Across the yard. Over the garden. Past the large oak tree that was once home to Roni's childhood swing. He forced her—tripping and stumbling—all the way to the shed, where he finally stopped. But he didn't let her go. Instead, he flung open the door, then shoved her inside. She hit the wooden floor, and as it cracked and splintered under the impact, her father spoke in a cold voice.

"If your boyfriend dies without God's forgiveness..." he said. "Then that's on your soul."

Roni's heart dropped, and her own suffering slipped away long enough for her to utter a reply. "Wh-what?"

"Someone tried to kill him. Gutted him, and he probably deserved it."

"I don't understand."

"Well, you probably should. Because Ellis Black has *you* listed as his next of kin."

He started to close the door, and Roni realized what his intention was.

"No, Dad. Please don't."

"This is what I should've done with your mother," he said. "Maybe if I had, she would've learned a lesson. And maybe you wouldn't have had such a bad example to follow."

Tears sprung up, but before they could make their way out, the door slammed shut, enveloping Roni in darkness. She wanted to scream. To pound on the walls. It would do no good.

There was no one near enough to hear her.

42

Ten Years Earlier
Twenty Hours Before Arrest

The Policeman

lip paused, glanced over his shoulder, and peered into the night, searching for watchful eyes. He was in deep now. Both in the forest, and in too far to look back. Some time ago, he'd crossed the threshold onto the Black property, and he wasn't entirely convinced that he wasn't being followed. In fact, he was kind of sure someone was tailing him. He half-suspected it might be Cliff. After all, he didn't know how far the other man would go to ensure he followed orders.

Order. Like the guy has any real *authority,* Flip scoffed.

He pushed on, mentally cursing everything that surrounded the current moment. The need for proof. The fact that he had to prod the other Meridian officers to do their job because they thought he wasn't good enough to trust. The more time that passed, the more it bit at him. Who had they called out to investigate the dropped 9-1-1 calls? Who had been on the force the longest? Not Cliff. Not even Captain Dax had been there are long as Flip. What made them so deserving of promotion and prestige?

Nothing. Not a damn thing.

Neither of the other two men had ever solved a major crime. But maybe that was because they ignored anything more striking than a jaywalker. This thing with the Blacks wasn't going to stay buried. Flip had to get ahead of it. Had to be the one to provide the solution. Preferably in a tidy package. If that meant slogging his way through the woods like this—no uniform, pilfered weapon in tow—then so be it.

He was so enmeshed in his internal mutterings that he very nearly missed the shadowy movement in front of him. Just in time, he stopped. There, in the woods, was a human form. Leaned against a tree. Hunched over a little. But unmistakable.

Ellis Black.

Eyes narrowed, Flip slid behind a tree to observe. Right away, the boy's rough voice carried out.

"I see you, Officer Farriday. No need to hide from me."

Flip didn't correct him to constable. He wasn't there to nitpick. Or start a fight. He was there for evidence. He stepped out from the failed attempt at cover with his hands lifted in a show of good faith.

"What are you doing out here at this time, son?" he asked.

"Could ask you the same," the kid replied, ornery as ever.

"I'm here because I'm concerned."

"Oh, yeah? What're you concerned about? Making your quota for hassling delinquents?"

Flip didn't address the sarcasm. "Is your mom still AWOL?"

The boy pulled out a cigarette and lit it. "Yeah. And before you ask, my dad's still dead, too."

"And your sister?"

"What about her?"

"Do you know where she is, Ellis?"

"Do *you*, Flip?"

"When did you first notice she was missing?"

"Did I say she was missing, Officer?" The boy took a long drag of his smoke and offered a glittering smile.

If there was ever a kid with a bigger chip on his shoulder, Flip hadn't met him. "Let's just say, hypothetically, that she isn't home."

"Is that when you decided to go inside our house and help yourself to a look around?"

"It's part of my job to investigate suspected crimes."

"And what is it that you suspect happened?" Ellis asked. "Because if you think something happened to my sister, you're probably obligated to tell me."

"I'm more interested in what you know about that," Flip stated.

"I've got nothing to say."

"Are you sure? What about if I tell you I'd like to end the grace period I gave you, and I send a team of cops up here? Have you got something to say then?"

"Should probably try social services instead. From what I hear, your boss isn't interested in me."

Flip narrowed his eyes. "How do you know what my boss is and isn't interested in?"

Ellis puffed away for a second before answering. "I don't. Well. I *didn't*. But I made a good guess, didn't I?"

"Has anyone ever told you that you're too smart for your own good, kid?"

"All the time. They say it'll get me in trouble one day. So far, all it's done is helped me outsmart douche canoes like you cops."

"You little—" Flip stopped himself before he could say something he regretted.

Ellis smiled again. "I'm a little shit. A little bastard. A thorn in the fucking side of Meridian at large. And if you don't have anything to tell me about my sister, then I'm going to ask you to leave. This *is* still our property."

"It might be easier for you in the long run if you tell me what you know."

"And do your job for you? Not a chance. You have a nice night, Officer."

"I'll be seeing you soon, Mr. Black," Flip replied.

He'd get what he needed. Soon. And the kid wouldn't know what hit him.

43
Fifty Hours After Escape

The Preacher's Daughter

Veronica froze with her hand midway to the box she was packing. Holding the rest of her body still so as not to make a noise, she shifted her eyes to the partially opened window and listened. No sound carried in. But she was sure she'd heard a rustle seconds earlier.

You're being paranoid, she told herself. *It was probably a squirrel.*

She let out a small, almost silent sigh. It was the fourth time in the last half-hour that she'd stopped what she was doing because of some phantom noise. It was also the fourth time nothing had come of it. And truthfully, even if it *wasn't* nothing, Veronica had no reason to worry. Or at least not any more reason than she'd had for the last two days. Her newest bodyguard was waiting outside in his car, and he'd been so eager that it had sounded like he *wanted* something to go wrong.

So why am I still not convinced that everything is fine? Veronica answered the thought as quickly as it came. *You mean other than the fact that Ellis has proven again and again that he can slip by every officer on the force??*

She remained unmoving, ears on alert. A good minute or so passed before she finally convinced herself to get back to the task. Sighing again, she set the folded T-shirt into the box and rested her hand on top of the growing pile of clothes. They were her father's. A lifetime of pants and tops. All stuff she didn't actually have to pack up because her sale agreement stipulated that she could leave the house as it was, contents included. Yet here she was, doing it anyway.

It'd started out as a practical thing. After burning the secret stash of suggestive pictures, she'd been concerned that somehow the new owner would accidentally stumble upon something more devious than pornography. What, Veronica didn't know. And she hadn't wanted someone else to find out before she did. But as she'd sorted the items, picking through her father's closet and drawers, the search morphed into a personal one. An angry one. What else had he been hiding from her? What other deviances had he been projecting onto her?

When her search turned up nothing, it hadn't been relief that had settled in. It was grief. The first mark of sadness she'd truly let herself acknowledge since her father's death. Since his murder. And while she wasn't going to deny that he'd often made her life a terrible and scary place to be, he'd also been the only parent she'd really known. It was okay for her to feel grief. But the more things she boxed up, the better she felt. It was cathartic. And it offered a sense of closure. Which made her keep going. In fact, the T-shirt she'd just folded marked the last of his clothes, and it was time to move on to something else.

Maybe I'll do his books next, she thought, closing the box's lid.

It wasn't an entirely unappealing idea. But as she reached for the packing tape, a new noise carried through the window. This one was not only definite; it was also recognizable—the sound of a car approaching. Veronica's heart automatically sped up, and she ordered herself to stay calm. No one who was trying to sneak up to the property would do so with an engine that loud. And it *was* loud. Not in a sports car kind of way, but rather in a missing a muffler kind of way.

It could be a reporter, she reasoned.

A few had tried to contact her. Except she couldn't imagine a member of the press flying through the hills in an old beater, which was what the continuing rev brought to mind.

Deciding she had to take a look for herself, Veronica slowly stood and crept over to the window. She sucked in a small breath, then leaned in to steal a peek. For a moment, the darkness surprised her. She hadn't realized how late it had gotten. The sun had thoroughly set now, and clouds covered the moon. But it worked in her favor, as did her position on the second floor, because it meant the flash of headlights in the distance was easily visible. Yes, the noisy car was definitely headed her way.

Tension ramping, she watched the vehicle get closer and closer. She wasn't sure what—if anything—she ought to do about it, and when it neared the end of her long driveway, she hazarded a glance toward the squad car that sat a dozen feet from her porch. The policeman inside *had* to be hearing what she was hearing. Any second now, he'd be able to see the headlights, too.

C'mon, c'mon, Veronica willed.

Finally—just as the approaching car got to the final little hill before the house—she saw the constable's door swing open. His thick legs appeared first, followed by his stocky body. In line with the eagerness she'd noted earlier, his hand rested beside his weapon as he squared his body into a waiting stance.

Veronica waited, watching the other vehicle slow as it got near. Its appearance was exactly as she'd pictured. An indiscernible color marked with rust. A cracked front windshield. The chug emanating from under the warped hood was practically a noise violation, and it drowned out any hope of hearing anything else as it coasted to a stop past the waiting officer.

Veronica was pretty sure someone opened the door and got out, but the porch's overhang blocked her view of the driver. She leaned forward a bit more and shifted to try and get a better vantage. It was to no avail. If she wanted to see properly, she was going to need to move. But she didn't get a step away from the window before the too-loud engine revved, the headlights flashed, and the vehicle disappeared with as much gusto as it had arrived.

What just happened?

A half dozen unpleasant scenarios played through Veronica's head. Most—maybe all—ended with the cop lying on the ground, staring dead-eyed at the sky. So when a firm *tap-tap-tap* sounded on her front door a second later, she jumped. She forced herself to make her way out of the room and down the stairs, but she couldn't quite muster up the courage to actually respond to the knock.

"Ms. Hollister?" said a muffled voice.

It was the policeman, alive and well. He knocked again, and Veronica expelled a breath.

"Coming!" she called.

She hurried to the door, where she paused to quickly compose herself, then opened it with a polite smile. The cop was waiting on the other side with a pizza box balanced on one hand. The smell of garlic and cheese wafted into the house, and Veronica's mouth watered as she greeted the uniformed man.

"Thank you," she said.

He shrugged and smiled. "Not a problem. But you might want to give me a warning next time. I just about dropped the poor kid before I spotted the food."

"I didn't—" Veronica stopped herself before she could admit she wasn't the one who placed the order.

"What?" A little frown dimpled the cop's forehead.

She didn't immediately answer. There was no reason not to tell him she hadn't placed the pizza order. And there were probably a dozen good reasons *to* tell him. But something made her keep it to herself. She cleared her throat.

"I didn't expect you to pay for it," she said lamely.

His frown only deepened. "Kid told me you prepaid. Tip, too."

Veronica's face warmed. "Oh. Right. Sorry. I clearly need the food."

"No worries. Here you go." He held out the box. "Checked the inside to be sure it was copacetic. Looks delicious."

Gingerly, she took it. "Do you want a slice?"

The stout man shook his head and patted his stomach. "Wife keeps me too well fed already. But you enjoy that."

"I will."

He nodded. And as he turned away, Veronica bit her lip.

You really should tell him.

But she didn't. She closed the door and watched through the window as he walked back to his car. When he was done climbing in, she carried the pizza box over to the dining room table. Her hands shook with nerves, but she managed to flip it open.

For a minute, all she saw was the pizza. Double pepperoni and light cheese. Her favorite.

She stared and stared, certain there must be a trick. But it wasn't until the steam wore off and the inside of the box took on a wavy appearance that she realized what it was. An extra layer of brown paper had been taped to the underside of the cardboard lid.

Chest burning, she peeled it back. And there it was. A message.

HE'S WATCHING YOU, it read in Ellis's familiar block lettering. *BE A GOOD GIRL AND EAT YOUR PIZZA.*

Veronica swallowed. Her skin crawled. And she could've sworn the words made it real; she could feel unseen eyes on her, and a flash of movement from outside drew her attention. What was it? Was someone actually there?

Silently, she counted to ten, waiting for another sign that there was something more than her imagination lurking in the shadows of her yard. Stillness reigned. But suddenly, she wasn't hungry at all.

243

44
Fifty Hours After Escape

The Policeman

Farriday slunk backward, mentally cursing himself for taking a couple of steps too far out of the trees. Veronica's silhouette stayed in the front window, unmoving.

In turn, he stayed still, too.

C'mon, he urged silently. *Chalk up whatever you saw to an overactive imagination.*

Until a minute ago, he'd barely caught a glimpse of the girl. A flash by the window now and then. Nothing more. But when she'd opened the door for the on-duty cop, Farriday had seen the necklace. It had caught the glow of the porch light and sent out an unmistakable sparkle of blue. For a second, he'd forgotten his need to stay hidden. He'd automatically moved closer. He couldn't help himself. After all, it was the necklace that had brought him here.

Since the second he'd spied the pendant resting at the base of Veronica's throat, the *why* and the *how* of its presence had been eating him up. He didn't believe it had come to her randomly. Maybe a friend *had* picked it up. But it would be the world's biggest coincidence to have acquired that exact piece of jewelry. And if he trusted his gut—which he did—then he had to conclude that the necklace had come from Ellis. Somehow. Some way.

His mind drifted to the past in search of a hint.

He remembered perfectly well how the public defender had harped on the missing chain. At the time, it hadn't mattered to the overzealous lawyer that Ellis Black had pleaded guilty. It was like the words on the written confession meant nothing to the man. He'd insisted that the necklace had been taken by the "real" killer. Plucked from Emily Black's body and hidden away for some unknown reason. Forensics, probably. But Farriday was the one who'd noticed it was missing in the first place, and he'd thought it was ridiculous nitpicking. Why obsess over such a minute detail, when there was a mountain of evidence already in existence?

Farriday almost wished he could call the lawyer now. He'd open the conversation by asking if the other man still believed Ellis wasn't the murderer. He'd follow that up by asking if the guy also still believed the actual killer had taken the necklace and stashed it. Then he'd whip out this little tidbit. The part where the chain was not only found, but found around the neck of the very same woman whom Ellis had used in his escape plan.

Put that in your pipe, you windbag, he thought.

Farriday's amusement faded quickly. Veronica wasn't standing in the window anymore, but she was seated at the dining room table—a position where she could still easily see him if she looked in just the right spot at just the right moment.

Or the wrong *moment, as far as things go for me.*

His fingers tried to strum his thigh as he continued to wait where he was, and he ordered them to hold still. He couldn't afford to lose focus on the present. If the girl spotted him— or decided she'd seen something worth looking into— then two hours of waiting and prep would be wasted. Not only that, but he'd also have to come up with a good excuse for his appearance as well as his presence. Something he wasn't sure he could do.

Head to toe, he was dressed in army green. He'd traded in

his Meridian PD ballcap for a camouflage fisherman's hat, and his face and neck were slathered with grease paint in shades designed to blend in with the foliage. There wasn't exactly a reasonable explanation for slinking around a woman's property geared up the way he was at the moment.

Might be able to pass it off as going the extra mile to protect her from Ellis, he told himself as he kept a steady eye on the window.

It was an empty self-reassurance. The cop he'd appointed to guard the house—Constable Roberts—would never buy it, even if Veronica could be convinced. And Farriday had made an effort to avoid his subordinates finding out about this little side endeavor by carefully timing his arrival with the shift change between Roberts and the man who'd been there before him. He needed to keep *not* getting caught. Which meant sticking with the plan of maintaining his distance, being patient, and staying out of sight. No more attempts to get a better look at what was going on inside. He was there *because* of the necklace, but he wasn't there *for* the necklace. The jewelry was just the catalyst for his epiphany, which had hit Farriday while he was eating a sandwich. He'd almost choked on his tuna. Because it was so obvious. He was still kicking himself for not seeing it before.

The necklace had found its way here, to Veronica. So had Emily Black's dress. The cross and its ribbons were within walking distance from this house. Of course they were all connected to—provided by—Ellis, and they all related back to his case. But that wasn't the takeaway. The key here was the fact that in order to time things perfectly, the escaped man would have to know where Veronica was. He was keeping tabs on her. *Physical* tabs. The easiest, most logical place to do that was at her home. Heck, Ellis might be holed up somewhere very close. In shooting distance, maybe. Either way—sooner or later—he would show himself.

Farriday watched as Veronica at last stood up. She barely even paused at the window before flicking out the light. Five minutes more, and *all* the lights were out. The only glow came from Constable Roberts' squad car, and that was just about perfect for illuminating the space around the house.

Farriday let his eyes travel the perimeter. What would he do if he were in Ellis's shoes? Avoiding detection was clearly no challenge to the man. So what was the next item on the agenda? Presumably to wait until he was sure that the girl was asleep, then sneak up for a peep. He had no problem picturing it. The big man standing in the corner, a hulking shadow. Veronica, blissfully ignorant of the danger, tucked into her bed, sweet and vulnerable.

Unconsciously, Farriday took a small step forward, but the crack of a branch behind him made him spin. He squinted into the dark. For a second, he didn't see anything. Then a faint white glow bobbed in the distance, flickering in and out. It looked as though someone was moving through the woods with a flashlight.

And there's only one person who'd be doing that out here at this time of night, isn't there?

"I've got you now, haven't I, Mr. Black?" he whispered.

Feeling triumphant, he cast a glance over his shoulder toward the house, then slid deeper into the trees. He moved as fast as he dared, working to close the gap between himself and the other man while also maintaining his stealth. For five minutes, he was secure in his success. The light bounced steadily but never picked up speed. The distance between it and him narrowed. Then, abruptly, his target vanished.

Farriday stopped and squinted again, expecting the light to reappear at any second. It didn't. He turned his head in search of it. Where had it gone? And more importantly, where had the man carrying it gone?

Farriday turned again, this time with his whole body. There was nothing to see. Almost literally. Aside from the closest trees and the barest sprinkle of stars overhead, his surroundings were a wall of shadows. He flexed his fingers in irritation. The last thing he wanted was to give up and turn back. But his only other option was to take a wild guess at which direction Ellis had gone.

Might be worth a shot to at least try.

Nodding to himself, he lifted his foot. His booted toe immediately caught a root and sent him to the ground, chin first.

"Or not worth it at all," he muttered, spitting out a mouthful of dirt.

He grabbed hold of the nearest tree trunk and started to stand. He stopped on one knee. Right in from of him was a campsite, maybe ten feet in diameter. A circle of stones had been set up as a firepit on one side, and a triangular lean-to sat on the other. The remnants of the bushes that had been cleared to create the spot were spread wide around the edges of the camp, and despite the dark, Farriday could tell it'd been done on purpose. He imagined that even in daylight, the spot would be hard to notice unless someone was looking for it.

"Pretty clever, aren't you Ellis?" he said, smiling. "But not quite clever enough."

45
Three Months, Seven Days Before Escape

The Preacher's Daughter

Roni drew her knees up to her chin and wrapped her arms around her bent legs. The movement was agonizing. It was also all she'd managed to do since the ache in her head had subsided enough to think at all. Now, she almost regretted the restoration of her cognitive abilities.

She'd already been inside for how long? How many hours? Had a whole day passed? She had no way to tell. There was no light. No sense of time.

She was scraped, bruised, and thoroughly battered, that much was for certain. And cold. So cold. But the idea of taking a more specific inventory of her injuries scared her, so she focused instead on really looking at her surroundings. As she did, it struck her that the space wasn't unlike the one where Ellis had spent the last decade. Six by eight. Cold and impersonal. Roni could practically feel the walls tightening around her. A thread of renewed fear worked its way through her veins. What if she died in here, like Ellis might die in *his* prison?

Ellis might be dying.

The thought shouldn't have been a surprise. It was the reason she was in there. But for some reason, it hit her anyway. And Roni felt guilty. She felt responsible for *his* injury. As she huddled in the corner of the shed, trying to fend off the cold and the damp, her mind insisted it was somehow her fault.

You could've refused to go back after the very first session, she told herself as yet another shiver wracked her body. *You didn't have to confront him about tricking you into believing he was Bobby Lines.*

She tried hard to be reasonable. She didn't know why someone had attacked Ellis. There were probably a hundred different things that could've led to violence in the prison. And what were the chances that her personal interaction with Ellis was *the* thing, in this case? Pretty much zero.

But he put me down as next of kin.

And that pricked at her.

"Why would he d-d-do that?" she whispered through her chattering teeth.

She had no answer. But she knew she needed one. More than that. She had a *right* to one.

"D-d-don't I?"

As if in reply, a gust of wind slapped hard against the exterior of the shed, making it shake. Was Mother Nature agreeing with her, or was the increasingly inclement weather a sign that she ought to suffer her punishment without protest?

She eyed the door. Whether her father had locked it wasn't a question. Even though she'd been crying too hard to hear him do it, she knew he wouldn't have left her with a way out. But there had to be an alternative. She just had to find it. With a shuddering breath, she released her knees and made herself get up off the floor. Her muscles—maybe her bones— screamed in response, but she didn't let the pain win. The extent of her hurt was only going to grow.

Swallowing back a whimper, she examined the wood sides of the shed in search of a weak spot. The construction was old but solid. Built by hand by some past owner, in a time before prefab was a thing. Her father had told her about it many times, sounding as proud as if he was the one responsible for the good craftsmanship. Airtight. Practically bulletproof.

That's what he'd said. From what Roni could see, it almost appeared to be true. There were no cracks. No splits. And despite the chill and the howl, there was no palpable breeze creeping through the boards, either. She looked up at the underside of the roof. No gaps caught her eye.

"But there has to be some way."

The idea that there might not be... It wasn't something she wanted to consider.

Then, quite abruptly, she remembered. The shed was solid. But it wasn't on solid ground. It'd been constructed in pier and beam style in order to compensate for the uneven terrain below. It was only two feet in the tallest spot. But that spot exited out the back of the shed. So if she could break her way through the floor... "I can crawl out."

Roni dropped to her knees. New adrenaline took hold, and her pain abated. She crawled along until she found the spot that had split when she'd landed. Mentally, she marked it. Then she moved away from it, tap-tap-tapping until she heard a hollow sound.

There. She leaned down, pressed her ear to the floorboards, and tapped again. *Yes.*

It had to be the spot. There were roughly three feet between it and the broken piece of flooring. It wasn't perfect, but it was about as close as she could hope for. Sitting up, she swung a look around in search of something she could use to pry up the damaged boards so the two points could be connected to provide an escape route. A plastic milk crate— which sat in one corner of the shed—drew her eye.

Dad's gardening tools, she recalled.

Bubbling with anticipatory triumph, Roni shuffled toward the container. She reached in and pulled out a trowel, then moved back to the splintered section of wood and got to work. It wasn't easy. It wasn't particularly quick. She cut herself more than once, and she ripped back a pinkie fingernail, and she cried a little more.

"You can do this," she said to herself as she stared into the beginning of the hole she'd created. "You'll be out before you can even think about claustrophobia."

She drew in a breath and pressed her feet to the ground between the wood slats. It was soft. Wet. Unpleasant. A sick feeling welled up in her stomach at the thought of dipping the rest of her body into it. She ordered herself to go in anyway.

Taking a deeper breath, she slid into the space and wriggled toward the fresh air. The mud squelched around her. She swore she could feel the weight of the structure pressing down on her. But in less than two minutes, she felt the rain on her feet instead. Thirty seconds after that, she was pulling herself up from the ground and wiping dirt from her face. She didn't waste a single second after that. She tossed a single glance toward the house, and then she ran, not pausing or looking back once. If her father had seen her go—if he was going to come after her—then she didn't want to know.

By the time she reached the edge of their property, she was breathless. She ached everywhere. Her freedom, though, made it worth it. She wasn't even sure if the tears that streamed down her face were from the pain and exertion, or if they were made of relief. Most likely the latter.

It took an eon, but at last, she reached the main road. The sound of an approaching car reached her almost immediately, and she stumbled out, arms waving. The car slowed, then sped up again and kept going. A second car did the same. A few minutes passed, and then a truck zipped by, sending a spray of water over Roni. Her hope deflated.

Can you blame them for not stopping? said a little voice in her head. *You're a mess, and you wouldn't stop for yourself, either.* A sob threatened. *What am I going to do?*

She couldn't go back and face her father. She thought he might actually kill her if he found out she'd escaped. At the very least, he'd find a way to punish her. Maybe permanently. But the thought of voluntarily getting back into the shed made her throat constrict.

"I can't."

Her shoulders sagged, hopelessness weighing them down. She could barely lift her head as yet another vehicle— a minivan this time—approached. But when it slowed, a tiny spark ignited in her chest.

Please, please.

And sure enough, the minivan came to a coasting stop a few feet in front of her position.

Heart jumping, Roni jogged toward it. The driver's side window opened, and when she caught sight of the man sitting inside, recognition clicked.

"You're the tow truck driver," she said.

"Stan," he replied. "And you're... I'm sorry. I know I should remember your name, but I don't."

"Nic." Her face heated as soon as she realized what she'd said.

Ellis responded in her head, too, sounding amused. *Really?*

She brushed off her subconscious, straightened her shoulders, and corrected herself in a firmer voice. "Veronica Hollister."

Stan looked at her like he was trying not to frown.

"Right. Veronica. Did you break down again?"

"No. I just need a ride."

"I can do that. Hop in and give me your address."

"No." She said it too quickly, and now the tow truck driver did frown.

"Sorry?" he said.

"I actually need to get to the prison."

"The prison?"

She gritted her teeth to keep from screaming. "My friend might be dying."

"Your—"

"Please."

"Shit. Yeah, okay. I can get you there."

Roni let relief sweep through her as she walked around to the other side of the van to climb in and fasten her seatbelt. But tension was quick to follow. She could feel the curiosity in the glances Stan shot toward her every few seconds. She couldn't blame him. The circumstances begged for more information. After a minute of increasingly awkward silence, Roni tipped her head toward her window and closed her eyes so as not to invite any conversation. Thankfully, Stan didn't push it. He just turned the radio up a little and said nothing until they pulled into the parking lot at Meridian Penitentiary.

"Here we are," he announced as he brought the van to a halt almost directly in front of the gates.

"Thank you, Stan," she said, flinging open the door with undisguised relief. "A lot."

"Yeah, no problem. Hang on a sec, okay?" He reached into the backseat, pulled out a smallish canvas bag, and held it in her direction. "Here."

Hesitantly, Roni took it. "What is this?"

"Clothes," he replied. "My wife's a nurse, and she always keeps something to change into."

His wife?

Roni's eyes sought his ring finger. It was bare. Just like she'd remembered. It made his kindness so ironic that she almost wanted to laugh. She might've, if not for the fact that there was a real woman on the other end of the tow truck driver's duplicity.

"Take it," Stan added. "Please. It's probably not a great idea to go into the prison looking like that."

She glanced down, belatedly realizing that her state was far more than bedraggled; it was downright scandalous. Her pale blue nightgown was a second skin.

Her face flushed. "Thank you. Again."

"I hope your friend pulls through."

"Me, too."

She hopped out, closed the door, and clutched the bag to her chest until Stan and his minivan disappeared into the rain.

46

Three Months, Seven Days Before Escape

The Preacher's Daughter

The clothes supplied by the tow truck driver consisted of a pair of jeans, a pale blue t-shirt, and a pair of ballet flats. With the exception of the shoes, which were probably half a size too big, everything fit Roni perfectly. They were also clean and dry. Two things she was extremely grateful for as she huddled under the scant awning and pressed the buzzer on the after-hours gate for the second time. The rain hadn't abated at all, and now a wind had joined it. It wasn't getting any warmer, either, and Roni was starting to wonder if anyone was actually monitoring the entrance. But as she lifted her finger to press the button a third time, a disembodied, male voice carried out from some invisible speaker.

"Can I help you?" said the unseen man.

"It's Veronica Hollister," Roni replied, knowing she ought to work on sounding calm and professional. "You guys called me about Ellis Black. Someone talked to my dad?"

"Hang on."

A feedback noise cut through the air then went silent. Another two or more minutes ticked by before the man spoke again.

"I'll buzz you through the gate and send somebody out to let you into the building," he told her.

Roni shifted from foot to foot, shivering. When the gate clicked, she could barely stop herself from flinging it open and running to the relative cover of the front steps. She was glad the guard appeared almost instantly. And she was gladder still that it was someone she recognized, and who she knew would be understanding. If it'd been one of the less kind guards, she might not have been able to hold it together.

"H-h-hi, Rodrigo," she said through chattering teeth.

"Ms. Hollister." The sixty-something guard swept his gaze over her. "Aside from the obvious stuff regarding Ellis... is everything okay?"

"It's a long st-st-story, Rodrigo," Roni replied. "I'm h-here for Ellis. But I f-f-forgot my I.D."

His brow wrinkled. "Well, under the circumstances, we'll forgo a few formalities. Let's get in out of the cold, shall we?"

She nodded and followed him inside. He guided her quickly to an area of the prison she hadn't been to before, taking the halls with sure turns. She didn't complain about the clipped pace. At least it got her blood flowing enough to drive away the chill.

"Your guy is in rough shape," Rodrigo said as they walked. "Took a knife to the gut and bled pretty fierce. Pierced a few things. I won't gross you out with the details. Multiple surgeries. Gotta say, though... he's about as lucky as someone can get under the circumstances. Wouldn't have made it if he'd had to be lifted out. But there was a surgeon here already, doing an in-house consult. Stabilized him long enough to pull in the needed medical personnel to do what had to be done to save his life. Damn lucky we're all but full-service in the healthcare side of Meridian Pen, too. Speaking of which..." He gestured to the door they'd reached. "Here we are."

Roni's stomach fluttered nervously, and she didn't step forward as Rodrigo swiped his keycard along the reader. She held back as the door opened. She wanted to ask him if he thought Ellis was going to pull through. But she was afraid of the answer.

"Change your mind?" asked the guard after a few seconds of stillness.

Roni swallowed and made herself shake her head. "No. I'm coming."

It still took some effort to follow the uniformed man into the hallway, but when she did, it was almost like entering a different place. It smelled like a hospital. It *looked* like a hospital. Even the slightly plump nurse who sat behind the desk gave off a non-prison vibe. She pushed her glasses up on her nose, tightened her gray-speckled ponytail, and smiled a genuine smile

"Evening, Rodrigo," said the other woman.

"Evening, Lorraine." The guard tipped his head. "I've got Mr. Black's guest here."

The nurse turned her smile in Roni's direction. "Hi there, sweetheart. Glad you were able to make it in."

"Me, too." Roni said it with more vigor than she meant to, but if the nurse noticed, she didn't comment.

"Are you ready to see your husband?" she asked instead.

A blush crept up. "He's not my husband."

"He's not?"

"No."

"I was sure I heard—well, never mind."

Rodrigo cleared his throat. "I'll be outside the doors if you need me."

"Thanks, hun," said the nurse.

She jotted something down on the paper in front of her, then rolled back her chair and indicated that Roni should follow her. She led the way past two closed doors and stopped in front of an open one.

"This is him," she said. "He's sedated, but I'm sure he'll know you're here."

Something in her tone made Roni think she still didn't quite believe that she and Ellis weren't married.

"We aren't in a romantic relationship," Roni stated.

"You don't have to worry," Lorraine said. "I'm way past the point in my career that I'm judging. Neither rhyme nor reason applies in these places. Plenty of women find themselves on the other end of an inmate's wedding vows."

Roni shook her head. "We're not involved, I swear. I'm his..."

His what?

Spiritual advisor was what she would've said a month ago. Now, it seemed off. But next of kin was a little more than she wanted to commit to. Her mouth opened, then closed. A heartbeat later, a pager on the nurse's belt went off, saving Roni from having to come up with an answer.

"Dammit," said the other woman as she read the little screen. "Emergency in one of the wards. I've got to go, but I'll let Rodrigo know to watch the door."

Roni glanced toward the room where Ellis's still form lay waiting. She could see the bumps made by his feet under the blanket, and she could hear the gentle beep of some piece of machinery. Her heart sped up.

"Is it okay that we'll be sort of...alone?" she asked.

"Yep. He's secured, and it's doubtful that he'll be awake anytime soon." The nurse paused. "Unless *you're* not comfortable?"

"No, I'll be fine.

The pager dinged again.

"I heard you the first time," the other woman grumbled before sending a raised eyebrow in Roni's direction. "Just remember that conjugal visits aren't permitted in the infirmary."

Roni's face flamed. She spluttered to find a retort, but the nurse was already out the door. Roni stared after her. Part of her wanted to chase down Lorraine and protest a little more heartily. What kind of woman did the nurse think she was? But her conscience spoke up, stopping her from moving.

She thinks you're the kind who kisses a man like Ellis, it said, *because you* are *that kind of woman. Literally.*

"I didn't kiss him. He kissed me."

As soon as she realized she'd spoken out loud, she whipped her attention to Ellis and waited for one of his dark chuckles. But he remained as immobile as he'd been before she'd blurted out the words.

"Ellis?" she said softly, easing into the room.

She stopped a few feet from the bed and studied him. He had one hand strapped to the rail with a padded cuff, and the other was attached to an IV. He looked pale and—for the first time since Roni had met him—vulnerable. Maybe it was the fact that he was dressed in a hospital gown, or that his eyes were closed and his face set in repose. Or maybe it was the combination of all of it at once. She couldn't say for sure. Whatever it was, it made Ellis Black seem more human. Breakable. And it drew out a strange protectiveness in Roni.

Feeling conspicuous, she stole a quick look over her shoulder to make sure Rodrigo hadn't come in, then stepped closer to the bed. For some reason, she expected Ellis to react in some way.

Like what? she thought. *For him to* know *you're here like the nurse thought he would?*

He didn't, though. As far as she could see from where she was, he didn't even let out a breath. And Roni had a sudden compulsion to check that he *was* breathing. She moved in and lowered her head to his chest. It rose and fell very softly. And the slow, steady beat of his heart filled her ear. Reassured, she leaned away. Or at least she *tried* to lean away. She didn't get far, because Ellis's hand—the one with the IV attached to it—landed on the back of her head, dug into her hair, and held her in place.

47

Fifty-One Hours After Escape

The Policeman

It only took minutes for Captain Farriday to decide that the best thing to do was to leave the campsite as quickly as possible. There was little doubt in his mind that Ellis was the light-bobbing figure he'd been following before landing smack dab in the middle of the hideout. Which meant that if he hung around and waited, the other man would undoubtedly come back. A confrontation would ensue. One Farriday wasn't necessarily prepared for at the moment. Definitely one where he wasn't confident that he had the upper hand. He'd followed the man because he wanted to know where he was holed up. What Farriday needed to do now was to stack things in his favor. To ensure that Ellis was completely unaware that he'd stumbled into the campsite in the first place. That way, he could set a trap.

"I need to make this *my* secret instead of his," he said in the barest whisper.

Except as he glanced around, he realized he'd already inadvertently made a mark. His feet had left distinct prints in the mud. His push through the woods had broken branches in a clear path to the other man's camp. Even in the dark, he could see both things. What other evidence had he left of his presence? He didn't dare use the light on his phone to check. If he tried to cover up what he *could* see, would he be close to successful? He couldn't leave anything to chance.

He strummed his fingers on his thigh for a second before a solution came to him. He didn't need *less* evidence. He needed more. It needed to be spread wider, too. Chaos to cover the real discovery. A feint. A trick inside a trick. He would cover his tracks by *un*covering them. Strategically, of course.

Smiling a little, Farriday pulled out his phone. Carefully shielding the screen with his hand, he pulled up his GPS map. He set a digital pin in his current location so he could find it again, this time on purpose. Then he began his exit. And he got messy.

He tripped on purpose.

He fell twice, his body marking the ground where he landed.

He backtracked and left more footprints.

He caught his shirt on a bark-heavy trunk and made sure to deposit some threads when he pulled away.

In several places, he paused to smear a few leaves with a bit of the grease paint on his hands and face. Briefly, he considered scraping his skin on a rock to ensure that there was some solid DNA evidence linking him to the search before deciding it was overkill.

Not like Ellis is gonna have access to a forensics lab, he thought with a smirk.

When he finished snapping a branch that hung at eye level, he felt he'd done enough damage to make it obvious that he'd found the camp and wasn't trying to hide that fact. Let Ellis think he was as stupid as a bag of rocks. It would make the convict more confident. He'd expect Farriday to return and be lying in wait.

But I'll know. And be watching you try to watch me. There was more than a hint of glee in the thought, and the captain didn't bother to tamp it down.

He was still careful enough to avoid detection by the man guarding Veronica's house—he didn't want to complicate things—but when he was off the property, he returned to his car with far less subtlety than he'd left it. After he reached his vehicle, he feigned a call to the station, speaking in a hushed voice about his frustrations over the case. He cursed Ellis out twice, for his own pleasure.

Satisfied, he climbed in and drove home, where he continued with the façade by going through the motions of getting ready for bed. A warm glass of milk. A quick shower. Farriday did everything he would normally do, including propping himself up on his pillow for a perusal of the local paper before clicking out his bedside lamp. For fifteen minutes, he lay under the covers. But he didn't stay there for a single second longer than that.

In the dark, he slid out from under his blankets and crawled across the floor to his discarded clothes. Stealthily, he shimmied into the camo gear and smothered his face in grease paint yet again. He strapped on his weapon, grabbed a folded-up hunting net from the open door of his supply closet and tucked it under his shirt, then used his back door to head out into the night.

The trek was far too long to make on foot, but Farriday had already come up with a secret weapon—an unmarked police vehicle that sat at the town's tiny impound lot, a mile away. On silent feet, he slipped through his neighbors' yards. He knew which spots to avoid in order to not be caught on camera. He was well aware of which of the Meridian citizens in his area were night owls, so he was able to bypass those as well.

Once he'd successfully exited the residential neighborhood, his feet moved faster on their own, and Farriday wondered if he ought to be tired. He wasn't a man who enjoyed late nights. If anything, it was the opposite. On most evenings, he would've been in bed for hours by now. But by the time he reached the lot, unlocked the late model sedan, and jammed his key into the ignition, he wasn't fatigued at all. He felt invigorated.

Ellis Black hadn't managed to keep himself out of custody by taking risks and being stupid. Not even close. The convict had done everything with careful planning. Every move calculated. Precise. Now, Farriday was going to do things the same way.

I'm going to catch that son-of-a-you-know-what, he thought, *and I'm going to do it tonight, and I'm going to do it right.*

It took some effort to keep from grinning as he pulled onto the road, and he had to remind himself that a cheerful whistle wouldn't be appropriate. But he did let himself hum a tune in his head for the duration of the drive.

In a few minutes, he was back at the edge of Veronica's property. He was careful to park in a different spot, though, than the one he'd used before. The vehicle might not be recognizable, but there was no sense in taking the chance. Still humming silently, he stepped out. He took a deep breath, enjoying the crispness of the night air for a moment before reaching into his pocket to pull out his phone. Exhaling, he put the screen on the dimmest setting, then opened the GPS app.

"There you are," he murmured when the dot appeared and gave a little blink.

He took a few steps, and an arrow appeared an inch from the dot. He stepped again, this time toward the treeline, and the arrow swung, guiding him in the right direction.

"Perfect."

Moving as noiselessly as he could, Farriday followed along with the virtual map until it brought him to the edge of the campsite. He approached carefully, seeking out any sign that Ellis was nearby. But the spot looked just as it had when Farriday had left it a couple of hours earlier. Whatever nefarious thing the convict was currently up to, he clearly hadn't returned yet for the night.

Suits me fine, Farriday thought, yanking out the hunting net. *More time to set up.*

He flicked the net open, then stilled as a branch cracked somewhere in the trees. He stayed where he was for a frozen moment, then spun toward the noise. There was another snap, this one in the other direction. He swiveled to face that way instead, heart rate increasing. A pop sounded straight ahead, pulling his attention in yet a third direction.

What the hell is—

A blinding pain on the top of Farriday's head stopped the thought, halfway. He wobbled. Then he collapsed, the world around him zapping into oblivion.

48
Fifty-Four Hours After Escape

The Preacher's Daughter

A boom jolted Veronica from sleep to wakefulness so abruptly that the gentle moment between the dream world and consciousness was completely eliminated. One second, she was folded in nothing, and the next, she was sitting straight up on her couch. Her heart smashed against her ribcage. Her eyes darted around the room, seeking the source of the sudden disruption. Thoughts of gunfire and explosions flitted through her mind. But a far more logical explanation showed itself a second later when another reverberation made the house shudder.

Thunder.

Veronica threw aside her blanket, stood up, and stepped across the living room to the window. Sure enough, black clouds with crimson edges heralded the arrival of both the morning and a storm. The rain hadn't started yet, but it would come soon. The tall tops of the forested area on the edge of her property whipped back and forth, and she shivered a little in a physical response to the visual display.

She gave her shoulders a roll. She hadn't meant to fall asleep on the couch. In fact, she'd wanted a good sleep, because she'd decided late the night before that today would be a day of self-care. A day of reinvention. The hairstylist—located in a bigger town about an hour's drive away—was booked for after lunch.

And since she was heading out of Meridian, Veronica also wanted to take advantage of being close to a bigger variety of clothing stores. A wardrobe update was more than in order.

For a few moments longer, she let herself watch the bruised sky. Then she rolled her shoulders again and decided to get ahead of the impending chill by making herself a cup of tea. She started to move away from the window, but before she could fully turn, she spied the policeman who'd been stationed at her house all night. He wasn't inside his car. Instead, he stood to the side of it with his phone in his hand and a concerned look on his face.

Automatically, Veronica pressed closer to the window, trying to discern the source of his worry. She saw nothing nearby that warranted the crease in his forehead. As she watched him, he lowered his phone to look at the screen, then squinted into the distance. What was going on?

A flash lit the clouds up, and yet another roll of thunder rumbled through the air. At the same time, a new squad car crested over the hill and came into view. For a moment, her anxiety spiked. She held her breath as the second official vehicle eased to a stop beside the first one. But as a uniformed officer—this one closer to Captain Farriday in age—climbed out and approached his colleague, an explanation popped to mind.

Just the changing of the guard. The thought came with a drip of sarcasm and a noisy sigh. *Nothing to lose your mind over.*

Except the moment the two men started talking, Veronica knew it was more than a simple shift hand-off. There was head shaking. Even a bit of hand waving. Then they both turned toward her, and she jumped away from the window so they wouldn't catch her staring. But a second later, she remembered that *they* were outside *her* house. She had at least a little right to be curious.

And if it has something to do with Ellis...

Then it was way more than a "little" entitlement to know what was going on.

Maybe they'd caught him. Maybe they'd done *more* than caught him. Her heart jumped nervously at the thought. She hadn't seen Captain Farriday since showing him the necklace. It hadn't been *that* long. But still. She was pretty sure it was still the longest he'd been absent since the moment she'd escaped through the motel window.

With her pulse thrumming harder than she would've liked, Veronica hurried back to the couch. She grabbed her blanket, wrapped it around her body, then flung open the front door and stepped toward the policemen.

"Ms. Hollister." The younger one—she really ought to start learning their names—actually sounded surprised to see her.

She tightened the blanket across her chest. "Is everything all right?"

The two men exchanged a look, and the older one gave a tight nod. "Nothing to worry about."

Veronica didn't buy it. "Is this about Ellis? Did something happen?"

"No. No updates there, I'm afraid," said the first man, his tone just grim enough to sound true.

Overhead, the sky crackled with lightning. Almost right away, the accompanying thunder ripped through the air. Both men flinched. But Veronica didn't budge.

"Should I call the captain?" she asked, careful to make the question sound genuine rather than threatening in any way.

Now the two policemen exchanged another look, and she knew that whatever was going on, it had something to do with Captain Farriday.

What did Ellis do? she thought. But aloud she said, "Is he okay?"

The younger cop sighed and averted his eyes away from his counterpart. "When was the last time you *did* talk to him?"

"I…" She cleared her throat. "Yesterday."

Was it really only the previous day? Why did it seem like so much more time had passed?

"Did he mention to you that he had anything specific

CONVICTION

planned?" the older man asked.

She thought about how he'd disappeared into the woods after their talk about the pornography, and how she'd been certain he'd come out of there, too. The necklace, which still rested against her throat, felt heavy. But she didn't mention either thing.

"I don't think so," she said instead. "He told me he'd see me soon. Is he all right?"

Yet another look passed between them, and the older one let out a little cough. "Captain Farriday hasn't done his usual check-ins, but it's nothing to worry about. He sometimes does his own thing and fills us in later."

Now Veronica's heart didn't merely jump; it climbed into her throat and stayed there. Her emotions must've been playing across her face despite the way she tried to school them, because the older policeman gave her arm a kindly pat.

"We really don't want you to worry about the captain, Ms. Hollister," he stated. "He's been working hard these last couple of days, so it wouldn't be out of line for him to catch a quick breather. In the meantime, you can count on us to keep you safe."

She had her doubts, but she made herself nod.

"Thank you," she replied. "Oh. And I'm sorry to ask, but are you going to be able to give me a ride out for an appointment in a short bit? I don't feel like driving, and I know you'd have to follow me anyway."

"Happy to."

"I'll let you know when I'm ready."

Veronica tightened the blanket again and hurried back into the house. Her mind hung on the captain's whereabouts for a moment. She could imagine a whole host of terrible things that could've been done to him. All courtesy of Ellis. But she didn't have time to dwell. Her new life was waiting, and if she stood around worrying about the old one, she'd never get a chance to move on.

268

49
Three Months,
Seven Days Before Escape

The Convict

Ellis was either dead or dreaming.
I'm gonna go ahead and rule on the side of dreaming.
The thought slipped through the haziness of his brain with remarkable clarity. *'Cause when you die, it'll be straight to hell for you, Black. Not in heaven like this.*

If he'd had the energy, he might've laughed at the cheesy undertone. He definitely had to admit, though, that his current position was the closest he'd been to heavenly in as many years as he'd been alive.

A soft body was pressed to his. A fistful of even softer, damp hair was in his hand. A damp, muddy scent filled his nose, and then a wincing voice carried to his ears.

"Ellis, you're hurting me."

His eyes flew open. A green gaze met his stare. Flushed cheeks filled his vision.

Veronica. Her head was on his chest, her face forced up by the grip he had on her hair. *Not dreaming after all.* A flood of recent, violent memories washed over him, battling against a lag that made him sure he'd been given a painkiller or three. *So.*

Not dead, either. Pretty lucky about that, I'd say.

"Fuck," he grunted, the word burning his throat.

The girl's cheeks got pinker. "My hair. Can you…"

He released his grip. It was easier, actually, than holding on. His hand ached. His whole fucking *body* ached. Except, that is, for the parts that had separated from Veronica, who eased away from him.

"Not that I'm complaining," he said, "but what the hell are you doing in my bed?"

"I'm not in your bed."

"Could've fooled me."

"I'm *beside* your bed." As if to prove it was true, Veronica stepped back a bit more.

"Potato, potato," Ellis said, pronouncing the word the same both times. "Why are you beside my bed, so close to it that you might as well be in it?"

"I was just…"

"Just what?"

Her face was burgundy now. "Just checking if you were still breathing."

"How fucking sweet of you," he replied.

"You listed me as your next of kin." She tipped up her chin. "How sweet of *you*."

"How *fucking* sweet of me," he corrected.

"Why did you do it?"

He opened his mouth, a flippant reply on his tongue, but she put up a hand before he could speak.

"Save the lie," she said. "I'm in the middle of some of the worst hours of my life, and if I don't believe your answer, I'm going to turn and walk out of here, and I promise you that I will never, ever look back."

Her tone was weary—beaten-down, even—and for the first time since coming to, Ellis took a good look at her.

"Jesus Christ," he muttered.

Now that the red had faded from her skin, he could see it was marked in other ways. Far worse than the last time her father had hurt her. Bruises, cuts. Dirt, somehow ground into her chin. A swollen lip. Other things, too. Like the fact that her hair wasn't damp; it was nearly soaked. It'd dripped down onto her clothes, which were far different than her usual style. Ellis didn't know what'd happened, but he was going to kill the son-of-a-bitch who'd done it to her.

"Don't look at me like that," she said.

"You're a fucking mess."

"You got stabbed."

"Right," he growled. "Because I'd fucking forgotten that."

She sighed. "Can you stop swearing at me, Ellis? Please?"

"I'm not swearing *at* you, I'm—"

"Are you going to answer me, or not?"

"Your father did this to you."

"Why did you put me down as your next of kin?"

He ground his teeth together, but the honest answer she was looking for slipped out anyway. "I don't know anyone else. Not a single other f—not a single other person. When the paperwork came in from my caseworker for an update the other week, I let impulse get the better of me."

Her expression softened. "So you didn't do it to manipulate me into coming here when you got hurt?"

"You think I got shanked in the gut on purpose? Mighty bold assumption. Little narcissistic, too."

"That isn't what I meant."

"No?"

Unexpectedly, Veronica came closer again. Her hand landed on his chest and flattened there. Then—even more unexpectedly—she seated herself on the bed beside him, the curve of her hip resting against him.

"Are you still hoping that I'll help you get free?" she asked.

There was no point in lying. "Yes."

"Then maybe instead of playing games—and I'm not talking about you almost getting killed—you should think about what *I* want."

"I can't give you what you want."

"You haven't asked what that is."

"I don't have to ask," he said. "What you want is for me to

be innocent. But I killed her. I murdered my sister. And maybe you could accept that, I don't know. Maybe you're the most forgiving person in the world. There's one problem, though, sweetheart. I'm not sorry for my crime, and I never will be."

That silenced her for a moment, and when she spoke again, there was far less conviction in her voice. "You can't be sure of that."

"I can, Nic, and I am."

"You can't—"

"I can." He let a finger land on her knee, then trailed it up.

"I'm not going to give up on you, Ellis." Her words were fervent, and they dug at him.

"If your God wanted me, he could've taken me in the mess hall. Easy." He lifted his free hand to snap his fingers in a deliberately trite way. "Just like that."

He slapped his palm to her leg again, dangerously high on her upper thigh. He squeezed. She didn't flinch away from his rough touch. Instead, she touched him back. Her fingers slid between his knuckles and stayed there.

"What the fuck are you doing?" he said.

She looked him in the eye. "The same thing you're doing."

"I highly doubt that."

Her mouth flattened into a stubborn line, but before she could form the argument Ellis knew was coming, a throat clear from the door stopped her.

"Ms. Hollister," the prison nurse said. "I'm afraid that touching the patients is frowned upon."

Veronica stood smoothly, a complacent smile on her face before she was all the way up. "Mr. Black needed a bit of an adjustment with his blankets. He woke up a little chilly, and I knew you were out on that emergency, so I didn't want to bother you. But it's taken care of. And now that I know he's okay, I should probably get going. It's late for all of us, isn't it?"

The nurse smiled back, fully invested in the cheer the girl was selling. "Well, he'll be stuck in the infirmary for about six weeks or so."

"Six weeks? That seems excessive."

"This isn't like a regular hospital, love. They did some serious damage in there, and we can't have him near gen pop while he's healing." She offered a nod in Ellis's direction. "That's the thing about abdominal perforations like this one. Can't take the risk, can we?"

"I'd prefer not to," Ellis replied.

Lorraine looked back to Veronica. "He did remarkably well, though, so don't you worry. Mr. Black is tough. Most guys would've been in the ICU for days before being popped to the surgical unit and then kicked back here. But my patient here managed it in forty-eight hours."

"That's me," said Ellis, flashing his teeth. "Take a stabbing and keep on grabbing."

Veronica's face pinked. "I don't think that was their aim."

Lorraine wagged a finger at him, and Ellis almost laughed. She had to be the most relaxed person on the entire prison staff.

Veronica cleared her throat. "I'll see myself to the door."

"The guard will show you the rest of the way out," replied the nurse. "But don't be shy about coming back."

"Oh, I won't be." Veronica turned to Ellis. "Goodbye, Mr. Black. I'll see you soon."

"Night, Ms. Hollister," he replied.

He watched her go, smug. Two months ago, he would've believed the sweetness in her voice to be nothing but genuine. The *nurse* obviously believed it. Which was a victory. The preacher's daughter, deceiving someone for his gain. Ellis was that much closer to seeing his plan come to fruition.

50
Sixty Hours After Escape

The Policeman

An insistent drip—cold, wet, and spattering across his face—yanked Farriday to consciousness.

Rain, he thought.

But that made no sense.

He'd been readying himself to hide under the hunting net. Then he'd heard the sounds, and—

Ellis.

Farriday's eyes flew open. He tensed for another blow, but it didn't come. There was no sound except for his own shallow breaths and the chirp of a bird in the distance.

What in God's name happened?

He was on his back, staring straight up. That explained the rain on his face. So did the heavy clouds overhead. What was confusing was the color of the sky. It no longer held the thick darkness of night.

Struggling to make sense of the moment, he sat up. It was a mistake. A throb drove through his skull. His stomach heaved in response, and he leaned to the side and vomited. When he'd emptied out his stomach, he sagged in place and took a slow look around. He was still at the campsite, but it was definitely past dawn now.

"Dammit," he muttered, putting a hand on his aching head.

The curse was an understatement. He'd clearly been

knocked out for hours. It had to be Ellis who'd done it, though it made little sense. Why the hell would the other man not kill him when he had the chance? Bury his body in the woods and leave while he could?

Farriday didn't really expect an explanation, but he got one anyway. He spotted it as he started to stand. The hunting net had been folded tidily and set beside him. His gun rested on top of it. And next to the weapon sat a note, crafted in Ellis's bold black lettering and encased with eye-rolling thoughtfulness inside a plastic sandwich bag to protect it from the elements.

With dread overriding his nausea, he reached out, picked up the piece of paper, and let his eyes comb over the words.

DID YOU REALLY THINK THIS WAS CHECKMATE? the note read. THE TIME ISN'T RIGHT. NOT YET. BUT IT'S COMING.

There was a break in the sentences, and half an inch down, Ellis had added, CLEVER. BUT NOT CLEVER ENOUGH.

The other man had been watching him. He'd been listening. Maybe he'd even *baited* Farriday there with his stupid flashlight.

His fist balled up, crushing the paper. How dare he? How dare Ellis Black—that low-level scumbag—throw Farriday's words back at him like that? Mocking him. Taunting him.

"You bastard," he said in a low voice. "You fucking bastard."

The accusation hung in the air, impotent. Truthfully, he didn't know if he was talking to Ellis, or if he was talking to himself. He'd underestimated the other man. He'd overestimated himself. The perfect plan was nothing but a delusion, and the convict was still a step ahead.

51

Three Months,
Seven Days Before Escape

The Preacher's Daughter

R oni couldn't go home. She didn't even want to. But as she sat in the back of the cab, she was acutely aware that she had nowhere else to go.

She couldn't help but think about Ellis's words. *I don't know anyone else,* he'd said, the truth of the statement palpable. And she'd never felt a connection more acutely. The aloneness.

The people she knew weren't the kind to whom she could run. Not because they wouldn't take her in. They would. For sure. Then they'd call her father. Maybe while she was out of earshot, but they'd do it. Because they were *his* people, not her own. The townsfolk knew him. Or thought they did. And if she tried to tell them what had happened with him...

She swallowed back new tears. They wouldn't believe her. Why would they? Who would believe that an old widower—a retired preacher, no less—was the kind of man who locked his adult daughter in a shed and called her a whore? Hadn't Roni had time—*years*—to get some help? Wouldn't there have been some sign? Sure, she was sheltered. But she wasn't a complete shut-in. She came into town to get groceries. She had coffee at the shop on the corner, and she took books out at the library. Sometimes, she babysat local children.

Roni could practically hear the doubtful whispers as they

discussed her dubious claim. A grown woman. Twenty-two years old. Tasked with caring for her father, the resentment finally building to a crescendo, and this was how it came out. Revenge in a lie. Because her claim was that dubious.

Why didn't I get help sooner?

"Miss?" said the driver.

She lifted her eyes and caught his questioning gaze in the rear-view mirror. Guilt stabbed at her, though it shouldn't have. She was paying him by the mile. He wouldn't have been making more money driving someone to a known destination. In fact, he was probably earning more circling aimlessly around while he waited for her to make up her mind. But she *was* charging the trip to her father's card. Handing over the memorized number had been automatic. She couldn't retract it without being conspicuous. And if she had any hope of eventually getting home, then landing her dad with an enormous taxi bill probably wasn't going to help.

"Have you decided where you want to go?" the driver added.

Roni started to shake her head, then stopped as an idea struck, and she spoke up before sense could stop her. "Do you know where the Blacks used to live?"

His forehead wrinkled, then his eyes widened. "You mean the guy who—"

He stopped short, and Roni knew his brain had put the pieces together. He'd picked her up from the prison. Now she was asking about the home of a known murderer.

She cleared her throat. "Yes, it's the one you're thinking of. Does anyone live there now?"

"Can't say for sure. But I've never been asked to make a trip out there. Don't know anyone else who has, either. Driven by a few times for other reasons, though, and the place looks pretty overgrown. Safe bet that it's empty." He paused. "That's where you want to go?"

"Yes."

"You're sure?"

She gave him a look that she hoped would pass as scathing,

and he shrugged and pressed his foot to the gas.

Exhaling, Roni leaned back and focused her attention out the side window. She avoided thinking too much both about what she was feeling and what she hoped to accomplish by going to Ellis's childhood home. Nothing good would come of the analysis. After a few minutes, she didn't have to try to keep her thoughts elsewhere, because the taxi driver was bringing her closer and closer to a place she knew well—her own home. Had her father somehow gotten wind of her escape from the shed? Did he have a connection at the cab company? She told herself she was being paranoid. But when they didn't change course, and the familiar green scape continued around her, she couldn't help but voice her spiking worry aloud.

"Where are you taking me?" The question was just this side of a demand.

The cabby sent her a look. "The Black place. You change your mind?"

"The Black place is out here?"

"Where'd you think it was?"

"I…" She steadied her voice. "I guess I didn't realize how far out of town it was."

"Miss… sorry to ask again… but are you sure this is where you want to go?"

"Yes. I'm really sure."

"Okay. Just a short bit more, then."

Roni could tell her choice didn't sit right with the driver. And she didn't blame him for his concern. If their roles were reversed, her unease would've been equally piqued. But she ignored him in favor of again watching the scenery. Soon, they got to the turnoff that led to her house. She held her breath as they went past it, then released it in relief when they were far enough along that she was sure it wasn't some kind of trick. But only a minute later, she found herself gulping in another lungful as the cabby guided his car up the very next roadway. It was more of a country mile than it was a single block, but it was still close enough that Roni's hands tingled, and her vision blurred.

Ellis had been her neighbor. Like, really her neighbor. Not just someone in the same town. It was an unnerving coincidence. One that made her so tense that she almost didn't notice when the taxi came to a stop.

"Miss?" said the driver. "We're, uh, here?"

Once again, his uncertainty was easy to understand. The spot where the car sat idling was straight out of a horror movie. The headlights bathed their yellow hue over the crumbling remains of a building. The surrounding forest was dark and foreboding, promising a hiding place for a dozen unsavory fates. Roni had to order her hands not to shake as she reached for the door, pushed it open, then climbed out.

"Thank you," she said.

"Do you want me to wait?" the cabby asked.

"No. Thank you. I'll be fine."

"You're—"

"Sure? Yes."

"I could—"

Pretending not to hear him as he persisted, she closed the door and strode across the overgrown lawn in a purposeful way without looking back. Thankfully, it worked. A few seconds later, tires crunched on the gravel. The headlights faded. And Roni was left alone in the middle of the remnants of Ellis Black's childhood home. She didn't move right away. She let her eyes adjust to the new darkness, inhaling and exhaling the rain-dampened air, waiting for some unknown inspiration to prod her onward. It came in the form of a nearly errant thought.

If I were up high enough, I bet I could see my house.

Giving in to the compulsion to find out, Roni picked her way over the grass until she reached the trees, where she grabbed the lowest branch and hoisted herself onto it. Through her borrowed jeans, her knees scraped unpleasantly against the tree trunk. She ignored the sting. It wasn't anything worse than she'd experienced in the last day, let alone over the course of her lifetime. She clambered up even more, confidence building as she moved. At last—with aching hands —she reached a spot near the tree's top, where the branches were sparse enough to see through while also providing enough stability.

Roni leaned out. And there it was. The house where she'd lived for the last twelve and a half years. There were no lights on. No sign that her father had rethought the punishment he'd doled out. And for a moment, the weight of that fact pushed down on her chest, stealing her breath.

He doesn't care.

But a heartbeat later, her ribcage loosened. He didn't care, so why should she? Maybe she didn't owe quite so much to her father as she'd always believed.

52

Ten Years Earlier, Fifteen Hours Before Arrest

The Policeman

F lip needed a better plan. What he'd done so far had led him to a fat pile of nothing. Less than nothing. He was a step behind because he didn't have the support of the force behind him. With that in mind, and with his goal of making Ellis culpable, the first thing on the to-do list was to follow the boy as closely as possible. The only problem was, of course, that the kid was wise to his intentions. His boss, too. So Flip had to do something smarter. Something more off the books. It didn't take long to come up with a scheme and to put it in play.

First came the easy part. Calling in a favor that got him a not-strictly-legal tracking device. Next came the challenge. Getting the bug onto Ellis's person. For that, Flip suited up in camouflage and a whole lot of patience. Confident that the boy wouldn't suspect a second visit from him in such a short span, he made his way back onto the Black property. This time, he succeeded in getting in undetected.

Under the cover of trees and a pitch-black sky, he waited until the lights went out in the boy's house. Then he waited some more. At last, he was satisfied no one was coming in or out.

His initial thought was that he ought to simply put the

tracker on the kid's motorbike. But that would mean risking losing Ellis every time he went somewhere on foot. That wouldn't do. After some more thought, Flip took a risk. He sneaked away from the trees and headed for the house itself. Every couple of steps he paused and listened. His approach was unimpeded. Carefully, he let himself into the house. It really only took a second. An open door. A grimy boot. The tracker firmly planted in the footwear's sole. And then it was just a matter of waiting again. Something Flip was happy to do in order to see his plan come together.

53
Sixty-Six Hours After Escape

The Preacher's Daughter

Veronica scrutinized her appearance in the bathroom mirror at the salon. Her curls were no longer the brown she'd grown up with. In fact, they were no longer curls at all. The stylist had deepened the color into an impressive shade of auburn and straightened the unruly mess into a sleek bob. Veronica had wanted the latter to be permanent—she'd really tried to insist upon it— but the stylist had suggested trying something temporary first to see if she liked it, so she'd settled for a treatment that was promised to last the week unless it got wet. It would have to do. And she had to admit that she'd done a doubletake during the big reveal.

"I don't even look like *me*," she'd said, unable to keep the astonishment out of her voice.

The stylist had laughed. "You still look like *you*, honey. But a sophisticated you."

"You think?"

"I know."

So maybe it would more than do. But for now, Veronica didn't want to draw any extra attention to her new look. And she'd come prepared. With a nod at her supposedly sophisticated self, she pulled a floral scarf from her purse and carefully secured it over her head using bobby pins to hold it in place. A single strand of hair still managed to escape from under the silky fabric, and she made a face. But she also quickly tucked it up with the others, making sure no other pieces got exposed in the process. Then she stepped back and gave herself another once-over.

"All right," she said to her reflection. "If anyone asks, the bad weather could ruin my new style, so I'm keeping it under wraps."

And it had the bonus of being true.

She slung her new purse over her shoulder and headed out. She paused outside the doors, wincing at the sight of the gray-haired cop—*Constable Salmon*—Veronica reminded herself for the third time—waiting in his car. He'd been nothing but patient. Even now, when he spotted her, he offered a congenial wave. But he was still a policeman with a pile of shopping bags sitting where he ought to have a criminal in cuffs. And her little package from the dentist—a kindly man who'd fixed her chipped tooth and given her a new toothbrush, too—sat in the console, looking out of place.

Forcing a smile, Veronica hurried toward the passenger side door, grabbing the handle before he could try to get out and open it for her. Something he'd done twice already today.

Constable Salmon eyed the scarf on her head, but all he said was, "This mean we're done?"

She nodded. "We're done. And I'm sorry that you have to run me around like this. I really do feel bad that you guys have all been turned into my watchdogs."

"Not a problem. I've got a wife and three grown daughters, so I'm pretty used to sitting outside stores while they try things on." He winked. "And if you're anything like my wife and kids, what you're thinking about now is a glass of wine and putting your feet up."

"Tea and feet up," Veronica said. "But otherwise... exactly."

"Let's hit the road, then." Constable Salmon winked again, then flicked on the flashing lights and pulled a questionably legal U-turn.

The hour-long trip back passed quickly. The aging policeman was easy to chat with. Good at small talk. And fatherly in a way that Veronica's own father never had been. She wondered what it was like, growing up with a man like him sitting at the head of the table. If his family knew how lucky they were. Veronica let herself enjoy it.

But her indulgence backfired. She'd relaxed just enough that when a figure darted out in front of the squad car and stopped directly in its path, it was all the more jarring. The constable slammed the brakes. Veronica jerked forward, the tires screeched along the pavement, and an acrid smell filled the air.

She couldn't tear her eyes away from the man on the road.

Move, move, move! she willed.

He didn't budge. The car continued to sail toward him, fighting the concrete.

Veronica clapped a hand over her mouth to contain the shriek that tried to escape as she braced for impact. At the last second, Constable Salmon pulled on the wheel. The tires screeched again. The vehicle careened and finally came to an aggressive sideways stop. And the person in the middle of the road stood there, unbothered by any of it.

"Holy shit," breathed the cop beside her.

Trying to stop herself from hyperventilating, Veronica dropped her hand. Her eyes immediately widened. A gasp slipped out, too. It wasn't so much the fact that they'd narrowly missed killing someone—although that by itself was frightening. But what really gave her a start was recognition of the man in question. And her current bodyguard realized it at the same moment as she did.

He let out a cough and muttered, "Farriday? Are you kidding me right now?"

It was definitely the captain. But his appearance had taken a strange turn. Instead of his usual rumpled uniform, he wore what looked like army gear. His face was streaked with... something. Dirt? Veronica couldn't say for sure. He also had a white bandage stuck to his forehead, and its haphazard placement looked almost like an afterthought. A smear of crimson that could only be blood dotted the corner of his lips. If any of it bothered him, though, he didn't show it. He put his hands on his hips and stared at them.

Constable Salmon closed his eyes for a tenth of a second, seemingly to compose himself, then flung open the door.

"Captain?" he said. "You okay? Scared us more than a bit, I think."

Farriday lasered in on Veronica. "I need you."

"Me?" Her pulse somehow managed to leap even higher. "What for?"

"Bait."

54

Two Months,
Twenty-Nine Days Before Escape

The Preacher's Daughter

Roni shifted in her chair and bit her lip. For ten minutes now, she'd been sitting a few feet from Ellis's bed, trying to find the right words.

Almost three weeks had passed since she'd made her way to his old property. She'd stayed there the whole time. Putting up with the weather as it beat on her. Foraging for what little she could find to eat. Climbing the same tree every few hours to survey her own house and check if her father had mounted an alarm, which he hadn't. She didn't know if that was good or bad, but at least she didn't have to hide from the authorities.

This was her third visit to Ellis in that timeframe. Mostly, he'd been too injured to do anything but lie there. But Roni didn't care. Her mind had been occupied anyway, trying to find a solution for what to do next. Today, an answer had finally hit her. She knew *exactly* what she had to do. Maybe she'd known it all along. But for some reason, explaining it to Ellis was proving to be exceedingly difficult.

"You might as well say whatever you came to say, sweetheart," he said after another minute of her pensive silence. "They took away my morphine forty-eight hours ago, and it hasn't exactly put me in a good mood."

Roni bit her lip harder. So hard she tasted blood. She saw

Ellis's attention find her mouth, his eyes glittering despite the fact that he was confined to the bed, and she forced herself to relax her jaw.

"I have to leave," she said.

Ellis lifted an eyebrow. "By all means. Come in. Wake me up from an entirely pleasurable dream. Sit there silently. Then leave. Don't let me keep you from whatever the fuck else you should be doing."

"I don't mean I need to leave *here*. I mean I need to leave Meridian completely."

"Leave and go where?"

"I'm not sure yet. Anywhere else. My dad keeps a stack of cash hidden away, and he doesn't know I know about it. I think there's enough there that I could make a fresh start. All I have to do is sneak in when he's sleeping, and..." She trailed off as she caught the impossibly flat look on Ellis's face.

"So you came here today to do what? Tell me that you wouldn't be coming here?" His voice matched his expression. "Seems like a waste of both of our times."

"I felt like you should know," she replied.

"Why? Why would I give a fuck that you've decided it's moving day?"

She didn't know. She couldn't even think of a plausible answer. Not with Ellis staring at her like that. Not with him looking at her as though—if he were a different person—might make her think he *did* care.

"Just so we're clear," he said. "You running off means that all the stuff about not giving up on me was all bullshit."

The statement made her blink. "Does that matter?"

"Not to me."

"Oh."

"Maybe it should. Integrity, godliness, and who knows what else?"

"Ellis."

"Veronica."

She blinked again, bothered by his use of her full name,

then bothered more by the bothering itself. "I can't stay here with my father."

Ellis's face stilled. "Did he—"

"No," she said quickly. "Not that."

"Good."

"But I still can't stay."

"So the son-of-a-bitch gets to stay, while you're forced to leave your home," he said. "That's fucking poetic."

"It's not as though I can make *him* go," Roni replied.

"Let him stay, then. Only make him do it six feet under."

From anyone else, the words would've sounded like a joke. From Ellis, it sounded like a suggestion. A solution. Roni fought a shiver.

"What do you want, sweetheart?" he said after another silent moment. "My permission to go? I'm not gonna give it. You haven't helped me in any way. Not in the way that I want. Not in the way that you want. So seek a blessing from someone else."

Guilt pricked at her, and she had to clear her throat. "And how many times have you told me that you can't be redeemed? That you *won't* be?"

"Still true."

"I don't understand."

"What if I told you a different story?"

There was an unusual edge in the question, and as much as Roni wished she weren't drawn in by it... she was.

"Like what?" she asked.

"The truth."

"You're going to have to be more specific."

His eyes sank shut, and the grimace on his face was full of genuine pain. "The truth about me."

Roni's breath caught in surprise. What was he saying?

He opened his eyes again, meeting her gaze. "Don't look at me like that. Like you think I'm about to tell you I'm not guilty. I *am* guilty, Nic. And I need you to accept that."

"I do."

"Do you?"

"Of course I do."

"Come closer."

Roni flashed a look toward the door. "You know that I can't do that."

"You can. I paid her to leave us alone for thirty minutes," Ellis replied.

"Lorraine wouldn't do that."

"Okay, fine. I paid some guy named Shorty to ask some other guy named Duck to fake a stomach pain that might or might not be a bout of appendicitis."

"That sounds... complicated."

"Come closer," he said again, this time far less gently.

Roni knew she shouldn't do it. She was already riding a horribly dangerous line. But a part of her brain demanded to know what she had to lose.

Why not? it said. *Once you walk out that door, every move you make is going to be a new risk.*

With a nervous little inhale, she stood up and walked to the side of the bed.

"Sit down," Ellis ordered.

She did.

"Lie down," he added.

"What?"

"Lie. The fuck. Down."

Taking another breath, she did that, too. For at least a full minute after, Ellis said nothing. But his silence only made Roni acutely aware of her position against him. She was lying in bed with a very dangerous man. A monster. And for what? To prove that she really believed he *was* the monster in question? It made no sense, even in her exhausted state. But she made no move to get up.

"Tell me something." Ellis's voice was a rumble above her ear. "Would you really climb into bed with a man who you thought was guilty of rape and murder?"

The question was a stab. And a trap. Who was she if she

said yes? But saying no meant he was right; she thought he was innocent. And she didn't. Did she? *Oh, God.* Maybe she did. Maybe she really, really *did.*

Ellis's finger pressed into the top of her spine, and it dragged slowly down her back, stopping just above her waistband. "I'm not innocent, Nic. I'm not a good man. I didn't start out that way and being in here has only made me worse."

There was an enormous, immovable lump in Roni's throat, and it burned when she answered him. "If you're trying to manipulate me into staying so I can help you get out to become a better man, it's not going to work."

"Look at me."

Even though every bit of her brain screamed at her not to do it, Roni tilted her head up. Ellis's blue gaze shot straight into her, immobilizing her just as it'd been doing since the first time. The familiar fear bubbled up. But under it—and God help her the sickness that must be driving her to feel this way—was an undeniable attraction. As she stared at him, she thought of the violent kiss they'd shared. She craved another one. Her stomach roiled. The rest of her quivered.

Ellis Black isn't the only monster in this room, she thought.

She whispered his months-old promise in a shaky voice. "You'll chew me up and spit me out."

"I will do *any*thing to get out of here," he said.

"I really am leaving."

"I fucking heard you."

What happened next, Roni didn't want to admit to. Or at the very least, she would've liked to have blamed Ellis. To say that he forced her. He was the perfect scapegoat, after all. His past. His present. But in truth, she was the one who reached for the drawstring on his pants.

55
Seventy Hours After Escape

The Policeman

Captain Farriday glanced at Veronica. She sat in the middle of her couch with her hands folded in her lap and her eyes closed. She looked smaller and more vulnerable than usual. Her fear was manifesting itself in ways he could actually see. A slight tremor as she drew a breath. A film of sweat below the edge of the scarf she wore on her head. The way her lower lip kept finding its way between her teeth. He felt bad about it. Yes, he wanted her to look scared. If Ellis was watching—no, not if... because he was watching — the more real the fear seemed, the better. But Farriday wanted her to trust him, too. He needed her to comply with his unconventional plan.

He pulled his eyes away from her, stepped to the window, and flicked the curtain open a smidge.

I know you're out there, you bastard, he thought.

It was simple, really, what he wanted to do. Draw the convict out. Then let the chips fall naturally where they ought to.

He turned back to Veronica. "You ready?"

She opened her eyes and bobbed her head the smallest bit. "Yes."

Anticipation jumped through him. He picked her suitcase up and held out his hand. She didn't move. Trying to maintain his cool, he counted to ten. She stayed where she was, her gaze sliding to the window he'd just abandoned.

"Hey," he said, not letting any of his impatience show. "It's gonna be okay."

She looked up at him, her eyes wide and wary. "Is it?"

"I promise."

"How can you be sure?"

"Because I'm the good guy, Ms. Hollister. And the good guys always win, don't they?" He offered a smile.

"Did Ellis's sister win?" Roni replied. "Was she the bad guy?"

"Emily Black was a victim. Her brother's actions... he took evil to the next level. Which is exactly why we need to catch him now. So all the good guys—like us—can go back to our normal lives."

"Is that what you really believe?"

"Of course."

"All right." She took a shuddering breath. "Let's go."

He held out his hand again, and this time, she pressed her damp palm into his and let him help her to her feet. Farriday gave her his best reassuring squeeze.

It was showtime.

Every move from the front step to the car was orchestrated.

The way he had Roni lock the door and hand him the key.

How, as he led her down the walkway from her house, he paused to tie the shoe he'd deliberately left undone.

And the fact that when he opened the car door, he leaned closer and spoke in a voice that was a little too loud.

"Here you go, Ms. Hollister," he said. "We'll be out of town faster than you know it, and all of this will be behind you."

She delivered her practiced lines, too, the cadence of her words impressively natural. "Could we stop at the diner on the way? I could use one of their lattes."

"Absolutely. Whatever you need."

He gave her a pat on the back, and she climbed in. Once he'd closed the door behind her, he walked to his side of the car and placed a phony call to dispatch.

"Danielle?" he said into dead air. "I've got Ms. Hollister all loaded up. We should reach the town limits in about twenty minutes." He paused as though listening. "Yes. The main drag out. Not a lot of point in messing around and trying to find a different route. It's not as though Black has a vehicle." Another pause. "Okay. Thanks."

He tapped the phone as though turning it off, purposely didn't look toward the treeline, then climbed into the car and started the engine.

Roni spoke up, her voice soft. "You're sure he's going to follow us?"

Farriday nodded. "Without question. Ellis won't let us get much farther than the diner."

"What if he can't get there?"

"Trust me. He'll find a way."

In silence, they pulled away from the house and started down the long driveway. They made it to the road and hit cruising speed—not so fast as to be reckless, not so slowly as to be suspicious. The trap was set. There was no need to hurry. All they had to do was follow the staged timeline, and everything would happen just as Farriday wanted it to.

56

Two Months,
Fifteen Days Before Escape

The Preacher's Daughter

Roni stared up at the silhouetted house, marveling over the way it already felt so separate from her. So other.

The chipped white paint seemed foreign. The window she knew was her own didn't call to her. It was as though everything that had happened over the last weeks and months had changed her so completely that she was no longer Roni Hollister at all. And yet she'd lived here, in this house, for most of her life. But she wasn't here to dwell on the past. Or to dwell on the present, either. She hadn't been back to see Ellis since she'd degraded herself the way she had. But she also hadn't done a thing to move forward. And she'd delayed this long enough. Too long. She'd come with a purpose, and she needed to see it through.

This is it. Last chance to back out without the possibility of being caught. One more step out of the trees, and Dad might see me.

Steadying her mind, she took a breath, lifted a foot, and moved forward. There was no responding threat. No lights flicked on. Her father didn't holler from the porch, demanding to know who was out there in the dark. She took another step, and another. Everything remained hushed. And while the stillness didn't exactly embolden her—she couldn't afford to get reckless—it did bolster her confidence.

On sure feet, she hurried to the front of the house. There, she paused again. She surveyed the windows that were in her sightline. She could see the outline of the living room furniture and the staircase that led upstairs. There was the barest glow of yellow light, but it didn't worry Roni. She knew it emanated from the snowflake-shaped nightlight in the hallway, and the fact that it was plugged in meant her father had gone to bed. Another good sign.

"Okay," she said in a whisper. "You've got this."

She ducked down and crept toward the front steps. Avoiding the creaky third stair by habit more than intention, she made her way up to the porch and stopped in front of the door. Her hand closed on the handle, turning oh-so-slowly. Her father hadn't locked it. He never did. He'd once told Roni that only God could help a man who broke into their home. At the time, she hadn't thought of it as a threat. Now she realized that's exactly what it had been.

Swallowing back a jump of anxiety, she pushed open the door and waited. Hellfire didn't rain down. And her father didn't jump out from somewhere with his baseball bat raised to strike, either.

Only a minute or two more, Roni told herself. *Then I'm gone for good.*

She tiptoed over the floor to the coat closet—which was really more of a coat cubby, since the bi-fold door had fallen off years ago—and dropped silently to her knees. She pushed aside a shoebox and pressed her fingers to one of the floorboards. It shifted under the pressure, but as she started to lift it, it also let out a scraping noise that made her wince. Biting her lip, she glanced toward the staircase. She counted to ten. When there was no sign that the sound had disturbed her father, she pulled up the wood again, a little more slowly this time. And there it was. The tightly bound stacks of cash her father had hidden away, thinking she was clueless.

Roni didn't know how much was there. She'd never been

bold enough to pull it out and count it. All she was sure of was that there was a lot of it. Thousands, at minimum. Definitely an amount that would ensure that yesterday would be her last night sleeping on the cold ground out near Ellis's place. And after that? There was plenty enough to get her out of town and started somewhere. Wherever.

Roni took it all. She tucked the money into the waistband of the tow truck driver's wife's jeans, pulled her shirt overtop of the stacks, then put everything back exactly as she'd found it. It could be months before her father realized it was gone. And even if he figured it out right away, she didn't care. Because it wasn't stealing. Not really. It was an early withdrawal of her inheritance.

Maybe it's more than that, she thought. *Maybe it's payment for everything I've suffered.*

She nodded to herself, fully satisfied with the explanation. She stood up. But a noise from overhead carried through the thin boards between the first and second floors, stilling her. The sound came again. A thump. And what might've been a groan. Then another thump.

Panic tumbled in. Was her father simply moving in his sleep? Or had he woken? Had *she* woken him? Was he headed downstairs now? Were her chances of escape better if she hid or better if she ran? Indecision made her feet stay where they were. And as a few seconds ticked by, there was no indication that she was about to be caught in the act.

Why she did what she did next, she didn't know. Maybe it was just years of conditioning. But for whatever reason, instead of making her quick exit, she headed for the stairs. She took them, one at a time, conscious of the light tap of her feet on each one. She headed straight for her father's room. The door was ajar. It only took a few seconds for Roni to realize how unfortunate that was.

Her father stood near his bed, his eyes closed. In one hand, he held what appeared to be a dress, possibly one of her own. In the other, he held his own erect penis.

Shock and revulsion swept through Roni. And so did Ellis's familiar voice.

Why does he do it? She heard him say. *Why does he keep a beautiful, twenty-two-year-old woman all locked up at home and punish her for any transgression against his wants?"*

Now she had an answer. For a single moment more, the horror of it kept her rooted to the spot. Then sense and self-preservation kicked in, and she fled.

57

Ten Years Earlier
Twelve Hours Before Arrest

The Policeman

One of the advantages of the GPS tracker was that Flip didn't have to have eyes on the kid to know where he was. In turn, no one would have eyes on him. He could watch Ellis's day unfold from the comfort of his own living room without Cliff or Danielle or a single person in town being the wiser. He sipped his coffee and ate his cookie, watching the little red dot on the map on his laptop.

For the first bit, Ellis didn't leave his property. Flip imagined him smoking in the yard. Roving the house restlessly. Stopping in his sister's room a few too many times and peering out the window. The last bit made Flip feel smug.

Yeah, spend time in there, you delinquent, he willed. *Think about where she is.*

He ate another cookie, and the minutes started to drag, and the smugness waned. His coffee settled to lukewarm, then room temperature. But just when Flip wondered if the boy would go anywhere at all, the red blip finally came to life with some force. It zipped away from the Blacks' address and slid along the highway. Ellis was on his bike, no doubt.

Flip sat forward, eager to see what he could use to incriminate the kid. But what he saw made him scratch his jaw.

The first stop was Meridian Trust—the primary bank in

town.

"You getting ready to perform a robbery?" Flip murmured, biting into yet another cookie.

He waited, tapping his thumbs on the desk as the seconds ticked into minutes. Twenty of them. Maybe the kid really *was* robbing the place. But then the dot moved again, and it only went two blocks. Not exactly fleeing the scene.

"Where are you now, Mr. Black?"

The address wasn't one Flip was familiar with—a rarity — and he had to take an extra moment to look it up online. It was an insurance place. A new one.

Odd choice for a kid.

Frowning the whole time, Flip waited out Ellis's visit there. And on to the next. The red dot blipped along from the broker to a gas station. After that came a longer trip. Forty boring minutes of watching the kid go from Meridian to the outskirts. Another address that Flip had to look up, which turned out to be a mechanic's shop. For a short while after that, the policeman debated what to do. He felt like there had to be an underlying thread between the stops the kid made. Except he couldn't see it.

Time for another trip out to the Blacks' place, he decided.

He knew there was a risk that Cliff might catch wind of it somehow. He also knew it might be the only real opportunity to perform another search under the radar, and the only time he could be sure he had enough time to do it.

He snagged his keys, downed the rest of his completely cold coffee, and headed out. He took the side roads as a precaution, and he went the speed limit until he hit the piece of highway that led out to the boy's home. There, Flip all but floored it. In record time, he reached his destination, exited the car, and cautiously approached the house. His intention was to look around. Go after those photos of the girl, maybe. Find something that would toss guilt in Ellis's direction. But he only made it as far as the living room.

A suitcase sat in the middle of the coffee table. It was packed with the boy's clothes, and it provided the connecting clue Flip had been missing. Those seemingly random stops in town? They weren't random at all. They were a part of the kid's exit strategy.

Ellis was going to make a break for it.

58
Two Months,
Thirteen Days Before Escape

The Convict

Ellis woke to the feeling of someone touching his hand. A palm, pressing against his own. A thumb, stroking his wrist alongside the skin-to-skin pressure. The sensation wasn't altogether unpleasant though, and his sleepiness softened his reaction. Instead of swinging a violent fist at the intruder, he simply tightened his grip on the invading hand and dragged his eyes open.

Veronica's gaze was locked on him, expectant. For a few seconds, he had that same dreaming-or-dead sensation the last time he'd come into consciousness and spotted her leaning over him. The same dreaming or dead sensation each time he'd woken up *without* her leaning over him for the last two weeks. Since she'd fucked him and left and not shown up again.

Now, the dreamlike feeling swept itself away quickly. She was there for real. She still wore the same odd outfit she'd had on during her last visit, though it looked as though she'd put it through the wash. Her hair was damp again, but when Ellis drew in a breath, he could smell its freshly shampooed scent. The bruises and scrapes on her face had faded, but the rim of red around her green eyes was fresh.

"What the fuck happened?" he asked.

"I don't want to talk about it," she said. "I don't want to talk at *all*, actually."

"Then why are you here?"

She said nothing. It didn't surprise him.

Truthfully, he hadn't fully expected her to come back. Not after what had happened last time. Not after the way she'd tugged on her clothes and scurried out, shame in her eyes and self-loathing rolling off her like a fucking tidal wave. In fact, seeing her here now, Ellis half-wondered if he'd imagined everything that came before that hasty escape. If sepsis had set in and poisoned his memory. Sex. An unlikely fucking truth.

Lust raged anyway, and he ground his teeth together. "Stop fucking around."

She stayed silent, and he loosened his hold, sure he was going to do something he regretted if he didn't let go. She inched back. Still silent. He opened his mouth but closed it again as she reached down, grabbed the hem of her T-shirt, yanked the fabric over her head, and tossed it aside.

59

One Month, Five Days Before Escape

The Convict

I t was amazing, how quickly Ellis got used to it. How it almost became an expectation to wake up and find Veronica there.

Twice more, he opened his eyes just as she reached his bed.

Two other times, he stirred earlier, when she stepped through the door.

Once, she was under the covers already, her hand sliding past the waistband of his ridiculous hospital pajama pants.

Always, she came to him the same way. With a pink face. Embarrassed. Eager. Deliciously sneaky as she confessed that she'd arranged, yet again, for them to have a half hour alone.

She was so fucking soft and sweet that he forgot he was supposed to want to hurt her.

Still.

He kept waiting for the violence to rise up. For his fingers to climb to her throat so they could squeeze the life from her pliable body. For his vision to get clouded with bloodlust. Each time the smell of her filled the room, he expected it. When her hands slid over his chest, shy and cautious, he knew it must be coming.

Except it didn't. For each of those thirty-minute sessions, all pre-arranged with Nurse Lorraine, Ellis was a different man. A man who he knew he *wasn't*. Who he'd never been and could never be.

"I'm leaving Meridian for good," she'd said fervently each and every time she slipped her clothes on and got ready to leave.

Yet a day or two or three later, Ellis would see her again. Taste her again. Live inside the prison version of a fucking fairy tale with her, just one more time.

60
Twenty Days Before Escape

The Convict

V eronica's head had been resting against Ellis's chest for far longer than usual today. He was starting to think she'd fallen asleep when she spoke up, her voice soft and serious.

"How much more time do we have before the nurse comes back?" she asked.

"Only one of us is allowed to have a watch, sweetheart," he replied. "And it isn't me."

"I think I left mine somewhere I'll never get it back from." Her finger traced a little circle around the bandage that covered his wound. "You were right, you know."

Instinctively, he knew she was referring to her fuckwad of a father, and he felt himself tense. "What did he do?"

"Nothing."

"Bullshit."

"Nothing to *me*," she amended. "I've been staying at the Meridian Motel, so I haven't seen him."

"All right," he said. "I'll play along. You wanna clarify what I'm right about, then?"

"Why he kept me around the way he did."

The tension in his body amplified. "You know this because?"

"I saw something. A while back now. I'd rather not go into

detail, but it made me think and wonder if…" She bit her lip, worrying at it.

"What?"

"It doesn't matter." She sat up and swung her bare legs off the bed. "I'm leaving Meridian."

"So you've said." He shifted, watching as she slipped her top over her head and pulled on her pants.

She leaned in and gave him a ridiculously normal kiss on the cheek. "I'll see you soon."

As she made her way out of the room, unease slithered into Ellis's chest. He couldn't pinpoint the source, and that made it worse. He was used to being in control. He *liked* being in control. Right now, though, he had a suspicion he wasn't.

61
Ten Days Before Escape

The Convict

Ten days. Ten fucking days. That's how much time had passed since Veronica had her mysterious and undisclosed epiphany. In the last however many weeks, it was the longest stretch of time she'd gone without coming to the prison infirmary. It made Ellis antsy.

The gut wound was getting damn near recovered. It would've healed already if not for a setback with an infection. Something he never thought he'd have been thankful for, but which had worked in his favor just this once. Now, though, he was feeling better. Up to par, really. He'd tried to keep that little fact to himself, playing up the injury as much as he could. Pretending to struggle with his physio like some fucking weakling tool. But he'd heard Lorraine and another nurse talking about how they were going to put him back in gen pop sometime soon.

"Then what?" he muttered to himself.

Then nothing, his subconscious replied. *Were you expecting this to carry on forever?*

"Obviously not," he said.

"Obviously not what?"

He jerked his head up at the unexpected reply. Veronica stood in the doorway for a second, as though waiting for him to answer. When he didn't, she stepped the rest of the way into the room and closed the door behind her.

Ellis narrowed his eyes. She looked different. The blue T-shirt and jeans—which had somehow become her uniform—were gone. Her hair, which had grown with remarkable speed, was pulled into a small ponytail. It wasn't only that, though.

She's still in control, said a dark part of Ellis's brain. *And that's a problem.*

He eyed her up and down in the slow, lascivious way he'd often done before actually getting access to the curves she tried to keep hidden. "Don't know why you bothered with the new dress. Not like you're going to keep it on for long."

Her cheeks went pink, and she smoothed her hands over the dress in question. She didn't, however, take the bait.

"I called your lawyer," she blurted instead.

It was almost a relief to have her immediately say something that pissed him off. "You did what?"

"Morris Trail," she clarified.

"I know his fucking name," he replied, embracing the anger like an old friend.

"He says you had a shot at winning your case in court."

"He's a liar."

"He told me there was evidence that might've helped you. Something to create reasonable doubt. And he—"

"Did you fuck him?"

She sucked in a sharp breath. "Pardon me?"

"Morris fucking fuck-face Trail." Ellis growled, the steadily unleashing rage making his hands flex and his blood burn. "Did you fuck him?"

"Why would you even ask me that?"

"This is me, sweetheart. Maybe you've forgotten who I am. Now answer me. Did you let him put his shady lawyer cock inside your—"

"No! You're the only person I've—" She stopped, and her hands, clenched, her hurt palpable. "You don't get to do this. You can't twist things up. And I haven't forgotten who you are. I called Morris because I was doing what you wanted me to do."

"How?" he demanded. "Just how the *fuck* is talking to my lawyer doing what I wanted you to do?"

"You want to get out of here," she said.

"What does Morris have to do with that?"

"He's your lawyer. It's his job."

He could hear the bitterness in his own laughter. "Do you think that's how it works?"

"That *is* how it works," she stated, a frown creasing her forehead before her eyes widened with an innocence that seemed like a parody. "You wanted me to help you break out literally?"

"You know what I did to my sister. No amount of lawyering is going to change that."

"You feel responsible for her death, I understand that. You were her brother, and you didn't protect her. But you're leaving something out. I've known it since the second we met."

Something in him snapped. This sweet girl really believed what she was saying. The look on her face—the stubbornness in her eyes, the set of her mouth—told him so. She'd been inside his dark world for *months,* and she still didn't get it.

"Christ," he said. "Listen to me, Nic. Really listen. My guilty plea wasn't a result of a guilty conscience. I *confessed.* They aren't going to let me out of here. No legal fucking loopholes. No appeals. No retrials. I described in court exactly what I did to her. Do you want to hear it, too, so you can stop playing this game?"

A hint of uncertainty passed over her pretty features. "No. I don't think that—"

He cut her off, his tone wooden. "She was lying on the ground, and I was on top of her. She was bleeding from everywhere. You know the expression 'beaten to a pulp'? That's what I think of when I remember it. The way parts of her skin were pulverized."

"Ellis. Please."

"Her face was barely recognizable. Broken nose. Smashed jaw. If it hadn't been for her eyes... they were the same as mine. Same color. Same shape. Looking into them was always, always like looking into a mirror. A freaky, funhouse mirror. One where I didn't know that the world's a pile of shit."

"Ellis," Veronica repeated.

He ignored her; he was in the zone of his darkest memories. "I wondered why she wasn't dead already. How anyone that damaged could be breathing. But she was. Blood was puffing in and out of her mouth in bubbles. I even thought something along the lines of, *'Just die, already.'* She didn't. So I finished the job. I put my hands on her throat and I squeezed as hard as I could. I closed my eyes, and I kept squeezing. I have no idea for how long. The next thing I remember is Farriday, pulling his gun."

Now Veronica was silent. But she didn't need to say anything. Her expression spoke on its own. Her skin had gone from pink to ashen to green. If she leaned over and puked, it wouldn't surprise Ellis at all.

"Now you know," he said. "And while I'm being honest with you, I didn't just kill my sister, sweetheart. I killed two men. One because he thought it was a good idea to regularly fondle my balls and one because he killed little girls with drugs after he raped them. And believe me when I tell you that I've got at least one more asshole on my list before I'm done."

"I don't understand." Her shoulders were hunched, her voice small.

"Which part?"

"Any of it. Any of... *this.*"

"I've been saying it all since the beginning, haven't I sweetheart? Out of the two of us, I'm not the one who's been living in a fantasy world."

"I have to leave." The words were faint, her gaze vacant as she stumbled back toward the exit.

"You do that," Ellis said contemptuously. "Just try to keep out of my lawyer's pants."

She was gone so fast that he had no idea if she'd heard him or not.

62

Ten Years Earlier
Six Hours Before Arrest

The Policeman

Flip needed the kid to stay put. As he stared down at the open suitcase, it was an overwhelming thought. The kid had to be made to stay. He knew he was the one who had to do it. He had to pivot again. Adapt to this tangent. If Ellis Black managed to get out of town, the chances of finding him again became so slim that Flip estimated them at zero. Degenerate kid. Degenerate family. *Good riddance to them,* is what the local people—and the local PD—would say. They wouldn't seek Ellis, let alone his sister. No crime to investigate other than two runaway kids.

Flip couldn't tear his eyes away from the bag. His mind churned.

Even if by some miracle the report *was* made and taken seriously, how long would they search? How wide? A couple of towns over? A week or a month? The Ellis twins were minors, but they weren't young. It wasn't their first time alone, and if their parents were gone for good, that just meant an added burden on the system. And since no one believed that something nefarious had gone on, it wouldn't be too hard to think that Ellis had taken his sister somewhere else. Maybe they'd think it was somewhere better. Safer for the two kids.

Another minute passed, and Flip considered whether

making a final appeal to his would-be boss might be worth the effort. Except he had a feeling that Cliff wouldn't have any interest. The other man might use the prod to do the very thing Flip had narrowly avoided having done to him two days ago. And getting fired was the last thing he wanted.

What if they found something after the fact?

He puzzled that over for a second. If they did—if Cliff did —then surely that would be enough to spur a search. But again, he could easily imagine Ellis disappearing with an extraordinary amount of thoroughness.

That's when it hit him. What he needed wasn't yet another plan. What he needed wasn't evidence. What he needed was a body.

63

Two Hours Before Escape

The Preacher's Daughter

Roni sat in a corner booth in the Meridian diner with her hands clasped around a long-cold cup of hot chocolate. She wasn't sure how long she'd been there. Enough time for the staff to have done a shift change. Enough time that her muscles had grown stiff. But not enough time to make a decision about what came next. For a month now, she'd felt like she was at an impasse. She needed to move on. Physically. Emotionally.

She'd counted and recounted the money back at the motel. There were eight thousand, four hundred and five dollars in the pile. And fifty-two cents at the bottom of the box. Roni was ready to leave Meridian behind. Ready to abandon her belief that she was in some way beholden to her father. That much she knew. But she had yet to let go of whatever strange thing bound her to Ellis Black.

Part of her wanted to blame the sex. It was an easy excuse. It was also simple to accept. She couldn't control her physical attraction, however misplaced, however depraved. Lust was its own animalistic thing. Except she knew it was more than that. An invisible bond. A connection she could feel in her bones, even as she knew she ought to rail against it.

She couldn't quite pinpoint the magnet that drew her to the man who'd committed such atrocities, but she was one hundred percent sure that if she didn't confront it head-on, it might hold her back forever.

And I'm done being held back, she thought.

But she couldn't stomach the thought of going back to the prison. She didn't know what would happen if she tried to face off with Ellis. Would her urges win out over her conscience? Likely. Just considering the idea made her ache to climb into his bed. Dredging up his graphic descriptions of his sister's murder did nothing to ease the want, either.

She *wanted* to go back. She *wanted* to look Ellis in the eye. And that was the exact reason she couldn't do it. But she had to speak to him.

"*Have* to." She meant to whisper it to herself—or maybe not aloud at all—but she said it with so much fervor that a passing waitress jumped, rattling the tray of glasses she held.

Roni started to offer an apology then stopped.

"Do you have a phone?" she asked instead.

The waitress bit her lip. "Not usually for customer use, but if it's an emergency..."

"I think it is."

"It's behind the counter. I'll show you."

"Thank you."

Covering her eagerness, Roni rose smoothly to her feet and followed the other woman to the phone. She waited for the waitress to get back to work, then reached for the receiver, dialed the operator, and asked to be connected to the prison's main line. She counted off the rings as they vibrated in her ear.

One.

Two.

Three.

The line clicked, and a woman's crisp voice greeted her. "Meridian Penitentiary. For your safety and ours, all calls placed to this institution will be recorded. How can I help you today?"

"Hi there. My name is Roni—" She paused, quickly decided that the cutesy moniker no longer suited her at all, then smoothly corrected herself as she gave the rest of her rehearsed response. "Veronica Hollister. I'm the next of kin for an inmate named Ellis Black. He's currently in the infirmary, and I'm wondering if I could speak with him?"

"I'm sorry, ma'am, but that's not possible," said the woman on the other end. "Outgoing calls only."

Roni—*Veronica*—felt her shoulders sag, but she tried again anyway. "I need to tell Mr. Black something urgent."

"I'm sorry again, ma'am, but unless it's a death in the family —"

"It is."

There was the briefest pause. "Sorry?"

"It is," Veronica said more firmly, the lie coming with no effort. "I need to inform Mr. Black that his mother has passed away."

There was another pause. "Could you repeat your name?"

"Veronica Hollister."

"Hang on one minute, Ms. Hollister."

Veronica closed her eyes, anticipating a drawn-out wait followed by disappointment. She was surprised instead by the brevity of a response.

"Ms. Hollister?" said the woman on the other end.

"Yes?"

"This is highly irregular."

What is? Veronica thought, but aloud she said, "I see."

"Can you be reached on this number in another minute?"

"I think so."

"Okay. Stand by."

The line went dead, and Veronica's heart rate quickened. She glanced across the diner. The staff members were all presently out of view, but she didn't want to risk being asked to abandon the phone. Keeping the receiver to her ear, she pressed her finger onto the hang-up mechanism on the hook. Again, she didn't have to wait long. Under two minutes, and then the phone started to ring.

Breathless, Veronica lifted her finger before the sound could fully form.

Without any preamble, Ellis's growl filled her ear.

"My mother, sweetheart?" he said. "You really think I'd care if that bitch was dead? She left me to rot at home before I was ever rotting in here."

Veronica tamped down the reflexive ache. "It's not that."

"What is it then? Couldn't stand to see me face-to-face?"

"Why did you kill Emily?"

She blurted the question without meaning to, and until the second the words were out of her mouth, she didn't realize it had been on her mind.

Why *had* he killed Emily? For all the horrific details Ellis had shared, that wasn't one of them. She waited for an answer. Something dark. Something that would chill her. But the line went silent for so long that Veronica thought they'd been cut off.

"Ellis?" she said tentatively.

It was his turn to respond with a query. "Does a man like me need a reason?"

"You gave me the details about why you killed those other two men. The one who molested you and the drugdealing pedophile."

"So?"

"So... those were *reasons*. They might even be reasons that someone could justify. But you haven't said a thing about why you killed Emily. Not in all the months that I came there."

Silence dominated again. Veronica pictured Ellis on the other side of the call. Still in bed. Hand gripped tightly around a portable phone of some kind, eyes piercing some spot on the wall.

"How many times have you told me how terrible you are?" she added. "I think I deserve an explanation."

"I told you about my shitty family life."

"Sure. You told me that your dad was abusive like mine, and that he abandoned you and then died, and that your mom left you and your sister alone for longer and longer times until one day she didn't come back at all. But you didn't *have* to tell me any of that. It was in all the newspapers I saw when I looked up your case."

"Isn't that enough?" he asked.

"No, as a matter of fact," Veronica replied. "It isn't enough. You never talked to me about Emily. You never told me anything about your relationship at all."

"She's dead."

"Did you love her, Ellis?"

"Of course I fucking loved her."

"But you really did kill her?"

"I've been saying it since day one, sweetheart. Guilty as sin."

Veronica took a breath. "Then I'm going to ask again. Why did you do it?"

His responding exhale was so thick and heavy she could practically feel it through the phone. "She wasn't going to live, no matter what I did."

There was something in his words that made her frown. "What really happened that day?"

"Nothing anyone would believe."

"I'd believe it."

"Would you?"

A niggling of suspicion tried to work its way into her brain. She just didn't know quite what it was. But she did suddenly know she needed to see him. To watch his face as he told her whatever secret it was that he'd been harboring all these years.

"I'm coming to the prison," she said.

There was a pause, and then he spoke in a resigned voice. "Better hurry if you want to get me alone. They're moving me back to my cell the day after tomorrow."

"I'll get there as soon as I can."

Veronica set the receiver into the cradle of the antiquated phone, then hurried back to her table, where she dropped more than enough cash to cover the cost of the drink she never finished.

Almost blindly, she left the diner and made her way back

to the motel, intent upon giving herself a quick tidy-up before heading for the prison. She didn't get quite that far. She no sooner opened the door to her room than a hand shot out and yanked her inside, bringing her face to face with an imposing figure.

Her father.

64
Seventy-One Hours After Escape

The Convict

Ellis was straddling his newly acquired motorcycle—a passable bike, which hadn't even cost him the entire grand that he'd pilfered from Veronica's stash—on top of a hill that overlooked the road that led out of town. He'd chosen the spot for two reasons. One, because the cover of trees hid him well enough from prying eyes. Two, because it gave him a perfect view of the Meridian Café. He wanted to be sure that Veronica and her best buddy, Captain Farriday, were going to follow through on their plan to make a stop.

From his vantage point on top of the hill, Ellis would be able to see the policeman's car as it came around the bend. When it did, it would reach the café in a minute or less, and that would be his signal to leave. Right then, though, he had some time.

He lifted his paper coffee cup and took a sip. Absently, his thumb slid across the raised logo on the side, and his eyes momentarily drifted to the matching logo over the shop's door. It'd been a risk, going in there. Especially this close to the final pieces of his plan. But he hadn't been able to resist. He'd met the barista's eyes from behind his sunglasses, daring her to somehow know who he was. *And shit.* When not the barest hint of recognition crossed her face, he'd been tempted to *remove* the sunglasses. Maybe give her a nudge. As he'd contemplated doing it, her smile had wavered for a second, but then she'd held out her hand.

"Your change, sir?" she'd said.

He'd been so focused on waiting for her to gasp his name and take a frightened step back that he'd ignored what she was actually doing—her job.

He'd waved a hand. "Keep it."

"You paid with a fifty."

"I know."

The young woman's face had pinked, and as Ellis had turned away, he'd wondered if she thought he was flirting with her. It'd been a long time since anyone had looked at him and not known at least a small piece of who he was—*the villain.*

It was the second time it'd happened today. First with the purchase of the motorbike—a cash transaction where he was damn sure the seller was worried about being the shady one himself—and now this. It made Ellis scoff.

Farriday, his lackeys, and the prison guard retrieval team hadn't issued a public warning. A murderer-slash-rapist on the loose, and no one was the wiser. Only the captain would be that arrogant. That self-centered. Undoubtedly, Farriday wanted to bring Ellis in himself. Be the same bullshit hero he'd been all those years ago.

Not this time, you son-of-a-bitch.

He lifted his cup a second time, but he lowered it again before he could get it to his lips. The weather-beaten sedan had just made an appearance. Ellis leaned forward, straining to get a glimpse of the occupants. His lip curled when Farriday's balding head came into view, and he fought irritation as he realized he wouldn't be able to see Veronica until they stopped. The car was on the wrong side of the road to allow it. It was probably an extra hint that he ought to get going. Yet once again, he couldn't suppress an urge to take a risk.

He watched as the car came to a stop in the Meridian Café parking lot. The driver's side door opened first, but Ellis paid little mind to the cop as he exited. His eyes were focused almost solely on the passenger side. A pair of familiar slim legs poked out first, followed by the flounce of a black, knee-length skirt, then a pink-clad torso and a head topped with a colorful scarf.

"There you are, sweetheart," Ellis murmured, battling a surge of automatic lust as he eyed her from top to bottom and back again.

He wasn't quite close enough to see Veronica's face, but her mood was readable, nonetheless. The repeated smoothing of her skirt. The way she darted a look around before closing the door. It all told him she was nervous.

Can you blame her?

He shook his head to himself, rolling his shoulders as Veronica started toward the diner with the cop following close behind. No, he sure as shit couldn't blame her. She had to know he was out there, waiting for his chance to pounce. Better than anyone, she was aware that there was no way in hell Ellis was going to let Farriday go. Even if that meant allowing the cop to think he'd outsmarted him. For now.

Smiling a little at the thought, he downed the last of his coffee, crushed the paper cup, and jammed it into his pocket. He put on his helmet and turned over the motorcycle's engine. Under him, it hummed. It was a pleasant sound. A pleasant feeling. Not loud and overdone. Exactly the right amount of power for the job. He'd missed being on a bike more than he'd known.

Smiling wider, he lifted a foot and prepared to take off. At the last second, though, he glanced down toward the Meridian Café one more time, and what he saw made him freeze. Farriday had paused outside the coffee shop's doors. His head was tipped up, his hand poised at his brow, his attention seemingly lasered on Ellis's hilltop position.

Had the captain heard him despite the relative quiet of the engine? Could he see him? Maybe he'd caught a glint of the sun's reflection off Ellis's helmet?

Mentally—hurriedly—Ellis calculated how long it would take him to tear down to the café. He didn't know if he could get there before Farriday packed up Veronica and booked it. He'd have to try, though. But a heartbeat later, the point became moot. The captain gave his forehead a flat-palmed wipe, then swiveled and headed into the coffee shop at a leisurely pace.

Ellis's shoulders dropped. A stab of disappointment flashed through him, and he realized he wouldn't have minded an excuse for immediate conflict. An ending.

Soon, he told himself.

This time, when he lifted his foot, he didn't pause for a final look. He wanted this to be over.

65

One Hour Before Escape

The Preacher's Daughter

A breath. Or half a breath, to be more accurate. That's all the time Veronica had to react to her father's next move. It was just enough. She took a step back as he swung his arm in an open-palmed hit. His hand whipped by her face, so close that she felt his fingers brush her skin. Thankfully, the momentum sent him off kilter. He stumbled forward and hit the ground. Veronica managed to get farther out of reach, but he was still blocking the exit. Vaguely, she wondered why the commotion hadn't drawn any outside attention. Of course, she knew the answer. She'd chosen this motel because it was the exact kind of place where people didn't pause and ask questions. The only person who was going to help her was herself.

She straightened her shoulders and hoped the calmness in her voice would have some effect. "Dad, you need to leave."

His reply was a sputter. *"Leave?"*

"Dad—"

"You paid for this room with my money, and you think *I* should be the one to leave?"

"I'll call the police," Veronica warned.

"And tell them what?" said her father as he grabbed a hold of the wall and pulled himself up. "That you stole from me and holed up here like the whore I've always known you'd turn out to be?"

He lunged, and Veronica sidestepped to avoid the attack. But it didn't matter. Apparently, she wasn't his target. He moved past her, took hold of the old-fashioned phone, then yanked it out of the wall. He sent the phone flying toward her head. At the last second, her hands came up to protect her face. The base of the phone glanced off her knuckles. The receiver spun wildly on its cord then dropped and smashed her foot. It hurt. But her father had done far worse, far more violent things to her in the past.

She lifted her chin and met his eyes. "I'll tell them who you really are. What you're really capable of."

He snarled wordlessly and lunged again. Veronica moved out of his way.

"I'll tell them what you do when you're alone at night," she added as her father crashed into the tiny table in the other corner of the room.

He steadied himself and rounded on her. She'd never seen him this angry. His face was so red it was nearly purple. Almost comically, a vein bulged in his neck. But at the same time... he was somehow frail. His knobby shoulders were hunched in, and liver spots were visible on his coiled hands. His thinning hair appeared sparse and brittle, and his lips tremored as a tiny bead of blood formed in the center of the lower one. Catching his breath was a visible struggle. He looked old. Of course, he *was* old. Older than her mother by twenty years. Closer to fifty than to forty when Veronica had been born. But never before had she realized how pronounced his age had become. And Veronica realized something more important than that, too. He looked beatable. She had an opening to escape now. Her father no longer blocked the path to the door. Why wasn't she running? She blinked at the exit, then shifted her attention back to her father, holding fast to her position.

"What are you going to do?" he said, sneering despite his wheezing. "Hit me?"

"The night Mom died, she locked me in a closet and told

me she'd come back for me," Veronica replied, the memory suddenly overtaking her. "She was bleeding from her eye, and even though I knew you'd done it, the blood was scarier. She told me she loved me, and she closed the door."

"I don't know what you're talking about."

"I let myself out. I broke the latch on the closet, and I went looking for you to tell you she was gone. I was so mad at Mom for leaving me there, and I wanted to punish her."

"She was a whore who *deserved* to be punished."

Her father was breathing easier now, and a little voice in Veronica's head screamed that the window to get out was closing. She went on anyway.

"She was just trying to be free," she said softly. "And she wanted me to be free, too. But I thought I killed her. I thought she died because I didn't wait for her."

"She was—"

"A slut. A whore. I know. You've been telling me that for as long as I can remember. But was she *having* an affair, Dad? Or did you need to believe that so you could make yourself the victim?"

She wasn't expecting him to answer. And he didn't. His eyes darkened. The vein pulsed. And he came at her once more. This time, she didn't move out of his way. She simply braced for his weight. Her readiness didn't completely stop her from losing her footing, but it was obvious he hadn't been expecting as much resistance as he received. When his body hit hers, he bounced backward, stumbling. His rear end hit the bed hard enough to make the springs squeak a protest. His eyes were wide with surprise.

"I really think you should go, Dad," Veronica said.

He swiped a hand over his mouth and stood up. "Not until I get what I came for."

She didn't know if he meant the money or if he meant her, and she didn't care. "I'm not saying this for my own sake. If you don't leave, I think you'll regret it."

In response, he dived yet again, clearly still not seeing that she wasn't going to let herself be easy prey. Veronica angled herself away from him. For the second time, he smashed into the table. But now the cheaply made piece of furniture couldn't withstand the pressure; the top cracked, one of the legs fell off, and her father's head hit the wall, eliciting a cry.

She thought he might give up. Or at least take a moment to recover. Instead, he seized a newly created weapon—the table leg—and he didn't bother to stand up before using it. He took a swing from his spot on the ground. And while he wasn't close enough to hit her, several chunks of splintered wood came flying her way. The onslaught made her cringe back and close her eyes when she should've been forging her own attack. Her father pressed his advantage. In the three seconds it took to open her eyes, he'd already pushed to his feet, brandishing the table leg.

Now she had no time to react. No time to defend herself.

The makeshift weapon jabbed into her stomach. It swiped her hip. It pressed to the underside of her chin for just long enough to make her choke, and then her father dropped it. He shot out his hand and gripped her throat. While Veronica flailed, he backed her to the wall, squeezing harder and harder. Spots dotted her vision. But through those, she could still see that a smile—far more sinister than any Veronica had ever seen even Ellis Black flash her way—graced her father's face. It was no longer about punishing her or about getting his money. This was sheer enjoyment.

Nausea rose up, and sickness gripped Veronica's heart. Broke it, even. How had it come to this?

Ever think that it was always like this? said Ellis's voice in her head.

Maybe it was, she thought in response.

And the idea brought a resurgence of self-preservation. She lifted a knee and drove it between her father's legs. She hit him with far less force than she would've liked, and while it was enough to make him fall back, it wasn't enough to completely deter him. He immediately snapped the table leg up from its discarded spot on the ground and came at her with it again. This time, it became a club instead of a lance. It sliced through the air. Wildly, once, then with a bit more precision. On the third swing, Veronica ducked low, then turned herself into a battering ram. With a cry, she slammed her shoulder into her father's chest. He teetered. He stumbled. He fell, his head smacking the nightstand as he went down. But he wasn't done.

Pressing the table leg to the ground for leverage, he righted himself, wiped away the blood that gushed from a fresh split above his left eyebrow, then lifted the weapon. It had further splintered on the end, now sharp and spear-like and deadly. All details that Veronica noticed as he ran straight at her.

Gasping, she jumped out of the line of fire. There was a sickening noise. A *squelch*. And her father finally—abruptly — stopped. His body sagged in a strange position, about a foot from the wall. It only took a moment for Veronica to grasp what had just happened. The blunt end of the table leg had stuck into the wall, while the sharp end had stuck into *him*.

"Dad?" A sob escaped along with the word.

Veronica started to take a step closer, but she jerked away again as his head suddenly lolled back. Grotesquely, the motion drew him off the table leg that had impaled him. In near slow motion, he folded to the floor. The whites of his eyes were on display and pointed straight up at the ceiling while a contrast of crimson pooled from his stomach. Veronica could see things no one but a surgeon ought to see.

She covered her mouth with her hand and whispered against her palm. "Not like this. Please."

And like an answer to the plea, his chest rose then fell.

He was breathing.

Dear God.

He was unconscious and gutted. But somehow still alive.

Veronica choked back another horrified sob. "Dad."

His hand twitched. His eyes closed.

There was nothing she could do. Nothing anyone could do. There was no coming back from a wound like this. No way to help him except—

Ellis.

His name slammed through her head like an echo. *He* could help. He'd done it before, for his sister. The unthinkable. The necessary.

She needed him, and she needed him now.

66
Five Hours Before Arrest

The Policeman

T he old barn was the answer. Flip didn't have to think too hard to come to the conclusion. But the problem wasn't a location. The problem was the bait. He needed to draw Ellis out there. Bring him in. Have the kid do what Flip wanted him to. And the hours were running short. Any time now, the kid would finish whatever other errands he had planned. He'd come back to the house. He'd grab that bag, and he'd go. He'd evaporate. Flip had to stop him.

Bait.

After a few moments, he realized there was an obvious way of doing things. A good old-fashioned trail. In this case, made of Emily Black's things.

Smiling, Flip got to work.

67
Thirty Minutes Before Escape

The Convict

Ellis was expecting Veronica. She'd literally told him she would come as soon as possible. Yet somehow, she still managed to surprise him when she stepped into the room, quickly closed the door, then turned a wild-eyed look his way.

"Ellis…" She hitched a ragged breath. "I need your help."

He'd anticipated a barrage of questions about Emily. A press for more truth about what had led to his crime. A lengthy discussion. In fact, anything other than a plea for help would've surprised him less.

"Ellis?" she said again. "I don't think I have much time."

He ran his eyes over her face with new scrutiny. Over the past few weeks, her abrasions had all but healed. Now, though, he saw fresh marks. The beginnings of a bruise above her eyebrow. Tiny cuts, marking her cheeks. Like she'd been in a fight with a handful of fragmented glass. An explanation came to mind right away, and the familiar anger surged up.

"The son-of-a-bitch found your hiding place," he replied.

She nodded. "Yes."

"Well, fuck."

"Fuck, indeed."

Genuinely startled by the word coming out of Veronica's mouth, Ellis lifted an eyebrow. "Cursing? That's new."

She swallowed. "The situation calls for it."

"What situation might that be, sweetheart?" he asked.

She stole a glance over her shoulder then stepped closer to the bed and dropped her voice low. "He's dying."

"That's a bad thing?"

"In a bad *way.*"

Ellis couldn't give fewer fucks if the man died as badly as he'd lived. "And *that's* a bad thing?"

Veronica's lips pressed together for a second before she answered. "I can't let him suffer."

"I'm not the man you need for this."

"You're the only person I know."

"Well that fucking sucks, because what you're looking for is either a hitman or 9-1-1. Not some poor asshole tied down to a hospital bed inside a prison infirmary."

She pushed a small breath out. "I'm willing to make a trade."

"For what?"

"The only thing you want."

"You don't know what you're saying," he replied.

She almost laughed. Was he going to try to talk her out of it?

"You told me you had a plan," she said. "You told me to say the word."

"I know what I told you."

"So. I'm saying the word, Ellis."

She opened her hand to reveal a metallic object. It didn't glitter. But it might as well have. Ellis's eyes hung on it for a long second before he pulled them up to her face.

"That's a Leatherman," he said. "How the hell did you get it in here?"

"I didn't," she replied. "It was in the nurse's desk."

"What did you—"

"Nothing. I didn't do anything to her. She's running an errand. Like usual. We only have the same half-hour we always have. If we're going to do this, we need to move."

He eyed the knife again. "If you free me, I won't be coming back."

Her fingers closed, covering the tool. "I know."

"If you wait for five more minutes, maybe your father will die without my help."

"You want to argue? Now? You've been telling me for months this is all you want."

"No shit."

"So I don't understand the problem."

In truth, Ellis didn't understand it either. What was he worried about? He'd been working up to this moment since the second Veronica walked into the room on that first day. She'd been a gift. Wrapped in pretty fucking paper. Why was he questioning it?

A frown put a deep crease in between her eyebrows. "Are you really not going to help me?"

"Fuck," he said. "Yes. Cut the fucking zip-tie."

Relief made her face relax. "Thank you."

Eagerly, she leaned in and used the knife on the thick plastic that held Ellis to the bedrail, and in less than ten seconds, a sharp *snap* indicated his new freedom. He immediately used it. Slickly—easily—he wrenched the knife from Veronica's fingers, grabbed a hold of her hair, and pulled back her head. Roughly, he pressed the point of the Leatherman to her exposed throat.

"Still want to do this?" he asked in a low voice.

"Yes." She said it without a trace of worry, and there was no indication that she was bothered by his abrupt regression into violence.

He pressed a little harder, watching as a tiny drop of blood formed between the metal and her skin. "Those guards out there won't hesitate to use lethal force, Nic. And they won't stop to say, 'pretty please' like I'm doing now."

She still didn't flinch. "They will if you're using me as a shield."

"So that's your plan? To play the victim?"

"I *am* the victim. You tricked me into believing you were someone else. You manipulated me into coming back here

— over and over—by giving me hope that you might become repentant. You made sure that I *had* to come back by making the police contact my father and by putting me down as your next of kin."

"All true," Ellis conceded without letting the blade drop. "But what are you leaving out?"

"Can you please let me go?" The question had the sound of deliberate avoidance.

"Don't know why I should."

"Did you rape Emily?"

"What the fuck does that—"

"Because I don't think you did. I think you killed her because you had to kill her. Because she was suffering. And I think that your *real* reason to get out of here has nothing to do with a simple hatred of being locked up."

Silence hung in the room after she spoke. Her words begged for discussion, but the seconds were closing in on them, becoming minutes. Soon, the window to escape would close too.

"All right," he finally said, letting his hand fall away from her delicate throat. "Tell me the goddamn plan before I change my mind."

68

Seventy-One Hours,
Thirty Minutes After Escape

The Policeman

As he navigated the car toward the Meridian town boundary, Captain Farriday couldn't stop himself from playing out all the ways Ellis Black might make his grand entrance.

Some were plausible. Like the idea that the other man might simply try to run him off the road using a stolen vehicle.

Others were a bit more unrealistic. Like wondering if the convict might've managed to acquire a set of rollout spikes, which he was going to toss into Farriday's path.

A few were downright insane. Like Ellis descending in a parachute—something that actually flitted through the captain's mind before he gave his head a shake and refocused his thoughts.

But one thing he didn't anticipate was that the man might make himself a target on purpose. In fact, it was so unexpected that the captain didn't realize it was happening. Part of that, Farriday blamed on a simple lack of recognition. He'd seen the escaped convict recently, of course. And he knew what the boy had grown into. A foreboding character. A dangerous one. But apparently, despite knowing that, Farriday was still mentally chasing the kid.

So when they were about ten miles out of town, and he

spied a figure—tall and broad and still—in the middle of the road, all he felt was irritation at the potential slowdown. The wide-shouldered man blotted out the sun with an oversized motorcycle. He was also literally in the center of the lane. And the other side of the road appeared to be blocked by some kind of cement barrier. If the biker didn't move on his own, there was going to be little choice but to come to a complete stop and demand that he get out of the way.

For crying out loud, Farriday thought, tapping down on the brake.

But as his foot lowered, then lowered some more, a lightbulb finally went off. It was Ellis. Right out in the open. No road rage, no spikes, no parachute. Just standing there. Waiting.

"You're kidding me," Farriday said under his breath.

He blinked, half expecting the figure in the road to disappear like a mirage. He didn't. And as the captain continued his now slow approach, Ellis crossed his arms over his chest. As though his pose made him impenetrable. As if he couldn't possibly be run over.

Then another lightbulb went off. Because whatever else Ellis Black might be, he was most definitely subject to the general laws of humanity. He would *have* to move. Because if he got hit, he'd fall. If he got hit *hard* enough, he'd die. And it'd be his own fault, really.

Farriday's foot shifted from the brake to the gas. He gave it a push. The car accelerated. He pushed a little more firmly. A small smile made its way onto his face. But his expression froze as a sharp gasp from the passenger seat interrupted his enjoyment of the moment.

Veronica.

He jerked his eyes toward her, momentarily losing control of the steering wheel. She'd been so quiet since they pulled away from the coffee shop that he'd thought she'd fallen asleep. Then he'd become so immersed in his own thoughts that he'd half forgotten her presence. Now she was definitely awake. Her eyes were wide, her hands clutching the seat on either side of her legs.

"Captain!" Her voice was frantic. "Look out!"

Cursing himself, he yanked his attention back to the road. Back to Ellis. Remarkably, the man still hadn't budged.

This is it, Farriday thought. *This is how it ends for him.*

But as he accepted what was about to happen—what he was about to do—and started to brace for impact, Veronica's small hand landed on the steering wheel and gave it a hard tug. The vehicle heaved, then it careened to the side. The tires skidded. Burning rubber filled the air.

Automatically, Farriday lifted his foot from the gas. The sudden loss of fuel made the car jolt a few more times, and the jarring motion sent his teeth slamming together while also throwing Veronica toward the passenger side window, where she slumped into stillness. It took a few moments for Farriday's vision to clear. When it did, he found himself staring straight into Ellis's cold eyes.

69

Twenty Minutes Before Escape

The Preacher's Daughter

Veronica took a breath, then pulled Ellis's arm a little tighter around her waist. He had his other hand wrapped around the knife, and he held the point pressed to her throat. It stung. So did the spot he'd actually pierced a few minutes earlier. She didn't care. The pain and the blood added to the authenticity of their ploy.

"Are you ready?" she asked in a whisper.

"I dunno," Ellis replied into her ear. "Can someone ever be truly prepared for a prison break?"

"I'll take that as a yes."

"Then by all means, lead the way."

"I think you have to take charge from here."

"Right," he said. "Now get the fuck out there before I kill you."

Holding her firmly against his body, he nudged her forward, then pushed her out of the room toward the infirmary's nurse station. The desk was empty, as she'd known it would be. Lorraine was off doing whatever it was that she did during the unofficial conjugal visits. A tiny stab of guilt pricked at Veronica. The woman had been genuinely kind. Genuinely indulgent. She'd probably even been risking her job over the last few weeks. But there was no time for remorse. Not now. Every second from here on out would be recorded.

Right then, one of the guards could already be watching the live footage. They had mere minutes before the prison staff converged.

And they had to keep up the show.

Veronica fought an urge to seek the camera overhead as Ellis touched her cheek with the knife.

"Don't do or say anything without my order," he said.

"I won't," she replied.

"Promise."

"I promise."

He flicked his hand, palming the knife, and Veronica exhaled. But she relaxed too soon. Ellis traded the blade for his fingers. Hard enough to make her eyes water, he grabbed her jaw and leaned in to give her a kiss so aggressive that she didn't have to pretend to fight it. She even tasted a hint of blood as he finally pulled away.

"You're a bastard," she said.

"I know. Give me a minute, and you'll see what I'm really capable of."

"A minute's probably all you have before they come for you." It was more of a warning than a threat, and the slight lift of Ellis's eyebrow told Veronica that he knew it.

"Don't worry, Nic," he said with one of his dark smiles. "We'll be out of here faster than you can imagine, and then you'll have me all to yourself." He stepped back and pressed himself to the wall beside the door. "Now, call for the guard. Nicely, mind you. Wouldn't want him to worry."

Veronica swallowed, then lifted her voice. "Rodrigo? Are you out there?"

There was the sound of boots hitting the ground from up in the hallway, and two seconds later, the uniformed man's silhouette darkened the doorway. "Right here, Ms. Hollister. What do you—"

Ellis darted out, snaked his arm around the guard, and pulled the other man into a chokehold. The guard's attempt to fight him off was hopeless. Ellis was too big. Too strong. Too experienced.

"Gonna need your help with this one, sweetheart," he said. "Something to tie him up, something to stop him from screaming for his buddies."

Veronica did as she was told. From inside the closest cabinet, she retrieved a few items she thought might serve the purpose—a roll of gauze, a strip of bandage tape, and a piece of rubber tubing. But when she tried to hand them over to Ellis, he shook his head.

"You've gotta do the dirty work, too," he said.

She flicked a look from him to the guard and back again. "I can't."

"You can. Because you won't like the consequences if you don't."

Shaking, she stepped closer to the guard. His face was purple. Maybe with anger, maybe with strain, maybe with the lack of ability to breathe properly. Veronica wanted to close her eyes to block him out. But she couldn't secure him if she couldn't see. And Ellis was right. She did have to do this. She steeled herself and got to work.

The gauze, she stuck into his mouth. The bandage tape, she used to cover the gag. And the rubber tubing, she wove into a secure knot around his wrists.

"Good enough?" she asked Ellis.

"Almost," he replied. "We just need to make sure that our friend here doesn't call *his* friends. Slide that chair over here."

Veronica nodded and obeyed again. She stood back and watched as Ellis completed the task she'd started. He removed the guard's baton and radio, then pushed him onto the seat. With sure movements, he tightened the knot, stretched the rubber tubing to its max, and used the extended piece to tie down the other man. He surveyed their combined handiwork, then nodded.

"It won't hold forever," he stated, "but it'll sure as shit stay for the next little bit."

He slipped behind the counter, lifted a bare foot, and

smashed it into the cabinet there. Once. Twice. And a third time. On Ellis's fourth kick, the cabinet at last gave way. And so did the alarm.

Veronica's heart zigzagged as shrillness filled the air. It would take minutes—not many, but some—for the control center to catch up.

Hurry, she willed as Ellis yanked a few items from the cupboard.

"You can still let me go," she said when he finished.

"Drop it." Ellis's tone was flat and menacing. "Let's get moving."

He grabbed hold of her elbow, dragged her toward the door, and pushed her out of the infirmary.

70

Seventy-One Hours, Thirty Minutes After Escape

The Policeman

C aptain Farriday was thrown back in time as Ellis Black held his gaze through the driver's side window. He was suddenly ten years younger, standing in the courtroom as the judge handed down the sentence. The boy had pled guilty already. It'd been the right move. The only move. The evidence against the boy was so strong that his own lawyer had begged him to take the deal. Or so Farriday had heard. But nothing was foregone. Not until the gavel had been banged. Not until the bailiff led the defendant away. Farriday had been waiting with bated breath. His job was on the line. This boy's murdered sister was the one thing standing between him and his career. Make or break. And Ellis Black's conviction was the solution. And at last—long, long last—the judge made the pronouncement.

Life in prison. No chance of parole.

There'd been more. God knew what else. Farriday missed it all. He'd turned his attention to Ellis, who'd been looking his way, too. Cold, cold blue eyes. Just like now.

Then the illusion of the past shattered. Almost literally. Ellis—the current one—drew back his arm, then shot it forward. As the other man's hand drove toward the window, Farriday saw the rock gripped there, and he squeezed his eyes shut before the glass exploded inward. Shards hit his face.

Pinpricks of pain stung his skin. One particularly large chunk split his lip, and blood gushed free and slid unpleasantly down his chin to his neck. A hand landed on his collar. Yanked him forward, then straight through the window.

A guttural yell—animalistic, even to his own ears— escaped Farriday's throat as the remaining glass tore off chunks of both clothing and flesh. Then he hit the ground. He was vaguely aware that his gun had become dislodged from its holster and skittered across the concrete. He knew he should find it. Or fight back. But all he could do was brace for further attack. It didn't come. What he got instead was a long moment of pain-filled silence, followed by an order.

"Look at me, you asshole," said Ellis. "Open your fucking eyes and look at me."

The captain forced himself to obey, wincing as the motion drove a few shards even deeper. But the added sting was quickly forgotten when his attention landed on the convict. The other man stood over him, his legs wide, his hands in fists, his foot on the freed gun. His gaze was full of contempt, but under that was something else. A need, Farriday realized. Ellis Black still hadn't reached his endgame. He was after something more. And that gave the captain the slightest bit of hope.

"Whatever it is that you want, Mr. Black…" he said. "Maybe I can get it for you."

"Do you have the power to play God? A divine ability to reincarnate?" Ellis asked. "Because what I want is to bring Emily back to life."

"We both know I can't give you that. But maybe—"

"How about ten years, then?"

"Mr. Bl—"

"*Those* are the things I want, Captain. My sister. And my life. Since I think we can both agree that neither is likely, I'm going to have to settle for something else, aren't I?"

Farriday shifted on the ground, trying to stem any hint of

real eagerness. "Money?"

Ellis chuckled, low and dark. "Maybe a little fame? Or some power? No, thanks. None of the above. But I *will* take something equally banal. Ask me what, Captain. Please."

Farriday gritted his teeth. "What?"

"Revenge."

71
Seventeen Minutes Before Escape

The Preacher's Daughter

They made it only halfway up the corridor before Ellis stopped and bent his mouth to Veronica's ear. "I'm afraid we have a problem, sweetheart."

He slid his hand down her arm—knife-first—then clasped her wrist and lifted it up to point at the security camera at the end of the hall. Veronica had deliberately held back from doing it in the infirmary because it might've given away her personal concern over being watched. Now she let herself look up at the blinking red light at the 'T' at the end of the corridor.

"The big bad prison men are going to get a show," Ellis added, his voice tickling against her skin. "They might even be getting one *now.*"

"I don't think they let people walk out of here, Mr. Black," Veronica replied.

"Well, we'll have to do something about that, won't we?" He dropped her arm and stepped away from her, a thoughtful look playing over his features. "You know what? Pretty sure I know how to fix it. You just worry about standing here and holding still. And in case you happen to be considering *not* behaving... remember how my sister died."

He loped to the end of the hall. There, he paused under the camera. He reached into his pocket, pulled out the roll of bandage tape, and tore off a piece with his teeth. There was something feral about the action, and Veronica couldn't fight a shiver. She watched as he stood on his toes and tapped the tape over the lens. When he was done with the coverup, he cast a quick, dark smile at her over his shoulder, then went left at the 'T' and disappeared.

Veronica knew he must be blinding the other nearby cameras. It made sense. But the silence was a vice, squeezing her. She inhaled and exhaled, just to hear a sound. How long would he be gone? Never mind that, how much time had passed already? It felt like an hour. But it couldn't have been more than a few minutes.

She glanced toward the infirmary door. How many minutes were enough that she ought to consider freeing the bound guard so he could call for help? Veronica bit her lip. She ignored the taste of blood that hit her tongue. Maybe the authorities would argue that seconds mattered. Maybe they would say that a mere fifteen heartbeats would give the guard enough time to mount an alarm. But the point became moot a moment later anyway. Ellis came jogging back around the corner, his breaths slightly short as he reached her side.

"Knife to your throat?" he said. "Or can I trust you to behave without it?"

"You can trust me."

"I hope so. I'd hate to have to punish you for lying."

She met his eyes and narrowed her own. "I'm not sure I believe that."

His teeth flashed, wolf-like. But as his mouth opened, the sound of heavy boots—prison-issue guard boots—carried in from somewhere not too far away, cutting him off. Any trace of a smile slipped off his face. Grimly, he grabbed a hold of her arm and pulled her the rest of the way up the hall. At the end, he veered to the right when Veronica expected to go left.

For a second, she thought he'd made a mistake. Hadn't he covered the cameras in the other direction? But she didn't get a chance to ask. With a rough tug, Ellis pulled her to a door she hadn't even known was there. He opened it—it was a utility closet of some kind—then dragged her inside and clicked the lock shut. And it was just in time, too. Immediately, after the darkness surrounded them, the footfalls stopped. There was a brief moment of silence, and then two muffled male voices cut through it.

"How the hell did they get by us?" said the first one, sounding frustrated and puzzled at the same time. "They should be right here."

"How do you know where they should be?" replied the second man, this one with a hint of a British accent. "He covered the bloody cameras, didn't he?"

"Yeah. Shit."

"Absolute shite," said the Brit. "Maybe we should double back."

"Hang on," said the first guard. "What's—"

A third voice cut him off, more muffled, but loud, nonetheless. "Fuck! Guys! Rodrigo is all tied up here! Not sure he's breathing. Little help?"

Veronica's shoulders sagged as boots clattered in the other direction.

Immediately, Ellis found her ear again, speaking in a low tone. "Have I ever told you how I earn my keep here in prison?"

"I don't think I knew you *could* earn any kind of keep in prison."

"All about reform and rehabilitation, sweetheart. Gotta earn skills. Learn a trade. Pay your way in case you ever get out. That's the beauty of our system."

Veronica couldn't think of a single beautiful thing about Meridian Penitentiary or the system that it represented, but she didn't argue.

"What did you learn?" she asked instead.

"How to wire a house. Or *un*wire it." He paused. "And here it goes."

"Here *what* goes?"

The answer came in the form of a click and a zap, and then the air was suddenly too still. Darker, even, than before.

Veronica sucked in a breath, her brain doing a jog to figure out what had happened. Ellis had somehow cut the power. Rigged a switch on an electrical box to blow, maybe. The moment she made the mental leap, chaos erupted outside their hiding place, confirming her suspicion.

"Where the hell's the generator?" hollered one of the men.

"Fuck should I know," another yelled back. "Must be on its own goddamn loop."

"Call for backup. Now!"

There was some equally frantic but less distinct conversation, all of it in raised voices. And a lot of thumping. A bang. Then Ellis took hold of Veronica's arm again, and he tugged her out of the closet. Fear made her feet freeze. It was pitch black. Far too dark to see their way, wherever that might be. What were the chances they wouldn't crash straight into a guard? Or multiple guards, for that matter?

When she didn't move—not even after he gave her a nudge—Ellis leaned in close and whispered, "I'm leaving with or without you, sweetheart, so you'd better make up your mind. Me? Or them?"

He didn't wait for her to respond. Instead, he swung away from her and stalked in the other direction with a stealth that belied his stature. And very quickly, Veronica realized she was going to lose sight of him. His back was already no more than a blob. Staying behind wasn't really a choice, anyway. She wasn't going to let herself become collateral damage in a prison break. And she needed to get back to her father.

Her father.

It was enough to propel her forward at last, and— careful to keep as silent as possible—she hurried after Ellis. They reached the end of the corridor, where they came to a stop in front of another door, its outline visible despite the blackness. On her own, Veronica would've hesitated. At the very least, she might've checked for an alarm. But with Ellis at the helm, there was no waiting. He simply put his palm on the handle and gave it a hard push.

Air rushed in, startling Veronica. She didn't know what she'd been expecting, but it definitely wasn't an unventilated breeze and the accompanying moonlight. Automatically, she inhaled. The acrid scent of tobacco filled her nose, and as hard as she tried to cover it, she couldn't stop a cough from sliding up her throat and escaping through her lips. The sound cut through the silence. It also brought a guard out of the shadows. He was clearly off-duty. No radio on his shoulder, uniform shirt unbuttoned and askew. And the man's surprise was evident in the way the orange-tipped cigarette slipped from his fingers, hit the ground, and rolled toward them while he stood still.

There was a moment with no more reaction than the dropped cigarette. Relative silence. Then the guard seemed to remember who he was and what he was supposed to do. He lifted a foot. That was as far as he got. Ellis slid out from behind Veronica, drew back his fist, and soundly coldcocked the other man. The impact made a fleshy snapping noise, and the guard dropped to the ground, his eyes rolling back in his head as he crumpled.

For several seconds after that, Ellis stood there. With the guard at his feet, his hand relaxed in and out of a fist, and Veronica watched him as he looked up at the sky then over to the mountains in the distance.

Finally, he spoke in a gruff voice. "Looks about the fucking same, doesn't it?"

"What do you mean?" she replied.

"It's been ten years since I've been outside without the backdrop of barbed wire. I thought it might be different somehow. But it's not." He shrugged, cleared his throat, then gave his head a small shake and tipped it to his left. "That piece of shit car over there yours?"

Veronica looked in the direction he'd indicated. Her car *was* there, sitting alone at the farthest end of the parking lot. She was surprised that they'd exited so close to it. But then again, she was surprised that they'd managed to exit at all.

"Should all of this have been so easy?" she asked.

Ellis's gaze glittered silver. "The hard part comes when we get to the motel."

She opened her mouth, then closed it as she shivered in a way that had nothing to do with the ruffle of the evening air.

72

Seventy-Two Hours After Escape

The Policeman

Keeping a calm face despite the chill that cut into his chest, Captain Farriday shook his head and echoed Ellis's word back at him. "Revenge?"

The convict's teeth flashed. "Are we really going to play this game?"

"No idea what you mean, Mr. Black."

"Okay, so we *are* going to do that, then." The other man dropped into a crouch. "Tell me a story."

The new position brought him closer to Farriday's level, but it also emphasized his bulk, driving home the fact that if the captain wanted to come out on top, he was going to have to outsmart Ellis. Overpowering him was out of the question.

"Why don't you tell me something instead, Mr. Black?" Farriday said, using his best good-cop voice. "Explain to me what you think we're doing here. I want to understand."

Ellis sneered. "Don't bother with that shit."

"I'm sorry?"

"Don't play the white knight. We both know that's not what you really are, Captain."

"I still don't know what you mean."

"Tell me a fucking story, Captain." His tone was cold. "Make it start ten years ago on the day before you showed up on my doorstep, looking for Emily."

"I don't remember that day," Farriday lied.

"Then let me remind you."

The big man stood again. Then slammed his foot into the policeman's stomach with enough force to elicit a gag.

"On that day, my sister went out for a walk," Ellis stated. "It was something she did all the time. Especially if she was mad. Better still if she wanted to make *me* mad by disappearing. Running away, she called it. She always came back quickly, though, because she didn't like to be alone. It scared her. Any of this sound familiar yet, Captain?"

Anger mixed with the throb in Farriday's gut, and he fought to keep it from getting the better of him. But as the convict stared him down, fury making the man's jaw twitch, the policeman realized it might be better to let it out. Ellis's own short fuse and his sensitivity on the matter of his sister's murder might be the only way of distracting him long enough to give Farriday an edge. So he seized on it.

"How would I know what she did or didn't do on that day or any other day?" he said derisively.

Ellis's reaction was immediate—he sent his foot out again, this time aiming for Farriday's ribs, then the shin, then once more in the stomach.

"You should know because it was literally your fucking job to know," he snarled. "Who she was with. What she was doing. Her habits. And where she was, all those minutes and hours leading up to her murder. Unless you disagree, Captain?"

Farriday wheezed out his response. "No."

"No, what? No, you disagree? Or no, it wasn't your job?"

"I *did* my job."

"How do you figure?"

"I brought in the man who murdered her. Caught him red-handed, actually."

Ellis's face darkened, and he drew back his foot yet again. But this time, Farriday was ready for the blow. He rolled to the side. The convict stumbled, and the captain used the extra moment to spring from the ground. He dived into Ellis's legs, and even though he practically bounced off, the impact forced the other man to try to retain some kind of foothold. So Farriday dived again. The second attack sent Ellis toppling. The captain ignored him as he fell and concentrated on the thing that mattered more. Getting his hands on his weapon.

73
Escape

The Convict

Ellis eyed Veronica's hands on the steering wheel. Despite the that fact that they were traveling well within the speed limit, her fingers were white-knuckled, her posture rigid. She'd been silent as they pulled out of the prison parking lot. Which was fine. Under-fucking-standable. There was still a good chance of being caught, especially while they were on the prison grounds. But she'd stayed quiet as they got onto the road. Lips pressed tight. Eyes straight ahead. Even now, as she flicked on the turn signal and guided the car to the exit that promised to lead to the Meridian Motel, she said nothing. Almost ten minutes of silence. The longer it went on, the more suspicious Ellis became. What the hell was she hiding under her stiff façade?

It irked him that her mood affected him. He should've been reveling in his new-found freedom. Maybe looking out the window at the kind of scenery that had been nothing but a memory for a decade. Definitely, he ought to have been plotting out the first steps of the plan he'd had in mind for the last few months. Instead, he was stealing glances at Veronica's pretty face. He was ordering himself not to ask trite questions about her thoughts. Clamping his own jaw shut to keep from disobeying his self-directed commands, but somehow still unable to enjoy the that fact that he was fucking *free*. And it wasn't until they were pulling into a spot at the motel that she acknowledged his existence.

With the engine idling, she expelled a breath and spoke without looking at him. "You don't have to do this."

"Don't I?" Ellis replied.

Her hands didn't leave the steering wheel. "I shouldn't have made this a contingency of helping you get out."

Ellis reached over and turned the key into the off position. "Tell me something, Nic. When did you start planning this?"

Puzzlement clouded her face. "Planning what?"

"Your father's murder. Was it when you first saw me? Or when you realized that I wasn't Bobby Lines? Maybe when you went to the library and found out what my crime was?"

"Whatever you're accusing me of, Ellis, it isn't true."

"I'm not accusing you of anything," he said. "I'm asking you. Flat out. When did you decide that I needed to be your scapegoat for your father's murder?"

She flinched. "I didn't decide that."

"Hurting people is what I do, sweetheart. What I'm good at. If that weren't true, I'd be of no use to you. Using me like this... It wouldn't be the first time it happened."

"Well, it didn't happen *this* time."

"Then let me ask you something else," he replied. "Do you think you could stop me from leaving?"

Her response was soft—barely more than a sigh—and her eyes dropped down. "No."

"Do you think I give a shit about owing you a favor?"

"I don't know."

"Well, let me unravel the mystery. I don't, sweetheart. Why would I? Some prison code? Honor among thieves? It's a fucking myth. Dog eat fucking dog is more accurate." He brought a finger to her chin and forced her to meet his eyes. "I hate whatever your dad's done to you. He's not a man. He's a coward. If it hadn't played out like this, I might've gone after him just for the years of abuse."

Her expression softened, and her eyes warmed with

misguided appreciation. *Fuck.* Ellis dropped his hand, cursing himself for his own continued weakness, then snapped open his seatbelt and flung the door wide.

"The longer we sit here, the more likely it is that we get spotted," he said over his shoulder. "What room?"

"Two-oh-eight."

He moved quickly, ignoring the fact that Veronica had to scramble to catch up. When they reached the door—which was marked with faded numbers and had a damaged frame—and she clutched the keycard without reaching out to use it, Ellis let his impatience take over. He yanked the card from her fingers, swiped it, then pulled the handle. He entered the room without discussion, and the second Veronica stepped in behind him, he closed and locked the door behind her.

Briefly, he skimmed his eyes over the room, taking in the details. Evidence of the struggle abounded. Broken furniture sitting in a heap. Blood stains, already turning brown on the carpet. Shattered glass. And the main event. Her father, who was laid out in the center of the floor. He had a gaping wound marking his stomach, and Ellis knew why Veronica had been concerned about a slow, painful death. Why she'd sought mercy for him.

Unbidden, his sister's face filled his vision. Broken and suffering. The pain of seeing her in the state—of knowing he was going to lose her, of realizing he was the one with the power to end it—renewed itself and seared his chest. His hand came up to press against the burn. Emily had deserved better. She still deserved better. More than the fucker on the floor for sure.

Jesus, Black. Let it go for now. Get this shit over with so you can move on.

The feeling refused to be shoved aside. It was like mourning her all over again. Like reaching in and yanking out the parts of his heart he'd been able to ignore for so long. Jesus, he missed her. Hell. Maybe being free reinforced it. Christ knew he'd give up another ten years of his life to bring her back.

"Ellis?" Veronica said tentatively.

He let his eyes sink shut for the briefest moment before answering. "Yeah, sweetheart. I'm on it."

Her voice stopped him before he could take a step toward following through on the promise. "Wait."

He turned her way. Her gaze was fixed on a far corner of the wall, nowhere near her father's still form. It was clear the avoidance was deliberate.

"Second thoughts?" Ellis said.

"No. I just..." She swallowed, her eyes bright with unshed tears as they came to rest on his face. "How are you going to do it?"

"This suit you?" He reached into his pocket and pulled out one of the opiate-filled syringes he'd swiped from the infirmary.

She exhaled. "Yes. Yes, okay."

He stepped closer to the man, and as he focused on the ravaged body there, he immediately realized something. The man really *was* just a body. He was dead already. No breath. No pulse. Eyes partially opened and devoid of life. Ellis stood still, staring down at the carnage.

"Is something wrong?" Veronica asked.

He eased away from the dead man, an explanation on his lips. Except when he glanced over and caught the look on her face, he thought better of it. He hadn't agreed to kill her father because he felt any pity for the man. He'd agreed for Veronica's sake. She was the one who didn't need to suffer.

"I'm getting ready to euthanize my girlfriend's abusive father," he said. "What the fuck could be *wrong*?"

He didn't wait for her to answer. He jabbed the syringe into the preacher's arm and pressed the plunger. When the liquid was all gone, he counted to thirty in his head before pulling the needle free and swiping his palm over the other man's eyes to close them. Then he lifted her father from the ground and deposited him on the bed. At least it gave the illusion that someone cared about the fucker.

He faced Veronica, and he kept his tone impassive. "It's done."

"It's that quick?"

"Your dad might not have seen it as quick. But yeah."

"Thank you, Ellis."

"Weird fucking thing to say in this situation." He tossed the needle into the trash can beside the bed.

"I know." Her skin was pale, her tone hollow. "But I can't think of anything else that fits."

"I could hold you and stroke your hair and feed you some bullshit about how it's going to be fine."

"Before you put a knife to my throat again, you mean?"

"Fair point," he conceded. "Maybe you could cry."

"I actually think I'm done crying. At least for now." She paused and studied him for a second. "What about you?"

He couldn't stop a brow from arching. "Are you asking if I'm going to cry, Nic?"

"What if I am? You did just... you know."

"Kill a man?"

"My father was already dying."

"Without a doubt," Ellis replied, no hint of the truth in his voice. "And my eyes are dry."

She nodded, but a moment later, her face somehow managed to fall even more. "Ellis... what if you were right? What if, this whole time, the only reason I kept coming back to you was because I hoped you'd kill him for me?"

"Honestly?"

"Yes."

He shrugged. "I'll get over it. A hundred worse things have happened to me."

"I don't want to become a hundred and one," she replied.

He let a rare moment of sincerity take him. "You won't be. That much, I can promise you."

"So what now?" she asked, her attention flicking to her father then quickly away again. "What will you do?"

"Doesn't matter."

"It matters to me."

"If I tell you, you don't have plausible deniability, sweetheart."

She shook her head. "I don't want plausible deniability. I want to help you."

"No. You really don't," he said.

"Why not? Is it any more fucked up than my life in general?"

After she said it, Veronica's mouth curved up in a quick, sad smile that pulled at the split in her lip. As it dropped away again, her tongue darted out to clear the fresh drop of blood, and lust reared up.

Forcing his eyes away from the temptation—he had work to do—Ellis cleared his throat. "Should I expect you to keep dropping curses from here on out?"

"If it bothers you, I won't do it."

"You don't have to give any fucks about what I think. That's the whole fucking point of being free."

"I don't feel very free," she said.

"Stuff your cash into your skirt and drive as far the hell away from Meridian as you can, and that might change," he replied.

"Or you can let me make my own decisions, and maybe I'll actually *be* free," she countered.

"Veronica…"

"Nic," she corrected, her voice firm. "I already started the process of legally changing it."

A new bubble of crimson dotted her lip. Ellis flexed a hand. His fingers wanted to squeeze something. Some part of her. *Any* part of her.

"Whatever you're after, I'm not that man," he stated.

She tipped her head to one side, licked the blood away again, and took a step closer. "I know exactly who you are."

"You think you do, but you have no idea what I'm thinking about doing to you. Right here, right now, in front of your father's corpse."

The way she was looking at him, sure and expectant, made

Ellis question his denial.

"Do your worst," she said. "Because I've been sleeping with a man who went to prison for raping and murdering his sister. Today, I asked him to kill my father, and he did. Whoever I was ten months ago… she's gone. Dead. You did what you told her you would. You chewed her up and spat her out, and now here *I* am."

"I'm going to kill the fucking police captain, sweetheart." The confession burst out. "But first, I'm going to make him suffer. I have a plan. Things organized to the goddamn minute. A list of places I need to go and errands I need to run. All I needed was to get out those doors in just the right way."

"All you needed was me."

"You resent that yet?"

"No." Veronica—Nic—said, her tone easy and accepting. "Tell me why you want to make him suffer. And maybe I can help you."

74

One Hour Before Arrest

The Convict

A little flap of pink hung from the oversized latch on the barn doors. It waved in the breeze, out of place in both its shade and its placement. It didn't belong there. That much would be obvious to anyone who happened to see it. And for Ellis, who stood at the top of the hill, watching it, it was much worse. His heart was a stone, sinking into his thin chest and pressing hard against his ribcage. Even from as far away as he was, he knew what the fabric was—a ribbon in his sister's favorite shade. Bubble gum.

It was just the final item in the trail that had led him here. There was a shoe, too. One of her stupid boyband magazines. A picture. And now this.

Ellis took a step forward, not realizing what he was doing until his conscience spoke up.

This is a bad idea, it cautioned.

And it was. Most definitely. So his feet stalled for a moment. Something in him, though, told him that it might be worse to wait it out. He took another step. And another. Then he was running hard. His army boots smashed against the ground. Dirt and rocks flew up under the impact. Ellis paid no attention as the muddier bits spattered on his clothes, and he was oblivious to the particularly large pebble that smacked his cheek and left a slash of red.

By the time he reached the barn, his body was in a full sprint. He was moving so fast that he couldn't quite stop in time, and he had to put out both hands to keep from crashing straight through the door. As it was, his splinter dug into his palms. The wood shuddered, and Ellis stayed there for a few seconds, waiting for it to go still before pushing away from it.

Swallowing back his nerves, he lifted the ribbon. He slid his fingers over the satin. He was aware that he might be contaminating evidence. Absently, he also acknowledged that putting his fingerprints on the strip of pink could have consequences. Really, though, his mind was on his sister. On her innocent blue eyes. On the fact that she'd most definitely had the ribbons in her hair when she'd run away, and on the knowledge that the last words he'd spoken to her had been angry ones.

Please, God, he thought, sending up the first-ever prayer of his sixteen years of existence. *Please don't let this be what I think it is.*

The wish was futile. When Ellis pushed open the door, light streamed in, and the carnage it revealed was a freight train. The carnage was *Emily.* His sister, bloody and broken. More than broken. Destroyed. Nearly unrecognizable, save for the dress she wore and the blue of her eyes.

He stumbled back, an inhuman noise escaping his mouth as the depravity and loss and utter horror swept through him. He turned to run. It was cowardice. An inability to face what lay before him. He didn't care. Better to be spineless than to see this. Except, he couldn't help but take one tiny glance over his shoulder. And he saw movement. At first, he assumed it was a trick of the light. Then Emily twitched, and Ellis knew it wasn't.

Shaking, he stepped closer again and dropped to his knees at his sister's side.

"Em?" he whispered.

A bubble of red-hued spit formed on her lips. Her eyes seemed to focus on him for the briefest second, full of more pain than any human being should have to suffer, and then they went blank again.

"Em?" he repeated, trying and failing to stifle a sob. "Can you hear me?"

This time, he got nothing in response. But he did see his sister's chest rise and fall in the world's smallest breath. How she was alive, he didn't know.

She shouldn't be, said a voice in his head. *You can't let her be. What are you going to do about it?*

He answered himself aloud. "I don't know."

The moment he said it, though, he *did* know. He knew exactly what he had to do. What the universe was demanding of him.

"I can't."

His gaze stuck on his sister, and he willed it to happen naturally. For death to come, right then, as he watched. It didn't. The seconds ticked by, and with each one, he imagined the excruciating pain she must be in. He had to deliver her the mercy she needed. But a hundred memories slid through his mind and stalled him. His sister's laugh. The time she broke a glass and tried to tape it back together. The wrinkle in her nose every time she saw a slug. All the things she would never get to do again.

Sorrow slammed into Ellis. He wanted to sink into it. To let himself ride it into oblivion. He couldn't, though. Not unless he wanted his sister's pain to continue.

Violently, he shoved aside the sadness and the memories and reached out to put his hands around her neck. Her skin was sticky with blood, and he had a disturbing moment where his hands nearly slipped off. He had to take a breath and try again. As he started to squeeze, he closed his eyes. Tears flowed with blinding thickness. His breath hitched, and hitched, and hitched some more.

Under his hands, Emily shook. She gagged.

God, oh, God. Make it stop.

Instead, a millennium passed. The memories crowded in

again, fast and hard. Emily, on a swing. Emily, ducking out of the way as their father takes a drunken swipe at her. Him, waking up and finding her sleeping outside his own bedroom door, curled up and shivering from a bad dream.

Ellis heard the gurgle of blood.

Make it stop.

"Please."

The appeal only brought more remembrances. His sister, telling him a story about a squirrel. Him, giving her a ride on the back of his motorcycle.

Make.

It.

Stop.

Ellis's nose was snotty now. Like that of a small child crying inconsolably. Like *he* was the one suffering. And his mind remained relentless.

Emily, dancing in a circle in their living room as her favorite boy band blasted in the background. Him, sneaking up on her and dumping a box of packing peanuts on her head.

Then, when he didn't think he could take it anymore, his sister ceased her weak movements. But it wasn't a relief. It was hell. An ending crafted by evil. Ellis held onto her for a single moment more—as though it might make any kind of difference—then let her go and vomited. There was still no reprieve, but a sound did make its way through his nausea, and he lifted his head in search of the source, peering with swollen eyes through the dark. A figure came into focus. It was the cop who'd been hounding him for days. The man stood in the frame of the barn door, his weapon raised and aimed at Ellis. *Flip Farriday.* That was his name.

"Step away from the body," Flip ordered, his voice full of authority.

Ellis's pulse pounded thickly through his skull. "I can't."

"I have a gun, Mr. Black. You might want to consider taking me seriously."

"She's gone."

"I saw it all."

"I can't leave her."

"There isn't going to be a choice here, Mr. Black."

Ellis knew the cop was right, but he still didn't move except to drop a quick look toward his sister's broken form. To her open, dead eyes. To her pretty dress. To her bruised and bare neck.

Her bare neck.

Ellis jerked his attention back to Flip. "Her necklace. Emily isn't wearing it."

The cop kept his weapon exactly where it was. "So?"

"She never ever takes it off."

"So?" the cop repeated.

"So whoever killed her must have it!" Ellis said, his frustration bursting through his anguish. "He could still be out there!"

"Son... *you* killed her."

"But I didn't do it."

"I saw you do it."

Ellis gestured over his shoulder without looking. "I didn't do *this.*"

"You didn't do *this,* or you didn't do *it*?" asked the cop.

Confusion clouded Ellis's brain as he tried to sort out what the question meant. Clarity didn't come.

Emily is dead. Why does anything else matter? He answered himself right, almost manically. *Because maybe I can find him. Maybe I can find the guy who did this.*

"You need to move away from your sister," said the cop.

"I loved her," Ellis replied, hating that it came out in the past tense already.

The cop's eyes flicked past Ellis's shoulder. At Emily. At her body. Without thinking about it, Ellis angled himself to block her from view. This man didn't deserve to see her looking the way she did.

"Mr. Black, you—" The cop stopped short as a voice carried in from outside the barn.

"This is Captain Cliff Sunder of the Meridian PD!" it called. "Step out with your hands up, or I'm coming in hot!"

Flip swung toward the door and the voice, and Ellis saw an opportunity for escape. He pushed to his feet and leaped at the cop. Except his maneuver wasn't smoothly executed. The policeman sidestepped easily, and the move sent Ellis smashing to the ground. As his chin scraped over the barn floor, a bang pierced the air, and he waited for a bullet to hit him. Maybe he even welcomed the idea of dying. But death didn't come. Instead, there was a grunt and a thump that made no sense until Flip Farriday spoke.

"Son," he said in a cold voice. "You thought you had a problem before? That bullet was intended for you, but it hit my boss. And now you're responsible for the death of a police captain, too. So when your court-appointed lawyer offers you a plea bargain, I suggest you take it."

Ellis opened his mouth to protest, but his jaw snapped shut before the words could form. A concrete shell was forming around the hole where his heart had been. He could feel it. Because who would believe that he—an already troubled kid with no parents, no money, and a juvenile record as long as his arm—was innocent in all this? Hell. He didn't believe it himself.

75
Ten Days After Arrest

The Convict

The judge was speaking. Saying she understood that a plea agreement had been reached. Reading the terms aloud. Commenting on the speed and asking if Ellis understood.

He nodded, but he barely listened. Managed only the smallest of nods. Spoke up only when his lawyer, Morris, nudged him to do so.

Ellis wanted to go home. And he was going to get to. Sort of. In exchange for his confession, he'd be allowed to serve his time at Meridian Penitentiary. Close to Emily. Or as close as his new circumstances would allow. That was all that mattered.

The judge finished. A uniformed man—Ellis didn't know if he was a cop or a guard or what, and he didn't care— made a motion. Stiffly, Ellis held out his hands. Let the cuffs make a home on his wrists. They were cold. Uncomfortable. Somehow not tight enough for what he'd done. Been forced to do.

Emily. I'm sorry.

With the uniformed man's guidance, Ellis turned away from the judge and faced the courtroom at large. It was empty save for a solitary figure who waited on the benches. Flip Farriday. The goddamn cop who'd caught him in the act.

Ellis's lawyer paused to shake Farriday's hand. Ellis barely noted it. A black feeling—thick and tarry—was building up his chest.

The fucker. The absolute fucker.

Flip Farriday had *known* Emily was missing. Ellis had been told that the cop had been investigating her disappearance and had been suspicious of Ellis, placing his focus there instead of trying to find his sister before it was too late.

His fault, his subconscious snarled. *You might've done it, but if it weren't for him...*

Ellis latched onto the voice. The anger. He held it close to his heart. And let it take over.

76

Ten Months, Five Days Before Escape

The Convict

E llis rarely paid attention to his peers. Barely looked at them, if he could help it at all. Primarily because he fucking hated the fact that they were his peers. Low-life, piece-of-shit scumbags. That's what they were. The dregs of humanity, all screaming about their own innocence. It was bullshit. They all knew it. He knew it. The difference between him and them was that he didn't pretend it wasn't true. But on that particular morning, as Ellis made a rare trip into gen pop to grab breakfast, he happened to glance in a fellow inmate's direction.

The other man—Stillman... Stedman... something like that —sat on one of the common area benches with a newspaper in his hands. Normally, Ellis wouldn't have noticed either thing. Not the man, not the paper. He had no idea what made him do it then. Fate? Someone else might've said so. Not him. He didn't believe in that shit. Whatever the reason, though, his brief glance stopped him dead.

"What is that?" he said.

Stillman/Stedman lowered his newspaper, looked up at Ellis, and blinked. "Are you talking to me?"

"You see anyone else here in front of me?"

"No, but—"

"So answer me. What the fuck *is* that?"

Stillman/Stedman blinked again. "What's what?"

"In your hands," Ellis said. "The fucking newspaper."

"Uh. It's exactly that? A newspaper?"

"I know that, you—fuck. Just tell me if it's from today."

Stillman/Stedman flipped the paper over, glanced at the front page, then shook his head. "Yesterday, I guess."

Close enough, Ellis thought.

"I'll give you fifty dollars in commissary credits if you let me have the paper," he said.

The other inmate laughed. "You're kidding me, right?"

"I don't even want the whole fucking thing. Only that front page."

"Why?"

"I said fifty bucks for the paper, not fifty bucks for the paper and my life story," Ellis snapped, his fists curling at his sides. "Yes, or no?"

Stillman/Stedman shrugged, peeled the front page from the rest of the sheets, and held it out. "Whatever. Take it."

"Money'll be there by tonight."

Ellis grabbed the paper. He itched to study it then and there. To prove that he was right. But he needed to be alone. So he ordered himself to wait, stalking all the way back to his cell without so much as a look down. Once he was there, he sat himself on the edge of the bed, set the newspaper on the mattress, and carefully smoothed it out before finally letting himself peruse it, starting with the headline and its subtitle.

Local Police Captain Makes Good on Promise: Don't miss Darla Johnson's interview from inside Francis "Flip" Farriday's own home!

Ellis read it no less than five times, partly because he felt a compulsion to commit it to memory, and partly because he kind of expected the message to evaporate. In truth, though, it wasn't the words that mattered anyway. It was the accompanying photograph. That's what had made him zero in after his casual glance, and it was the reason he'd been willing to hand over fifty dollars—pretty much all he had and for which he'd made questionable trades to gain—to get a closer look.

"Oh, really?" he muttered to himself as he realized he'd unconsciously closed his eyes. "If that's true, then why *aren't* you looking at it, asshole?"

A full minute more still passed before he managed to do it. Even then, he took his time. He let his gaze rest on the man at the center of the photo.

Flip Farriday.

He'd aged some, and not entirely well. There were doughy bits around his chin that begged for jokes about cops and doughnuts. His hair was thinning in the front, and someone— probably Farriday himself—had done a shitty job of trying to cover his gray. A man like that wouldn't last five minutes in Meridian Penitentiary. He'd be a resident bitch before he could finish changing into the prison-issue jumpsuit. It made Ellis's lip curl with derision. He wished he could enjoy the other man's visible decline, but he had something more important to do.

Stifling an urge to crumple up the newspaper and throw it across the room, he shifted his focus away from the policeman—who was now the goddamn captain, apparently— and concentrated on the background of the picture. He zeroed in on one particular object there. It looked innocent enough, peeking out from under the lid of a decorative box on a shelf behind Farriday. A hint of blue. Familiar blue. Blue that he could practically feel sliding through his hands.

Ellis lifted the page and squinted. He had to be sure.

Yes, said a voice in his head. *That's definitely it.*

The mental affirmation was a punch in the gut. No. Worse than that. Worse than a punch in the fucking face, actually. Ellis was versed in taking a fist to both places, so he was certain. This was like having the rug pulled out from under him, then finding out that the rug was covering a hole that dropped into a fifty-foot pit with spikes at the bottom. But it was also a relief. An understanding. A justification for his decades-long rage.

"You absolute *fucker*," he said to Farriday's visage. "You lying, cock-socking piece of garbage."

He drew back a fist and drove it hard into the newspaper. There was no satisfaction in tearing through the policeman's image. Ellis needed to tear through his life.

He could call his lawyer. Maybe he *should* call his lawyer. Except it wasn't what he wanted to do. What he wanted to do was to destroy Captain Flip Fucking Farriday. Rip him apart, the same way Emily had been ripped apart.

How are you going to do that from in here?

He snarled. He started to ready another punch. He stopped, though, before he even finished curling his fingers. Wanton destruction wouldn't help. What he had to do was to find a way out of the prison. He'd been locked up for this long already. He could be patient a while longer. All he needed was for the right opportunity to present itself, and he was quite suddenly full of conviction that it would come.

77

Two Hours After Escape

The Preacher's Daughter

Nic met Ellis's eyes as he finished talking her through his incredibly elaborate but remarkably thorough plan, and she reiterated her offer. "Just tell me what I need to do, and I'll do it."

"It's not going to change who I am," he replied.

"And I don't want it to."

"It's not going to be fun."

"I don't expect it to be."

"You'll never be able to set foot in Meridian again," he warned.

"I wasn't going to anyway," she said.

"This won't save my soul, if I even have one."

"That's between you and someone other than me."

"They'll need to believe you were taken against your will," he said.

"I think I can manage to convince them," she told him.

"You sure?"

"Yes."

"I might have to hurt you," he added. She exhaled. "I'll deal with it."

"You'll have to do exactly what I say."

"I can deal with that, too."

Ellis studied her as though he expected her to change her

mind under the weight of his heavy look. But Nic didn't waver. She didn't cast her eyes down.

Finally, he sighed. "Book the room next door. Get me something hard to drink and find me a rope. And don't look eager while you're doing it or not a single person will buy this."

She nodded, careful to keep her feelings in check. But truthfully, she'd sensed a shift in her *own* soul, and she knew it was her who was meant to be changed by this, not him.

78

Seventy-Two Hours After Escape

The Policeman

arriday's hands closed on the weapon. The cool metal couldn't possibly have been more reassuring as his fingers wrapped around it. Triumphant, he rolled over. He fumbled to level the barrel at Ellis, who was still steadying his balance. He didn't hesitate. Not this time. Not like he had, ten years earlier, when he'd walked in on the boy in the barn. Back then, he'd wanted a live scapegoat. Today, he needed nothing more than a dead convict. So he found the trigger, and he squeezed. Nothing happened.

What in the ever-loving hell?

He squeezed again. And this time, there *was* an echoing bang that carried through the space between him and Ellis. Immediately, pain seared through Farriday's left shoulder. And while it was truly the worst thing he'd ever felt — world-blackening in its intensity—for the briefest second, puzzlement overruled it.

What happened?

Then his brain caught up. *He* had been shot. Not the other man. Belatedly, his body reacted to the fact, too. His hand loosened, and the useless gun dropped to the ground. The captain collapsed after it, curling to one side as the burn radiated from the wound to his arm and to his chest. His vision blurred. His teeth chattered so hard that he bit his tongue, and blood filled his mouth. And through it all, he swore he could hear his phone ringing. Which made no sense. Or at least it didn't. Not until he spied the girl, standing in front of him with the familiar electronic device in her hands. Even then, Farriday didn't really understand what was happening. Why would she get out of the car? Why was she looking at him expectantly?

"Help me," he croaked.

"That was the hospital," she said as the phone went silent.

"The... what?"

"What's your voicemail password?"

"What?" he said again.

Why wasn't she helping him? The interaction felt surreal. And it only grew more so when the girl held out the phone with the screen facing up.

"They left a message," she told him. "I think we should listen."

Farriday half-wondered if the gunshot wound was making him delirious, which was probably the only reason he answered. "It's four-three-two-one-two-one."

"Thank you," said Veronica.

Through his haze of agony, he watched her punch in the code and set the phone on speaker. A second later, a disembodied female voice crackled into the air.

"Captain Farriday? It's Dr. Yves, from Meridian Hospital." There was a pause. "I need to tell you something. I didn't want to do it on a voicemail, but it's important—urgent, I think—so I'm going to go ahead. Ms. Hollister's bloodwork came back, and... Lord, help me. Veronica's pregnant, Captain. Eight weeks. I have a feeling it's... call me back when you can, okay?"

Farriday blinked up at the girl, panic mixing with his pain as he clued in to what the doctor had concluded.

Veronica nodded. "Yes. It's exactly what Dr. Yves thinks it is."

"What do you want?" the captain rasped.

It was Ellis who replied, stepping closer. "What I want is for you to tell the truth about what you did to my sister."

Farriday stared up at the other man's face, fury bubbling at the self-righteous contempt he saw there. How dare the murdering trash degenerate look down at him like that?

"I'm the head of the goddamn police," Farriday spat.

"You're a piece of shit," Ellis stated.

"*Me?*" If he *could* have, the captain would've laughed.

"Yes, you fucker. Tell me what you did to her, and maybe I'll let you live."

"I don't remember."

Ellis strode over to him, lifted his foot, and planted it directly against the gunshot wound. "Ten years, ten months, nine days ago. Tell me what you did."

Ellis ground his toe down. Hard. A scream tore from Farriday's chest.

He could hardly breathe, let alone think about speaking. But his mouth had other ideas, and the words came anyway.

"I fucked her, and I set you up, and you performed *so* much better than I could ever have hoped. So thank you, Black, for making sure that I had the chance to keep my job, shoot my competition, and become captain."

79

Ten Years Earlier
Fifty-Four Hours Before Arrest

The Policeman

F lip tipped back the vodka bottle and let the burn slide down his throat. This afternoon, he'd been a constable at the Meridian Police Department. Now, a mere seven hours later, his career had teetered into the abyss.

You're not fit to be a member of this force, Farriday, or any force, for that matter. We both know it. His boss's words ground at him, along with the accompanying threat. *Quit or be fired. Beginning of the day tomorrow, you give me your answer, or I'll give you mine.*

Like it was any kind of choice.

"Not fit to be a cop," Flip muttered.

What evidence did the man have to prove that? Flip made arrests. Doled out speeding tickets. So what if he'd had a complaint or two filed against him? What good cop didn't?

"Bastard."

He brought the bottle to his lips again. Filled his mouth, held the liquid in until it burned enough to make his eyes water, and swallowed. Bitterly, he slid off the hood of the police cruiser he'd liberated from the station on his way out —permanently or temporarily, he hadn't decided yet—and plopped himself on the grass.

After another swig, he set the vodka down and lay back to

stare up at the sky. He pointed a finger at the stars and began pegging them off, one by one, with an imaginary handgun. It did little to ease the burn of his anger.

He narrowed his eyes, imagined his captain's holier-than-thou face, and started to pull back his trigger finger once more. But he froze as a rustle carried to his ears.

Slowly, he sat up and squinted at the bushes on the other side of the embankment where he'd haphazardly stopped the car. The rustle came again, closer and louder. Flip tensed. His fists clenched in expectation of a fight. Maybe in hopes of one. He didn't get anything close. In fact, when the foliage parted, he almost laughed. It was a girl. A young woman. Pretty. Clad in a dress that looked about a size too small, exposing an amount of cleavage that he didn't pretend not to notice as she stepped cautiously toward him.

"Are you a policeman?" she asked.

With a sigh, he brought his attention away from her chest. He took an exaggerated look around, resting his eyes on the cruiser, then looking down at his uniform before he lifted his gaze and offered a crooked smile.

"Why, yes," he said. "Yes, it seems like I am."

"Oh. Good."

"Why? You got a crime you need solved?"

Her delicate brow puckered for a second before a laugh escaped her lips. "You're making a joke."

"I sure am. I'm off duty." Flip swigged the vodka, then held the bottle out to her. "Do you want to sit down and have a drink with me?"

"Is it fizzy?"

"Nope."

"Okay."

The girl hiked her dress up to her knees then plopped herself down beside him. She took the bottle and gulped a mouthful that made her choke hard enough that Flip felt a need to whack her on the back. As he lifted his hand, though, her coughing tapered off and she took another hearty sip.

"It tastes funny," she said.

"Yeah, well. I ran out of orange juice." He could hear the slight slur in his words, but if the girl noticed, she didn't say.

"I like orange juice," she told him.

"Me, too."

He watched her take yet another gulp. Vodka trickled from one corner of her mouth, dribbling to her chin and then her throat. Flip's eyes followed it.

"Do you have a name?" he asked her.

"Emily."

"Hello, Emily. I'm Flip."

"That's a funny name," she replied.

He grinned. "Do you like funny things, Emily? The funny drink. My funny name. My funny jokes."

She smiled back. "Yes. I like funny."

Flip eyed her curved lips and licked his own as his mind swirled. "Do you like them enough to give me a kiss?"

A hint of nervousness passed over her features. "I've never kissed a boy before."

"Would you like to?"

"I think so."

Flip leaned over, but the girl pulled away. Irritation flickered through him.

"Maybe this isn't a good idea," she said. "Maybe I should go home."

"Or maybe you shouldn't," Flip countered.

She shuffled back. He moved forward, his anger growing. She moved as though she was getting ready to stand up.

"I don't think so, honey," he said.

His hand shot out and took hold of the hem of her dress. Roughly, he yanked it toward him. She hit the ground, a yelp slipping out as her head smacked the dirt behind her. The sound made Flip smile.

Serves her right, he thought.

For the first time in a long time, he felt powerful. In control. He crawled up and pinned her underneath him, forcing his mouth to hers, laughing when her teeth gnashed his tongue.

Vaguely, he knew she was crying now. Whimpering, really. Flip didn't care. If anything, it goaded him on. Let her cry. Let her suffer. He'd spent years protecting people like her. For what? Ungrateful bitches.

"Shut up," he grunted. "Shut up and take it."

He put his hand on her throat, silencing her with his palm while he yanked her dress to her hips. He snapped open his pants, held her in place, and forced himself into her until he was satisfied. It wasn't until he eased off her limp body that he saw the blood pouring from her head. Her eyes were mostly closed. The powerful feeling slipped away, leaving him weak.

Empty.

Oh, fuck. Oh, fuck, fuck, fuck.

"Fuck."

He put his head to her chest. She was breathing.

But for how long?

Flip shoved himself away and pushed to his knees, his eyes darting around. The air was still, the space empty save for him, the car, and the girl.

She's not going to live, said a little voice in his head. *And you need to get the fuck out of here.*

Staggering a little, he stood up, grabbed the nearly empty vodka bottle, and picked his way over to the cruiser without looking back. He flung open the door and climbed in. Panic made him drop the keys twice.

"C'mon, c'mon," he said, as he finally got them into the ignition and turned it over.

He hit the gas, but too late, he realized he hadn't put the car into reverse. The tires spun and sent the vehicle forward. Right away, Flip's foot slammed onto the brake. But not quickly enough. The undercarriage crunched. The tires thumped. And for a second after that, he sat utterly still. He told himself that he didn't know what had just happened.

No reason to investigate.

He took a shallow breath, shifted to reverse—triple-checking this time that the gear was correct—and pressed the gas once more. The cruiser groaned a protest and didn't budge.

"No. Just fucking... no."

He opened the door again, but he didn't immediately set his feet on the ground. The air felt colder. Like it'd dropped ten degrees in the last minute. The thought that it was a sign of something worse to come enveloped Flip.

What could possibly be worse than this?

But the answer was obvious—he could get caught.

"Not happening," he said, swinging his legs out.

Moving quickly, he stepped around to the front of the vehicle and dropped his eyes. She was there. Her legs were invisible under the bumper, and one of her arms was bent at an unnatural angle. Blood still seeped from her head wound. For a single moment, Flip's conscience pricked at him. He shoved it aside. Regret was a luxury that would cost him a hell of a lot more than his job. No way could he leave her there. Not now. Paint chips. Tire treads. Something would connect the girl back to the cruiser. It'd give his former peers a reason to look at him. A reason to ask him for a DNA sample.

He gave the surrounding area a quick scan, then bent down, closed his fists on the girl's dress, and yanked. She slid out with enough resistance to make Flip break a sweat, but not enough that he had to pause to recoup his energy before leaning over to pick her up. He slung one arm under her bare legs and the other under her back. He sucked in a breath, pulled her close, and stood up again, nearly dropping her in the process. She was heavy. Far more than he would've expected. Cursing every movie that made it look like hauling a human being around was easy, he shifted, trying to distribute the exertion a little better. The effort didn't help much, but it would have to do.

Only gotta make it ten steps, he reminded himself. *Maybe twelve.*

With a grunt, he circled to the rear of the cruiser, adjusted the girl again, then popped the trunk. Clumsily, he deposited her inside. He adjusted her arms and legs, fitting her into the small space like a piece into a puzzle. Finally, he closed the lid and made his way back to the driver's seat and racked his brain for what his next move ought to be.

Think, Farriday. You have to be smart about this.

But a solution didn't pop to mind. Not immediately, and not after a full five minutes had slid away. The longer he sat still, the more slippery his brain seemed to get. Exhaustion and alcohol tugged simultaneously at him, and when his eyes closed on their own, he let them stay that way. Just for a second. Just a short rest.

The next thing Flip knew, the squawk of the in-dash radio was dragging him into consciousness.

80
Seventy-Two Hours, Thirty Minutes After Escape

The Convict

The cop finished speaking, his voice rasping as he spat out the truth at last, confessing to how he'd gotten away with the crime. Admitting to destroying the DNA sample before it ever got identified. Explaining how he suppressed every piece of potential evidence and rushed everything through court. Then he closed his eyes and said nothing more.

Ellis watched the other man's shallow breaths, and he waited for some kind of weight to lift off his shoulders. Some sense of closure. Anything, really, other than the thick anger and boundless grief he'd felt for the last decade. It didn't come. Hell. Maybe it was a myth. Maybe there *was* no such thing as closure. His sister was still dead. He was still guilty of taking her life. The man who'd raped Emily and lain the crime at Ellis's feet would never be able to pay. Not enough. Not if he went to prison forever, not if the wound on his shoulder festered and killed him, and not if Ellis slit his throat and let him bleed out there on the side of the road.

So what now? What was the point of it all?

"I don't fucking know," he said under his breath.

Nic's hand landed on his elbow. "Do you want me to shoot him again?"

The question made him want to laugh a bitter laugh. "Do you really think I'm unwilling to kill him with my bare hands?"

Her slim shoulders lifted and dropped. "I know you can, but you don't have to if you don't want to."

"And if I *do* want to?"

"Then go ahead."

Ellis eyed the unconscious cop again. "Is it too much of a mercy to let him die?"

"If it changes anything… I recorded his confession on his phone," said Nic.

"Is there something poetic in that?" he replied.

"I doubt it. But we could give it to the police." She paused. "The *other* police, I mean."

"Or we could drop it off with that lawyer"

"Or that."

Ellis stepped over to Farriday. He stared down at him for a single second more. Mercy crossed his mind again. But then again, he was nothing more than the monster this man had created, was he? That was a fact.

He lifted his boot and drove it into the policeman's throat with all of his strength.

THE END

MELINDA DI LORENZO

Author's Note

Something interesting that I discovered whilst going through this book with my editor is that American and Canadian prisons are very (very) different.

Case in point, the small matter of Ellis having a pair of drawstring pants. During edits, this brought in a comment along these lines: A prisoner could never have drawstring pants because the string could be used as a weapon. Wait. Is this story not set in the United States? Because if so, a lot of what I've said might not apply. And then began the comparison/contrast and the entire re-edit!

P.S. If you're interested in having a virtual look inside a Canadian federal prison, I highly recommend this site:

https://www.csc-scc.gc.ca/csc-virtual-tour/index-eng.shtml

12918102R00214